VIRAGO
MODERN CLASSICS
639

D1330215

Mary Renault

Mary Renault (1905–1983) was best known for her historical novels set in Ancient Greece with their vivid fictional portrayals of Theseus, Socrates, Plato and Alexander the Great.

Born in London in 1905 and educated at the University of Oxford, she trained as a nurse at Oxford's Radcliffe Infirmary where she met her lifelong partner, fellow nurse Julie Mullard. Her first novel, *Purposes of Love*, was published in 1939. In 1948, after her novel *Return to Night* won an MGM prize worth $150,000, she and Mullard emigrated to South Africa.

It was in South Africa that Renault was able to write forth-rightly about homosexual relationships for the first time – in her last contemporary novel, *The Charioteer*, published in 1953, and then in her first historical novel, *The Last of the Wine* (1956), the story of two young Athenians who study under Socrates and fight against Sparta. Both these books had male protagonists, as did all her later works that included homosexual themes. Her sympathetic treatment of love between men would win Renault a wide gay readership.

By Mary Renault

THE MASK
OF APOLLO

Mary Renault

Introduced by Charlotte Mendelson

virago

VIRAGO

This edition published in Great Britain in 2015 by Virago Press

1 3 5 7 9 10 8 6 4 2

First published in Great Britain in 1966 by Longmans, Green and Co. Ltd

MIX
Paper from
responsible sources
FSC
www.fsc.org   FSC® C104740

Virago
An imprint of
Little, Brown Book Group
Carmelite House
50 Victoria Embankment
London EC4Y 0DZ

An Hachette UK Company
www.hachette.co.uk

www.virago.co.uk

δάκρυα μὲν Ἑκάβῃ τε καὶ Ἰλιάδεσσι γυναιξὶ
Μοῖραι ἐπέκλωσαν δὴ τότε γεινομέναις,
σοὶ δέ, Δίων, ῥέξαντι καλῶν ἐπινίκιον ἔργων
δαίμονες εὐρείας ἐλπίδας ἐξέχεαν.
κεῖσαι δ' εὐρυχόρῳ ἐν πατρίδι τίμιος ἀστοῖς,
ὦ ἐμὸν ἐκμήνας θυμὸν ἔρωτι Δίων.

Tears were for Hekabê, friend, and for Ilion's women,
Spun into the dark Web on the day of their birth,
But for you our hopes were great, and great the triumph,
Cancelled alike by the gods at the point of glory.
Now you lie in your own land, now all men honour you—

But I loved you, O Diôn!

PLATO
Trans. Dudley Fitts

INTRODUCTION

Mary Renault was an Ancient Greek.

It's true. Yes, she was writing in the mid-twentieth century, an English doctor's daughter in South Africa, and her own direct experience of wrestling techniques and human sacrifice was fairly limited. So what? Were *you* there, in the colonnades, arguing with Plato, or in the Syracusan fortress–palace, flirting your way to survival, or seeing the eyes of your greatest foe glinting through his helmet slits, then stabbing him deep in the neck?

No, I thought not. Neither was I. But when we read her novels, the worlds of fifth-century Athens, of revolutionary Ionian city states and tiny tyrannies are as real as London or Hogwarts or Antarctica, and that's what counts in fiction. Unlike most historians, she was a glorious writer; unlike most novelists, she knew a colossal amount about the past. And so when she described the complexities of Alexander or Socrates, or the stage-hands and soldiers she invented, it seems inconceivable that they could have died over twenty centuries before her birth.

Dorothy Hartley, the great historian of English food and folk-lore, was so immersed in her subject that she'd sometimes answer the phone with: 'Go away, I'm in the fourteenth century.' Mary

Renault found her element too, and it was even stranger. She was lucky. For most people, the fear of their own ignorance, or dry text-book translations, kill the thrill of the classical world. However, for those of us fortunate enough to discover for ourselves the gloriously nasty gods of Mount Olympus, the rippling warriors of Homer and the vertiginous brilliance of Greek myth, there is nothing better. Their weird glitter stays with one for life. Mary Renault's greatest blessing as a writer was, I suspect, her lack of a classical education. Instead of four years studying the syntax of boundary-stone inscriptions, she spent her time at university reading Shakespeare, falling in love and, voluntarily, finding out about some of the most barbaric, dramatic and mind-expandingly complex aspects of Greek civilisation, such as the Minoan bull-leapers of Crete whose world, one and a half millennia before Christ, incorporated bare-breasted snake goddesses, astonishingly sophisticated ceramics and a flushing toilet.

What makes a novelist change direction? Renault was nearly fifty when she began to write *The Last of the Wine*, her seventh novel and the first to be set in Ancient Greece. Depending on perspective, one can ascribe this to the parallels she saw between the decline of Athenian democracy and South African politics in the early 1950s; or to her desire to write a love story which happens to be homosexual, whose protagonists would not be shamed, imprisoned or hounded to death. Or, perhaps, it was simply the evolution of an artist: the wisdom to wait until the flames of her ardent love for Crete and Macedon and the Peloponnese had died down before ordering parcels of books, researching for two years and then, in command, beginning to write.

More than almost any novelist, Mary Renault understood the deliciousness of mundane and technical details. Like Alcibiades, she 'knew [her] Athenians as a potter knows his clay' and, just as we know exactly the feeling of turning on a light-switch or ordering a sandwich, from her reading of anecdotal accounts and linguistic analysis, and her own study of vases and friezes, Mary Renault could describe perfectly Greek daily life: the pattern of scarring 'you see' on the arms of a cavalryman and the shock of seeing bare-faced Etruscan actors; hairstyle fashions and naked sculptors' loin-protecting arrangements; the practicalities of acting in an eighteen-thousand-seater Corinthian theatre where 'in the top row they can hear you sigh'; the way mourning women have to stop for a chat when they're tired out with wailing; and how men yawn as they bleed to death. Most of us, despite what academics think, don't care about Demosthenes's rhetorical techniques or oligarchic legislation; we want to imagine life as one of them, sharing their sexual secrets and financial worries and mundane preoccupations, and then get on with the story.

And Mary Renault was an exceptional story-teller. If she hadn't been female, and a writer of historical fiction, she would still be patronised and underrated because of this; her novels are much too enjoyable to count as literature. Her sense of suspense and drama were extraordinary, whether she was describing a wrestling match or a coup, a family argument or the way one loiters while waiting for a love object, pretending not to be trying to catch their eye. She also understood perfectly how to handle pace: to level the heightened emotion with wit ('at a peace conference, it went without saying that everyone would be looking for slights and insults') or bathos (the uncleaned temple at Olympia buzzing with flies) or a perfect one-liner: a foreigner 'like a carp in a corselet of golden fish-scales'.

Without gorgeous writing and background detail, a description of even the most spectacular battle quickly palls. However, what gives Mary Renault's fiction depth is her psychological insight; she understood the difficulty of being human, and knew that under their corselets and ornamental plaits the Ancient Greeks felt as we do. Heartbroken Lysis in *The Last of the Wine*, ugly Simonides in *The Praise Singer* and dry Nikeratos in *The Mask of Apollo* are just like us: disgusted by their teenage bodies, furious with their ageing parents, ashamed and libidinous and lonely and full of regrets. And she is, of course, particularly skilful at describing love. When Lysis says: 'I saw a boy. So one begins', the emotion he feels makes sense to every reader, of every sexual inclination: we all know that hope, and pain. And isn't that one of the joys of fiction: that sensation of being understood? At times, reading Renault is like talking to a kindly bachelor uncle who has seen every type of love, and knows how to survive it: 'My dear, there is no terrible face of Eros. There is just the one charming one, which he may decide to turn away. The furies who follow him are all begotten by men.'

Yet Renault's feel for less operatic impulses, the mundane drama of our lives, was just as strong. She understood the motivations which drive us, particularly at our most difficult to understand: hero worship, racial hatred, resentment, sycophancy and *Schadenfreude*. She could see straight into the heart of a 'fragile anxious lady' who 'had always leaned on her menfolk', or a man who was 'a hater of many things, beginning I think with himself'. And, for those who are interested, she is unrivalled on the development of creativity; particularly in her portrait of the artist as a young Greek, *The Praise Singer*, where Simonides wants to be a poet 'before I knew what a poet was', but also on actors: their vanity, the perforated line between performance and prostitution. The scene in *The Mask of Apollo* where Nikeratos calms the battling Phigaleians while channelling Apollo on a tumbledown roof would compel any listener, however resistant to theatre, or the classical world, or fiction generally.

It is always a terrible moment when one discovers that a hero has questionable views. Thankfully Renault, a white immigrant to South Africa, was one of the first members of the Black Sash anti-apartheid movement. She was, admittedly, a reluctant gay icon, but that was her prerogative; she lived openly with a woman, Julie Mullard, and if they didn't call themselves lesbians, who cares? Only in her attitude to women in general was Mary Renault a disappointment. They barely figure in her Greek novels; men have the best characters, the best bodies and best lines. However, had it not been for her view that 'men have more fun', for her Darwinian, or Spartan, appreciation of physical and intellectual perfection and her rejection of the woolly-liberal discomfort with inequality, her evocation of great men in a male world would have been both less powerful and less convincing. Renault's Greece succeeds because she thought like an Ancient Greek; we may wince at her characters' attitude to female babies, or wives, but they were accurate.

On Renault's deathbed, in 1983, she was cheered to learn that an Oxford Professor of Ancient Greek was recommending her novels. However, despite great commercial success, her later novels were rarely treated as literature. Like crime fiction, historical fiction continues to be met with with appalling snobbery. As the great Hilary Mantel points out, writers of historical literary fiction do make things up, but so do historians, and literary novelists, and even sometimes journalists. Moreover, as Mantel, an admirer of Renault, wrote in 2009 in the *Guardian*, the sneering belief that novels about the past are somehow escapist, and therefore inferior, ignores the facts: those 'events and mentalities that, should you choose to describe them, would bring you to the borders of what your readers could bear. The danger you have to negotiate is not the dimpled coyness of the past – it is its obscenity.'

Yes, some historical novelists are too impressed by their own research, the battle manoeuvres or the bodices and night soil, but the greatest, like Mantel and Renault, hold up their lens so close to the reader's eye that it is invisible. When Renault wrote that Delphi 'smelled of bliss, danger and gods' or of the way ancient men have a scent of 'old green bronze', she isn't bringing them to life. To Mary Renault, we are all Ancient Greeks, and that is the secret of her novels' brilliance. She is merely telling us what we already know.

Charlotte Mendelson, 2015

Not many people remember Lamprias now in Athens. But his company is still talked about in the Peloponnese. Ask in Corinth or Epidauros, no one will have heard of him; but down in the Argolid they will go on about his Mad Herakles, or his Agamemnon, as if it were yesterday. I don't know who is working his circuit now.

At all events, he was in Athens when my father died, and owed him more money than anyone else did; but as usual was nearly broke, and trying to fit a tour out on a handful of beans. So he offered to take me on as extra; it was the best he could do.

As I suppose everyone knows, my father Artemidoros was an actor before me; the service of Dionysos runs in our blood. Indeed, you could call him a sacrifice to the god. He died of a chill he caught here in Athens, playing second roles in the *Bacchae* of Euripides, which was that year's classical revival. It was one of those bright spring days you get at the Dionysia, warm in the sun but with a cutting wind. He came on first as King Pentheus, wearing a heavy-sleeved costume, red cloth with thick embroidery; also some padding in the chest and shoulders, since like me he was a slender man. I don't know what possessed him to put on under all this his maenad dress for Queen Agave. There is plenty of time after Pentheus' exit; but he was always proud of changing quickly. Of course he sweated; when he changed masks and came on again in this damp thin robe, the sun went in and he got chilled to the bone. One would never have known it. I was on as a Maenad, and thought he was at his best. He was famous for his women's roles, especially the crazy ones, like Agave and Cassandra, or tear-wringers like Niobe.

He had no luck that day; for the leading man, who had played the god, got the actors' prize and gave a party. My father did not like to leave early, in case it was misunderstood, so he stayed drinking till past midnight. The cold went to his chest with a high fever, and on the third night he died.

Though I was nineteen at the time, it was the first death in our own house since I was born. I felt half-dazed, and confused with the noise of the rites; the house all upside-down, my father on his bier, feet to the door, my mother and grandmother and sister flinging their arms across him wailing; the small room full of neighbours and actors edging and shouldering in and out to pay respects and hang on the door their black-ribboned locks of hair. I can still feel the pull on my scalp as I stood in a dark corner, hacking at mine with my mother's scissors. It was short already, like every actor's; being fair and fine it seemed to go to nothing, however close I cut. I tugged and hurt myself, my eyes running with the pain, and with grief, and from fear I should not have enough to show up in the grave-wreath.

From time to time the wailing broke off as some new caller spoke his lines. The neighbours left soon – outsiders don't know what to say about an actor – but his fellow-artists hung about, for he was always a well-liked man. So indeed they kept saying; how good he was to work with, and always ready to help a friend. (My mother, I thought, would sooner have had the news that he had

2

saved a little.) He never dried, they said, he could keep going through anything; and they told some tales that made me stare, not having learned yet that anything can happen on tour. What talent he had, they said, poor Artemidoros! A disgrace he was passed over at the Lenaia; no one remembers seeing Polyxena done with more feeling; but the lot fell on some poor judges, this year.

I put down my scissors and ran inside, my hair half-shorn like a felon's, leaving my clippings on the towel. As though everyone would not have approved of my weeping, I hid like a beaten dog, gulping and choking on my bed. It was not the mourners I was hiding from, but my father on his bier, as silent as an extra, masked in his dead face, waiting for his exit.

I'm not sure how long I had known I had more talent than he had. Two years – no, three; I was sixteen when I saw him as the young Achilles in *The Sacrifice at Aulis*, and I doubt if it came new to me even then. He always moved well, and his hands could say anything. I never heard his voice more charming. He made Achilles a delightful youth, spirited, sincere, with an arrogance too boyish to offend. They could have eaten him; they hardly noticed his Agamemnon, waiting for him to come back as Achilles. Yes; but the shadow of all that darkness, of that black grief beside the shore, the dreadful war-yell whose rage and pain scared all the horses, it is close ahead, his goddess mother knows already. One ought to feel it breathe. It crept in my hair, where he speaks of his slighted honour, I shivered down my backbone. And I heard another player, hardly yet knowing whom.

If he had been self-satisfied, jealous or hard to work with, I should have learned to justify myself. But he had all an artist needs, except the spark from the god. No one knew better than I did what he was like backstage. I had been on with him almost since I could stand alone.

3

At three, I was Medea's younger son, though I can't remember it; I don't suppose I knew I was on a stage. My father told me later how he had brought home his Medea mask beforehand, in case it frightened me; but I only stuck my fingers through its mouth. It is hard to make actors' children take masks seriously, even the most dreadful; they see them too soon, too near. My mother used to say that at two weeks old, to keep me from the draught, she tucked me inside an old Gorgon, and found me sucking the snakes.

I do remember, though, quite clearly, playing Astyanax to his Andromache. I was turned six by then, for Astyanax has to work. The play was Euripides' *Women of Troy*. My father told me the plot, and promised I should not really be thrown off the walls, in spite of all the talk about it. We were always acting out such tales as a bedtime game, with mime, or our own words. I loved him dearly. I fought for years to go on thinking him great.

'Don't look at the Herald,' he said to me at rehearsal. 'You're not supposed to know what he means, though any child would that was right in the head. Take all your cues from me.'

He sent me out in front, to see the masks as the audience saw them. Climbing up high, above the seats of honour, I was surprised to find how human they looked, and sad. While I was there he did his part as Cassandra, god-mad with two torches. I knew it by heart, from hearing him practise. It was his best role, everyone agrees. After he changed masks, ready for Andromache. This is the play where they bring her in from the sacked city on a cart piled up with loot, her child in her arms, just two more pieces of plunder. A wonderful bit of theatre. It never fails.

I was still small enough to be used to women's arms; it was odd to feel under the pleated dress I grasped at, the hard chest of a man, holding each breath and playing it out with the phrases, the rib-cage vibrant like the box of a lyre. If one thinks, I suppose

4

most men's sons would die of shame to hear their father weep and lament in the voice of a woman. But as he never missed his exercises, I must have heard them from the first day I drew breath: old men, young men, queens and booming tyrants, heroes, maidens and kings. To me it was the right of a man to have seven voices; only women made do with one.

When the day came, I was still aggrieved there was no mask for me, though I had been told again and again children did not use them. 'Never mind,' said my father, 'the time will come.' Then he pulled his own mask down, the smiling face going into the solemn one. He was in the prologue as Athene.

Outside the parodos the cart was waiting, drawn by four oxen, with the gilded spoils of Troy. At last came the callboy, and my father in the pale mask of the shorn-haired widow. He clambered up, someone hoisted me after; he settled me on his knee, and the oxen started.

Out beyond the tall gateway was the great curve of the theatre. I was used to the empty tiers. Now filled with faces it seemed vast and unknown, murmuring and dangerous as the sea. My father's voice whispered, 'Don't look at the audience. You're sacred of strangers. Think how they chopped up your poor old granddad. Lean on me.'

This is not how I myself would direct Astyanax. He is Hektor's son; I like him alert and bold, thinking no evil till the time. But my father knew his business too. Even the men were sighing, as we came slowly on into the orchestra; I could hear the little coos and cries of the women, floating on this deep bass. Suddenly it took hold of me. My father and I, by ourselves, were doing this with fifteen thousand people. We could carry them all to Troy with us, make them see us just as we chose to be. I can taste it still, that first sip of power.

Then I felt their will reach out to me. It was like the lover's touch, which says, Be what I desire. All power has its price. I clung to Andromache my mother and leaned upon her breast; but the hands I answered to were Artemidoros the actor's. As they moulded me like wax and sculpted us into one, I knew the many-headed lover had caught him too; I felt it through both our skins. Yet I felt him innocent. He did not sell, but gave freely, love for love.

The Herald came, with the news that I must die. I remembered I was not supposed to heed him; but I thought I should look sorry for my mother's grief, so I reached up and touched the mask's dead hair. At this I heard sighing and sobbing rise like a wave. It was coming from the block where the hetairas sit; they love a good cry more than figs. But it was a few years yet before I knew to look for them.

When the Herald bore me off to die, I thought everyone back-stage would be there to pay me compliments; but only the wardrobe-master's assistant came in a hurry, to strip me naked and paint on my bloody wounds. My father, who had exited soon after me, ran over to pat my bare belly as I lay, and say, 'Good boy!' Then he was off; it's a quick change from Andromache to Helen, what with the jewels and so on. It is always a splendid costume, meant to show up against the other captives. The mask was most delicately painted, and had gold-wreathed hair. He went on, and I heard his new voice, bland and beguiling, answering angry Menelaos.

Soon after came my cue to be brought on, dead. They stretched me out on the shield, and a couple of extras lifted it. The day was warm, but the breeze tickled my skin, and I gave my mind to lying limp as I had been told. The chorus called out the dreadful news to my grannie Hekabe; lying, eyes shut, while the Herald made a long speech about my death, I prayed Dionysos not to let me sneeze. There was a pause, which because I could not see seemed to last for ever. The whole theatre had got dead silent, holding its breath. Then a terrible low voice said just beside me,

Lay down the circled shield of Hektor on the ground.

I had been well rehearsed for this scene; but not with Hekabe. I had nothing to do but keep still; and this was Kroisos, the leading man. He was then at the peak of his powers, and, fairly enough, did not expect to tutor children. I had seen the mask, and that was all.

I had already heard him, of course, lamenting with Andromache; but that is her scene; and I had my own part to think of. Now, the voice seemed to go all through me, making my backbone creep with cold. I forgot it was I who was being mourned for. Indeed, it was more than I.

No sweetness here, but old pride brought naked to despair, still new to it, a wandering stranger. At the bottom of the pit a new pit opens, and still the mind can feel. Cold hands touched my head. So silent were the tiers above us, I heard clearly, from the pines outside, the murmur of a dove.

I was not seven years old. I think I remember; but no doubt I have mixed in scraps from all sorts of later renderings, by Theodoros or Philemon or Thettalos; even from my own. I dreamed of it, though, for years, and it is from this I remember certain trifles, such as the embroidery on his robe, which had a border of keys and roses, glimpsed between the eyelids. When I think of these dreams it all comes back to me. Was it Troy I grieved for, or man's mortality; or for my father, in the stillness that was like a wreath of victory on Kroisos' brow? All I remember for certain is my swelling throat, and the horror that came over me when I knew I was going to cry.

My eyes were burning. Terror was added to my grief. I was going to wreck the play. The sponsor would lose the prize; Kroisos the crown; my father would never get a part again; we would be in the streets begging our bread. And after the play, I would have to face terrible Hekabe without a mask. Tears burst from my shut eyes; my nose was running. I hoped I might die, that the earth would open or the skene catch fire, before I sobbed aloud.

The hands that had traced my painted wounds lifted me gently. I was gathered into the arms of Hekabe; the wrinkled mask with its down-turned mouth bent close above. The flute, which had been moaning softly through the speech, getting a cue, wailed louder. Under its sound, Queen Hekabe whispered in my ear, 'Be quiet, you little bastard. You're dead.'

I felt better at once. All I had been taught came back to me. We had work to do. I slid back limp as his hands released me; neatly, while he washed and shrouded me, he wiped my nose. The scene went through to the end.

> *In vain*
> *we sacrificed. And yet had not the very hand*
> *of God gripped and crushed this city deep in the ground we*
> *should have disappeared in darkness, and not given a theme*
> *for music, and the songs of men to come.*

As the extras carried me off in my royal grave-clothes, I thought to myself, surprised, 'We are the men to come.' As well as everything else, I had been responsible to Astyanax. His shade had been watching from the underworld, hoping I would not make him mean. What burdens I had borne! I felt I had aged a lifetime.

My father, who had been standing behind the prompt-side revolve and seen it all, ran up as they slid me off the shield, asking

8

what had come over me. If it had been my mother, I dare say I should have raised a howl. But I said at once, 'Daddy, I didn't make a noise.'

Kroisos came off soon after, pushing up his mask. He was a thin man, all profile, like a god on a coin except that he was bald. When he turned our way I hid behind my father's skirts; but he came towards us, and fished me out by the hair. I came squirming; a disgusting sight, as you may suppose, all smeared with blood-paint and snot. He grinned with big yellow teeth. I saw, amazed, that he was not angry. 'By the dog!' he said. 'I thought we were finished then.' He grimaced like a comedian's slave-mask. 'Artemidoros, this boy has feeling, but he also knows what he's about. And what's your name?'

'Niko,' I answered. My father said 'Nikeratos'. I had seldom heard this used, and felt somehow changed by it. 'A good omen,' said Kroisos. 'Well, who knows?'

While the women wailed over the bier, a dozen such scenes from my childhood up came back to me. My father always got me in as an extra when he could. Outside came a lull; Phantias the maskmaker had come to condole, bringing a gravepot painted to order with two masks and Achilles mourning by a tomb. The women, who were getting tired, broke off to talk awhile. I was master of the house, I ought to go out and greet him. I could hear his voice, recalling my father as Polyxena, and turned over again, biting the pillow. I wept because the god we both served had made me choose, and my heart had forsaken him for the god. Yet I had fought the god for him. 'What a house today,' I would say; 'they must have heard the applause at the Kerameikos. That business with the urn would have melted stone. Do you know I saw General Iphikrates crying?' There was always something one could say, and something true. But the great things every artist hopes for, the harsh god closed my mouth upon, and pushed them back down my throat. He missed them; I know he missed them; I saw it sometimes in his eyes. Why not have said them, and left the god to make the best of it? The gods have so much, and men have so little. Gods live for ever, too.

I could not lie there like a child. I got up and wiped my face, greeted Phantias, finished cutting my hair for the grave-wreath, and stood at the door to receive people. I was there when Lamprias called.

When he made his offer, my mother, without asking me what I thought, thanked him with tears. Lamprias coughed, and looked at me with apology, knowing what I knew. His great black eyebrows worked up and down, and he glanced away at my father. I too, as I accepted, half looked to see him sit up on his bier and say, 'Are you mad, boy?' But he said nothing; what indeed could he have said? I knew I should have to take it. I would do no better, now.

At nineteen, one is good for nothing in the theatre but extra work. To get into a company, even as third actor, one must have the range that will let one play, not only youths and women but warriors, tyrants and old men. No lad of that age can do it; whereas a good man, who has kept his voice in training and his body supple, can wear juvenile masks till he is fifty, and do everything else as well.

So long as my father lived, I always got work, singing in choruses, carrying a spear, or doing silent stand-ins, when two roles played by one actor overlap, needing an extra to wear the mask and robe for one of them. Lately I had even got odd lines here and there, in modern plays where the rule of three is not so strictly kept, and the extra sometimes speaks. Though I knew little else, I knew the theatre; and I was not fool enough to think that any more of this would come my way. Any actor good enough to appear in Athens has got a son, or a nephew, or a boy friend training for the stage. From now on, I would be like the little orphan in the *Iliad*, who gets no table scraps. 'Outside!' say the other boys. '*Your* father is not dining here.'

I reckoned I would need three years to make my way, at the very best, before I got parts in good productions; and even for three months, my mother could not keep me idling. We had been left really poor; she would have to sell her weaving, my sister to earn her own dower or else marry beneath her. Somehow I must pick up a living at the only trade I knew.

Lamprias was pleased I agreed at once and said nothing to embarrass him. He would be getting something for money he owed outright, when cash down was what we needed. 'Good boy, good boy,' he said, patting me on the back. 'The choice of a real professional, and your father's son. The range will come, we all know that; meantime, you've a head start over most lads I could get. You've lived backstage since you could stand, you know something of everything, from lyre-playing to working the crane. A tour like this will be the making of you. No artist knows himself till he's done a tour.'

I did not tell him I had toured only last year, with my father, playing Samos and Miletos as extra in a first-class company, berthing aft and eating with the captain. I would make what was coming no better by putting on airs and getting resented. It might have been worse. Boys left like me have had to choose between selling their favours to some actor in return for work, or going right to the bottom: the village fitups where, if they don't like you, you can make your supper off the fruit and greenstuff they throw. At least Lamprias' company played in theatres, though only in the little ones.

At sunset they buried my father. There was a very good turnout; it would have pleased him. Philotimos himself showed up, with a tale of some scrape my father had got him out of when he was young and wild. When it was over we went home and lit the lamps, straightened the room, and looked about as people do, not wanting to think what next.

I would be leaving within the month. I went out and walked about; everything looked strange. On my way I passed the door of an old hetaira I had had a night with when I was seventeen, because I was ashamed never to have tried a woman. I could hear her now inside, humming to her lyre. She was always kind to boys. But I owed my father more respect; and all I had really wanted was a little mothering. My first real love affair was still fresh in my heart, though it was three years since. An actor visiting from Syracuse had come for a month, and stayed another for love of me. We had had a beautiful parting, quoting from *The Myrmidons*; a whole year after, he had written to me from Rhodes.

Before we started rehearsals, I was asked to sup at Lamprias' house and meet the company. We lived at Piraeus near the theatre; he had lodgings on the waterfront. I walked there anxiously, picking my way over fishy nets and around kegs and bales.

'The scourge of a third-rate tour,' my father used to say, 'is the second actor. He's the failed one. As a rule he makes everyone pay.'

This time he was wrong. Old Demochares had had his taste of honey, and it had kept him sweet. More than once he had worn the victor's ivy crown; he had come down through serving Dionysos all too well in a crown of vine. When I got there he was pretty drunk already; and in the end, to keep him from falling in the harbour, I helped carry him home. He was as jolly in his cups as Pappasilenos, except when we were putting him to bed; then he clasped my hand and cried a little, and quoted *O fair young face, sorrow and death pass by you*, in a voice that still showed some beauty through the fog. As we walked back after, Lamprias coughed, referred to his triumphs, and gave me to know I would be expected, along with my other duties, to share the common task of getting him on stage sober.

The third actor, Meidias, had gone home already in a pet; if you will believe it, because I, rather than he, had had compliments from an old drunk who could not see straight to walk. My father had been half right; here was the failed man; not six and twenty, yet he had outlived his hopes. Some mocking god had given him a handsome face, the one beauty an actor can do without; it had brought him some success offstage, which he owed his start to; and made him think the world was at his feet. Now he was learning that feet are to stand upon, but did not want to know it. We had barely filled the first cups when he began telling me what splendid roles had been offered him, if he had cared to sell his honour. He was as free with great names as some old madam showing the girls her jewels. Though young-looking for my age, I knew enough to guess he had gone through whatever his honour would fetch, before he signed on with Lamprias. I fear he saw this in my eye.

Next day we started rehearsals. We had a repertory of two or three modern plays, without chorus; and a couple of classics in case some sponsor hired us for a festival.

Of course we were by-passing Corinth. Corinthians know what is due to them, and throw things if they don't get it. We were opening at Eleusis, then on through Megara and south around the Argolid. When Lamprias went on, as he did every day for both our good, about the fine experience I would be getting, what he meant was that we would hardly see a bit of modern equipment from first to last, or, probably, a sponsor; we would cart along our own costumes, masks and props (stuff bought second-hand after the Dionysia, when richer companies had had their pick), fix up the skene with whatever we found when we got there, and practise making do. Though I never thought I would live to say so, one can make worse beginnings.

It seemed a pity that in the last week of rehearsals I had to knock Meidias down. Even though he took against me from the first, I had tried to get along with him for the sake of peace; but that day he thought fit to quote me a piece of envious bitchery about my father, from one of his fancy-friends. He was bigger than I, but had not troubled, as my father had made me do, to go to a good gymnasium where one learns how to stand and move. One also learns some throw-holds. We had been rehearsing in the Piraeus theatre, and were walking up the steps between the benches, when I hit him and tipped his knee; so he did not fall very soft, and rolled a good way down. Some little boys, who had perched at the top like sparrows to watch us act, were glad to get so much for nothing, and cheered the scene. Luckily he broke no bones, and his face was no one else's business. So Lamprias said nothing. I knew I should be made to pay; but that could not be helped. Little I guessed, though, how far along my life that blow would cast its shadow.

The day of departure came. My mother saw me off by dawn and lamplight, shed a few tears, and warned me against temptations, which she did not name, guessing no doubt that I could have instructed her. I kissed her, shouldered my bundle, and went whistling down the twilit streets where half-wakened birds replied. The shouts of the night-fishers, bringing in their catch, rang far over the grey water. At the meeting-place I found that Lamprias, to show we were a troupe of standing, had hired a handyman for the baggage-cart, asses and mules. This cheered me; I had thought I might have to do that too.

It was a chancy year for touring, he said as we moved off. It was; like most other years. Lately the Thebans had amazed the world by throwing the Spartans first out of their citadel and then

14

out of their city. They had run them clear of Boeotia; we Athenians had beaten them at sea; all over Hellas men stretched, and breathed more deeply. However, with all this, troops were for ever marching about the Isthmus; Lamprias said he would be glad to leave it behind. No doubt Megara would be quiet; they are apt there to mind their own business; but in the Peloponnese the cities were working like a pan of yeast, throwing off the dekarchies the Spartans had set over them. We might run into anything.

People are always saying what fine free lives we actors lead, able to cross frontiers and go anywhere. This is true, if it means that hired troops have nothing against us, and others respect the sacred edicts. You are likely enough to get with a whole skin where you are going, and can count there on roof and food at least from your choregos, always provided this sponsor is alive, and not exiled overnight. But for a company working its own way, to arrive is hardly enough, if you find that the men have taken to the hills, the women have battened themselves inside the houses, while a squadron of cavalry has hitched its horses in the orchestra and is chopping up the skene for cook-fires.

However, it was a fine morning; the straits of Salamis glittered against the purple island; remembering my Aischylos, I peopled the water with grinding oars and crashing prows, and rammed galleys spilling gold-turbaned Persians into the sea. Eleusis was just ahead; we would be playing there tomorrow, setting the skene today. I rode my donkey, getting the cart when I could between me and Meidias. Lamprias led on his riding-mule; Demochares liked to start the day on the cart, where he could have out his sleep on the bundles and favour his morning head. I looked at him hopefully, planning to ask him if he had ever met Euripides. He looked old enough.

There is nothing really worth telling about the first part of the tour. A hundred artists could tell it for me. I had the hardest bed at the inn with the oldest straw; ran everyone's errands, mended the costumes, put laces in the boots, combed the masks' hair and beards, and daubed on paint when some old skene needed freshening. I did not mind, except when Meidias told people it was what I had been hired for.

He was the gall under my harness; not the fleas in the straw, nor the hard work, nor looking after Demochares. I loved the old soak, even when he drove me mad, and soon learned to manage him. In his heyday, as he let me know, he had been a great amorist; it was some while, I think, since he had taken to a youth whom he trusted not to mock him. Being the ruins of a gentleman, he was never disgusting, even in his drink; more like some old dancer who, hearing the flute, steps through his paces where the neighbours will not see. Self-respect kept him in bounds when sober; after the play, when he started drinking, he had no time for lesser interests. All it came to was that he taught me a great deal, which has been of use to me ever since; and recited me some beautiful epigrams composed by Agathon and Sophokles for youths they courted, with the name changed to mine wherever it would scan.

It was only in the morning, before the play, that he gave me any real trouble. Then he would slip off for a cup to warm him up and, if I did not watch out, go on and finish the jar. I would run to the wine-shop for him, mix in the water on the way, and keep him talking to spin it out. With luck I would have him dressed in time to get my own work done.

'The theatre is in your bones,' he used to say to me. 'You have the open face. Not like that oaf Meidias, who is in love with the mask he happened to be born with, and soon won't have even that, since his fatuous conceit is already marking it. The artist flows into the mask the poet offers him; only so will

16

the god possess him. I have seen you, my dear, when you have not seen yourself. I know.'

He spoke to comfort me. No one was kinder, when he could be kind sitting down. I never hoped of him that he would stay sober to fight my battles. He was near sixty, which seemed very old to me; but he still moved like a man who knows he looks distinguished, and behind a mask it was surprising how young he could sound, on a good day. I bore him no grudge for Meidias, who would snigger to strangers in taverns about the old man's darling.

So things were jogging on, till the day we put on Philokles' *Hektor*. It calls for Homeric battle-dress, showing one's legs to the thigh. Meidias was thin-shanked, had to wear padded tights, and still had knock-knees. He was cast as Paris.

We were playing at a little market town between Corinth and Mykenai. Such places always have the local wit who gives his own performance. Paris exits saying, 'What do I care, while Helen shares my bed?' This man yelled out, 'She must have got thin, to fit between those knees.' It stopped the play for some time, and worse was to come. Meidias was playing the Greek herald too, and Paris, who must be on to hear his challenge, is a stand-in bit. Backstage, Meidias gave me his kilted corselet and his mask as if he wished they were steeped in poison. Sure enough, when I came on this joker cheered, and set the whole house off.

After this they had Paris in a long robe for *Hektor*, writing in a line about his unwarlike dress; and Meidias, from plaguing me in spare time, became a serious enemy.

Let us omit the daily chronicle of his devices. Sit down in any wine-shop by any theatre, and you will hear some actor pour out the ancient tale as if he were the first man it had happened to; but at least the listener has been bought a drink. We will pass by, then, the thorn in the boot, the sewn-up sleeve, the broken mask-string, and so forth. One morning I found a dark sticky splash and a broken wine-jar by the seat where Demochares had taken the air. The wine had been neat, and I guessed who had sent it; but that time he reckoned wrong. Demochares might be too easy with himself; but he was not easy enough to let a Meidias make use of him. I think at this time he warned Lamprias we should have trouble. But Lamprias wanted to hear of no more troubles than he had; and he knew about Meidias all that signified; namely, that there was no chance till the tour was over of getting anyone else.

We had an engagement in Phigaleia, a small town near Olympia. This was an important date, because the city had hired us. They were celebrating, on the feast of their founding hero, their liberation too.

This was one of the towns which the Spartans, after they won the Great War against Athens, gave into the power of their oligarchs to keep the people quiet. Here as usual they had chosen their Council of Ten from the worst of the old landowners, who had been exiled by the democrats and had most to gain from holding them down. These Dekarchs had paid off old scores tenfold; done as they chose, helped themselves to any pretty young wife or handsome boy they fancied, or any man's best bit of land. If anyone complained, the Spartans would send a troop there, and when they had done with him he thought he had been well off before. Then came the Theban rising; Pelopidas and the other patriots there had shown the world that Spartans are made of the same stuff as other men; and while the Sons of Herakles were rubbing their heads and running about to look what hit them, the subject cities seized their chance. The Phigaleians had been prompt in this; but as they had begun by rushing with one accord to tear in pieces the most hated Dekarch, the others with their faction had got away to the hills.

The City Council had sent us word beforehand, and asked for a play to suit the feast, no expense spared; some of the Dekarchs' gold had been saved from looting. Lamprias had found just the thing for them; a *Kadmos* by Sophokles the Younger, glorifying Thebes. It was a new, middling piece, which no one has thought worth reviving; Kadmos, punished for killing the War-God's dragon, is redeemed from bondage, made King, married to Harmonia, and so on to the finale with wedding procession. For good measure Demochares, who doctored scripts well when his head was clear, had written-in some prophecies for Apollo, somehow dragging in Phigaleia. The Council was delighted. We had a week rehearsing with our chorus, who were about as good as you would expect when leading democrats' sons had been chosen first and voices afterwards.

I looked forward myself to this production, because it gave me more than usual to do. I had a few lines as an extra (one of Kadmos' earth-born warriors) and for the whole finale I was standing-in for Apollo, since Meidias, who played him, was doing Harmonia as well.

This was the first time I had worn the mask of the god. Meidias, who sneered at all our costumes to show what he was used to, despised more than anything this Apollo mask. He said it must be all of fifty years old; and in this I found he was right. It was heavy, being carved from olive wood, but no hardship to wear, for it was finished as smooth inside as out, a real craftsman's job. No one makes them to last, nowadays.

I remember the first time I unpacked the hampers, at Eleusis, and saw it looking up at me. It gave me a start. It was a face, I thought, more for a temple than a stage. I know I sat back on my heels, among all the litter, looking and looking. Meidias was right in calling it old-fashioned, one must allow him that. No one would say, as they do before a modern Apollo, 'Delightful! What a nice young man!'

Demochares, whom I asked about it, said it had been left to

Lamprias by some old actor who had thought it brought him luck. It was supposed to have been made for the first revival of Aischylos' *Eumenides*, where the god has a central role. That would be in the great days of Alkibiades and Nikias, when sponsors were sponsors, Demochares said.

Our overnight stop, before Phigaleia, had been at Olympia; I had never been there, and could not stare enough. In fact the place was stone-dead, it not being a Games year; but youth is easily pleased, and I set out with Demochares to see the sights. Like an old horse to its stable, he plodded to his favourite tavern near the river; and, seeing in my eye that I was going to move him on, said in his priest voice, 'Dear boy, you were asking me about the mask of Apollo. It has just come back to me, whose workshop it came from, as I was told. Go along to the Temple of Zeus, and you will see. Let me think, yes, the west gable.'

I gave in, not sorry to get on quicker. Heat filled the wooded valley, for spring comes like summer there. Already the river was shallow in its pebbly bed; the dust was hot to the foot, the painted statues glowed. A tender Hermes, dangling grapes before the baby god he carried, made one want to stroke his russet flesh. Further on were the penalty statues, given as fines by athletes caught cheating; shoddy hack-work done cheap. The giltwork dazzled on the roofs, the white marble glared. The great altar of Zeus, uncleaned since the morning sacrifice, stank and buzzed with flies. But there are always sightseers for the temple. The porch and colonnades were noisy with guides and cheap-jacks; pedlars sold copies of Zeus' image in painted clay, quacks cried their cures, kids and rams bleated, on sale for sacrifice; a rusty-voiced rhetor declaimed the Odyssey while his boy passed round the plate. I went in from the hot sun to the soft, cool shadows, and gaped with the rest at the great statue inside, the gold and ivory, the throne as big as my room at home, till my eye, travelling upward, met the face of power which says, 'O man, make peace with your mortality, for this too is God.'

Going out, I had to shake off a low fellow who seemed to think a free supper would be my price, and nearly forgot to look at the west gable. But a guide was herding a gaggle of rich women with their children, nurses, and big straw hats; I saw him pointing, and talking of the sculptor Pheidias. My eye followed his finger.

The triangle of the gable end was full of the battle between the Greeks and Kentaurs. Theseus and Pirithoos and their men were battling to save the boys and women: men against half-men, wrestling, bashing, trampling, swinging axes; and in the midst, tall and alone, his right arm stretched above the mellay, was the Apollo of the mask.

You could not mistake it. But here the mouth was closed and, the face had eyes. I walked back to see better, so lost that I bumped a lady, who scolded me. I scarcely heard. My flesh shivered with delight and awe. Even now, sometimes, at Olympia, that shudder will come back to me.

He stands above the battle, needing only to be, not do. The world is still green and raw; he alone knows it is for him the Greeks are fighting; yet some light from him shines back in young Theseus' face. The Greeks must win, because they are nearer his likeness; his prophetic eyes look far beyond. He has no favourites. He is stern, radiant, gracious and without pity. A perfect chord is the friend of him whose strings are tuned to it. Can it pity the kitharist who fumbles?

I walked back doing a speech for him, boyish nonsense in the hack-verse any actor can think in. There was no time to finish it, for Demochares had drunk himself silly, and had to be got back while he could still stand. He greeted me as his lovely Hylas, making the other drinkers laugh and cheer; but I was used to that. 'Hylas?' I said. 'You know what happened to *him*. Herakles let him

21

go sightseeing on his own, and the local nymphs took and drowned him. And Herakles lost his passage in the Argo. Heave-ho, shipmate; come back on board, before the skipper casts off.'

But when I unpacked the hampers at Phigaleia, and hung the mask of Apollo on its peg, I plucked a bay-sprig to stick above it, and poured a few drops of wine on the floor below. As I went with my flickering lamp out of the old wooden skene-room, I half-thought as I turned that there were eyes in the eye-holes, watching me off.

On the morning of the performance, long before sun-up the audience was pouring in. Every soul who could walk must have been there; indeed, I saw one old granddad carried from his donkey to his seat.

I made sure Demochares took his breakfast watered; buckled him into the panoply of Ares; laid out everyone's things, and tuned my lyre, which I should have to play for the bridal song. Then I got dressed as the Theban Warrior.

Everything went quite smoothly, as far as I remember, until about two-thirds through. Lamprias and Demochares were on stage as Kadmos and Telephassa. Meidias had exited as Harmonia, to do his change for Apollo; presently he would appear and prophesy, on the god-walk above the skene. I was still on as a warrior, with nothing to do but hold a spear.

Standing up stage centre by the royal door, I was looking out beyond the theatre at the hillside it was carved from. Suddenly I noticed a crowd of men coming down towards it. My first thought was that the citizens of some neighbour town had come to see the play, and got here late. When I saw they all had spears and shields I still did not think much of it, supposing they were going to do a war-dance at the festival. Looking back, I find this simplicity hard to credit; but when you work in Athens, you get to think the world stops still for a play.

Lamprias went on with his speech; the men got nearer; till suddenly, down in the orchestra, one of the chorus gave a yell and pointed upward. The audience stared; first at him, then at where he was pointing. Then chaos began.

The troop above gave the paean, and charged downhill. The Phigaleians, all weaponless, started tearing up the wooden benches and their struts, or running away. The women, who had been sitting in their best on the other side, began to huddle, scramble and scream. One young man, a quick thinker, jumped up on stage from the chorus, and snatched my spear from my hand. I hope he got some good from it; it was a property one with a wooden blade. I offered him my shield, which he would need still more; but he was off, with his bearded mask pushed back on top of his head.

I don't know what I would have thought of doing next. But, booming away close by, I heard the voice of Lamprias, still speaking his lines.

Those people who did not say that actors are mostly mad, said afterwards that a god possessed us. But in fact, there is more sense in going on at such times than you would suppose. At least everyone knows who and what you are; we would have stood a far better chance of being speared, or trampled on, if we had bolted than we did by staying on stage. Man's nature asks a reason, say the philosophers, so there I offer one. I doubt if I thought of it at the time. Theatre, to me, was still the Dionysia at Athens. I was used to ceremony, respect for the sacred precinct, priests and statesmen and generals in the seats of honour; everything done decently, and the death-penalty for violence. This brawling outraged me. We had rehearsed the play especially for this one festival; and I had not done my stand-in as Apollo yet.

The turmoil was getting worse. Here and there men in the audience had jumped up, paused in two minds, and run round

23

outside to join the oligarchs. Some women had clambered over to the men's side to grab their kin and keep them out of it. Now men who had run away at first, not in fear but to fetch their weapons, were coming back armed. But Demochares had come in on cue, and was fluting gravely as Telephassa. He even had an audience; one ancient priest in front, who had noticed nothing amiss, and some children, who it seems were used to faction fights but had never seen a play.

I had just noticed, startled, that blood was flowing out in front – the first I had ever seen shed in war – when Lamprias adlibbed something, beckoned me near, and said out of the side of his mask, 'Get Apollo on.'

I made an exit and ran behind. Before I reached the skene-room I knew what I would find, which of course was nothing. I even looked in the hampers. He must have run off still costumed as Harmonia. His own clothes were there.

The robe and mask of Apollo were where I had put them out. I stripped and scrambled into them, picked up my lyre, and went out to the back. The skene-room was just a flat-topped shed, with a crazy ladder to the god-walk on its roof. Meidias, but not I, had rehearsed getting up there, holding on with one hand and managing with the other both lyre and skirts. As I floundered up, tearing my sleeve on a nail, I cursed the oligarchs of Phigaleia who had got so rich without spending a drachma on this wretched theatre. Down with them, I thought; up with the democrats. Apollo blesses their cause.

As I waited under the entrance-ramp for my cue, I ran over all I knew of Apollo's speech from hearing Meidias ploughing through it. It was just the thing for the Phigaleians, if anybody listened. I touched the mask for luck, saying 'Help me through this, Apollo, and I'll give you something'; there was no time to think what. Then I swept up the ramp, striking my lyre.

From on top, I could see a proper battle. About half the citizens were now armed, if only with knives or cleavers. There were spears and swords too, serious business. To stand up here, mouthing away unheard, seemed stupid in an actor, and undignified in a god. I raised my arm, in the pose of the Pheidias Apollo, and cried out, 'Victory!'

Some women exclaimed and pointed. A few men started to cheer. At once the speech of prophecy went clean out of my head. For a moment I felt like dying. Then – how sent, I leave you to decide as your nature prompts you – there came back to me my own childish voice, declaiming the Messenger from Salamis, in Aischylos' *The Persians*. It was the first long speech my father had made me learn. I slammed a loud chord on the lyre, stepped to the god-walk's edge, and threw it out for all I was worth.

> *Onward, sons of the Greeks! Set free the land of your fathers!*
> *Rescue your sons, your wives, and your holy places,*
> *Shrines of ancestral gods, and tombs of those who begot you!*
> *To battle! Winner takes all!*

The theatre at Phigaleia was short of everything else, but at least it had good acoustics. The cheers came back from right up the hill. Later, I was assured that some of the women thought it really was Apollo; from what I have seen on country tours, it would not much surprise me. The men, if less simple than this, still thought it a lucky omen, believing it was in the play. I heard them calling on the god, as they pushed the oligarchs backward.

The rest of the speech would take the Greek sons to sea, which I feared might spoil it. But I was sure it would disgust my father, to think I had dried because of a slight mischance on tour; besides, down below, on stage, Demochares was blowing kisses and saying 'Go on! Go on!' So I took it all as it came, bronze beaks, rammed sterns, shattered oars, corpse-strewn beaches, wallowing keels, wailing upon the waters. I broke off now and then and played Dorian marches, to spin it out.

I forget how far I got before the oligarchs fell back out of sight beyond the hill-ridge. (They ran till they got to Sparta, where they stayed, and just what they deserved.) So I had lost most of my audience, the citizens going in pursuit. Since the play seemed over, I tagged it off, from Euripides this time,

> In vain man's expectation;
> God brings the unthought to be,
> As here we see.

Then I came down, and tore my sleeve on the nail again.

The evening's party went on all over Phigaleia. They had a great krater in the Agora the size of a well-head, full of free wine. I left Demochares to enjoy Dionysos' bounty – he had earned it – and wandered off. People kept asking me who had enacted Apollo; a man of towering stature, they mostly said, who had appeared as if from heaven. I had been meant to wear lifted boots, but had not had time to lace them on. It is a fact that you can make an audience see nearly anything, if you yourself believe in it.

I missed Lamprias for some hours, and wondered where he had got to. Later I learned he had spent all that time in the skene-room, sitting on a hamper-top as patient as the Fates, waiting for Meidias to come back for his clothes.

He had a story ready, how he had seen some citizen being set upon and rushed to help. This ungrateful fellow never came forward; and Harmonia's wedding-dress was ruined, all over muck from a near-by pig-house, where there had not been room to stand.

26

The City Council begged us to do *Kadmos* again next day, to celebrate victory. We did so, with much acclaim. When it came time to pay, they said they could not give more than half-fee for the first performance, since we had not finished it. I still laugh when I think of Lamprias' face. For myself, I had no complaints, being cast this time as Apollo and Harmonia, while Meidias stood in for me.

As I was saying, anything can happen on tour. At all events, that is how I got my first chance as third actor.

2

By the time I was twenty-six, I was not quite unknown in Athens. I had played first roles at Piraeus, and at the City Theatre done second in some winning plays. But they had had big male roles for the protagonist, and my best ones had all been women's. It would be easy to get typed, being my father's son; while anyone casting a great female part would think first of Theodoros. It was a time which comes to many artists, when one must break away.

It would take more than applause at Piraeus to get my name on the City Theatre list of leading men. Competition was deadly; the books were full of old victors who could hardly count their crowns. But there were still contests in other cities; it was now I should try to bring home a wreath or two.

My mother was dead. I had dowered my sister decently and got her settled; nothing held me in Athens; and I am footloose by nature, like most men of my calling. For all these reasons, I went into partnership with Anaxis.

It is a good while now since he took up politics full time. His voice and gestures are much acclaimed; and every rival orator, who wants a stone to throw at him, accuses him of having been an actor. Well, he chose his company, and is welcome to it. But though he might not thank me now for saying so, at the time I am speaking of he was very promising; and I have always thought he gave up too easily.

He was older than I, past thirty, and had a name for touchiness; but one could get on with him if one did not tread on his corns. His family had been rich, but lost everything in the Great War; they never got back their land, and his father worked as a steward. So Anaxis, though he had talent, only wanted to be an artist with half his mind; with the other he wanted to be a gentleman. Any fellow-artist will understand me.

He was the only actor I've known to wear a beard. How he bore it under masks I can't think, but even in summer he only trimmed it. He valued the dignity it gave him, and he certainly had presence. But he was growing no younger, and had not got on the list; so he was getting anxious.

Under our contract, we would take turns as directing protagonist. He was fond of the stately parts, like Agamemnon, which meant that even when the choice was his, he would be handing me some first-class acting roles. Always the man of breeding; on the other hand, he did live up to it. He might be pompous, but was never sordid or mean; which is worth something, on tour.

We had a booking at Corinth in a brand-new play, Theodektes' *Amazons*. Anaxis, who had choice of lead, took Theseus, leaving me Hippolyta which to my mind was the better role. Herakles was done by our third actor, Krantor. He was the best we could afford to hire, a steady old trouper, long past ambition but not gone sour, who stayed in theatre because he could have borne no other life. For extra we had a youth called Anthemion, who was Anaxis' boy friend. Anaxis likened him to a statue by Praxiteles. This was true at least of his head, which was solid marble; for the rest he was harmless, and would do as he was told. I could have improved on this choice, but had known

29

Anaxis would never stir without him; so kept quiet, rather than have words right at the start.

The Corinth theatre is one of the best in Greece. It has seating for eighteen thousand, and in the top row they can hear you sigh. The revolves turn smoothly; the reveal runs out on oiled wheels; you won't find Clytemnestra, brought forth in the final tableau of the *Agamemnon*, come jerking and tottering with a couple of bouncing corpses at her feet. The crane swings you up over the god-walk as if you were really flying, and puts you down like a feather right on the mark; it will lift a chariot with two life-sized winged horses and two actors, without a creak.

Our sponsor, who like all Corinthians was so rich that gold ran out of his ears, had hand-picked a chorus of the loveliest boys in town, to do the Amazons. I spent all my free time with one of them, a splendid creature, half Macedonian, grey-eyed and with dark red hair.

Anaxis was very happy there. In Corinth actors are asked to the very best houses. So are charioteers and wrestlers, though I knew better than to point this out to him. What a pleasure, he used to say, to be among gentlemen, away from theatre talk with its narrow jealousies. Still, theatre men do know what one is doing and what it is worth; even their jealousy is a kind of praise. For me, I would rather sit drinking with a paid-off soldier from Egypt or Ionia, telling his tales, or swap advice on inns with some ribbon-seller who knows the road, than share a supper-couch with some rich fool who thinks that because he owns three chariots his notice must delight you, who does not know good from bad till the judges tell him what to think, but who has you in his supper-room like the Persian tapestry and the talking jackdaw and the Libyan monkey, because you are that year's fashion; and tells you without fail that he feels it in him to write a tragedy, if his affairs would only give him time. All you can say for such a host is that he does hire the best hetairas. I can live very well without women, on the whole; but any sensible talk you get at such a party, you get from them. They really know the tragedies, starting with the texts. One soon learns, at Corinth, where their block is in the theatre; everyone plays the subtleties to them.

The Amazons is one of Theodektes' better plays, and won the poets' prize. He had ridden over from Athens, and was so pleased with us that he never said a word about the places where I had sharpened-up his lines. Our sponsor put on a victory-feast, truly Corinthian; it took us all next day to get over it, and I lazed with my grey-eyed Macedonian, in a rocky pine-shaded cove near Perachora. An actor's life is full of meeting and parting; one can't tear one's heart out every time; but I was touched when he gave me a necklet of blue beads to ward off the evil eye. I have got it still.

Our next engagement was at Delphi.

Anaxis was full of this prospect. With every year as his hopes in the theatre fell, he went further into politics, scouting out the land; and he had got wind of this booking from afar. The reason for a play being put on outside the festivals was to entertain the delegates at a peace conference, a very big affair.

Peace of some sort was overdue; for some years artists had had trouble in getting about at all, what with Spartans marching on Thebes, then Thebans marching on Sparta. Everyone was for Thebes in the early days. But since all her victories, the old neighbourly jealousy had waked up in Athens; and we had an alliance with Sparta now. I suppose this was expedient, but it disgusted me; it is things like this which make a man like me leave politics to the demagogues. The one good thing was, that those dour-faced bullies needing to ask our help proved they were down to third roles for good and would never play lead again. They had been thought invincible, only because they were in war-training from the cradle to the grave; but the Great War went on so long that other Greeks too got this professional experience, though against their will. By the end of it a good many had borne arms since they were boys, and barely knew another calling. So, like actors short of work, they went on tour. There were still nearly as many wars going on as drama festivals; and all of them needed extras.

No sooner had the Spartans been put down, than the Arcadians, who had been content till now with fighting here and there for hire, thought to try ruling the roost on their own account. So the Peloponnese was full of smoke and soldiers, just when it had looked like a good season with clear roads.

Most other cities, however, had had enough. Hence this peace conference at Delphi. Anaxis assured me, too, that backstage promoting it were powerful states outside of Hellas altogether. They had learned the worth of good Greek mercenaries; were grieved to see them wasted fighting for their own homes, and wanted them back in the open market.

Anaxis was full of lore about intrigues. I tried to attend, but found it hard. We had come by sea to Itea; now on hired mules we were hauling up the twisted track through the Pleistos valley, following the river in the shade of the olive groves which wind up through the gorge. Sometimes the trees would open wide, and one could glimpse Delphi high above, tiny against the huge flank of Parnassos, shining like a jewel.

It was warm in the olive-fields, the sunlight came dappled, and one was never far from the sound of water as the river lapsed towards the sea. Now and again the boughs would stir, and a different air blow from the mountain, cold, bright and pure. It made my nape shiver, as a dog's nose twitches before he knows why. But Anaxis had been as busy as a squirrel in Corinth, getting informed, and did not like to see my eye wandering. Pharaoh of Egypt, he said, and the Great King, would be sending agents for certain.

'Good luck to them,' I said. 'At least in peacetime, Greeks can choose whether to fight or stop at home.'

Anaxis cleared his throat and looked about; a needless bit of business, since only the mules were in earshot. Anthemion had got bored, and fallen back to bore Krantor. 'They say, too, there will be an envoy – unofficial, of course – from Dionysios of Syracuse.'

I slapped my knee, startling my mount, which nearly threw me. These words had waked me up. 'By the dog of Egypt! Only envoys? Are you sure? Perhaps he'll come himself; we might even set eyes on him.'

Anaxis frowned, and clicked his tongue, hearing levity in my voice. We were talking, after all, of the most famous sponsor in the world.

'Of course he will not come. He never leaves home except for war, when he takes his army with him. Thus they cannot be corrupted; and are at hand if treason springs up behind his back in Syracuse. He would not have held power for forty years, in Sicily, if he were not one of the shrewdest men alive. On the other hand, the envoy he sends may well be someone high-ranking at his court, who has been told to look out for talent.'

I had read this in his eyes before he brought it out. His solemnity tempted me. 'Leave me out,' I said. 'He might want to read us one of his odes, as he did to Philoxenos the poet. He was asked for his opinion, gave it, and got a week in the quarries to mend his taste. Then he was forgiven and asked to supper. When he saw the scrolls coming out again, he clapped his hands for the guard and said, "Back to the quarry!"'

I must own to have heard this story at my father's knee.

Philoxenos had been dining out on it for twenty years, improving it all the time, and I daresay had made it up on the way home, after hailing his host as a second Pindar. But it was too good to waste. 'And then,' I said, 'there was that Sophist who keeps that school, the man Dionysios' young kinsman fell in love with and brought to Syracuse, hoping, poor lad, to change the tyrant into a second Solon; how touching young love is! When the poor professor opened his mouth too wide, wasn't he not only chased out of Syracuse, but put on a ship for Aigina when they'd just passed sentence of slavery on any Athenian landing there? And his learned friends had to bid for him at market. I forget his name.'

'Plato,' said Anaxis, breathing slowly to keep his temper. 'Everyone agrees he is a stiff-necked man, who missed his chance for fear of being called a sycophant. He was asked to a party, but wouldn't wear fancy dress; he wouldn't dance—'

'Can he?'

'Nor, when he discoursed, would he avoid political theory—'

'What was he asked to discourse on?'

'Virtue, I suppose. What does it matter? All I am asking is that you keep your eyes open at Delphi, and look what you are doing. Opportunity only knocks once.'

'Well,' I said, 'if Dionysios is as rich as people say, no doubt he can stand his envoy a theatre seat. It only costs two obols.'

'Niko, dear boy, you know I think the world of you.' He was trying hard. 'You have a gift; audiences like you; but never think you can't end where *he* is now' (he looked back at Krantor, who had slid off his mule to piss) 'if you take no trouble to get known by people of influence. That boy in Corinth! A charming creature for a night, but to spend your days with him! And that party you said you were too tired to go to; do you know Chrysippos owns the biggest racing stables in the Isthmus? Everyone was there. Yet you were not too tired to go round the wine-shops with Krantor.'

'Krantor knows the best. Everyone was there; why didn't you come too?'

'In a city like Corinth, an artist of your standing should not be seen drinking with a third-part actor. I assure you, such things are not understood at all.'

'Thanks for the compliment, my dear. But if I'm too good for that, then by Apollo I'm too good to play in third-rate fustian, even if the Tyrant of Syracuse writes it and puts it on. Let him hire Theophanes, and put him in purple boots; they deserve each other.'

I could see Anaxis holding himself in, remembering, as I ought to have been doing, how quarrels ruin a tour. Men can't get away from each other long enough to cool off; I have known it end in blood.

'Very well, Niko. But an artist should know whether it is art he is talking about, or politics. In this case, I doubt you do.'

'Look!' I said pointing upward. 'That must be the Temple of Apollo.' I had had politics enough.

'Of course. The theatre is just behind it. Tell me, Niko, have you yourself seen one of Dionysios' plays performed?'

'Not I; I've never set foot in Syracuse.'

'His *Ajax* won second prize at the Dionysia, in Athens, some years ago.'

'*Ajax*? Was that his?' It had been put on of course by an Athenian choregos, acting for him, and one gets wrapped up in one's own play. I had forgotten, if I had known, and own that the news surprised me.

'Yes, it was his. Athenians don't sit through trash without complaining, still less see it crowned. Let us keep things in their places. Dionysios, the ruler, is a despot and the friend of despots. He governs with spies. He plunders temples. He has sold Greek cities to the Carthaginians. He is allied with oligarchs everywhere.

He lends troops to the Spartans. To hate him, therefore, is the password of a democrat. In a speech to the Assembly, of course one must say his verse is bathetic and limps in every foot. If one said it is passable, do you think they would debate its structure? They would merely accuse you of wanting the Thirty Tyrants back. But we, my dear Niko, are artists and grown men; and nobody is listening.'

'Well, that's fair. But would you really act for him, even so? I shouldn't care to play to an audience an orator had been at first, like that one at Olympia.'

'My dear Niko! One can see you have been in theatre since you were born. That was more than four Olympiads ago. How old were you?'

'About seven; but it seems like yesterday.'

I had been there when friends of my father's, who had seen it, called with the news. Dionysios had entered some choral odes at the music contest. Not content with hiring first-class talent, he had not known where to stop, but had dressed them as richly as Persian satraps, adding a marquee for the show, of purple rigged with gold cords. It came, I suppose, from his never leaving Sicily. Cultivated people laughed, and all the rest cried 'Hubris!' Visiting the Games was Lysias the orator, then an old man but still impressive, who had been at war with oligarchs all his life; not without cause, seeing his brother had been murdered by the Thirty, and he himself barely got away. Seizing his chance, he made a fiery speech against Dionysios and urged the crowd to show what Hellas thought of him. They duly booed off the artists, pulled the pavilion down, and looted it of everything they could carry. At this point of the tale, I drew attention to myself by squealing out with laughter. My father, who never passed a mistake until next time, had fixed the thing in my mind for ever by the taking-down he gave me. Olympia, he said, was a sacred festival; if it was unlawful for Lysias to use violence there himself, he should not have done it through other men. And at an art contest, nothing should be judged but art. How would I like to be one of the artists pelted while giving their best work? He hoped I might never find out for myself. After this I had crept away. Even now, I shrank from telling Anaxis.

'He was provincial in those days,' Anaxis said. 'He is just a clerk's son, after all. But he has bought good advice since then; and he always was a worker.'

'I'll read his plays,' I said, to keep him quiet. We were getting up towards the shoulder Delphi stands on. The groves were thinning. A pure bright air blew from the peaks. The place smelled of bliss, danger and gods.

'In any case,' Anaxis was saying, 'one must remember he is a Sicilian ruling Sicilians. The old stock of Corinth has run pretty thin there. Fighting back the Carthaginians all these years, they've learned their ways, and bred with them. It's said Dionysios has a touch of it. The best they could hope for, as they are, would be to change a bad tyrant for a good one.'

For a moment the dark-browed face of my boyhood's lover came into my mind, and I wondered if he would still delight me. Then we came out from the trees, and stood upon the shoulder. Ask some poet to describe the awe of Delphi, and some philosopher to explain it. I work with the words of other men. I looked back down the valley, the olives winding and falling mile on mile to a rock-clipped blink of sea. Beyond a vast gulf of air were the highlands of Mount Korax, cloud-patched with sun and gloom; westward the iron cliffs of Kirphis; above us reared Parnassos, more felt than seen. Its head was hidden by its knees, the rock-towers of the Phaidriades, which themselves seemed to gore the sky. Truly, Apollo is the greatest of all chorus-masters. The town, with his temple in the midst, is tiny as a toy in all this vastness;

yet all those titan heads seem to stand around that and look towards it. They are the chorus round his altar; if he raised his arm they would sing a dithyramb. I don't know any other deity who could bring off such a show. At Delphi, you don't ask how they know it is the centre of the earth.

I looked up the great steeps of the Phaidriades, which stand behind the theatre like a skene reaching to heaven. 'Look!' I said. 'Eagles!'

'My dear Niko, they are as common here as doves. Do let us get to the inn while they have something left to eat. If this is your first visit, you need not tell the world.'

Next morning we looked over the theatre. We were pleased to find not a bit of obsolete equipment anywhere; after the big earthquake of five years back, they had had to refit completely. There was still scaffolding round the temple, and the roof a makeshift of pinepoles and thatch; Apollo and the Earth Snake kept up their ancient war. We shouldered back through the town under the tall proud statues, past the treasure-houses for the cities' offerings, Anaxis waiting patiently while I tipped the guardians and gaped at all the gold. We squeezed past sightseers and guides and pilgrims, soldiers and priests and slaves, temple-sweepers with brooms and whores with fans; stalls selling lamps, ribbons, raisins, books of oracles, and sacred bayleaves for lucky dreams. Looking up and about, I thought it was like dwarfs playing on a stage designed for titans. I suppose it was still a small, solemn place when Xerxes' army came to lift the gold, and they asked Apollo what to do. 'Get out,' he said; 'I can take care of my own.' They still show the rock-peak he hurled down on the Persians, blazing aloft the Phaidriades and yelling through the thunder. I bought, for keepsake, a little gilded bronze of the god drawing his bow. A pretty thing. The old statue in the temple, that is an Apollo to shoot straight.

But the shops don't copy it now; they say it is crude, and art must move with the times.

Presently came a slave to meet us, bidding us take wine with our choregos.

We were led to a fine painted house beside the Stadium, and saw at once that our sponsor was a syndicate. Three were Delphians; but by watching whom everyone looked at first, we guessed it was the fourth who was putting up the money. He was one Philiskos, an Asian Greek from Abydos. What with his clothes and his ivory fly-whisk, and Delphi being as full of gossip as a winter hive of bees, we added two and two. This was King Artaxerxes' agent, playing host to the Conference with Persian gold.

While sweets and civilities went round, we discussed the play. The citizens of Delphi weren't mentioned from first to last; it was the delegates who must be pleased. It was my turn to direct and choose a role, and I had proposed *Hippolytos with the Garland*. It was as good as settled, when some little man, who I'll swear only wanted to go home saying he had spoken, said it might give offence to the Athenians, by showing King Theseus in the wrong. We both assured them it was revived in Athens about one year in five, and was the surest hit in repertory. Too late; the damage was done, the panic started. At a peace conference, it went without saying that everyone would be looking for slights and insults. *Helen in Egypt* might affront the Pharaoh; *Medea* the Corinthians; *Alkestis* the Thessalians. Once or twice I stole a glance at Anaxis, meaning, 'Let's leave them at it; before they miss us we'll be in Thebes.' But he had set his heart and hopes on this production. When I whispered, under cover of all the dickering, 'Try offering them *The Persians*!', he looked down his nose and would not laugh.

From mere boredom I started dreaming; and dreams bring

memories. Next time they paused to scratch their heads, I said, 'Why not *The Myrmidons?*'

How often, if ever, you have seen this play depends upon where you live. It is a favourite in Thebes and well liked in Macedon. In Athens it is hardly ever revived; no sponsor likes to take the risk. Ever since Aischylos' own day, some people have always disapproved; and you never know when they will get on the judges' board. Demagogues have proclaimed that the love of man for youth is a relic of aristocracy (a politician will say any-thing, if it strikes where he wants to hit), and the last thing they want to hear is that the play is noble. They would rather those great avowals did not ring on so in the heart.

Today, however, it turned out to be just the thing. Having looked at it backwards, sideways and upside down, they could not find a single slur on anyone's ancestors, gods or city.

We went our way, stuffed full of Persian sweets and almonds, cursing the waste of time but satisfied with the outcome. Anaxis was content with his roles. I, being protagonist, would do Achilles; but Patroklos has some lovely lines, and so has Briseis later. Krantor would do Odysseus and the other odd parts, 'and', said Anaxis, 'I suppose Apollo in the prologue?'

Walking as we talked, we had come out on top of the theatre seats, and were gazing over the temple roof at the mountains. I said, 'No, I'll take Apollo myself.'

Anaxis raised his brows. 'Do you want to? It's a very quick change. Don't forget Apollo is flown on; you'll have the harness to get rid of.'

'I've a fancy for it. One's not in Delphi every day. Call it my service to the god.'

That evening we were summoned back to meet the chorus-master, the flautist and the skene-painter. The painter, Hagnon, was an old friend from Athens. Between rehearsals, I stayed to chat with him while he painted trophies-of-arms on the reveal and Greek tents on the flats. From time to time he would shout for his man to bring him ladder or paint, or shift his scaffolding, complaining that the fellow was never at call. He was lanky and spindle-shanked, with a straggling yellow beard; once I caught him staring at me, and it stirred some memory I could not place; but it was clear he would stare at anything rather than work, and I thought no more of it. Hagnon had had to take him on at Delphi, having come to do murals in a private house and getting this contract afterwards.

Rehearsals went smoothly. The chorus of Myrmidons were fine well-built men and could sing as well. I found a saddler to make me a flying-harness. The crane-man weighed me for the counter-weight; finding him skilful, I only did my fly-in once with him, and rehearsed the prologue from the god-walk.

I enjoyed working on *The Myrmidons*. I had steeped my soul in it when young, and it still moved me. I have heard Patroklos better done; Anaxis had technique enough to sound young, but fell short of charm; still he did bring out the character's goodness, without which nothing makes sense.

Delphi was filling up every day. Delegates were arriving; and, as Anaxis told me, all kinds of agents to watch the delegates, sent by the opposition in their various cities, their secret allies in rival cities, the interested kings and tyrants, and I don't know whom. I was more amused by the high-priced hetairas who had come in from other towns and set up house to the rage of the Delphi girls; they would make a better audience than all these peace-traders. Leaving Anaxis to smell about, I went walking on the thymy hillsides or through the olive groves, hearing for chorus the cicadas and moun-tain birds, while I ran over this speech or that. One day Anaxis came bustling up to say that the envoy of Dionysios had come at last, and bettered our hopes by being some great personage and the tyrant's kin. My mind was on the placing of a breath-pause, and the name went straight out of my head.

At my request, Hagnon was painting the masks for the principals; the local mask-maker was fit only for chorus work, but Hagnon worked wonders with his carving as a good painter can. He had done me a fine Achilles, and was working on Patroklos. The Apollo was not yet carved.

Ever since Lamprias died and his widow sold up his things, I had kept the mask of Pheidias hanging, in a box like a little shrine, on the wall of my room in Athens. Remembering Phigaleia, before every contest I would wreathe it and make some offering. There was no good reason why I should have brought it with me – one can always find a friend to mind one's things when touring – yet some reason had seemed good, and it was on the table at my lodging. That evening, when the lamp was lit and the shadows moved with the flame, it seemed to look straight at me with eyes inside its eyeholes, as if to say, 'Nikeratos, you have brought me home. Dionysos' winter reign at Delphi is past and gone. Have you not heard my music on Parnassos? I should like to smell skene-paint again.'

It gave me a start. I sat down at the pinewood table, chin in hand, as my father taught me to do before a mask, when one wants to think oneself into it.

'Glorious Apollo,' I said presently, 'are you sure? Wouldn't you like your face to be more in fashion? You could have anything; a solid gold wreath, jewelled earrings; it's nothing to the backers here. And they'll be at the dress rehearsal.'

A night breeze blew in from the heights of Korax; the lamp-flame quivered; Apollo looked at me with dark lidless eyes. 'At Phigaleia,' he said, 'you promised to give me something. Have I asked for anything before?'

In the morning, I took it to the light. The paint was dull and worn, but the carving perfect. Hagnon was in the theatre, touching-up; I opened the box, and asked him what he thought.

He looked long in silence, frowning and biting his lips. I waited for him to say the usual things: stiff, harsh, primitive. But he looked up as if some pain had gripped him, and said, 'Oh God, what was it like when men had certainty like that?'

'God knows,' I said. 'I'll wear it and see what comes to me. Can you repaint it?'

'Oh, yes; of course. I can touch it up and tone it down, till from in front you'd hardly tell it from a modern one. Listen, Niko. I'll buy you a new one and paint it free. Just give me this and we're square.'

'No; I meant can you do it as it was?'

He lifted it out, turning it in his hand and scratching the paint with his finger. 'I can try,' he said, 'God help me. Leave it with me.'

He put it by, and hauled his ladder along the skene. I gave him a hand, asking where his man had got to. 'I turned him off, and good riddance. It's quicker to work alone. Bone-idle, sullen, and drunk half the time. Niko, did you ever hire him?'

'Not I, by the dog.'

'When I paid him off, he said he supposed it was your doing.'

'Mine? What could he mean? It's true, there was some look about him ... What is his name?'

'Meidias ... You do know him, then?'

I told the story. I daresay in those days it would have pleased me to see him now; you would think he had been a seedy, shift-less day-labourer all his life. Maybe I might still have known him without a beard; but I think it was his legs had jogged my memory. Who else would have believed that after all these years, having got where I was, I would stoop to rob him of his wretched pit-tance? I suppose it was what he would have done himself.

43

'Well,' I thought, 'I've looked my last on him now.' Which indeed was true.

Next day Hagnon did not come to the theatre. Someone said he was shut in his room and would not open; he did not sound sick; he must have company in bed. At evening, he met me in the wine-shop. 'The paint's not set,' he said, 'but come and see.'

He had propped the mask on a table with a lamp before it. I gazed in silence, while the eyes of Apollo Longsight, full of unplumbed darkness, stared out beyond us. We had served his turn. He had come back to his mountain lair, like a snake in springtime, to have his youth renewed.

My long quiet made Hagnon uneasy. 'The room's too small. I should have shown it you in the theatre.'

I said, 'Did you do this, or did he do it himself?'

'I'll tell you what I did. I found it was a day for the oracle; so I sacrificed, and took this with me, and went down to the cave.'

I stared. He looked rather shamefaced. 'It was just to get the feel. But one must ask something, so I asked which attributes the god's face should show; and the Pythia answered – quite clearly, I could hear it without the priest interpreting – "Pythian Apollo". So I went home and started work.'

'Apollo Loxias,' I said. Before, rubbed down almost to bare wood, it had seemed to show only the Olympian, balanced and clear. But poring in the faded lines of mouth and eye and nostril, Hagnon had found lost curves and shadows. A shiver ran down my neck. Here was the Double-Tongued, whose words move to their meaning like a serpent in a reed-bed, coil and counter-coil; how can a man tell all his mind to children, or a god to men?

Presently I asked Hagnon what the Pythia had been like. He answered, 'Like weathered rocks. She had lost her teeth, and under the drug she dribbled. But the fact is, I didn't look at her long. In the back of the cave, behind the tripod, is a crack running into the

44

darkness; and in its mouth is a seven-foot Apollo cast in gold, with eyes of lapis and agate. It must go back beyond the Persian Wars; it has that secret smile. I couldn't take my eyes from it. But I heard what she said.'

I sent out for some wine, and tried to make him take the price of his time; but he said it would be bad luck. Before we drank, we both tipped our cups before the mask.

I asked him why, if these old forms moved him so, he still worked in the current style. 'Just put me back,' he said, 'in the glorious age of Perikles, and dose me with Lethe water, to unknow what I know. Once men deserved such gods. And where are they now? They bled to death on battle-fields, black with flies; or starved in the siege, being too good to rob their neighbours. Or they sailed off to Sicily singing paeans, and left their bones there in sunken ships, or in the fever swamps or the slavequarries. If they got home alive, the Thirty Tyrants murdered him. Or if they survived all that, they grew old in dusty corners, mocked by their grandsons, when to speak of greatness was to be a voice from the dead. They're all gone now; and here are you and I, who know just what became of them. What will you do with that mask, Niko, when you have it on?'

'Well may you ask. At least I'll play in Aischylos, which is what it was made for. Perhaps it will teach me something.'

The lamp soaked, and Hagnon trimmed it. As he pricked up the wick, there was a flicker on the face of Loxias, and it seemed that the dark side smiled.

At dress rehearsal, just as I had foreseen, the sponsors asked Hagnon why he had fobbed them off with old stuff repainted. When he showed that he had not charged for it, they said, amazed, that they had ordered everything of the best. The mask lacked grace and charm; it was too severe. Sponsors are sponsors,

45

so I did not ask them what Apollo needs charm for, coming to tell of doom in words like beaten bronze. Instead we said the god had chosen this mask expressly, through the oracle, for his Pythian likeness. That kept them quiet.

When these fools had gone, Gyllis the Theban courtesan – getting on now, but still famous for her verse-readings – came round to kiss us all. She had been in front, and vowed we should make a hit. Mikon the mechanic, who loved his work, asked if I found the crane ran smoothly. 'I like an artist to feel secure, or he can't do himself justice. Here in Delphi, we never make an old rope do. Twice for a man, once for a chariot, that's my rule. The last play was *Medea*, so you get a new one.' I assured him I had not felt safer in my mother's arms; and he scrambled back into his wooden turret with his oil-flask and his crock of grease.

That evening it rained, which damped our spirits; but day broke cool and blue, with barely a breeze. When we got to the theatre, the upper tiers were full, and the sponsors' servants were fussing about the seats of honour with rugs and cushions. Through the cracks in the skene, it looked like a real occasion. I stripped for my flying-harness, and belted over it Apollo's white, gold-bordered tunic, while my dresser worked the harness ring through the slit.

On my table stood the mask in its open box. From the mask-maker I had bought it a new, fair wig. It was young, strong hair, such as the peasant girls sell when they have to cut it for mourning. The life of the face flowed into it; I pictured it streaming from the head of the furious god, while his arrows clattered at his back with his angry strides, as he came down the crags like nightfall to the plain of Troy. That is the Apollo of *The Myrmidons*; straight from Homer.

I lifted my hands palm upward, asking his favour, and then put

46

on the mask. As the dresser arranged the hair, the flutes and kithara began, and Mikon from his turret signalled 'Ready'.

I ran out, waving on my way to Anaxis, who was kissing Anthemion for luck, and to Krantor strapping on the corselet of Odysseus. Behind the back of the skene-room was the hidden platform, with Mikon's boy waiting there to hitch me on the crane-hook. The music rose, to cover the creak of the machine; the rope at my back went taut. I grasped my silver bow, and leaned on the harness in the arc of flight.

Up I soared, out above the skene; the crane-jib, with its travelling screen of painted clouds, lifted and turned upon its pivot. The sea-sound of voices hushed; the play had started. Above the Phaidriades an eagle wheeled and cried, balanced like me upon the air. The jib slewed up and outward, and the music stopped for my speech. It was then I felt, quite close above me, a twang in the rope, and a slight sag down. A strand had parted.

At first I thought it must be just a jolt of the pulley. Mikon was trustworthy and the rope brand-new. I resolved to think no more of it. I was about one-third through, when I felt something go again. No doubt this time. I felt it strain and part; I sagged down a good inch.

. . . Zeus' battle-shattering aegis . . .

I could hear myself going on; while quick as a heart-beat the thought ran through me, 'A notched rope – Meidias. Thirty feet down, on stone.'

When the tawny eagle with his stallion crest
Swoops down, safety is hard to find . . .

Wise words. It was still coming out of the mask, one line

47

prompting the next. Two strands gone, how many left? The last taking all my weight could not last long. If I called out now, they might just get me back in time.

> *For I am Phoibos, zenith-cleaving, sun-shafted archer,*
> *Unforsworn tongue of truth . . .*

Brave words. I could hear myself as I spoke them, breaking off to yell, 'Help! Help! Let me down!' and the theatre echoing with a belly-laugh that would sound in my ears if I lived to three-score and ten. And it might be still too late. What a way to end, bawling like a scared child on a swing; what a line to be remembered by. The eagle circling the crags gave a long shrill 'Yah!'

I thought of the mask I wore. I had sat so long before it, I knew its face like my own. I thought of that human bleat coming out of it. And I thought, 'My father would have gone on.'

This had passed in moments. My voice still spoke the lines; now I put my will to them. The words, the light, the rock-peaks seen through the mask-holes; the smell of the mask, old and woody, mixed with new paint; the scoop of the hillside filled with eyes, struck on my senses clear and brilliant, as each moment passed which might be the last of my life. A kind of ecstasy, such as I have heard men can feel in battle, flowed all through me.

Suddenly the audience had got restless. There was a buzz; then someone shouted aloud, 'Watch out! The rope!'

It had started in the side-seats where they could see behind the screen. I wished they would keep quiet. I might be dead before the end of this speech; they could at least attend, not interrupt with stale news. I lifted my hand palm out, Apollo commanding stillness, and threw in the first tag I thought of, 'Lord of all gods is Fate!' Then I picked up the speech again.

Dead silence now. Each word dropped into a breathing stillness.

48

In the harness-straps I felt a tremor and strain from the rope above. The third strand was parting.

It went. The fourth must be the last, I thought; it was giving already; I was sinking down. Then as the audience groaned with relief (or else with disappointment) it came to me what was happening. Mikon had been warned; he was paying-out softly, letting me down on stage.

One moment, it seemed, I was dangling from death's forefinger; the next my feet touched ground. It was over. The silence broke then. Here I was right downstage, with nobody to unhitch me, and they expected me to stand there taking bows. I got my hand back and slipped the ring, and made some kind of exit. My last line was about flying back to high Olympos. I had just enough sense left to cut it. With a keyed-up audience, it would have been the very thing for a laugh.

By now it seemed I had been up there by myself for days. It was quite strange to have everyone grabbing me backstage and asking me how I felt. 'Later,' I said. 'Just let me change.'

Anaxis rushed up to me, his boyish Patroklos mask shoved back, his beard and eyebrows staring; he had gone quite pale. He pushed a wine-cup at me, but after one swallow I put it by; I was afraid of throwing up. 'Can you go on?' he asked. 'Would you like Anthemion to stand in for you?' I pulled my face straight just in time. 'No, thank you. In the name of the gods, get out on stage; nobody's there.'

My dresser unharnessed me, and strapped on my panoply for Achilles, clucking and chattering. Mikon came running, the frayed rope in his hands, waving it about. 'Later,' I said.

Achilles has a good while to sit sulking, before he consents to speak, which would give me a rest; but when he does break silence, he has got to be worth hearing. My blood was still stirred up, I felt ready for anything; I remember thinking, 'This is just how one feels when acting badly.' However, when I got to the lines where he chooses glory before length of days, suddenly a burst of applause broke out and stopped the play. I had never thought of that; I think it was the nearest I got to losing my lines.

At last it was over. The noise seemed to last for ever. Even after I went to change, I could have taken another call; but of a sudden I felt hollow as an emptied wineskin, sick, and deathly tired. Even the applause seemed empty; it would have been the same for some juggler who had jumped through a ring of knives. I thought with loathing of my performance, which I was sure had been ham all through. Stupidly I stood while my dresser stripped me, trying to be civil to the people who had come behind. Presently Mikon brought his rope again, and showed it round.

'I checked it overnight, every foot.' He pushed it under the noses of two sponsors, who had come behind to complain. 'Look here, at the cunning of it. The strands were opened, and a hot iron laid inside. With filing it would have frayed, and I'd have seen it as I ran it out. This was done in the night. That drunken loafer, the painter's man, I'm told that he was seen here.'

Hagnon said, 'I saw him, round about midnight. I thought nothing but that he'd picked up some odd job. Well, I hope they find him. The young men were off on the mountain trails; they reckoned he might have gone up there, to watch it work.'

'Maybe,' I could not feel concerned. Near by was the bier of the dead Patroklos; I pushed off the dummy corpse, glad of something to sit on.

Krantor said, 'Where's that wine-jar?' He poured, and held out a cup to me. I would have swallowed anything; but the rich Samian fragrance told me this must be the best in Delphi. It ran through me like new warm blood.

Anthemion tittered. 'It's a gift from some admirer in the audience. It came round before the end of the last chorus; the message just said, "To honour the protagonist". But you'll be hearing his name, I'm sure.'

I put it down. 'You fool! Someone's just tried to break my neck; and now you give me wine from you don't know who.' I wondered if I ought to take an emetic. It seemed less trouble to die.

'No, no, Niko.' Old Krantor patted my shoulder. 'Drink it up, my boy, I saw the slave who brought it. Groomed like a blood-horse; born and bred in good service, that one. It must come from a sponsor.' He looked at the two who had come behind; but they coughed and looked elsewhere.

He filled my cup again. The wine, though neat, was so smooth it went down like milk. On an empty stomach – I can never eat before I play – I pretty soon felt the difference. I started floating on air, needing no crane. Everything was golden, everyone kind and good and beautiful. I turned, the cup in my hand, and saw on my table the mask of Apollo, propped in its box. My dresser had plaited the hair and bound it, as I had shown him, in the style of Perikles' day. As the wine lighted me up, it seemed about to utter prophecies. I swayed to my feet before it. It was never I who had made that speech; the mask had spoken, I thought, while I hung like a doll in Apollo's hand. I tilted the cup, and poured him a libation.

'You do well,' said a new voice. 'Truly, the god must love you.'

I turned. The skene-room crowd had parted, just like extras for a big upstage entrance.

A man stood there, who might have stepped straight off a statue-plinth in the Street of Victors. Six feet and a handbreadth tall; dark curly hair, the temples greying, but the face still young; a face of the gravest beauty, austere even to melancholy, yet keen with life. Surely a face of those days Hagnon had talked about, when men deserved their gods. His eyes were dark, and fixed on me.

I don't know, with so much having come between, what I felt then. Only that he had come, as if sent, when I poured the offering.

All this, and the wine, had slowed me down. My answer halted; and Anaxis rushed in; all talk and civilities. The sponsors had come back and were edging up. I saw this was someone to everyone, not just to me.

While Anaxis talked, I had time to look. He was dressed very quietly for a feast-day, with the severity almost of a philosopher; a long robe, no tunic under it, the left shoulder bare. There was a great battle-scar running half the length of his upper arm. His robe was simple; barely an inch of border. But the wool was fine-combed Milesian; his sandals stamped Carthage work with gold clasps. This was the plainness of a man who only knows one shop, the best in town.

He spoke upper-class Attic, yet with a touch of Doric somewhere, and some other accent mixed with that, which I had no chance to define; for his answer to Anaxis was so short and formal that the compliments all dried up. Then, with his face still set in this sternness, he looked back at me, and swallowed. I don't know what cleared my eyes; I expect it was the truth of the grape; but I thought at once, 'Why, he is shy. But too proud to own it.'

I had gazed on him with awe; he seemed from another world. Now, discerning an infirmity which proved him mortal, I began to love him.

I got up from the bier, keeping one hand on it to steady me. I was not much put-out at being drunk; after all, he had sent the wine. He was here in friendship, never, as any fool could see, having set foot back stage before. He must feel all at sea; and I was his host.

'Thank you,' I said. 'The best drink I ever had, just when I most wanted it. You saved my life, next after Apollo, who stood by me like the gentleman he is. I'll give him a goat tomorrow. And I owe a grave-offering to my father Artemidoros. Did you ever see him as Cassandra?'

He half-smiled, looking easier, and saying, 'Yes, let me think.' He put his word to nothing lightly, that was clear. 'Yes! it was in the *Troades*, was it not; not the *Agamemnon*? I was a very young man then, visiting friends at the Academy; but I have never seen it rendered so movingly. If I remember, Hekabe was done by Kroisos.'

'Kroisos!' I said. 'Then you saw me too. I was the child Astyanax.'

He gazed at me intently, and said after a pause, 'Then you have always been an actor? All your life?' He seemed surprised; yet it was clear he meant no discourtesy. I told him yes. 'Why then,' he said, 'there are some true words in Euripides, about the many faces of the gods. How does it go?'

I said,

> *The gods wear many faces,*
> *And many fates fulfil*
> *To work their will . . .*

Was it that you meant?'

He smiled; without stiffness this time, but like a serious boy, 'Yes, and now I can complete it:

> *In vain man's expectation;*
> *God brings the unthought to be,*
> *As here we see.*

Words of good omen, this time.'

He paused, and looked about at the skene-room crowd, all

53

breathing down our necks. His smile faded; he said formally, 'We must talk more of all this. You will be needing rest now; but won't you sup with me this evening? Come about sunset, or a little before.'

'Delighted,' I said; more happy than surprised, for I knew we were ordained to meet. 'But whose place shall I ask for?'

I could hear the two sponsors cluck and suck their teeth; Anaxis gasped, and started making signs again. But I saw the man was not displeased. It is never bad to be liked for oneself, by anyone.

'I will send my servant for you,' he said quietly. 'I have rented a house on the bluff at present. My name is Dion, a citizen of Syracuse.'

3

By evening, when it was time to dress and go, I would just as soon have got out of it, I had slept off the shock and the wine, and for what seemed hours had listened cold sober to Anaxis, telling me what to say and still more what not to. For of course my host was the envoy of Dionysios. Perhaps, Anaxis said, he would ask me to give a recital.

'Don't count on it,' I said. 'He didn't look the man to make a guest earn his supper.' A citizen he had called himself, like any Athenian gentleman. Syracuse, one knew, still kept the ancient forms, but he could as well have said a prince, for it came to that. Such a man, if he is curious and has nothing else to do, may give supper to a touring actor, and will treat him with the breeding he owes himself; but that would be the end of it, as any fool could see. Very likely the place would be full of delegates and politicians, who, when they remembered I was there, would condescend with silly questions. In my heart, I cherished this meeting, sudden and strange like an act of fate; rather than spoil it with banalities, I would sooner we never met again.

It would have been something to dress in peace, without Anaxis fussing like a bride's mother. He even brought a barber to curl my hair. I nearly lost my temper, and asked what kind of monkey he meant to make of me, when my host had seen it that morning, straight as rain. Luckily the barber walked out, saying it was too short to work on. I had trouble to escape from wearing Anthemion's party-robe, red with embroidered borders, a love-gift from Anaxis. Like many actors who wear finery enough on stage, I like a rest from it. My spare robe was quite clean; a plain dark blue; one can't keep white fresh on tour. Having got my own way, I felt kindly to Anaxis. He would have given his ears for my chance; feared I would wreck all our fortunes with my careless tongue; and yet had not got spiteful. As the time drew near, I would gladly have changed places. Gyllis of Thebes was giving a party in her room, and I was the only one not going.

Presently came the slave and led me to Dion's house, which stood beyond the town, on the spur above the Pleistos valley. The sun was sinking, and Delphi had on its tragic robes. A blood-red light dyed the pale steeps of the Phaidriades, and filled the gorges with cinnabar and purple. From somewhere high up I heard hallooing, as if the maenads were running there. But it was long past time; it must be the young men, still hunting Meidias. They would have some light, for the moon was rising. I thought, 'He must be in Thebes by now. Poor wretch, let him go.' If he had really lurked somewhere to watch his triumph, I reckoned my score was paid. The square white house faced outward; its terrace hugged the edge of the bluff; beyond was space and the red sky. It was half dusk; on the terrace a torch in a gilded sconce burned with an upright flame. There were urns of trailing flowers, sweet-scented shrubs between the flagstones, a trellis with a vine. A young boy was singing somewhere to a kithara. The music ceased; my host rose from the shadows and came to meet me, his tall head brushing the vine above.

'Welcome, Nikeratos.' On his own ground, not stared at, he seemed ten years younger. The faded light showed him smiling; he touched my arm to lead me in. 'I am glad to see you. We are out here to catch the last of the day. But we will go in when the cold begins.' It was a mild evening; I remembered he came from Sicily.

The terrace was paved with coloured marbles. The low rush couches had cushions of white linen, whose embroidery looked like Egypt. There was no sign of a party; it was a good thing I had turned down Anthemion's robe. Only one other guest was there; a man of about sixty, grey-bearded, with a heavy brow and deep-set eyes. He was squarely built, but not fleshy with it, in good hard shape for his years, like an old athlete from those days of the gentleman amateur they talk about. There were white battle-scars on his left arm. Hoplites with shields don't get wounded there; he must have been a knight. Indeed, even standing by Dion he still looked quite distinguished. Not a Sicilian; Athens was written all over him. Not a politician; he looked too honest, and was too graceful when Dion presented me. But by accident both spoke at once, so I missed his name, and did not like to ask.

'We saw the play together,' Dion said. 'Do you know that neither of us had ever seen it performed before? But we had read it ... of course.'

He looked across smiling. One could not miss it. I suppose *Myrmidons* is the least acted and most read of all great plays. Lovers meet at it, as if it were a shrine like that tomb in Thebes. However long ago that had been, something of it hung about them still.

'Indeed, we have,' said the other. I understood this must be a thing the whole world knew about them; there is a certain air which tells one so; but it seemed to me, too, that it had surprised him to see Dion so unbend. As if to hide this, he added, 'And

57

then the mind hears an ideal rendering, which reality seldom equals. But you, on the contrary, enriched the play for me. I shall be many times your debtor.'

We walked over to the terrace balustrade. The sunset was rusting away, but Delphi seemed still to glow from the light it had drunk before.

'I have been making Dion envious,' he went on, 'by telling him how I saw you as Alkestis, last year at the Piraeus. The death scene was very fine. Her steadfastness, her loneliness, a voice receding, it seemed, with every line, as if already on her journey; that was memorable, far beyond the pathos most actors aim at.'

I was pleased, yet for some reason answered, 'Who wouldn't be lonely, dying for a wet stick like Admetos? I'm always glad to change masks for Herakles and the drunk scene, even though I do have to play it on three-inch lifts.' He made me nervous. I don't think he meant to; some men are used to distance. It had not stopped him from giving me, once, a certain glance which said that if I had been five years younger it might have been a serious matter. I don't think he meant to do that either. He had the nature he was born with, though he might never slip its leash.

I could tell my answer had disappointed him. But Dion smiled. One seldom saw him laugh aloud; but he had a certain smile, with the head thrown back a little, which was a laugh for him. There are men hard to be at ease with, whose walls one breaks by some stroke of chance; this was my good fortune here. And it comes, I thought, through a man who tried to kill me. Somewhere a god is working.

After more talk about the play, we went in to eat. The food was excellent, but simply cooked, and two courses only, not at all the Sicilian banquet of the proverbs. The flowers came in, small yellow roses; and the wine, the same he had sent me at the theatre. He had given his best. He was always all or nothing.

A splendid lamp-cluster hung from the ceiling; Etruscan work; a sunburst with outward-soaring nymphs whose arms held up the lampbowls. You don't get such things in a hired house unless you bring them with you. There was nothing in the room which did not serve some use; but what there was, was royal. I found it hard to take my eyes off him long enough for manners. Reclining wreathed on the supper-couch, cup in hand, he could have modelled for a vase-painter drawing a feast of gods. His bare arm and shoulder were like fine bronze; he could not make an awkward gesture; the dignity actors train for was bred into his bones. And his face passed the test of motion. Often beauty grows dull or common when speech breaks the mask; but here each change, like a change of light, brought out new quality.

Presently he sent out the slave, saying we would serve ourselves; the krater was set in the middle, the dipper laid on a clean cloth, our couches pulled up nearer. 'Now tell us, Nikeratos,' he said, 'about your escape this morning; and if I am intruding on your mystery, forgive me; for I am a soldier among other things, and I never saw such coolness in the face of death. Were you inspired? Or do you prepare for such things in training?'

He spoke as if to a guest of honour. I paused to think. 'Well, no,' I said. 'After all, a theatre is a sacred precinct. It's a crime to strike a man there, let alone shed blood. We don't train for such things, though we do reckon not to be put out easily; I've known a man who fell off the god-walk to change masks and play on with a broken arm. But today, I think ... You saw the mask of Apollo. It's not a face one would care to make a fool of.'

He threw a quick look at his friend, as if to say 'I was right'; then turned with his grave eager smile. 'Not without cause, then, these words were in my mind: *Do you think I have less divination than the swans? For they, when they know that they must die, having*

sung all their lives sing louder then than ever, for joy at going home to
the god they serve. Men, who themselves fear death, have taken it for
lamentation, forgetting no bird sings in hunger, or cold, or pain. But
being Apollo's, they share his gift of prophecy, and foresee the joys of
another world ...' He broke off, and said to his friend, 'I speak
without the book.'

'Near enough,' he answered smiling.

'No. I forgot the hoopoe.'

I had been listening with all my ears, and could hardly wait to
exclaim, 'What marvellous lines! Who wrote them? What is the
play?'

They looked at each other. I seemed to have made them
happy. Dion said, 'There is the poet. They are from Plato's dialogue, *Phaedo*.'

The name amazed me. These were the people whose story I
myself had told Anaxis! All those years ago – near twenty it must
be – and here they were still meeting. But I had thought this
Plato was some kind of sophist.

'The words are mine,' he was saying. 'The thought was a better
man's.'

'But the words!' They were still sounding in my head. 'Sir, have
you more like that? Haven't you ever thought of writing for the
theatre?'

He raised his brows, as if my little compliment had startled
him. At last, however, he said half-smiling, 'Not lately.'

'Plato!' said Dion. 'What is this?'

'Strange to say, in my youth it was my first ambition. I was full
of images and fantasies; they had only to knock and I would open;
only to ask, and I would feed and clothe them ... oh, yes, Dion,
surely I told you that?' I noticed again his expressive voice, like
a low-pitched aulos played by a master. But no volume with it.
With that chest of his, he could have overcome it in a month, if

60

I had had the training of him. Forcing would make it thin; it seemed he had learned that and no more. 'I assure you it is so,' he said. 'I once wrote a whole tragedy, and brought it as far as the Theatre bureau, to enter it for the Dionysia. From what I saw at the contest, it might have been considered; I cannot tell. But by chance – as men say who are content with ignorance – I met Sokrates in the porch (the friend, Nikeratos, who brought me to philosophy) who asked to see it, and put some questions, all too much to the purpose. I saw I had a lifetime's work before me, to find the answers I had given so glibly. Everything was there but truth.'

'Well, sir,' I said, 'even Euripides was a beginner once. Truth to nature can't all be learned in the study; it comes half the time from getting out in front to listen. The actors will soon show you if a line speaks badly. From what I've just heard, I should think you've let your friends put you off too easily. Believe me, the theatre is crying out for good new tragedies; just look at all these revivals. Why not get it out and go over it, and this time get it read by someone in the business? Would you care to let me see it, and tell you what I think?'

'Why not?' said Dion. 'Then I can read it, too.'

'I burned it,' he said, 'as soon as I got home.' Seeing my face he smiled – he could be a real charmer when he chose – and said, 'My friend, Apollo does not ask us all for the same offering.'

Dion filled up my cup. The bottom was painted with an Eros, playing the lyre; pretty, flowing work, heightened with white, in the style of Italy. 'Well, Nikeratos, if Plato has no play to give you, some other friend must step in as best he can. I intended asking you, but was diverted by the pleasure of our talk ...'

He broke off short. We all started bolt upright. From the sky, as it seemed, outside, had sounded a scream that stopped my breath. In all my life, I don't think I ever heard a sound so

61

dreadful. As a meteor plunges trailing light, so plunged from some great height above us this shriek of terror, then ceased as if cut with a knife. I put down my cup, which was spilling in my hand. It was Dion who, calling the slave in, said, 'What was that?'

The man beamed, like a good-news-bringer sure of his welcome. 'Why, sir, that must be the godless fellow they've been hunting since this morning, who tried to pollute the precinct with this gentleman's blood. The young men were saying, before they went up after him, that if they caught him they'd throw him off Aesop's Rock.'

The wine went cold in my belly. Dion said, 'Aesop's Rock?'

'It's called, sir, they tell me, after some old blasphemer who was sent off from there. It's above those great white cliffs, the Phaidriades. They go all the way down.'

'Thank you,' said Dion. 'You may go.' He turned to me. 'They have done justice, and avenged you ... What is it? You look pale.'

He is a soldier, I thought. Does he think I should have been up there, lending a hand?

'I was avenged already,' I said. 'He was an artist once.'

I thought of the long hunt, the quarry stumbling and thirsty like a wolf run down; and then they must have dragged him a long way to the place, knowing what he went to.

Both of them were staring. They did not look scornful; but then I was a guest. Dion said, 'He tried to take your life; yet you would have spared him?'

'I would have spared him that. After all, here I am, alive and feasting. Do you think me poor-spirited?'

His eyes opened. I have never seen such dark eyes so light a face. 'You are surely joking. Poor-spirited, after what we saw today? By Zeus, no! It is greatness of soul that spares the enemy in the dust. Better than vengeance, is not to share the evil.' He

62

leaned forward glowing like a man in love. I did not fool myself; honour was his darling. My head was not fooled, at least.

'It is an old bad proverb,' he said, 'that one should outdo one's friends in kindness, and one's enemies in cruelty. No; I have seen . . . ' he paused, and turned to Plato: '. . . too much.'

Well, I thought, Sicily must be the place for that. How does such a man come out of it?

'Believe me, Nikeratos, as much as for your courage I honour you for taking no joy in vengeance.' Being shaken and sick, I could have wept at his kindness; but that he would not have honoured. I said something or other, about having enough, in my work, of other men's revenges. I saw Plato stir at this; but after all he kept silent.

'Surely,' Dion went on, 'to crave revenge is to fall down before one's enemy and eat dust at his feet. What worse can we let him do to us? In hatred as in love, we grow like the thing we brood upon. What we loathe, we graft into our very soul. The man has more profit who beggars himself for a whore. The mind neglected; the soul starved of its true food; condemned at last to some base rebirth, if, as I am persuaded, Pythagoras taught us truly. Who in his senses would give that triumph to the man who wronged him?'

These words impressed me. I had never thought of any of it, and said so; adding, in apology, 'I was thinking about this wretched Meidias. All his life he wanted to be somebody, but without having to pay for it; which is always death to an artist. Now this. I couldn't have done it to a dog. But of course you are right about the soul. You have shown me the riches of philosophy.'

'Borrowed riches,' he said smiling and catching Plato's eye. 'It is the fate of the teacher, to hear his words come limping back from the pupil's mouth.'

'The pupil,' said Plato in that low light voice of his, 'who lives what he learned, is a teacher too. A city of such pupils could teach the world.' Then, as if he had lapsed from courtesy by speaking of some private thing, he turned to me, saying, 'You are clean of this death, having neither willed nor welcomed it. Remember, the man suffered it for sacrilege. It was the god's honour they avenged.'

I drank some wine, which I could do with, and held my peace. But I was saying within me, 'Is that what you think, wise man? If I had called for help up there, squeaking with fright through Apollo's mouth so that they all laughed and despised me, they would have beaten the cover round the precinct, from duty, and then gone home. But I pleased them; they took trouble for me; this is my wreath of victory. So wise, and you can't see it.' They were quoting Pythagoras to each other. I looked at their fine faces full of mind, and thought, 'I'm only an actor; the best I do will be gone like smoke when the last greybeard dies who heard it; these are great men whose fame will very likely live for ever. But for all they know, they don't know a crowd.'

'Your cup is empty,' Dion said, dipping into the mixer. 'We cannot have you melancholy. Did Achilles grieve for Hektor? And here's only a Thersites dead. Which brings me back, Nikeratos, to what I had to say. Would you like to play Achilles again, in another tragedy, at the next Lenaia?'

So it's come, I thought. For a moment I saw Anaxis with the barber. But in Athens? 'I am happy that you thought of me; but I'm not yet on the roll of leading men; and besides, the sponsors draw for them.' I had forgotten he was a foreigner. So near, so far.

'Apply again,' he said smiling. 'I think friends of mine can manage that. As for the draw, if we miss first turn we may still have the luck to get you, while your name is new on the list.'

I saw he knew what he was about. Past victors get chosen first;

the draw exists, indeed, to give sponsors a fair chance at them. He was telling me that even if his choregos drew first turn, he would still choose me. The door I had knocked for years on, was opening at his finger-touch. I thanked him as best I could. Even now, though, I had been too long in the business not to ask, 'What is the play?'

I guessed the answer before I got it. I saw him swallow.

'The title is *Hektor's Ransom*; a work by my kinsman Dionysios, the Archon of Syracuse.' He would rather not have looked at me, so he gave me a soldier's stare. 'As you will know, his work has been presented at Athens in the past, and won the lesser prizes; but like every poet, he sets his heart on the first.' He clapped his hands, and said to his slave, 'Mago, bring me the book from my bedside table.'

We talked while waiting, I forget of what. I was thinking he had done it well; he knew how to ask like a gentleman. The man being his kin and ruler, he could scarcely beg my pardon. And no one could say he offered a mean reward.

The book came; he said, 'Would you like my secretary to come and read it? He is a Tarentine, and reads quite well.'

'Thank you,' I said, 'but it is best to hear oneself. The torch still burns on the terrace; may I go out there?'

He hoped civilly that I would not be cold. I went into the cool garden, fresh with dew, and full of the sounds of a mountain night, trees rustling, a bell-like bird call, goat-clappers, tinkling across the gorges. Pavers of moonlight washed the Phaidriades as pure as crystal. The dark foam of the olives flowed to the sea. Vine-shadows crossed the veins of the marble pavement. The torch was burning low, but I hardly needed its light.

I sat down on a couch with the book closed in my hand. In the dappled shadows of the oleander I seemed to see a waiting face. I untied the ribbon from the roll, then paused again. 'Loxias,' I said, 'if there's good here it comes from you. Then I'll play in it, and people can say what they choose. But if it's pretentious bombast, it's not yours, and I won't touch it; not if I have to wait till I'm forty for another chance like this, besides losing the friendship of a man who makes one believe in men. I promise, Loxias. A man hasn't much to give a god in thanks for saving his life; it's the best I have.'

I unrolled the book, and read.

To Zeus on the god-walk, enter Thetis grieving for Achilles her doomed mortal son. It sounded quite well, Thetis especially. Nothing much developed, but it would pass in production well enough. Exeunt gods, enter boys' chorus (captive women) then men's chorus (Greeks). Centre doors open, Achilles within, discovered mourning, brought out on the reveal. So far, so-so.

Scene for Achilles, lifted from Homer with a touch of Sophokles. If one is going to borrow, by all means use the best. One could do something with it; there was no bathos, at least. I read on; the plot was not badly contrived, and had touches of originality, as far as it is possible with such a theme. After a scene for Phoenix and Automedon, chorus, while the actors change masks; then enter Hermes, fore-running Priam. Not a bad speech for third actor. Now for Priam; a chariot entry through the parodos, which always goes well. The chariot stops centre, and Priam speaks.

I had been skimming, to get the shape of the play. Now suddenly I was held, and started reading aloud. The old man speaks of his dead son whose corpse he has come to ransom from the victor: first as the hero-king he will never be, then as the child he was. The father recalls his scrapes as a daring lad, and how he beat him. It was a marvellous transition; even I, trained to read with my head, was near to tears. There was an entry for Agamemnon: non-recognition, cross-talk, irony, the usual thing. The play was just respectable, except for Priam. Then it breathed, and you could not fault it. The scene with Achilles would have melted bronze.

I was surprised, having heard from everywhere that Dionysios thought pretty poorly of his own son and heir. Here it was, at all events; a part one couldn't miss with.

I went back to the supper-room. They broke off their talk; Plato's cool eye told me, in case I had not known, that I had paused in the doorway to make an entrance. 'I like this play, it should act well. Did I understand you to have offered me the lead?'

'Certainly,' Dion said. 'How not?'

'The lead is Priam. Achilles only feeds him.'

'Any part you choose, of course.' He looked amazed. I might have known the Achilles in his own soul would hide the rest from him. But Plato, whom I had forgotten, said, 'He is quite right, Dion. The Priam has some freshness; the Achilles is everywhere derived. I did not tell you so; I doubted I could be just.'

In that moment I was as sure as if I had seen it that the tale was true about the slave-market at Aigina. Aristophanes, I thought, could have done something good with that. While we discussed the play, I trifled with this thought; but one thought leads to another. This was a proud man if I ever saw one. How he must have loved Dion, if he could love him still. It quenched my laughter.

Presently Dion said, 'You will want a good supporting actor. I thought of Hermippos, whom I have never seen give a bad performance.'

I ought to have foreseen this. I thought of Anaxis with his fancy cloak and his barber, fussing and nagging, simply because he trusted me not to be making what I could for myself alone; by no means a thing one can take for granted in the theatre. Well, I thought, I may not be much in this company, but I'll keep honest at my trade. 'I know Hermippos. A sound artist. But my partner is Anaxis, whom you saw today.' Our contract was only for the tour, but with laymen one has to simplify.

He looked rather put out. I suppose most people think theatre men live hand to mouth, taking what they can get. 'Forgive me,' I said, 'but we servants of the god have our honour too.'

'Say no more,' he replied at once, 'your partner is welcome.' It was Plato who had looked the more surprised.

But Dion had now started talking about plays; and I saw before long that here was a man who could teach me something. Nothing, as a rule, is more tedious than an amateur ignorant of technique and full of theories; and he was ignorant enough. But what he talked of, he knew. Most of tragedy is concerned with kingship, and the choices it compels men to; and what he said that evening has been of use to me all my life. The theatre, after all, can only teach one how; men as they live must show one why.

He knew war and command, what soldiers trust in a leader; how one must be strong before one dares be merciful. His favourite poet, he said, was Sophokles, who wrote about responsibility and moral choice; Antigone and Neoptolemos weighing their own decency and honour, which they knew first-hand, against causes they were asked to take on trust. 'A city,' he said, 'is only a crowd of citizens. If each of them has renounced his private virtue, how can they build a public good?'

'And Euripides?' I asked. 'We've said nothing yet of him.'

He said at once, 'I only like the *Troades*, which teaches mercy to the conquered, though no one shows it in the play. For the rest, his men and women are the sport of gods who behave worse than human barbarians. What can one learn from that?'

His heat surprised me. 'I suppose he shows how things are, and that men have to bear them. He lived in hard times, from all one hears. Hekabes ten a drachma.'

Plato said, 'He was dead before the worst.' It gave me a start, as always when one meets a man who lived it through; to me it was childhood tales. 'As it happens,' he said, 'I know what he wished to teach, though he died when I was still a boy. Sokrates told me. Euripides used to show him his work, before he sent it in, because their purpose was the same. Sokrates told him he would never come at it by the means he used; but he said he was an artist, not a philosopher. They had this in common, that it disgusted both to see the gods debased by crude peasant folktales which made them out worse than the worst of men. Sokrates called it blasphemy. For this fools killed him; but they could not kill his truth, because he did not destroy without offering something better. Not so Euripides, a maker of phantoms as all poets are. The truth is one, illusion manifold, and diversity makes a play. He believed it was enough to show these gods of the field and agora as the legends make them – capricious, lustful, lying outrageous in revenge, care-less of honour – and leave the audience to its thoughts. His cure for a leaky roof was to knock the house down. Sokrates taught that since it is inconceivable the gods should be evil, they must be good. But Euripides sent home his audience – and still does – saying, 'If those are the gods, then the gods are not.'

I thought this over; I could see what he meant. 'It's true,' I answered, 'that if we leave out the *Bacchae*, which is something by itself, he is not so successful with the gods as with human kind. You, sir, will know best whether he meant it so, or couldn't help it. But you will allow, I think, his skill in the second. He was the first to show men and women as they really are.'

'Say, rather, he was the first to say they can be satisfied with what they are, and need try to be no better. "I know," says his Medea, "what wickedness I am about to do, but passion is stronger than good counsel." "I am helpless," said Phaedra, before she deceives a just king into killing his innocent son. Men are seldom helpless against their own evil wishes, and in their souls they know it. But common men love flattery not less than tyrants, if anyone will sell it them. If they are told that the struggle for the good is all illusion; that no one need be ashamed to drop his shield and run; that the coward is the natural man, the hero a fable, many will be grateful. But will the city, or mankind, be better?'

Not being a sophist, trained to bring out answers pat, I could only say, 'But it's such marvellous theatre.'

Plato raised his brows; then he looked down into his wine-cup. An audience of twenty thousand, sitting on its hands, could not have produced such an echoing silence. I went hot right up into my hair.

Dion leaned over, and laid his hand on my shoulder. 'Plato, I won't have even you scold Nikeratos. Haven't we seen him risk his life only today, rather than a god should speak unworthily? He was a pattern for us all.'

Plato replied at once with something graceful, making amends. I think he even meant it. Though he was certainly not drunk, I daresay the strength of his own thoughts had carried him away. So, though it was time to go, I stayed a little longer to show there was no offence.

When I took my leave, Dion filled my cup to drink to the Good Goddess; then, when I had done so, dried it and put it in my hand. 'Please keep this,' he said, 'to remember the evening by, and in thanks for a performance I shall not soon forget. I wish there had been time to get one painted with Apollo or Achilles, especially for you.'

I went out into the sinking moonlight. Fathomless shadows filled the gorges. In the bowl of the wine-cup, Eros crowned with white flowers played his lyre. Behind me in the house I heard the voice of Dion, telling his friend whatever could not be said with strangers there. As for me, I knew I had met a man I would gladly die for.

4

The Delphi peace conference was a play that failed to hit, and won no prizes. Dion put this down to the delegates not having prayed or sacrificed beforehand. One would think that being in Delphi they might at least have consulted the oracle; but I suppose each of them was afraid of finding himself at the losing end.

'Some of our guests,' Dion said when he sent for me to confirm our contract, 'who had seats of honour at the theatre, should have gone to school there. If men with weightier business had shown half your piety, they might have prospered better.' I saw he meant this well; so I did not ask whether a jobbing treaty, meant to last till everyone goes home and thinks again, is weightier business than Aischylos, who has been with us a hundred years and looks good for another hundred.

Anaxis was in ecstasies, and had scarcely stopped talking since he got the news. Of course I never told him it was Hermippos whom Dion had wanted. Some actors never miss such chances; but they hadn't lived with my father. One pays for it later, too; and it's always at the bad time that the bill comes in. He was delighted I had chosen to take Priam; Achilles was just the sort of part in which he saw himself. He was like a cat in a cream-bowl.

'No year could be better,' he said. 'There was never less public feeling against Dionysios in Athens than there is today. If you remember, when he lent us troops in the Theban war he was given the freedom of the City. With any luck, the judges will vote upon the play and not against the author. Have you thought, Niko, that if it wins he is sure to want it put on in Syracuse with the original cast?'

'Spit!' I said. 'It's bad luck to price the unborn calf.' On this he went through every rite of aversion he could think of. I was afraid of his working himself into such a fever he would forget to act. Poor Anaxis, I could read his mind. He dreamed of getting his father's land back, and setting up as a gentleman.

I would be glad to make money myself. I had enough saved to eat in a bad time, if it didn't last too long; but not the money that lets one hold out for good roles. What took my mind much more, however, was the thought of getting launched in Athens; that, and something beyond. I knew what Anaxis guessed, that if the play won it would go on in Syracuse. Dion had told me. It would mean my seeing him again.

If you ask me what kind of love this was, I asked myself the same. I had known from the first he was unattainable as a god. I was too old for the love of a boy who reveres a man; nor, like a boy, did I wish to emulate. My calling was in my blood. Yet some need in my soul had known him for what it sought.

I walked out alone, the last night I was in Delphi, trying to reason with myself. It was late; the streets were empty; the votive statues looked at me, the bronzes showing the whites of their agate eyes, the painted marbles with a calm, blue gaze. 'What do you want, Niko?' they seemed to ask. 'Can you even say?'

I had found my way to the theatre, and was walking up hill beside it. The crane, that engine of the gods, poked up like a finger against a pale moonlit sky. I climbed higher, and came to a victor's chariot-trophy, done in bronze, a car and horses with a tall lad holding the reins; not in action as a sculptor would do it now, all straining muscles and flying drapes; but just quietly standing there in his long robe, waiting for the start. 'Here we are,' he seemed to say, 'I and my horses, trained and ready. We have made ourselves all we can be, but we are mortal. Now it is with the gods.'

I thought, Were you real, young hero, or just a sculptor's dream? But it works too the other way. The artist conceives the perfect athlete, the youth creates him. You were real; those big-boned hands and feet persuade me. You brought someone's dream to pass. Homer's? Pindar's? Plato called the poets makers of phantoms. Yes, but sometimes they take on flesh and come back to say, 'Hail, Father'. Well, here's one the parent need not blush for. It makes one think.

I thought of Dion. He had caught a dream from Plato, and willed himself to be. A proud creation. Yet I too had dreamed, and many more. How not? When the springs are brack, everyone's mind is on clear water. Look what Athens, and most of Hellas, has seen in our fathers' time and ours. First war; then weakness, tyranny, revolution; then the breaking of the tyranny and at last the good life could begin. But men's fires burned low; fighting the base with base weapons had shrunk their souls; before one can make the good life, one must remember what it is. There's always one more war to win, or one more election, before the good life; meantime, they wrangle about the good, those who still believe in it. So we dream. Of what? Some man sent by the gods, first to make us believe in something, if only in him, and then to lead us. That is it. We have dreamed a king.

I thought of the delight I had felt while he talked of kingship and its choices over the wine; of justice, mercy and command. I had thought it was because I was learning how kings and heroes should be played. Not so. When I had played kings and heroes, I had been making a likeness of what I wished for, like sailors whistling for a wind; it had been a conjuration. And that which I called had come.

Now I knew my own heart, I felt at peace. It made sense that I should love him just for being; there was nothing he need do for me, but be real. Beyond that, I would only ask the gods for a word with him now and then, to prove he still lived and walked the earth. In return I would do for him, if I could, whatever he needed done, like getting a prize for his kinsman's play.

I turned home, lifting my hand in salute to the horse-boy in the chariot. He had worked for it, and so must I.

We left Delphi next day, to go on with our tour. None of the sponsors stood us as much as a drink. They did not care two straws about the theatre, but would as soon have provided flute-girls if it pleased the delegates; in fact they did that too, so Gyllis of Thebes told me. However we were paid in full, which one can't always count on; so they were welcome to keep their wine.

It was a good thing I had told Anaxis that Dion liked his work, for he never got asked up to the house. Of course Dion should have done so, if he wanted to get the best from him; I had to cover it with some lie or other. It had been his bad luck to be sober in the skene-room when I was drunk; he had taken too much trouble, and Dion had written it down as sycophancy. There were people he was helpless with; rather than own it, he took refuge in his rank as in some high acropolis, out of their reach. All his life it made him enemies, and I suppose he must have known it; but he preferred this to showing weakness. That was the man.

When we got home, we put both our names down again for the protagonists' list at Athens. Before long, I heard that my name was on. Anaxis heard nothing, but he had got good roles, and if the play won would stand a better chance next year.

We had done well for money on our tour, between Delphi, Corinth, Thebes and Megalopolis. I could live quite well till winter, when rehearsals for the Lenaia would begin. I went about, treating old friends who had treated me, buying plays for my library, taking exercise at the gymnasium, and so on. I went most often to the one at the Academy gardens, though it was a good way from my lodging, just in case Dion, instead of sailing straight home, might be staying with Plato first. Though he never appeared I did not give up hope of him, knowing he was not a man who liked to be stared at in the streets.

Plato's school was not far from the gymnasium, behind a grove of plane-trees. One saw his young men, freshly bathed, oiled and dressed, going off that way after exercise; talking and laughing, but no horseplay. Sometimes two would stop by the Eros statue in the grove and offer a handful of flowers plucked on their way, touching hands, which I found charming. Once or twice when there was laughter I walked near to learn the joke; but I could never make head or tail of it.

They mostly dressed very well, some richly, though without ostentation. Those who were plainly dressed wore their clothes with an air, so one could not say if it was from poverty or choice.

Among the second sort, was a youth I saw often in the garden, though not in the gymnasium. His looks always caught my eye; he had a boy's smooth chin, but a fine clear profile, too serious for his age. Meeting him one day in the path, I took the chance to ask if Dion was a guest there.

'Not now.' He had a low pleasing voice, without the roughness of his years. 'You've missed him by a month or two. He went with Plato to Delphi. Have you come to see him?'

I passed this off, and to cover it asked some questions about the school. The boy had seemed shy, but this unlocked his tongue. 'It's not a school at all, in the sense you mean. We meet to work, and

75

think, and discuss, and experiment; and the younger learn from the elder. From Plato, everyone learns; but anyone can disagree, if he can make it good. Join us! It will change your life. It did mine.'

Plainly, he took me for a man of leisure. Before one has got known, one can hang one's mask up and go anywhere, free as air; nobody knows one's face. Even now I sometimes miss it.

I said, 'I don't suppose I could raise the fee. How much a year?' If he was not too high-born and rich, I was hoping to see more of him.

'Why, nothing. I've never paid one drachma. As Plato says, Sokrates never charged; he said he liked to choose whom he conversed with.'

I looked at the painted colonnades, flowers, and well-kept lawns. 'But didn't he spend all day in the streets and Agora? One can do that for nothing.'

'True. Plato isn't rich, though he has more than Sokrates had; but the school does accept endowments. Only from Academy men; he won't be beholden to outsiders. Dion gave us the new library. But no one, ever, is accepted for what he owns – except *here*.' He tapped his brow. He had grey eyes, with an inner ring as dark as smoke. 'Thank you for the pleasure of your conversation; I must go, or I shan't get a good place for Plato's lecture. This is his great one. He only gives it once in every few years.'

'Well, we may meet again here. What is the lecture?'

'On the Nature of the One,' he said, as if surprised at my asking.

When he had gone, I loitered on in the shade of the plane-trees. All the young men from the school had gone in; the palaestra gave out a different noise, louder but hollower. The gardens and lawns were empty. I walked nearer. A dolphin fountain murmured softly; the buildings, though newish, seemed to be at home like an old olive tree. There was an open door, with men's backs filling it. It seemed to me that one more would scarcely be noticed, and if Plato charged no fee one could not be defrauding him. I might learn what had made Dion the man he was.

As I got closer, I could hear a voice I recognised. Great God, I thought, these amateurs. Why does he throw it all off the top of his mouth? A beautiful voice, half wasted. The chest is there; he should be able to fill a theatre; even now, if a good professional took him in hand ... Nobody noticed me in the doorway. I could hear quite well; they could not have kept quieter for Theodores in *Antigone*. Well, I listened for as long as it takes to sing an opening chorus; and for all I could make out of it, he might as well have been speaking Scythian.

I slipped away, stopping for a last look at the house. There were words carved over the portico, and filled in with gold. But when I went up, all they said was NO ENTRY WITHOUT MATHE-MATICS.

The cobbler to his last, I thought. A wasted morning, except for those grey eyes. I went home to my exercises, and *Hektor's Ransom*, and took the air nearer home thereafter. It would have been different if the lad had ever shown himself in the gymnasiums; but, clearly, he was all for the mind and the Nature of the One. It could only end in grief.

However, one fine autumn day some weeks later, friends called me to come walking, and we found ourselves there. As we crossed the park, one of them nudged me, saying, 'Niko, you dog, you said you would go anywhere, but you took care to steer us here. Where do you find such beauties? Don't pretend you don't see him looking. It would serve you right if we didn't go away.'

I got rid of them, before he saw what they were laughing at, and went to meet him. He greeted me, and said at once, 'I know you now. I remembered as soon as you had gone last time. You are Nikeratos, the tragic actor.'

77

I said yes, feeling pleased, as who would not, that he should have remembered my face from those few moments at the theatre when one takes one's bow.

'I saw you,' he said, 'as Alkestis, at the Piraeus. I've seen the play twice before, but the other two were snivelling and self-pitiful, compared with you. You made the whole transit of the Styx, lying there all alone with the mourners round you. I wept; but as one should, with the soul and not the belly.'

There was not a hair on his face; he could hardly be more than fifteen, then; his poise and assurance startled me. I said, 'Then it's not all mathematics here?'

'Of course not. Why didn't you join us, as I said?'

'My dear boy, though one doesn't pay one has still to eat. But we can meet again, I hope?'

'You could come and study when you're not working.'

'No entry without mathematics. I'd be a white crow in the flock, you know. Will you sup with me this evening?'

'Is it because you are an actor? Plato is not conventional.' He paused in thought. 'I believe he would even take a woman, if he thought her fit.'

'You believe more than I can, then.'

'So everyone told me. Yet here I am.'

I opened my mouth to speak, and kept it open to gasp. Sure enough one could see under the man's tunic, once one was looking, the shallow curve of breasts.

'I am Axiothea from Phlios. At the Academy, everyone knows. I don't dress like this as a disguise.'

I could only stand blinking. If I had known from the first, no doubt I would have disapproved; as it was, I simply felt winded.

'I could see,' she said, 'it was getting unkind not to tell you. I hope you are not angry.' Her smile, and her frankness, won me over. I could not be cross, perceiving she was the same sort of

78

woman as I was a man. 'Friends are friends,' I said. 'May I take a friend's privilege and ask your age?'

'Nineteen. You thought me precocious.' We laughed, and I asked how she had begun all this. She said that when she was fifteen, she had won the girls' race at Olympia. Plato had been there; she had seen him, and heard the Academy spoken of. 'But,' she said, 'I thought of it as one might of driving in the chariot-race; splendid, but out of reach. I did the only thing I could; bought his books and read them. So I lived in my father's house, a white crow in the flock as you said just now, and suitors avoided me, which angered my father.' She had been through hard times; he had beaten her, and burned her books when he found them; those that were left, she had had to hide in the rocks and read by stealth. No one had spoken for her except her mother's brother, a man who had studied at Phaedo's school in Elis. But her mother was dead so no one heeded him. Then suddenly her father died, and this man became her guardian. 'Everyone, and I myself, was sure my father had disinherited me. But he had put it off, or changed his mind; and when this got known, suitors sprang up all round, like the Sown Warriors. My uncle, the best of men, not only understood my disgust but shared it. So we talked, and he granted me my wish. He would rather I'd gone to Phaedo; he said Plato was a man of dreams; but, he said, Plato was the likelier one to take me.'

She had cropped her hair and worn men's clothes to go to him, because she wanted her mind tested for what it was worth in itself, not as something remarkable in a woman; 'but,' she said, 'having got them on I found they fitted my soul. You, I expect, will understand it.'

'Yes,' I said. 'The theatre can give one that.'

'So I came before him, as it seemed, in my true likeness; which I expect was why he was deceived, if you can call it so; at all events he questioned me, and said I should be welcome. But by

79

then I felt such respect for him, I would no more have lied to him than to a god, so I told him everything. Truly, Nikeratos, he is a great-souled man. He might well have been angry, and thought I had meant to make a fool of him. But he said I had proved his thesis, that women can be taught philosophy if they are given to it by nature, and that I was welcome more than ever. As for my clothes, he said one must be true to the mind before the body.'

'And he has really kept to it? He gives you equality with the rest?'

She made a gesture so fierce and eloquent that I noted it in my mind to use at work. 'Equality! I hope I need never sink so low. That poppy-syrup! Does the soldier ask to be equal with every other? No, to prove himself. The philosopher? No; to know himself. I had rather be least of Plato's school, knowing the good and taking my own measure by it, than run back to Phlios where I could command what praise I chose. Equality! No, indeed, Plato doesn't so insult me. People whom such things concern you'll find at the schools of rhetoric. They don't come here.'

'I'm sorry,' I said. 'An artist ought to have known better.' We sat down on a bank under an olive tree. Once one got used to her, I found her easier to talk to even than easy-going Gyllis of Thebes. The one could have furnished a regiment from her lovers, the other had virgin written all over her; but she was used to men's companionship, friendly without brazenness and self-respecting without defiance. It seemed Plato had known his business.

After we had talked a while longer, I told her I had met Dion at Delphi. Her face lit up, and she said, 'He is our hope for all the world!'

I had expected praise of him, but this was a good deal more. 'You look surprised,' she said. 'Have you read nothing of Plato's, then, not even the *Republic*?' I confessed that this was so. 'You will find it all,' she said, 'in Books Four and Five, where he says mankind will never be free of evil till some great state comes under the control of a philosopher trained to kingship. Someone has got to begin, before people will believe it works. He says most politics today are like ships being steered by a half-blind master. The crew know he's off course, and plan to mutiny; but if they manage to seize the helm it will be no better, for none of them can navigate, they've not learned that such a science exists. If a real pilot came by and said, "Steer by Arcturus", they'd mock him for a star-struck zany. The philosopher is the pilot. He knows where the harbour is, and the reef; he knows the constant stars. But men still pursue illusions. Their prejudice will not be broken till such a man takes the helm and shows them. Once he has saved them from the rocks, that will be the end of guesswork. No man will drown if he sees the remedy; will he?'

She paused for a feed-line, as philosophers do; just like comic actors, though one must not say so. I answered, 'Surely not.'

'So, then, when Dion gets his ship, a new age will begin.'

'What?' I said startled. 'Is Dion planning revolt, then?'

'No, how could you think such a thing? He is a friend of Plato's. Plato has always taught that violence and treachery can beget nothing better than themselves. This was also the teaching of Pythagoras, the wisest of men.'

'Then what does he hope for? It's true, he is like a man the gods made for kingship. But Dionysios has an heir.'

'One he despises.'

'Blood is blood, when the last push comes.'

'Sometimes pride talks louder. Dionysios didn't build up the Syracusan power to bequeath it to the Carthaginians at his death.'

'Is that what he thinks of his son?'

'So everyone says. He has scared him since his childhood; now he despises him for a coward.'

'Is he really one?'

'Maybe. Maybe he just wants to keep alive the best way he can. Old Dionysios is brave enough in war; but he sees an assassin behind every chair. Did you know that even his own family can't come in to see him till they've been searched down to the skin? Almost since his childhood, young Dionysios, the son, has lived in dread his father may suspect him of some usurping plot, and decide to make away with him. He can't be got to touch any sort of public business; he'll scarcely offer a sacrifice at the games, or dedicate a fountain-house.'

'Well, you can't kill the cow and milk it too. What did his father expect?'

'Who knows what an untrained mind will think? One thing is certain; he trusts Dion further than any other man alive. He is even let off the searching, because the tyrant knows him for what he is, incapable of treachery. He is kin by marriage, not by blood; he comes of the old nobility, while Dionysios is a nobody; he is an envoy other states respect and will do business with, when they'd not trust Dionysios across the street; a soldier proved in battle, whom his men would follow anywhere. He has not always even carried out his orders; where he was sent to strike terror and make examples, he has done justice and won respect. Yet the heir is searched, while he is not.'

'I can believe all that. But only a philosopher, surely, would pass his own blood over and choose an heir for virtue.'

'Oh, yes. We don't expect it. But Dionysios has two sons by his other wife, Dion's sister. They're young yet, but he has helped bring them up; the elder thinks the world of him. Dionysios might decide to name him heir; and then Dion would have the chance he needs. It's not the show and pride of power he wants; only to change a city ruled by men for one ruled by laws.' I could tell, by the way she spoke these last words, that she was quoting; I suppose from Plato.

'Which laws?' I asked. 'Athenian?'

'Oh, Nikeratos, how can we talk till you've read the *Republic*? Listen. Wait here. I'll see if it's free in the Library. You'll take good care of it? If it gets lost, I couldn't afford to pay a copyist; I'd have to do it from the wax myself, and it would take a year.'

'Is it so long?' I asked, alarmed. But then I thought of Dion and said, 'Yes, I'll keep it safe.'

She was gone some time; at last I saw her hurrying through the trees, the dark curls ruffled on her brow. Certainly she had made her confession none too soon; I wondered if Plato had felt the same.

'I am sorry,' she said, 'it's out. And then Speusippos, Plato's nephew, kept me talking. But I've brought you this. It's quite short, and of course you will like it better. I should have thought of it at first.'

There was only one roll, not thick. I thanked her, perhaps too gratefully. 'Is this about law too?'

'No; love.'

'I shall surely like it. Tomorrow I'll meet you here to return it, at about this time.'

'I will be here. Do you know, you are the first man to be my friend, who has not been a philosopher? The rest have thought me a monster.'

'That would come ill from an actor. When I put on a woman's mask I am a woman; I could do nothing if I were not. There are two natures in most of us who serve the god.'

'You will like this book. I'm glad I chose it.'

'I that we met.' And there was more in this than civility.

I had meant to meet friends that evening; but it being too early, I untied the book and looked into it. It was called *The Drinking Party*, a cheerful start at least; and my interest quickened when I found it was supposed to take place at the house of

Agathon the tragedian after his first winning play. I had acted in his *Antaeus*; a charming piece, and the beginning of modern theatre, for he got rid of the chorus from the action and enabled us to have plots which don't assume the presence of fifty onlookers. Though to my disappointment there was no account of the production, the dialogue held me, and I kept reading. Presently they started a party game, a round of speeches in praise of love. The next thing I knew, it was getting too dark to see. I lit the lamp, and went back to the book, and did not move till it was done.

As one finds later, the early speeches are only supposed to show the bottom of love's ascent. But it was the dream of my boyhood, the knightly bond of Aristogeiton and Harmodios, Achilles and Patroklos, Pylades and Orestes. I remembered how I had lived it with my first lover, the Syracusan actor. He had worn the hero's mask for me, not in deceit, but, as I had long since understood, at my demand. Poor man, he would far sooner have had a listener for his little troubles, the rival who topped his lines or spoiled his big scene with bits of business, the tour that went broke in the wilds of Thessaly. I looked back at his kindness gratefully; he had been tender with my illusions; I had been lucky, as it mostly goes today. I had long since ceased to believe that the reality existed. Now I knew that it did, though not for me.

Plato and Dion had known it. I had seen proof. Twenty years after that torch was kindled, with all the heat burned out of it, it still gave light. It was bitter to me, though I had hoped for nothing for myself; such is man's nature. However, words and their sound being in my blood, I could not cease to read. I was like someone who, hearing a lyre upon the mountain, must follow it over rocks and thorns. The man wrote like a god. Now he is dead, people begin to say his mother conceived by Apollo. Well, he was mortal. I met him; I know. But I can understand the story.

Aside from all this, it was splendid theatre. One itched to put it on a stage. Alkibiades was a bravura role I would have given my ears for. Sokrates seemed to fall between tragedy and comedy (the modern writers are just starting to explore this ground) but the character arrested me, since I knew him mostly from the lampoon in *The Clouds*. If he was really such a man as Plato makes him, then his death was murder, and Aristophanes' hands are far from clean. This set me thinking that it was not wonderful if Plato had no time for dramatists, nor much for actors.

When I gave back the book to Axiothea I asked her if this was so. Though it was long before her time, she had heard the tradition of the school: that at Sokrates' trial Plato had got up to speak for the defence, which, considering the temper of the court and of the government, must have put him in great danger. He had opened with, 'Gentlemen, though I am the youngest who ever stood up before you—' planning to say he spoke for the young men Sokrates was accused of having corrupted. But the dikasts all bawled out 'Sit down!' and, being an amateur, he could not make himself heard. I suppose it was hardly surprising that he never got over this; but, as I told Axiothea, it was a real loss to the theatre. There was no doubt he had it in him.

I met her often in the park, because I liked her company, and for the sake of what she could tell me about Dion. Not having lost hope of bringing me to philosophy, she introduced me to her friends, one of whom was Speusippos, Plato's nephew. He was an elegant young man, spare and wiry, with a face like a handsome monkey's, who usually looked as if he had been up late, sometimes at his books, but sometimes not. In spite of this he missed nothing; Axiothea said he was one of their most brilliant men. He certainly had charming manners, and, though he knew every play worth hearing, always asked my opinion first.

On the other hand there was Xenokrates, a lean fellow with an untrimmed beard and dirty nails, who never moved any of his face but his mouth to talk, so that I often felt like telling him he could buy a better mask for ten drachmas. As coolly as if I had been a deaf post, he maintained to the company that it was casting nets for the wind, to try and philosophise an actor; a man (he said) who lent himself to every passion, not to learn the mastery of pain and pleasure, but rather to display their worst excesses for the applause of the ignorant. As well expound chastity in a brothel. No one rebuked him for his rudeness; it was their custom that any proposition must be debated before it was condemned. Perceiving this I kept my temper, the discussion lasted some time, but Speusippos took my side, and was agreed to have won the day.

They often talked about Dion without any prompting from me. They believed (getting it from Sokrates) that a memory of justice is born in man; and Dion was their favourite illustration.

His father Hipparinos had come of the highest blood in Syracuse, and had always spent like a king. What with race-horses, palace-building and banquets, he was nearly broke when he backed Dionysios' rise to power, and got his stake back five-fold. Dionysios must have liked the man as well as valuing him, for he bound their families as close as law allowed, marrying Hipparinos' sister, Dion's aunt, and, when she bore a daughter, betrothing the girl to Dion, whom he treated almost as a son.

Sicily, however, is not Greece, whatever the Greeks there tell you. Dionysios, a king in all but name, indulged a king's whim and took two wives. Aristomache, the sister of Dion's father, was for friendship and support at home; Doris of Lokri for foreign policy. It might have set the kindred at each other's throats, if he had not been a resourceful man. He avoided disputes about precedence by marrying them both the same day; what's more, he lay with them both that night, and no one was allowed to see which door he entered first.

It was Doris of Lokri who first bore a son; not, it would seem, what he had hoped, for after some time, Aristomache still not conceiving, he had Doris's mother put to death for casting a barren spell on her. (As I was saying, Hellas stops at the straits.) Doris's son was a growing lad, when Aristomache's first son was born.

Meantime, young Dion was growing up, all the gods' darling; as free of the Archon's house as of his own; so rich he need never ask what anything cost; ranking like a king's nephew, or rather higher; with the looks of some youth on a frieze by Pheidias. Courted both for his favour and his person, in that most dissolute of cities, he managed to keep his honour. It left its mark on him; though not vain, he learned aloofness in self-defence, and people called him proud. At sixteen he escaped, with relief, to war. The gods had stinted him of nothing; he was brave as well. Soon after, campaigning in Italy, he found time to study with the Pythagoreans. At twenty, with his brilliant youth dawning into manhood not less splendid, he got news that Plato was their guest. He dashed at once across the straits to offer homage.

By now I had read one or two of Plato's dialogues, written some time before this happened. There is nearly always, somewhere, a glorious youth, Lysis or Alkibiades or Charmides, as athletic in mind as body, who neglects his jostling suitors to alight by Sokrates; asks all the right questions, modest but keen; and goes off all radiant from the play of minds, sure to return. Here was the dream come true. I could imagine how Plato felt.

Before long they were in Sicily, climbing Mount Etna to view the craters. The pure form of the distant mountain, floating in ether, white as foam; the climb above the orchards among fierce shapes of black lava; the snows bathed in light sighing out dragon's breath; the fire-fuming stithy plunging unfathomed from the skies to the core of earth; nothing less, I daresay, seemed worthy of the elements released within them.

87

Meantime Dion had sent word to Syracuse; and Dionysios, who loved to think his court a Helikon of muses, sent the expected summons.

Young Dion was enraptured. Love and philosophy had opened his eyes; he saw all was not well in Syracuse where things had gone so well for him. But he had learned too that man only sins from ignorance. He must love the good, once seen. And – how not? – everyone must love Plato.

As I heard this tale in the Academy olive-grove, I must say I felt for the man. He had been brought up to politics; lived, in forty years, through the bitter end of war and three kinds of mis-government at home; had seen his own kinsmen, earnest reformers, turn to ruthless despots once they had seized power; had had to beg Sokrates' life from them; then, having cut himself off from half his family and given up his career, he had been forced to watch, helpless, while his friend who had defied the tyranny with unflinching courage was murdered by the democrats under form of law. Now here was the beloved youth, who believed in him like a god, inviting him to bring the good life to Syracuse. What could he do?

I was told in full, by my friends at the Academy, what Plato and Dionysios said to each other. Even philosophers are human, and I never knew a man repeat a set-to he had had with anyone, who did not improve it here and there; however, I believe most of it. Plato's manners were superb and he must have begun with courtesy. But having lived under the Thirty, he could not miss the smell of tyranny where it sweated from the very walls. Meantime he was made much of. In due course he was asked to do his act, and speak on the Good Life.

I don't know if Dionysios expected to be used as an exemplar; in Sicily it would not surprise me. It turned out that Plato's good life was that of just men in a just city, whose governors were chosen for merit without regard to rank, and trained up in temperance and virtue. He had been by now to one or two Sicilian banquets, where guests stuffed with food and soaked in drink finish up with an orgy on the supper-couches; this, he made pretty clear, was how not to make life good. He quoted Pythagoras upon Circe's swine.

Dionysios was not broken-in to free Athenian speech. He lost his head and his temper. Plato was as used to respect as he to flattery; there were high words. Dionysios was furious; perhaps he was jealous, too, of Dion's new allegiance. He lost the argument, but planned to have the last word.

Plato, of course, would leave at once; he only needed a ship, and this Dion had found him. It sailed with sealed orders from the Archon. It must have looked like a choice revenge, to have Plato betrayed to slavery by the man to whom Dion had entrusted him. When later he learned that Plato had never doubted Dion for a moment, I daresay he was astounded.

The well-off philosopher who bought Plato would not take back a drachma; he said it had been a privilege. Plato went home and kept quiet from pride; when it got about, he testified Dion's innocence. Old Dionysios, who cared what people thought of him, became uneasy; he wrote trying to patch things up, and saying he hoped Plato was not speaking ill of him. Plato replied that he had been too busy to recall the matter.

What Dion thought, when he heard the news, is not recorded. But his life was changed. When he was free to travel, he was already so much a man of the Academy that he seemed rather to have returned there than arrived. He was temperate as Pythagoras; he studied, he met philosophers; but in Sicily, any mission he was trusted with – war, embassy, judgement – was faultlessly discharged. If he departed from his orders for justice's sake, it was always in the open. No conspirator would have thought of breaking his mind to Dion. It was as if, because Plato had not been let stay in Syracuse to defend his own honour, Dion had made his whole life bear witness for his friend. As Axiothea had said, treachery was not in him; nor in Plato, who thought no cause greater than truth, and had lived through revolutions enough in Athens, each sowing hate, perfidy and revenge like dragons' teeth, to beget the next.

They had all failed, for the simple reason that men had got no better. Hate, he had found, destroys; only love creates; a state can be redeemed only by good men spreading goodness round them, till the lump is leavened, and there are enough just men to govern. All this they told me at the Academy; and I saw sense in it, if it could be got started. If any man could do it, Dion could.

Soon, however, it was time to forego these pleasures. They would be casting for the Lenaia, and then rehearsals would begin.

'You must win,' said Axiothea, when I told her this. 'It will draw Dionysios towards Athens and away from Sparta. That can't but be good.'

'Can't it?' I said. 'From what I've seen of politics, anything you can think of can go bad; it only needs bad will. I leave all that to the experts. Artists in politics are like the whore's child at the wedding; we remember things out of season, and get the stick.'

'Take care, Niko, how you shrug off public business. One day it may concern you whether you choose or not.'

'So may the black plague or the marsh-fever. Meantime I'll stick to what I know. The more time Dionysios spends writing plays, the less he'll have for his tyranny; a day's no longer for him than any other man. Besides, an artist has to know himself, which can't do anyone harm. Can it?' I added, remembering the method.

'No, indeed.'

Hektor's Ransom was passed by the selectors and booked for the Lenaia, a rich Syracusan resident standing choregos. Everything went as planned, except for one hitch over the casting. Leontis, our sponsor, had drawn third turn to choose his protagonist; and the man before chose me. He said he had seen my work at Delphi. There was a hasty conference; and the other sponsor changed his mind. I don't know what he got for it; but there was no cheese-paring in that production. When we heard who were doing the masks and costumes, painting the skene and training the chorus, and for how much, even the Persian-backed play at Delphi looked like a fit-up.

Phileas was a chorus-master who, if he had had to stand the chorus upside down, would still have got faultless grouping and each syllable crystal clear. I used often to sit in front just for the pleasure of watching him work. You may ask how I felt, playing lead and directing where Aischylos once did it; where Sophokles danced as a chorus-boy and, later, had only to walk on as an extra in one of his own plays to bring up the audience standing. Well, the place was my second home. I could not remember a time before I had known it. It was like being the son of a great house, who has come of age. I don't know when I have been happier.

I had lived with the play by now; I knew what the verse would give the actor, and where it would need heightening or throwing away. Just as I'd feared, Anaxis had got over-keyed and was ranting terribly as Achilles. 'My dear,' I said at length, 'you were splendid today, but you showed up the lines a little, if you understand me. We must cover for the old man here and there. Don't forget that to get us to Syracuse, it's the play that has to win.'

He took this pretty well, but complained that the third actor, Hermippos, was always trying to upset him, which was only too true. This was the man Dion had wanted instead of him. I had agreed he was a sound artist; so did not like to object, when Dion put him forward, that it might not answer to have a well-known second man playing third. The fee was big; there was also the golden lure of Syracuse; Hermippos had sunk his pride and accepted, but needed to show us he was somebody in case it got forgotten. This he did not by being pompous, which was not his style, but by playing the fool. He was one of the few actors to do well in both tragedy and comedy, and it was the latter which seemed to have shaped his face, which was round, with a big mouth and a button nose. On stage he behaved perfectly; but he was one of those men who, once having got their lines, can do anything they like up to the moment when they go on. He would crack jokes with the mechanics, lay bets on races, clown about in masks from other plays, to let us all know he thought as well of himself as ever. For myself, my father taught me to think what I was about, but not to be put off by trifles. I had met Hermippos' sort before. But Anaxis, who thought it proper never to put his mask on till he had brooded before it like an actor carved on a grave-stone, was driven mad and had not the sense to hide it. This was all Hermippos needed to egg him on. It was tiresome having to keep peace, when I wanted my mind on Priam.

Sometimes I got anxious about the role. I had turned down Achilles because it was too easy; I could have got the effects in my sleep. Perhaps I ought to have taken it, and proposed for Priam some good old actor, who had done the role in this or that play more times than he could count, and could get the effects in his sleep, too. That would have been the safer thing. I had wanted the part because it was something new for me; it was testing; I had thoughts about it; in a word, I had pleased myself. If I was not to break faith with Dion, and throw my own chance away, I had better be good.

I have never been the sort of actor who blusters about while rehearsing Herakles, smoulders for Medea, and so on. But this time I swear my bones would ache when it rained, and when I got out of a chair I leaned upon the arms. I read the *Iliad* through and through, coming back to the passage where Priam tries to keep Hektor from the death-fight. You are our last defence, he says; when you are gone, I shall see our house in ruins, Troy sacked, the women ravished, the children dashed on the stones, before I am cut down to lie where I am thrown until my own dogs eat me. *A young man fallen on the field, rent with sharp bronze, looks seemly even in his blood; death can lay nothing bare that is not beautiful. But an old man's corpse flung down, his grey hair and his beard and privates torn by curs, ah, that is the most wretched sight in all mortality.* These lines always came into my mind, when I played the scene with Achilles.

Then came the day for the Presentation of the Poets, which always makes the contest seem very near. We went to the Odeion in our festival robes and garlands, to make our bow while the subjects of the plays were given out. Our poet being in Syracuse, some sweet-voiced orator deputised, no doubt a good exchange. I was anxious lest our robes might be overdone – it is, after all, a ceremony, not a performance; one appears as oneself, without a mask, and should dress without hubris. But we were fitted out with sumptuous elegance; if our sponsor had not good taste, he knew where to buy it.

As Anaxis had foretold, the name of Dionysios got no booing; but Hermippos was greeted with a few laughs, because he had last been seen in comedy. A comedian, in the nature of things, gets more typed and known by sight than a tragedian; and if audiences remember you waving a string of sausages, with a great stuffed phallos bouncing about, it takes more than a gilt wreath to make them forget it. If Hermippos was displeased he did not let it show, but bowed as if to a tribute. He was a stout-hearted man; even when he was tiresome, I could not keep from liking him. I said to Anaxis, later, that it was a good thing he had been there to keep the public sweet.

'That clown! Let me forget him while I can. Dionysios took second prizes here while he was much more disliked than now. I can't think why you should be so anxious.'

I was about to deny it, but got a better thought and said, 'My dear, you must bear with me; the truth is, I'm strung-up like a lyre with this trouble between you and Hermippos. It's amazing you put up with him so well. But the fear of your being put off on the day, with so much depending on it, keeps me awake at night.'

'My dear Niko!' he said at once. 'I trust it would take more than Hermippos to do that to *me*. We are in the hands of the god; it may start to snow, the Chief Archon's wife may go into labour in the seats of honour, or the Thebans cross the frontier. These are real evils, which we may pray Iakchos to avert. But as for Hermippos, let us keep our minds on serious things.'

At dress rehearsal, therefore, he was all graciousness; and Hermippos, like the good artist he was at heart, found no time for foolery. 'It's going too well,' I thought. 'The bad luck will come on the day.' Then at my chariot-entry after Hermes one of the horses stretched its neck, picked up Hermippos' mask by the wig, which I suppose it took for straw, and plucked it clean off his head. We laughed ourselves sick and felt better.

Now came the fateful draw for playing order. It was raining that day, but we joined the crowd of artists and sponsors waiting in the theatre colonnade to see the lists go up.

The first days would not concern us; comedy is king at the Lenaia, and always opens. After that there were trilogies with satyr-farce finales, one day for each. Then came the single plays. The list went up, the word went round. Leaving out the comic closure, we were on last.

Now if this happens at the Dionysia, it is plain good news. But at a winter festival like the Lenaia, you can't tell if you are blessed or cursed till the very day. If it is showery, or there is a bitter wind, the older people, and the sickly, and those with thin cloaks, start going home. The rest get restless, going off to stretch their legs or relieve themselves; their minds are half on hot soup at home; they are getting sulky and fidgety and hard to please. On the other hand, if it turns out fine you have the best of the billing and of the day as well. The mildness and sweetness of the theatre on such afternoons is an artist's proverb. No wonder Zeus, and Dionysos, and Apollo Helios do so well for offerings beforehand.

On the eve of the festival, I lay listening to the noise of the midnight rites; the cries of the women trying, as they ran about the streets, to sound like maenads on a mountain; playing at danger in safety, as they do at the Lenaia, and garlanding King Vinestock to placate him for being pruned. Their hymns, and their squeals of 'Iakchos!' and the red light of torches sliding across my ceiling, would wake me whenever my eyes had closed. Towards morning, I heard a huddle of them go by with their torches out, shivering and grumbling, and complaining of the rain.

Next day opened cloudy; not the rank bad weather that gets the show put off, but grey and threatening. During the first of the comedies it looked so black that people stayed at home, and the theatre was half empty; if the cast had been less discouraged, I think the play might have won. Later it cleared a little; the theatre filled; a play no better was well received, and got the prize.

On the day when the contest of tragedies started, the wind got up. The audience came muffled to the eyes, their cloaks pulled over their heads, and with two cloaks if they had them. The wind snatched at the robes of the cast and chorus; the flute-player, who had to use both hands to play, had his skirts flung up till they showed his naked backside. This did not help the protagonist, playing Bellerophon and doing a solemn bit of recitative. In the next part of the trilogy he had to be flown in riding Pegasos. My heart bled for him as he swung to and fro, with the audience squealing or laughing. Of course the play was sliced in half; but it was middling work, which I doubt stood a chance in any case.

Next day started even windier. The chorus of women had trailing scarves, a stupid thing at the Lenaia; during a choral dance they got tangled up together and had to unwind. They were quite young boys, and started giggling; I don't suppose they sat down for a week, after the trainer got his hands on them. The play was uneven, the poet having put into the first part all he had to say, but being resolved upon a trilogy. During the last part the wind dropped and the sun came palely out; but by then the audience was bored, and waiting to see the slapstick.

The following day was ours.

I could not sleep. I thought of taking poppy-syrup; but it leaves one dull, and one would do better tired. Just as I was going off, a wedding procession passed, singing and shouting; there is one nearly every night in that month of marriages. I tossed and turned, and put out my hand at the window, and felt the air still, but very cold. Dim light from the sky showed me Apollo in his wooden frame. Since I was up, I lit a small clay lamp and stood it before the mask. The flame moved faintly in the air from the window; the eyeholes looked at me; they seemed searching, but calm. I went back to bed with the lamp still burning, and lay in thought. Suddenly I awoke to daybreak. The lamp had burned out; birds were chirping. The sky was clear.

I jumped up and looked out. A mild white frost furred the edges of the oleander leaves and the black fingers of the courtyard vine. My breath lay unstirring on the air.

I threw my blanket round me, and did my practice at the window. My voice sounded true and flexible. A ruffled-up bird in the vine whistled so like a flute that I did a bit of recitative as well. I blew up the embers in the hearth and mulled some wine, breaking some eggs into it and adding white meal and honey; an old-fashioned posset which suits my stomach at these times. I sopped some bread in, knowing I would eat nothing later. Then, having scattered the crumbs outside as my flautist's fee, I said an invocation before Apollo's mask and poured him an offering.

By the time I went out I felt warmed and brisk. My landlord and his wife, who seldom noticed me except of an evening to watch whom I brought home, called out to wish me luck, which I took for a good omen. The sky was getting quite blue. My feet and fingers tingled still, but I could feel the cold grow less.

I stopped at the barber's, and found Hermippos being finished. As soon as he could talk, he offered me a bawdy tale about two girls he had met last night returning from the rites. I was in a mood for quiet, but could see that under it all he was on edge, and this was his notion of keeping up both our spirits. So I gave him his laughs, and in return got his company all the way, since he waited till I was done.

When we got to the theatre, the public benches were full of

97

people bundled up in all they had, with hats pulled down on their ears. In the side seats, where actors sit to hear what they can of other plays, Anaxis had kept us places. Beside us sat the cast of the second play; they would have to leave halfway through the first. A little way below were the cast of the satyr-farce which would end the day, *Silenos and the Gorgons*. They greeted Hermippos as a lost brother, and asked when he would come back to comedy. Above us, right to the top, were the chorus men and boys, gossiping among themselves or swapping boasts and jokes.

Down below, in the seats of honour, ambassadors and archons, priests and choregoi and their guests were coming in, their slaves all laden with rugs and cushions to make them snug. Then came the greater priests and priestesses: the High Priestess of Demeter, the High Priests of Zeus and Apollo and Poseidon and Athene. Presently drums and cymbals sounded; the image of Dionysios was carried in and set down facing the orchestra, where he could see his servants play; his High Priest took the central throne; the trumpet sounded, and ceased. The theatre hushed. Out of sight, beyond the parodos, were heard the first notes of the flute playing in the chorus. Whether you are behind or out in front, there is nothing quite like this moment.

The first tragedy was an *Amphitryon* by a poet whose name escapes me; a new writer, who was never heard of again. He must have written himself out with this one, for it was far from bad. He had had his ear to the ground, and not missed one new effect, or bit of business, which had hit last year. It was polished like a racing chariot. Though everything had been lifted from something else, you felt the poet had hardly noticed this, it was done with so much confidence. The choral interludes were very striking, with Lydian obbligatoes for the flute; what, in those days when it was newer, we used to call belly-music. Even today, it puts me in mind of the wailing for Adonis. The flute-player was not quite up to such a tricky score, but I doubt if the audience noticed it. It was a brisk, sharp, neat piece, and was going down like hot spiced wine. Hermippos, I saw, was quite out of laughter. I said to Anaxis, 'This is a hit.'

He nodded, more calmly than I expected, and said, 'The judges are an elderly lot, this year.'

I craned over to look at the tribes' ten representatives. A man has to be of sober years to get into the ballot, and this year, true enough, there were some solid granddads. They did not look the men to relish that sobbing flute; and some were sure to take the wrong notes for modern music. I could picture the poet biting his nails each time.

However, the play had taken; the audience shouted, stamped, waved hats and shawls. The judges kept their own counsel. I was somewhat dismayed to meet such a challenge from this first play; it had been the second one I had had fears of. Anaxandrides, the author, was a prize winner from the Greater Dionysia; such poets seldom trouble to enter at the Lenaia at all. Perhaps he had something sharp to say; people prefer hearing the City criticised when winter has closed the roads and seaways, keeping foreigners out of earshot. In any case, he would be a strong contender; and besides, his sponsor, winning first draw, had got Eupolis, who had been getting actors' prizes for twenty years.

The opening chorus had some fine lines, yet was patchy, and not in Anaxandrides' latest style. I began to suspect this was some old discarded play worked over, which he had not cared to risk at the great festival. But he still had Eupolis who now came on as Telemachos son of Odysseus; moving beautifully, as he always did. I thought, 'What crazy hopes have I been feeding? We shan't even be placed.'

Hermippos leaned over to me. 'I thought he had more sense. He should have cast himself as Penelope.'

I raised my brows. Eupolis was famous for his juveniles; he was not much over forty-five, and graceful as a boy. Then he started to speak. I was amazed. He sounded twenty years older than he had last summer.

'Has he been sick?' I whispered.

'No; he's had three teeth pulled. He's been in torment with them half the year; at last his doctor warned him they'd be his death if he kept them longer. Hadn't you heard? But to think of his trying Telemachos.'

I have much to thank my father for; not least that he had strong teeth which gave him no trouble all his life, and passed on the same to me. Each actor, I am sure, who heard Eupolis that day shivered as if he had seen an owl in sunlight. It might happen to any of us next year. Once an artist is finished as an all-round man, he is mostly done for. It is rarely you get a play like *Troiades*, where the lead is old and need never change to a younger mask.

Our chance now looked better. But I could not rejoice, when I heard a fine player sing his swan-song, and the whole theatre knowing it. When Anaxis nudged me and said we should be going, I knew it was too soon. But I got up; I had not the heart to stay and listen.

Down in the skene-room there was the usual quiet scramble. I had known it since I was so small that I came and went like a mouse in a busy kitchen, scarcely seen if I troubled no one. After that I had been a chorus-boy, one chirping bird in the flock, giggling and gossiping and showing-off and mocking each other's suitors; then carrying a spear, delighted to get some bit of business; then standing-in for some real actor, sitting in front at rehearsal to study how he moved; at last, third man, the foothill one scales in triumph, to see from there the real mountain all to climb. Then second lead, where one may live and die unless one gets the chance and can take it. Now, for the first time, I came here as protagonist; here in the First Men's dressing-room was my table, the dresser waiting, my costumes on the wall-pegs, my masks and props laid out.

I put on the robe of Zeus for the prologue, a lovely thing, purple worked with golden oak leaves. The dresser rubbed-up the great mirror of smoothed bronze. It showed me at my back the other end of the room, with Eupolis' table. In the quiet, I heard clearly his voice on stage, and the audience coughing. From the sound of the lines, he would soon be due for his last exit. I picked up my sceptre, pushed back the mask on my head by its august beard, and said to the dresser, who was fidgeting with my girdle, that I would be back shortly. I expect he thought my bowels were griping, which is a common trouble with actors just going on; he did not keep me, and I got away in time. Eupolis had nowhere else to go, between his exit and his bow; and in his place I would have liked the room to myself.

I don't know where I went to wait; the next thing I remember is sitting enthroned down centre on the god-walk, eagle on left fist, sceptre in right hand; Anaxis in the mask of Thetis coming on towards me, and all the eyes of Athens skinning me to the bone.

As I sat, right foot advanced upon my footstool, in the pose of Olympian Zeus, it was as though I had sleepwalked here, and only just found out where I was. Suddenly I was gripped by terror. My first five lines sounded in my head, turning round on themselves, leading nowhere. When I was through them I was going to dry. You can't be prompted up there without the whole theatre hearing it. With a god it always gets a laugh. If this happens, I thought, I'll be a wreck all through the play. I thought of Dion; I was going to fail him; of Anaxis, whose hopes I would destroy. Here he came. In an instant I had lived an hour of fright. *Daughter of Ocean*, I thought, *Daughter of Ocean* ... My hands felt icy cold. I thought, 'My father would die of shame. He never dried. He was twice the artist I am.'

At once my lines came back to me. I started my speech, taking care of the little things about which he was exacting. I could scarcely believe he was not in front. Soon I got into the part; and when I came on as Priam felt no more fear than at rehearsal. But all through till the end I was aware of him, as if he had never been away.

6

I don't remember the victory feast very clearly. Gyllis of Thebes, who was in Athens for the festival, said she never saw a man drink so much and keep so sober. I am no great drinking man, but I daresay I drank whatever was put into my hand. My happiness must have burned it out.

The party was given by the Syracusan consul, and was the most lavish seen for years. In his speech on behalf of the author, he invited us straight away to Syracuse to play before our poet. He had bespoken our passage on the first good ship.

Anaxis and Hermippos sang a skolion together, their arms round each others' necks. Hermippos had forgotten he ever was in comedy, recalling only his tragic roles; each story ended with a laugh, though. We were all like brothers; I don't recall any prize party with so little bitchery. Anaxis had given a much sounder Achilles than ever at rehearsal, simply, I think, because he played down to give me a better chance, only protagonists being in the running for the actors' prize. I had worked like a dog to get the award for the play, but could scarcely believe I had been crowned as well. I kept putting up my hand to the ivy garland, as if to straighten it, but really to convince myself that it was true.

There was only one misadventure. Axiothea, though too discreet to enter a wine-shop or pass the gymnasium door, took a fancy to attend the party. Speusippos, as he told me later, knowing more than she did, tried to dissuade her; but she said she would not think of staying; to congratulate me would only take a moment and a friend could do no less. He agreed to escort her, if she would not leave his side. I was amazed to see her enter; and, feeling in love with all the world, went straight over and took her in my arms. The poor girl, cold sober, looked quite startled; some fool, who supposed she was Speusippos' boy friend, called out a joke which made people look; her blush made her still handsomer, and the joker declared he would cut us both out. Speusippos, who I was surprised to find had a blazing temper, would have set about him, and it would have ended God knows how; luckily I managed to keep the peace and pass it off. When I begged her pardon, she said I had only welcomed her like a friend. I think she was more put out than she pretended; but she was a generous girl, and would not spoil my victory.

Though the Lenaia prize was founded when money was worth more than now, it is still a pleasant sum, and with our expectations I saw no harm in spending it. I knew enough about Sicily to understand we must make some show off stage as well as on; so since I hate tawdry stuff I went to Kallinos. He made me a robe of fine-combed Milesian wool, cream-white, the borders embroidered in fine stitching with a deep band of crimson stars, edged above with pointed rays in blue picked out with gold. Unlike stage costumes, it looked good across the room but much better close up. I did not mean to come before Dionysios of Syracuse looking as if I owned nothing but what he chose to give me. There was Athens' credit to think of, besides my own.

Anaxis and Hermippos felt this still more. Anaxis' robe was embroidered nearly all over; he could have played King Midas in it, Hermippos even had his dipped in purple, having heard that in Syracuse it was common wear. I guessed this must have left him without a month's rent in hand; my ingrained caution, settled since childhood from hearing of artists' ups and down, nearly made me say 'Take it back'; but I feared he might think that I was jealous.

We waited some days for a ship, the consul being anxious we should arrive in style, and not be risked in storms on a small craft in the bad season. We set out, however, in very good weather for the time of year, and had a smooth run across from Korkyra to Tarentum. At Sybaris we put in, to unload a consignment of painted vases, which were packed and handled like eggs, being no doubt as costly as everything else in that city. Hermippos, who visited a brothel there, said it was like a noble's house, with murals in every room, the most instructive he had ever seen; put there, he supposed, lest thinking of the price should make the patrons impotent. He was now flat broke, but made nothing of it since we were so near Sicily.

There was nothing on at the theatre; but we saw a fit-up in the Agora, a mumming-show in the Italian style. As we all know, bawdry in comedy pleases the god, and I don't think I am prudish; but in Athens, we do keep inside the bounds of blasphemy. Dionysos, being master of the revel, is fair game; but with Zeus Almighty no one jests, and even in a satyr-play Apollo is done straight. Here he was being chased with a club by Herakles, and scolding from the roof of his shrine like a treed cat; tempted with cake, he leaned down, got walloped and fell into a water-tub. Worse still we had Zeus, with a big nose and phallos, scrambling up a ladder to debauch Alkmena; Hermes peeped in at the window after him and told the audience all about it. Even Hermippos, after laughing at the gags at first, finished quite shocked.

But this, disgusting as it was, did not so turn my stomach as a show put up by some Etruscans from up north. They are brown, sloe-eyed men, good dancers and flautists, whose forbears came, it is said, from Lydia. I don't know what story they were enacting; the Italians seemed to follow their jargon. All I can tell you is that their faces were quite bare; they were using them to act with.

It is hard to describe how this display affected me. Some barbarian peoples are ashamed to show their bodies, while civilised men take pride in making theirs fit to be seen. But to strip one's own face to the crowd, as if it were all happening to oneself instead of to Oedipus or Priam; one would need a front of brass to bear it. One knows, as one plays, that behind the mask one's face is speaking, as it must if one feels at all; but that's one's own secret, and the god's. Anaxis, outraged as a gentleman not less than as an artist, said one would feel like a whore.

Two days later we rounded Cape Herakles, and saw the cloud-white breast of Etna float high above the sea. Standing astern, to get windward of the rowers' stink which a springlike sun made ranker, we saw the loom of the land appear. The shipmaster, a friend by now, clapped our shoulders and said we should be made men once we got to Syracuse. Apart from Dionysios' own gifts, which were sure to be magnificent, we could play all the Greek cities along the coast, which had splendid theatres, and pretty well name our terms. This trip should set us up for life.

When he had gone, Anaxis said, 'This is his regular run; he must know what he is talking about. As I may have told you, before the war my family had a small estate near Marathon. A very good piece of land; the olives were sold by name in Athens. The man who owns it now lives in town, and farms it with a factor. One never knows; he might sell.'

'What I should like,' said Hermippos, 'would be to form my own company and do first-class tours. Three actors; two extras; a good flute-player who can train a chorus. One year, say, Corinth, Epidauros, Delphi, and north to Pella; another, Delos and Ionia. One hears great things of Pergamon. Samos I know; Ephesos – ah, there's a city! As for Sicily, while we're here I shall look about. Think of those top-rank companies, like Diphilos'; what really marks them out from ours? Only trimmings; costumes, masks, a good travelling turn-out, fancy-marked mules and some gilding on the cart. Once set up, one can stay there. I'd buy a little house in Corinth, in Theatre Street, to come back to between tours. I know just the girl to keep it warm. She'd jump at it; she's kept now by a paunchy spavined old banker who ...' And so on. After a while he said, 'And you, Niko? Why so quiet?'

I laughed, saying, 'Don't price the unborn calf.' I was as full of myself as the others; just more superstitious. My father bred it into me. We used to walk tiptoe before a festival, in case we should speak ill-omened words, or frighten the house-snake, or tell an unlucky dream. But nothing was so bad as counting on a win beforehand. I learned that for good the first time, he was so angry. Someone else won, too, and I blamed myself for years.

The wind favoured us so well that the rowers shipped oars. At sun-up we sighted Syracuse.

As we sailed into the Great Harbour, Anaxis said, 'So this is the place that made me an actor.' I knew what he meant. His family had been ruined in the Great War, and here Athens had lost it. We must just about be crossing where the boom had trapped our fleet. Over there – good drained land now – were the swampy flats where they had camped, and got the marsh-fever, which I'm told was unknown in Greece when our grandfathers were young. It was all flattish country; even the famous Heights of Epipolai one would call a ridge in Attica. But none of the actors in that old tragedy would have recognised the skene. The Upper Town was now armoured like a dragon, all walls and gatehouses;

and it had a dragon's head. At the end of its neck of causeway, scaly with towers, the island fortress of Ortygia thrust out into the sea, bristling with war-engines, and with walls like cliffs. All this was the work of Dionysios. The cost hardly bore thinking of; but then his rapacity was famous all over Greece; it was said, and I started now to believe it, that he taxed his subjects' incomes as high as twenty per cent. I asked the Captain how they bore it.

'You should soon know how,' he said, 'or rather why, if you'd been, as I have once, into a town the Carthaginians had just been sacking. I thought I'd seen evil, before that day. It's better, I tell you, not to know that men can do such things. Nothing here makes sense, without the Carthaginians. It was for fear of them, not of the tyrant, that free men worked on these walls like slaves; and the old man has kept power all these years for the same reason he got it: because they'd still sooner have him than the Carthaginians. Remember that when you go ashore, and watch your tongues.'

Presently the theatre came in sight, on the footslopes of Epipolai. We craned and stared, and Anaxis said, 'We may need extra rehearsals. It has that sound-cave.' I agreed, this being well known. It was a theatre where the low rake spoiled the acoustics and they had had to put in amplifiers. Some theatres use hollow bronze to throw up the sound, others wooden screens; but here they had worked on a natural cave hard-by. The echo chamber had the shape of a pointed ear; some wit had named it Dionysios' Ear, refer-ring to the ass-ears of King Midas, and it was so known by artists everywhere. I had been warned one needed to practise with it.

Some kind of bustle had started on deck; the sails were down, but the rowers sat idle. Instead of taking us in, the Captain was up in the prow with the pilot, shading his brows. When I came up he said, 'Are your eyes good, Niko?'

'What's to see?' I asked.

'Not enough by half. Too quiet; too few people about; and their heads together. No crowd to watch the ship in. Something's amiss on shore.'

I could see this too. If an odd man came from the upper town, people were stopping him for news; it looks the same anywhere. Then they would huddle in talk again. There was hardly any of the working noise and shouting one expects in a busy port.

The other two looked at me. I said, 'Whatever it is, it will take a good deal to stop Dionysios from seeing his play.' Some Sicilian passengers were starting to look uneasy. I said to the Captain, 'What do you think it is? The plague?'

'No; there would be smoke from the pyres. And in war they would all be busy. This is something political. If we stand well out, someone will come; a merchant for his cargo, or someone wanting a passage. Then we shall know.' A knot of Syracusans came up to him, demanding to disembark, while others argued against it.

'By the dog!' said Hermippos. 'Always some scare or other before a big performance. Well, whatever it is, they'll have had time to get over it before the end of rehearsals with the chorus.'

We dropped anchor where we were. The sun grew hot, the sights grew tedious. Some of the passengers chaffered with a fishing-boat to take them off, and we saw them on the waterfront, asking for news. It made us fidgety, and we said to each other that we would take the next boat ourselves. Soon we saw one. There was no need to hail it, it was heading for the ship.

Two men scrambled on board, the first clearly a merchant; Greek clothes, Greek barbering, brown skin and hooked nose from some Sikel or Carthaginian strain; Sicily has always been a meeting-place of races. In good Greek, he asked the Captain after a consignment of lapis from Ephesos. The Captain sent to the hold for it, and asked what news. You may suppose they could hardly breathe for eavesdroppers.

'No news since yesterday,' said the Syracusan. 'No one's been let through the posterns, and the guard won't open their mouths. The doctors have been in there three days, and even their own wives can't get word to them.'

The Captain said, 'My friend, you're starting the race at the turn-post. What's wrong with whom?'

'What, you know nothing?' He looked as if it should have been written on the air.

'Only what I could see. You're our first newsbringer.'

The man looked about him as if from habit; then, though there were a dozen of us breathing down his neck, 'It's Dionysios. Dying, they say.'

I could feel my mouth open, like the jaws of a landed fish. There was a gasp from Herakleides. Anaxis stood like stone. For longer than any one of us had lived, Dionysios had ruled in Syracuse. I had thought of pretty well every stroke of fate, except this.

Someone asked how long he had been sick. Six days, the merchant said, with fever; then his eyes went past us to the wharfside, where some stir was going on. He ran to the rail, waving at someone. The man on shore lifted his hand, and dropped it palm down. There was no need of an interpreter.

Someone, however, always explains. 'The news is out,' said the merchant. 'Dead.'

A babble broke out all over the ship, in three or four languages: bleating, barking, clucking; it was like a farm at feeding-time. Actors are said to be talkative; but I think we were the only ones dead quiet. Nobody dared speak first. Not that there was anything to say. We put off our hopes in silence, like gorgeous costumes and masks from a failed play; we would not be needing them again. After a while I said, 'Well, my dears. That's the theatre.'

Someone moved sharply. It was the merchant, who had turned to stare. He was waiting for his goods, while the other man from the boat talked with the Captain; he had a bundle with him and seemed to want a passage. Breaking in on this, the merchant pointed at us like one who complains that the cargo stinks. 'Are those men actors?'

Reminded of our troubles, the Captain said we were distinguished artists from Athens, who had been sent for to play at Court, but had lost our luck. At this, I saw the other man sidle away, trying to get the Captain between him and us. It made me notice him; there was something I half remembered. But the merchant had not done. 'Are they,' he said, still pointing, 'the actors from the Archon's play?'

I had had enough before and found this too much. 'Where do you think you are?' I asked. 'Pricing goats at market? Ask civilly, if you want to know.'

He neither took this up or begged our pardon; he was too full of his feelings to waste the time. 'Well, then, if you are for your own good you'd best turn straight round with the ship. How it will end what god can say, this day's work you did for our city, you and your fellow there.' He jerked his thumb, as it seemed, at the other man. 'I'm no politician, no sophist' (he was working right up into the next register) 'all I ask is to live in peace. Say what you choose about the Archon; but he built these walls, yes, hitched up his own gown and carried a hod, and made the quality do their stint too. He built them, and kept them manned, and saw the shipping got through. And now whom are we left with? What now?' He spun round at the second man, who had been creeping off, and gazed back like a snared rabbit. 'You! You badluck-piece, you cadging Athenian mummer with your money-bag up your shirt! May you never get fat on it. I hope it buys you a rope.'

We could make nothing of these Delphic ravings; but the Captain, sharp as a nail, said, 'What? What's this man done? Was it murder then? You, there, get off my ship before you're put over-side. Do you think I want the war-fleet out after me? Look alive; off!'

The man ran forward, gabbling. With one hand he grasped the hem of the Captain's tunic, with the other the breast of his own, where I suppose he had his money. Invoking every god from Zeus to Serapis, he vowed he had done nothing, nothing contrary to any law of gods or men. A babe unweaned was not more guiltless. I could not believe, with all this grabbing and swallowing, he could be any sort of actor; and yet something said 'theatre' in my mind.

Next moment Hermippos caught my arm. 'Niko. I know him now. He was in the chorus; the first line of the anti-strophes. That fellow who used to come in half a beat early. Don't you remember?'

He was right; it had happened as late as the dress rehearsal. 'But,' I said, 'how in the name of Hekate did he get out here?'

'Let us ask him,' said Anaxis. We all moved forward. The chorus-man clutched his brows and shook his head about, like Orestes beset by Furies. But there is a time and place for everything. So I stepped up sharply, and letting out suddenly my Angry Achilles voice, said, 'Enough! Tell us the truth.'

Wringing his hands till I thought they would come off, he gasped out, 'Oh, Nikeratos! I appeal to you, sir, I ask you, how could I have foreseen it? On my life, by all that's holy, I meant no harm to anyone. Somebody had to bring Dionysios the news, and get the good-tidings-gift; why some hired courier, why not me? I rode up to Corinth, and got a ship through the Gulf from there, and saved two days. Who could have thought of its harming artists like yourselves, who were sure of all the honours? Who could have known? Am I a soothsayer? A god?'

'No,' I said. 'Not by the look of you. So you shipped ahead of us with the news. What then?'

He showed the whites of his eyes, like a beaten dog. I would have shaken it out of him, but the merchant said, 'I can tell you quicker. When the Archon got the news, he paid Wing-foot Hermes here the price of it, and a good price too. Then he began the victory feast. It went on two days and I daresay they would still be at it, but that he took a turn in the gardens to get cool. He wasn't young; he'd had the marsh-fever more than once, and it clings then to one's bones. He went sick within two hours.'

The chorus man gazed from one to the other of us, his silence giving assent. Hermippos caught Anaxis' eye, and jerked his head at the water. They rolled back their gowns from their arms.

It was hard to blame them. I had half a mind to it, too. But the wretched man had only done what anyone else might who thought of it; and the sponsor's courier, no doubt, would still have got here before us with the same effect. Even when I had talked them out of it, they were all for putting him back on shore, saying he carried bad luck enough to sink a squadron. The only man more superstitious than an actor is a sailor, and I saw the Captain listening. The chorus-man – whose name I can't recall, though I thought it graven on my mind for ever – fell down and clasped my knees. I have seen it done better. Weeping he cried that his sole hope of life was to get away before the Syracusans started to blame him for the death; or he would be crucified on the walls, and his ghost would haunt us.

It was a good long speech, so I had time to think. I had been pretty late about it. Still, what need of time? A man who gets omens at the hour of fate should not turn back at the door and call it chance.

'Stop grizzling,' I said. 'No one can hear himself speak.' He choked it down, and I went on, 'Very well, you meant no harm.

But you did it. You've still come off with your profit, which I'm sure was a good one; while these artists here have lost the chance of their lives. As I see it, the least you can do is to stand them their fares to Athens. In that case, we will ask the Captain to let you sail.'

He could not offer fast enough. Anaxis said, 'Of course that includes Nikeratos, though he was too much the gentleman to mention it. As protagonist, he has borne the greatest loss.'

'Thank you, my dear,' I said. 'But there's no need; I shan't be sailing. I've a fancy to see Sicily.'

This line, as I had feared it might, stopped the show. Then the big scene started. Even the Captain joined in. Had I lost my wits, they asked. What would be doing in the theatre? Civil war was the likeliest thing, and then, maybe, the Carthaginians moving in while the walls were weakly manned. Even for a man tired of life, said the Captain, there are ways and ways of losing it. To all this I replied that I could look out for myself, and had always wanted to see Syracuse. After a while Hermippos and the Captain gave me up; but Anaxis drew me aside.

'Niko, my dear friend.' He grabbed my shoulders, a thing I had never known him do. I saw, surprised, that he really liked me. 'Don't, I beseech you, rush off like a boy into a battle, looking for the one he loves without helm or shield. I said nothing before the others, out of respect for your feelings; but it needed no oracle at Delphi to tell me how things were with you. Think! You have no head for affairs; you know it; you'll find nothing but trouble; and the man whose fortunes you want to follow, excellent as no doubt he is, won't be at leisure now to remember that such a man as Nikeratos walks upon the earth. You have no notion what can happen in a city, when a tyranny changes hands. Once faction fights begin, and throats are cut in the streets, men don't wait to ask if you are a stranger in those parts.

Come, sail home with us now, and come back later when everything is settled.'

'Don't fret so, dear boy,' I said. 'I toured with Lamprias at nineteen, on the second-class circuit, and came out of that alive. I daresay I can shift in Sicily.'

'How will you even eat?'

'I've some prize-money still in hand. Look, the boatman's shoving off; I must catch him now.' If I had to wait for another, I should have all this two or three times over.

When I had got my things, I brought Anaxis the mask-box of Apollo. 'Keep this for me, my dear. Set it up somewhere, and give it a pinch of incense now and then; the god is used to it; and ask him to keep me in mind till I come home.'

He promised; shaking his head over me as if it had been the boat of Charon I was boarding to cross the Styx. He and Hermippos both embraced me. They watched me all the way to shore. Further along the rail stood the man from the chorus, staring after me as if at a man bereft of his senses running into a house on fire. It stuck in my mind, as I set foot on the wharf of Syracuse.

7

I decided to do the natural thing, and make for the theatre. It would be a starting point; something would come to me there. I found my own way, seeing nobody I felt like asking.

Syracuse is a splendid city, taking after Corinth which founded it. But it was warmer, greener, dustier, stank more, and smelled already of spring. There seemed more of everything; more gilding, more marble, more shops, more people. They had traits of every nation under heaven: fair Hellenes and dark Hellenes; brown hawk-faced Numidians; black thick-faced Libyans; reddish little black-haired Sikels; and every kind of cross-breed these could produce. All they had in common was their Greek dress, and fear. The place was like a kicked ant-hill, before they start putting it to rights. Only they did not look to me like doing it, but as if they were waiting to see what would be done to them. There was a kind of meanness with it too; as if each watched his neighbour lest he might find a foothold quicker in the slippery time, and manage to make something out of it.

The theatre was empty. Even the caretaker and cleaners had gone off, leaving it unlocked. The streets had been full of people in their working clothes. I went in, and felt better for it, more myself. As I had expected, there was too much of the best of everything, coloured marble, gilding, painting, over-decorated statues; a place designed to make one think 'I am playing at Syracuse' rather than 'I am playing in Sophokles'. I had never seen such machinery as there was back stage and under it. Dionysios must have turned his war-engineers loose there when they had nothing else on hand. One huge device of wheels and levers left me quite at a loss; later I found it was to raise the stage or lower it, by pumping water in or out of chambers below.

However, as I had guessed I would, from here I knew where to go next. I went down into the street and found the theatre tavern.

One could tell it at a glance, as one always can: a barber's stand in one corner; a set of the tragic masks on one wall; on another a scene from the *Agamemnon*, with actors' names written in. Though the theatre had been empty, this was cram-full; the noise came out to meet me, the sort which, in cities all over Hellas, makes an artist feel at home. No muttering and whispering, as in the streets. An actor always knows that if one city gets too hot, there are others.

The barber's chair was free; so having shaved that morning I asked to be pumiced, a good long talkative job. News buys news.

The barber was a Corinthian, as every barber in Syracuse is, or claims to be. When he asked me whence I came, and so on, I told him everything, except that I knew Dion; there seemed no sense in hiding the rest. While he spread his towels he passed on the news over his shoulder; presently, to save him trouble, people got up and sat around. Some of them offered me wine. It was as unlike as possible to the city outside. Here one could feel one's footing. Actors understand actors, as dogs do other dogs.

No one was surprised that having come so far for nothing, I should stay to see the city before going home. The barber, who owned the tavern, introduced me to the leading actors who were there, and to some old ones who I expect sat there all day. Then he remembered that Dionysios' chorus trainer, who would have worked on *Hektor's Ransom*, lived near by, and sent someone to fetch him. Meantime everyone told me about Dionysios' fatal party, some adding that by habit he was a sober man, and might have lived if he had been better seasoned to it. They talked of the plays he had put on; there was a good deal of smooth backbiting among the leading men, far more than at Athens, which came, I should say, from their having had to compete for the tyrant's favour. The man I took to most was a second-role tragedian called Menekrates. As he seemed talkative, and I had learned nothing useful yet, I asked him whether young Dionysios would be as good a patron as his father.

For a moment everyone glanced round in search of eaves-droppers; even here one was still in Syracuse. But they seemed satisfied. Menekrates smiled, flashing his white teeth; he was dark almost to blackness, with a high-bridged Numidian nose. 'My dear Nikeratos, that is the riddle of the Sphinx. No one knows anything, about theatre or anything else. If you want my opinion, the man who would most like to know what young Dionysios is like, is the man himself. Since he left off playing with his toys, he's not dared to be anything that a man of rank could take seri-ously. He won't even laugh at a comedy till everyone round him has laughed first. He cries more easily. I made him cry once. That's as much as anyone knows. He may be sitting at this moment, like an actor without a mask, waiting for someone to write him a part.'

'Or,' said a man with a flute-player's flat-topped fingers, 'he may be taking off the mask he's been playing in all this time, to make his bow and show his face.'

Just then the chorus-master came in, a little bouncing man who knew artists all over Greece and demanded news of them, and I had to talk theatre. After all, it was the centre of these men's lives, and it was only chance that was making me any different.

What next? I was no nearer knowing than when I landed. If I had been anyone else, I could just have walked to Dion's house and asked how I could be of service. But what kind of entrance could I make, which would not seem to say, 'Here I am, stranded without work after coming all this way. You hired me; now look after me.'

The barber had done, and it was noon. But Menekrates would not let me order food, and shared with me a good fish stew. Then, when we had eaten, he said that since I had come to see the sights he would be happy to show me Syracuse, and to offer me the spare bed at his lodging.

Here was an omen at the crossroads. I had taken to the man; he liked gossip too, and might have some useful knowledge. All over Hellas, a web of guest-friendship binds the artists of Dionysos; it went without saying that when next he came to Athens I would return his hospitality. So I could accept it without loss of pride; a great piece of luck, with my passage home to think about.

'It will have been worth your visit,' he said, 'just to see the funeral. There is always a big show for an important man; but this should be the sight of a generation.'

'Of two,' said the chorus-master. 'Dionysios has ruled for two, by the common reckoning.'

I asked who would arrange the rites. 'Why, the heir,' he answered. 'Young Dionysios.' Plainly no one doubted who the heir was. I wondered what was going on in the island stronghold. There was not much chance of my ever knowing.

After this Menekrates took me to the small street where he lodged, in a good clean room with whitewashed walls opening to a courtyard. He showed me my bed, lay down upon his own and slept at once, as everyone does there at that hour. Even so early in the year, it was getting warm. Not being used to it, I lay thinking, looking out through the window at the court with its green shade of palms and guards.

When the shadows started lengthening, he woke up. As we splashed well-water on our faces, he said, 'Let us go and see if my cousin Theoros has got home yet. He should have got purified from the death-chamber by this time. We shall get something at first hand from him.'

As we slipped along a crooked alley where two could not walk abreast, I asked who this Theoros was. He answered, 'Oh, he is the great man of our family. He works for Leontis the physician; puts on his poultices, and so on. For three days now he and his master and the other leading doctor, Iatrokles, have been locked up in Ortygia. My cousin (he is my cousin's husband) has been at her wits' end, poor girl. She said if the Archon died they would all be executed. I told her not to fret; there was no one the old man's life was as precious to as it was to him.'

Apollo, I thought, you have not forsaken your servant.

'He does not approve of me,' said Menekrates. 'He thinks I should have had foreknowledge of so dignified a person marrying into the family, and chosen another calling. But we'll hear something from him; he is too self-important to keep it in.'

Some children playing in the street told us he was back. We went on, and found a small room fast filling up with kindred and acquaintance. The women had hidden inside, but the door-curtain bulged with them; two little boys ran about underfoot like chickens. There was no room to sit down. Theoros, a weighty fellow with a long combed beard and a manner copied from his master, held forth beside the hearth-stone. He received me civilly; but condescended to Menekrates. I saw that all the family, except for him, was quite fair and Greek. This often happens in Sicily.

I will cut Theoros' opening narration, which followed Dionysios' sickness from the first shiver through rigors, vomitings, sweatings, purgings, and so on, with all the treatment. He described how every time Leontis sent him outside for anything, before being let back into the sickroom he was searched to the skin by the guards; 'a foolishness, when so many means of healing can be means of death, misused. But they had their rule and no one dared change it; when Iatrokles, our colleague, complained of the delay, the Captain related how a guard was once put to death for handing a javelin to the Ruler's own brother, when all he wanted was to draw a siege-plan in the dust for Dionysios to see. He would not have a razor near him, even to shave himself, but singed his beard with glowing charcoal. So now, as you can understand, they feared he might yet recover and make them answer for it. When he began to sink, and they heard us say it was only a matter of time, they stopped searching young Dionysios; but you could see it made them anxious. If it had been Dion, that would have been different; the rule had always been waived for him.'

There was a buzz in the room. Someone said, 'Dion was not there?'

Theoros coughed, and stroked his beard. 'It was difficult. A very delicate matter. On the one hand, the patient was exhausted, and just the man (as his son had no need to remind us) to overtax what strength was left. On the other, he was the Ruler still. Yet to obey a sick man without discretion may be to make oneself his murderer.'

The company weighed this in a respectful pause. My question was burning my tongue; but the manners one is bred with stick. It was a white-haired old grand-dad, sure of his standing, who piped up, 'What? What? Did Dionysios ask for Dion?'

'That again, Glaukos, is a thing more easily asked than answered.' He nodded approval of himself, till I thought I should go mad. 'In the earlier phase, when the patient was full master of his faculties, he was occupied, as often happens, with trivialities, the gods having sent him no foreknowledge. He discussed his play, sent for Timaios the skene-painter, and talked a full hour with him against our advice, sending out more than once to learn if the actors had come from Athens.' Then he remembered, bowed, and said, 'Ours is the privilege denied him.' I bowed back. Menekrates caught my eye and winked.

'Dion of course visited his kinsman, but found him full of these affairs. Calling us to the anteroom he charged us to inform him at once if our prognosis altered. "I have seen these fevers in the field; they change quickly, either way. If he worsens, tell me directly, without fail." You know his manner. My principal said, afterwards, that a general he might be, but we were not his men though he seemed to think so.'

My heart sank. From the man one may infer the master, and I could see the scene.

'He was given the civil answer due to his rank. It went without saying that the heir must hear first of any change. And *he* said at once, "My uncle has never known how to spare himself. Nor has my father. It will be his death if we let them meet." When Dion returned, therefore, he was told the patient must have quiet. Indeed, with the fever's evening rise he grew restless, wandering in his thoughts, giving and cancelling orders, then demanding something to make him sleep. In the course of these ramblings it is likely that, as you, Glaukos, were asking, Dion's name came up. Had we obeyed them all, we should have had the sickroom full of mercenary captains, engineers, envoys, tax-collectors, masters of horse and actors; a chaos, as our new Archon put it. He himself behaved with great propriety. As for Dion, I believe he did come back once or twice, and latterly brought his sister's sons; and once Dionysios called out to him to come in if he wanted anything, not stand talking with the guard. But at once the patient had rambled off again, cursing us for calling ourselves doctors when we could not so much as dispense a draught of poppy. His son, who was there, begged us not to refuse this comfort, so likely to be the last. We therefore complied, and the end was peaceful.'

Peaceful for the doctors too, I thought. If you can't save your patient, it's next best to know when you can stop fearing him, and start fearing his heir. They were better off than the guards.

After this everyone started telling stories of Dionysios. It seemed even those who hated him were powerless to look beyond him; how not, when no man under fifty could remember the days before he ruled? But before Menekrates and I slipped off, I overheard Theoros impart to some favoured friends the last sensible words of the old tyrant. When he had had the draught, he beckoned his son and said, 'If these fools let me die, even a fool like you should be able to keep hold on Syracuse. I leave you a city bound with chains of adamant.' These words he repeated, like a craftsman speaking of a good job done; and closed his eyes.

As we walked away, I thought: Whatever part did I think to play here? This is not Kreon's Thebes, but the modern age, the hundred and third Olympiad. Well, I would stay on with Menekrates to see the funeral. It would give me a glimpse of Dion, since I could not think now of calling on him; he had trouble enough, without being touted by resting actors. I would just stand in the crowd, and see him pass.

Perhaps, I thought, he would spend more time in Athens now. I asked Menekrates his opinion. 'Rather less, I should think,' he said, 'unless young Dionysios is an even worse fool than his father thought. He never apprenticed him to his trade, for fear he'd want to own the business; he will need Dion at his elbow for years to come, to run the state at all. If that man is human, he must be waiting for his chance. Thank God I've no family of my own. I think I shall go on tour.'

'If you mean,' I said, 'that Dion might seize power, I don't think it likely. He doesn't hold with revolutions, or civil war. I met him once.' He might hear this any day from some actor lately in Greece; it would look strange to have said nothing, unfriendly too. I told him the story, dwelling only on the theatre part.

'Don't dream,' he said, 'of leaving before the funeral. No one will dare give parties, but we'll pass the time. Not with my father's kindred, whom I'm sure you have seen enough of. I don't mix much with them; there was a family quarrel over my birth. As you see, I'm dark; my father's sister, the fat frog, put it about I'd been got by our Libyan slave. Do I look like a Libyan? My father believed my mother, but the scandal soured him; he never had much use for me. When I was a man I searched the records. The Numidian strain's from their side, and I told them so, for which they liked me no better. Well, I vowed I'd turn out the best of them, and so I have. Theoros is a servant for all his airs. Last year, when my brother stabbed a man and they had to find the blood-price, whom did they come to? Me. He's as fair as you to look at; but inside, Numidian to the bone, savage as a desert wildcat. I am all Hellene; but they don't look below the skin. However, it's all one in the theatre, under the mask.'

Rather than I should lack entertainment, he offered to take me to the best boy-brothel in Syracuse, which he assured me would keep open. I thanked him and excused myself; I like Eros with unclipped wings, and the smiles of a slave, who might spit in one's face if he did not fear the whip, have no power to warm me. So we went back instead, that evening, to the theatre tavern, finding it fuller than at noon; where Menekrates told everyone about Delphi and the crane, so that I was forced to relate the story.

Then Stratokles, the chorus-master, said he had never seen the full text of *Hektor's Ransom*, having been given only the choral parts; and everyone demanded a recital. In no time they had got me up on the barber's stand, with an audience packed to the doors; some court gentlemen coming in who had no diversion that night, on account of the mourning, and who were eager to hear the play which, as they said, Dionysios had died of.

'The verse is not bad,' said one of them. 'Not quite Sophokles – except where it *is* Sophokles – but not bad at all. There was an oracle, you know, that the Archon wouldn't die till he had won a victory over his betters. He's let the Carthaginians off lightly more than once, when he could have pushed them into the sea.' Everyone started looking about in terror. The youth who had been speaking said, 'He's dead.' The green shoot bends quickest to the changing wind. 'They made it worth his while, and he needed them now and then, to keep the city needing *him*. But this was the destined victory, after all. Two-tongued Apollo laughs last.'

'I don't think so,' I said. 'I heard the other plays and I thought the judging fair. It usually is, in Athens.' My mind went back to Theoros' story of the old tyrant shouting for his sleeping-draught, with Dion at the door. Yes, he had beaten his better at the end.

Next morning Menekrates woke me early, to go sight-seeing in the cool. We were crossing the agora, when we heard a crier calling all the citizens to Assembly. I was surprised that under a tyranny such a thing existed; but Menekrates assured me all these forms had been kept on. 'Come and watch,' he said smiling sourly, 'and you will understand. My friend Demetrios, the coppersmith, will let you stand on his roof.'

The assembly place was down on the flats. On the way we passed the quarries where they put the Athenian prisoners in the Great War, and where so many died; they are not far from the theatre. Menekrates told me Dionysios had had them carved out twice the size and there was no knowing who might be in them. 'Well,' he said, 'things may change, who knows? Let's go and see.'

The assembly field had been cleared overnight of stalls, sheeppens, cockpits and so forth. A tall rostrum in the centre was hung with white, instead of purple. Menekrates had joined the citizens; from the roof of the smith I heard trumpets sound and the clank of armour. In marched about half a regiment, lining the middle of the square two or three deep. The Syracusans seemed to think nothing of it. They waited, chattering and shouldering, as women do for some spectacle others have prepared for them. I understood Menekrates' smile.

Through a lane of soldiers the new Archon rode to the rostrum, and mounted the steps without grace. My eyes strayed to Dion, who had gone up with royal dignity behind him, and stood there with a few other men of the family. Him I would have known anywhere by his bearing and his height. As for young Dionysios, the soldiers had raised a dust, and it was too far to see faces well. But as one knows in the theatre, the whole body speaks. He was thinnish, and held himself like a man with a stoop who never before pulled back his shoulders. Sometimes he forgot, and let his neck poke forward. You could have told at a mile that he had neither looks nor charm.

He started speaking, coughing now and again from the dust. His voice matched his deportment: forced, anxious, and striving for effect, which only brought out its faults. His speech seemed empty and formal stuff, written probably by someone else. From what I could hear of it, he praised the departed, deplored his own loss and the city's; and asked for the people's loyalty. There was some acclamation, such as you might expect with all those soldiers standing about. I missed a good deal, since the smith had had no notion of leaving his slaves to idle while he was gone, and the bursts of clattering from the workshop often killed all other sound. It seemed no great loss.

After one such din, I found he was speaking of his father's obsequies, which were to be worthy of Syracuse's greatest man. The people brightened, at news of a show, and there was some real applause. At this the young man picked up a little life, like a nervous actor with a good house. He stopped peeping at his notes, without which he would not have got far till now; and, with a sudden burst of eloquence, spoke of his father's poetic talents, the fruit of nights with the lamp while other men were revelling. (I am told this was quite true.) The hammers began again downstairs; after which I caught something about the gifted artist, who should have painted the skene, being at work upon a funeral pyre of no less splendour. You could tell, from the jerks and pauses, that he was now speaking extempore. After some more hammering, the loudest yet, I pulled my fingers out of my ears in time to hear '. . . will be spoken by the protagonist.'

'*Protagonist?*' I thought. 'What's this?'

Dion had been standing up there like a statue all this while. Now, even at this distance I saw him start, and look about. I knew then I had heard right.

I suppose the speech finished somehow. Menekrates met me at the door. He had been quite near the rostrum and heard everything. I was to speak the funeral oration.

'My dear,' I said, 'we must both be dreaming. It should be Dionysios himself.'

'Of course it should. He can't be such a fool as he looks. He couldn't do it, as we've seen; he's a stick; he loses his lines, he fluffs; he barely got through. At a state funeral, people expect something. The whole audience would have walked home saying, "Now Dion would have been worth hearing."'

'You must be right,' I answered. 'Nothing else makes sense.'

'If he'd hired an orator (and Demodoros must be spitting blood) everyone would know why. But this is a tribute to the old man's last achievement; you could call it clever. He was gagging, you know. It came to him on stage; he was playing to the audience. By the dog, Niko, your guardian god looks after you.'

'He sent me a friend,' I answered. Indeed, I was lucky in Menekrates. He was generous by nature; not a rival, being still a second-roles actor; happy enough as my host to share the event and spread the news. Some artists would have been so jealous, especially of a foreigner, that I should have had to move out.

We returned to the lodging, where I could be found. Just after siesta-time, when the sun was leaving the courtyard, the palace messenger arrived, with my summons to Ortygia. I was to go next morning.

At the hour, therefore, when the market opens, I put on a plain white robe, since I was going to a house of mourning, and walked in the cool sunrise towards the sea. Menekrates saw me halfway. He said it was against nature, for a Syracusan, to linger before Ortygia.

There was a thick-walled fort to pass through, before one even set foot upon the causeway. The swarthy Iberian mercenaries who manned it looked at my summons, and opened the triple gates. Any one of them would have done by itself for a small town. I came out on a cobbled square by the Little Harbour, with the causeway still to cross.

I never saw at one time so many ships of war. Here I had my first sight of a quinquireme, as high as a two-floored house. Strange engines were mounted on the decks, for flinging fire, or stones, or dropping weights from mast-height to sink the enemy. Their beaks glared with huge painted eyes. There was an eye on the pennants too; it was Dionysios' house-flag. The barracks of the galley-slaves, with their walls and guards, seemed to stretch for miles.

A thirty-foot gate tower closed the landward end of the causeway. Its roof was manned by Nubian archers, polished black men with ox-hide cuirasses and thick horn bows. In front of the gate below, fair as the men above were dark, stood eight towering Gauls.

They wore Greek armour, for show, because they were on guard. I had heard a good deal about these troops, mainly from soldiers who had run away from them. It was old Dionysios' rule that his mercenaries should fight in the panoplies of their homelands, which they felt at ease with; and the Gauls, as these men assured me, used to go into combat stark naked, singing paeans like the yowling of cat-a-mountains, tossing and catching their swords as they came on. They charged with wide, fixed blue eyes, seemingly insensible to pain and strange to the name of fear. A Gaul under six feet was reckoned a runt; altogether, one man told me, it was like facing a battle-line of insane gods. Afterwards they would cut off the heads of the dead for trophies. Some said they ate the brains.

Now here they were, just as described; shaved chins and long moustaches, braided ropes of yellow hair down to their waists and bound with scarlet; long swords with curiously-wrought hilts, neck and arm rings of plaited gold. I had not much time to stare; the Captain shouted to me, without leaving his place by the gate, and asked my business. Just getting the drift of his vile Greek, I went up and told him. He must have topped me by a head, and I am not short. I showed him my letter; he waved it off, as if it were my fault he could not read, and in their lilting tongue ordered a man inside to ask. At last the portcullis went up. A new Gaul beckoned me. We crossed the causeway, passing between the great catapults I had seen afar and their piles of throwing-stones. At the far end was another gateway, more Nubians on top, more Gauls below. My Gaul gave a password. This gate opened at once. I was inside Ortygia.

I had not got into a fort, but a hidden city. In fact, this had been the first Syracuse; the colonists from Corinth having perceived its strength at sight. They had held it against assault both from sea and land, till the city had burst its bounds and overflowed across to the rise upon the mainland. Dionysios had enclosed all of that in his defence-walls; then for his own benefit he had cleared Ortygia of all its ordinary citizens. Each man in this teeming town was in the Ruler's personal service. It was self-sufficient; all trades needed to maintain it in peace or war were established here. I saw a street of armourers; a great clattering forge; a tannery, with a leather-works as big as a small market; potters' and fullers' shops; and as for timber-yards, I passed three, not counting the shipwrights'.

The ground rose; going up steep cobbled streets and steps, we came to the barrack quarter. It was more like a soldiers' town, with a street for each race: Greeks, Gauls, Campanians, Iberians, Nubians, Egyptians. We went through that of the Spartans, whose officers would not let them mix with their fellow-Greeks for fear they should be corrupted. They stared from their doorways, haughty and stupid, and looking quite little beside the Gaul, which made me laugh. Now we were higher, I could make out the towers of a huge castle, jutting into the sea at the island's toe. I asked the Gaul if that was Dionysios' house; but he said it was the grain store. It was clear that this place could hold out for ever, if it had ships to command the sea.

At last we came into a much wider street, all one side of which was a great high wall studded with watch-towers. The Gaul knocked at a postern and spoke into a grille. The oak door opened. Sun sifted through green shade; there was bird song; water splashed and tinkled. We were in a garden. I don't know what I had expected; anything but this. It had seemed the core of Ortygia must be solid iron.

It was really a royal park; scattered among the lawns and groves were handsome houses, belonging to people of rank and office. There were a good many statues, modern ones, fluent and suave; the old man must have gone on collecting to the last. It was hard to believe in the Ortygia outside. At a fountain under a marble porch, women were drawing water in polished jars. Then I began to hear the shrilling of professional mourners, and knew we must be near the palace.

A tall portico, gilded and painted, was flanked with seated lions of red Samian marble. A guard of Gauls stood outside; but otherwise it was a palace, not a fort. So at least it seemed; but as I went through (the Gaul had passed me to a Greek chamberlain) I saw there was an inner wall fully six feet thick, before one got to the royal rooms. Outside its door of gilded bronze stood eight Gauls, the tallest yet. When they let me through, I was led into a place for all the world like the changing-room in an expensive bath-house. There were clothes stands, shoe racks, all full; even a mirror. Two of the guards had come in with me. Up from a chair got a fat Egyptian eunuch, bowed, and started without a word to undo my girdle. I was just about to hit him over the ear, when I remembered. This little ceremony had quite slipped my mind.

The eunuch stripped me, shook out my clothes, looked both sides of my sandals, and hung them up. Then he fitted me out from head to foot from the stands beside him. Some of the robes there were quite splendid; the one I got, second or third class I suppose, was better than my own. While he dressed me, the guards never took their eyes off him. Being used to putting on what I am given to wear, I suppose I minded less than most people.

When I was ready, the chamberlain scratched at the further door; listened; threw it open; and announced, 'My lord; Nikeratos, the Athenian actor.'

I entered the presence chamber.

But, after all this, there was nothing royal about it. It was just a rich man's room, and new-rich at that; over filled with valuables; statues, murals, enamel inlays from Egypt; an easel with a Zeuxis on it. The excess, though vulgar, had yet a certain air of sincerity; this was not bought taste; good and gaudy were one man's choice. By the window was the best piece in the room, a massive green marble table standing on gilded Sphinxes, Corinthian of the best period. I remember admiring it, before I really noticed who was sitting at it.

Perhaps old Dionysios was still loitering about somewhere; he can't have been one to let go easily. At all events, the young man at the desk seemed like some clerk, who would get up and ask me to wait. Luckily I have been taught how to come through doors, so these thoughts did not betray themselves. I bowed.

I can't remember how he greeted me, or told me what I was wanted for. He was not, as you will have understood, a man of memorable words. One's mind was inclined to wander. I reflected that this was no doubt the desk at which his father had written *Hektor's Ransom*; and that he himself was ill at ease here, having some homely lair of his own where he would rather be. When I looked at the room, it seemed natural he should keep me standing; when I looked at him, I remembered I was a prize protagonist of Athens, and thought I should have had a chair. I said what was proper; that I was honoured, and so on; adding something about his father's work and the loss to the theatre.

'Well,' he answered, fidgeting with a scroll before him, 'his last wish, almost, was to hear you in his play; so I hope it may please him to hear you speak his eulogy; at least, if the dead know anything, which we cannot tell.' He said this last like a man who liked to sound up-to-date. 'Here it is; may I hear you read some?'

What's this, I thought; an audition? But I suppose he thinks it due to him.

As I was unrolling it, he said, 'I hope you can read my writing. I worked late, and there has been no time to get it copied.'

It was quite clear, and I said I wished my theatre scripts were always as good. His face brightened like a child's. I asked which passage he wanted.

'Let me see,' he said, and fumbled through it head down, like a dog in long grass. He was near-sighted. 'This part,' he said.

I read a paragraph about the building of the walls of Syracuse. To my surprise the prose was excellent, an Attic style, restrained yet forceful, with beautiful speaking cadences. It almost spoke itself. Looking up I saw him eyeing me anxiously under a front of judicial calm. Of course, I thought, I should have guessed; he did not want to test me but to hear how his own work sounded. I had met such authors before. So when I came to a passage which was muddled and fidgety and without much shape, I gave it a pleasing contour, as one can if one learns the knack.

A very good piece came next; but he held up his hand and said, 'Thank you, Nikeratos. That was excellent. Do bring up that chair there; then we can talk.'

He could not wait while I did it, but ran on. 'I had heard you were in Syracuse. Among all my concerns, my father's death, my own accession, it must have stuck in my mind. For while I was addressing the Assembly, having prepared nothing at all upon the matter, it came to me as if sent by a god. I just spoke as my thoughts formed themselves. Is not that strange?'

I said nobody would have guessed it; and that is strange, if you like. I have never liked fawners, and can't imagine that I would have flattered his father so. But in the presence of this gangling youth (for with his awkward rawness he seemed no more) lank-haired, his mourning crop showing his pink scalp here and there;

sitting fidgeting with a writing-tablet, digging his nail into the wax, picking out bits and rolling them like a schoolboy; clutching at dignity, while his eyes begged like a dog's for notice; with him it seemed trivial to stand upon one's status rather than help him out. So I soothed him as well as I could without being familiar, since it was clear he must dread being taken lightly. In the end, he called for some sweets, which I hate at such an hour, but which he himself ate greedily, and started talking theatre, bringing out truisms about the classic tragedies as if no one had thought of them before. He dug down among the stuffed dates and candied rose-leaves, holding forth about the comedy element in *Alkestis*; and all the while my mind's eye retraced my steps that morning: the fort, the Iberians, the drawbridge and portcullis, the Nubians, the Gauls, the causeway with the catapults; the quinquiremes and triremes and pentekonters; the armament shops, the barracks, the walls, the grilles, the searching-room. Here we sat talking banalities about Euripides; while around us the greatest power-machine in Hellas, or the world, idled along by its own momentum, beside its dead engineer, its quivering levers awaiting the new master's hand; this damp pale hand with bitten nails, rolling wax along the table.

Presently he said I would no doubt wish to pay my respects in the death-chamber before I left, and clapped his hands for the chamberlain. When I had changed into my own clothes, I was led towards the wailing. Old Dionysios was lying in the banquet-hall, on a catafalque hung with black and purple in a chest lined with lead. They had packed him round with ice from Etna, to keep him fresh for the funeral. As it melted it ran into a tank below; there was a steady come and go of slaves, bringing fresh ice and emptying the tank with buckets. It had kept him from stinking; I saw his square fighting face, his black stubbly chin, his short pug nose. The hired mourners had got into the swing of it, howling and pummelling their breasts in a drugged rhythm. But at the head of the bier were others who were clearly kindred. One, who had a square face like the dead man's, and the same dark brows, I thought must be his daughter; maybe the one who was Dion's wife.

I took the shears on the offering-table, and cut off a lock of my hair and laid it on the pile, which was big enough to stuff a mattress. I was on my way out with the chamberlain, when in the outer courtyard a man, who looked like an upper servant, came up and said, 'If this gentleman is Nikeratos, the tragedian of Athens, my master would like to see him about the rites.'

I followed him into the park, past the fountain, and down to a grassy terrace. Beyond was a house, not very large, but perfectly proportioned, with a herm in front of it that looked like a Praxiteles. I had expected the lodging of some official; but even before I was inside, I knew. Everything spoke; the good lines, the plainness, the splendour of the few adornments.

The servant brought me to a white-walled study lined with shelves of scrolls. At a table of polished pine, by the open window, Dion was sitting. I stepped forward. 'Good day,' he said, as if to a stranger. I was shocked stupid, and just stood there. I'm not sure I even replied. He dismissed the servant; then at once his whole face changed.

'My dear Nikeratos.' He got up and grasped my hand. 'Forgive me that cold greeting. One moment.' He flung open the door; but the passage was empty. 'I have had my man ten years; but doubtful times, doubtful men, as they say. Sit down, and let us have some wine; I have been busy since dawn, and you too I daresay.'

He went over to a side-table, where a mixer stood in a big krater packed with snow. Having poured for us both, he offered me fresh bread to dip. Nothing could have surpassed the dignity with which he did these simple services. It had a charm too, like that of a well-bred boy looking after his father's guests.

We sat down near the table. On a trellis above the window was an old knotty vine just budding; its sharp shadows fell on the soft waxy shine of the wood, and his brown soldier's hand which rested there.

'The other actors, I hear, went back,' he said. 'You, Nikeratos, faced the change of fate with your usual courage. And it would have prospered as you deserve. Your speaking of the Eulogy would certainly bring you offers, not only hereabouts but in many other cities. I tell you this in fairness. When one comes to a man for help, one should let him know what it will cost him.'

He paused. I could find nothing to say. I feared I must be dreaming this. Had he really asked help of me?

'As for the mere money,' he said, 'of course I shall cover that. But a rising artist, still young, looks first for reputation. Don't think me ignorant of this. I know what I ask. You must judge if the cause deserves it.'

I said I would do anything. I could feel myself blushing like a boy, which seldom happened in my boyhood.

'You are a man I trust,' he said, not making a speech of it. 'When I heard you had been sent for here, it seemed like the hand of God. We have the business of the rites, and no one need know of any other.'

He took from a writing-box a letter folded small and sealed.

'To you, Nikeratos, who have heard us share our thoughts, I can say more than just, "Get this out of Sicily to Plato". In the first place, you won't fear its being seditious; you know our views on violence. No, the enterprise I urge him to is one of honour to us both. It can bring good beyond reckoning to our young Ruler, to this city, even to the world. But of necessity I had to write with frankness, which might give offence and spoil our hopes. Perhaps you understand me?'

I said I thought so.

'If Plato comes, as I have urged him here to do, the thought must seem to Dionysios to be his own, or he will resent it. This is natural in a young man new to power, following such a father. But Plato's welcome depends on this; and on his welcome, everything. As you too may have heard him say, philosophy is not a tool which can be passed about like a mason's rule; it is a fire struck from the glow of minds in search of truth. Without that fire, it is nothing.'

His voice, his face, took me straight back to that room at Delphi. The noble folly, the mad beauty of it struck me dumb. Twenty years, or thereabouts, since the golden lad in love brought his friend to Syracuse, to change the old tyrant with philosophy. (I thought of the square pug face in its bed of ice, the jaw clenched like a fist in death, the shrewd wary lines round the closed eyes.) And after everything – after that legendary clash of disparate prides, after the tricked parting; the slave-market at Aigina; all these years of half-stolen meetings; now in this man of forty, a diplomat, a soldier, the flame revived when the coals were blown on; he was ready to try again.

I must have been a long time answering. He said, 'Yes, speak, Nikeratos. There are few here I can share my mind with. You have met Dionysios. What do you think?'

After thinking how best to put it, I said, 'Plato won't stoop to flattery. Do you think it will matter less this time?'

He smiled, and paused. Then he said, 'I see you have the funeral speech there in your hand. Have you had time yet to run it over?'

Since he preferred to change the subject, I answered, 'Not much of it. Dionysios took me through a little.'

'What do you think of it?'

'Most of it is very good; he must have some of his father's talent. There are one or two awkward passages; do you think he would notice a cut or two? This, for instance, adds nothing to the sense, and it doesn't speak well.'

'Where?' he asked. I showed him the place. He said, 'I think you had better read that just as it stands. He put that in himself.'

Our eyes met. I could not believe I had been such a fool as to need telling. When one thought, his signature was all over it.

'And yet,' he said, 'when you read this to him, didn't you improve it as best you could?'

'I daresay. He is only young; and he looked so anxious.'

'You see, Nikeratos? You are not a servile man; you look for achievement, not for favour. Yet you flattered him. I am not servile either, yet I have done the same. As you see, he copied out the speech himself; by now he thinks he wrote it, but for a few hints here and there. Well, if you and I can feel for his untried hand and his unformed mind, don't you think Plato will? If you had heard him teach, you would know his gentleness with a beginner feeling his way. The will to learn is all he asks. And he knows how to waken that.'

I said I was sure of it. What else could I say?

'You have seen yourself Dionysios' hunger to excel. So far, the appearance is enough for him; we may blame his education, or rather lack of it. But as Plato always says, this is the beginning from which young men come to love excellence itself. Sokrates, he says, stamped these words on the souls of all who come to him: "Be what you want to seem."'

'That's good advice,' I said. But I thought to myself, Of course it is. But like the long-race, it needs staying power. In theatre, too, one picks out the stayers early on. If I were choosing a company, I doubt I would hire young Dionysios. However, fate did the casting; I suppose they can only direct him and hope for the best.

Dion, who had been sitting in thought, said, 'His father, in what concerned his own affairs, was a judge of men. He knew a son with his own qualities would have been his rival. He feared such a son; yet wished for one. Neither wish nor fear was realised. He admitted no regrets. Whether he felt them, whether the son guessed them, who can say?'

I thought of *Hektor's Ransom*. Much was now explained.

'One thing is beyond doubt; the young man wants to be something in himself. As yet, he cannot tell what. So it is now Plato must come. He must Nikeratos.' He looked dog tired. I doubt if he had slept all night. I don't suppose he would have talked like this to me at any other time. 'He has a gift from the gods of catching souls. No god has given it me. I hope I do my duty to my city, to my kin, to heaven. Plato made me love honour, and I can say I have not betrayed it. But I cannot light fires in other men. It has been a grief to me.'

'That is not true,' I said.

I could not help myself. I could have bitten out my tongue next moment. Not for having said it; it would have done well enough as a courtesy; but for saying it with my heart.

He had been looking at a golden lion he used to hold down his papers. Now he looked at me. He swallowed; I could see him thinking what one could say. I have made it sound like a painful moment; yet it was not, for through it all I saw him glad, not I daresay for the sake of the man who said it, but that someone should.

He lifted the lion from its place, set it down, and with the soldier's firmness he always turned to when he was shy, said, 'Well, though I did not share your danger at Delphi, I was there to offer the honours of the field. That gives a bond, as it does in war.' He was a great gentleman. It rescued us both.

He stood, and turned to a wall-niche at the far end of the room. There was a bronze Apollo in it; a calm searching face, the two hands held out; in one the bow of death, in the other the cup

139

of healing. 'Surely,' he said, 'the god you kept faith with then, whom Plato all his life has served; whom proportion pleases in men and cities; surely he led you here on the day of need.'

'I won't fail him,' I said. 'Or you. Let him be witness.'

A good exit line; but of course there was still the business of the rites, which took another hour. It was just as well; it made things easy between us.

Before I left he paid me an advance on my fee for speaking the Eulogy, more than I had expected for the whole. So, knowing I ought, I plucked up my courage and took Menekrates to dinner at the theatre tavern. At first the actors who were drinking there looked away, but I had known that would have to be faced. I went up to Stratokles and his friends, saying I should never forget I had them to thank for my good fortune; if they had not entertained me here, Dionysios would never have known I was in Syracuse, and I hoped they would give me the pleasure of standing wine all round. A few still looked sour, but no one left. In the end they all came round, and we spent a pleasant evening. I was glad to have done it; it seemed to me that Dion would have thought I should.

All next day I was rehearsing for the funeral, which would take place the following evening. The shop of the royal robemaker had been at work two days and a night upon my tragic robe. It was of black dipped in purple, with foot-deep borders crusted in bullion, amethyst, agate and pearl.

The procession set forth at sunset, down from the palace through the fivefold gates of Ortygia, on through the old town and the new; then between lines of torches down into the plain again, where Timaios the skene-painter had prepared the pyre.

First walked a men's chorus, singing the Lament for Hector from the dead man's play, to the music of double flutes; singers and flautists wore dead-black robes, and cypress garlands. After these came a troop of soldiers, dragging their spears, their helmets under their left arms; then a car shaped like a warship, draped in black, with an effigy of the Spirit of Syracuse, in a pose of mourning, twice life size. Then fifty boys, singing the Women's Chorus for Hector's wake. After these, the priests of Dionysos, the dead man's name-god, with their sacred emblems. Then torch-bearers, their torches made up with precious incense, for the kindling of the pyre. After that, walking before the corpse, came the male kindred; young Dionysios, and his half-brothers by Aristomache Dion's sister, and Dion himself.

The funeral car stood fifteen feet high, and was drawn by an elephant, taken from the Carthaginians in war. They are most fearful beasts, left over as it seems from the Titans' age; as high as two men, grey, hairless, wrinkled, with a tail both ends, the bigger before; one can tell the head by the great ears. It pulled patiently, guided by a man upon its neck. On a bier draped with black and purple, Dionysios lay clothed in white and wreathed with gold. In spite of the ice, he was starting to go off by this time; I got the whiff of him all the way. I walked just behind in my tragic robe, and a wreath of gilded laurel, carrying his prize vase from Athens. It was of course the usual kind, painted with a chorus and the god; against the other grave-goods it looked as simple as a kitchen pot. But it had got there before he lost his senses; and till his eyes closed for good he never let it out of his sight.

After me came the women of the household keening; then a great catafalque with his arms and ensigns and trophies of war. His war-horse, and the other victims to be sacrificed before the pyre, were led by Gaulish warriors. Here was a glimpse of the chains of adamant; but the murmuring never got very loud. I suppose it was true that even the poor, whose children scratched in the middens while he ate off gold, preferred a hungry lifetime within his walls to one night of sack by the Carthaginians. I had heard things, by now, which made me understand it.

It was now nearly dark, with just a deep red glow where the sun had set under the sea; but the space around the pyre was lit with cressets whose flames rose six feet high, making it almost as bright as noon.

I should like to have seen Timaios' designs for *Hektor's Ransom*. They must have been worth looking at. However, he had spent himself on the pyre instead, and they talk of it to this day. It was so high, the onlookers' necks were cricked from watching the dead man hoisted. The gilded bier-stand would have served to throne a Pharaoh, the offerings to equip a banquet-hall; the sides of the pyre, which sloped inward like a pyramid's, were boarded flat and painted all over with pictures of Dionysios' victories. Sicilians love paint. They cover their houses with it, their chariots, even their carts. These battle-scenes were framed in every kind of scroll and flourish, touched-up with gold. To an Athenian it looked gaudy beyond words; but the Syracusans were squealing and groaning with admiration, and it has got into the histories as a major work of art. It was certainly remarkable, and I should think would have kept the poor of the whole city in bread and oil for a year. At all events, they got the old man settled up there among the pitch and terebinth and scented oil and tinder. There he lay, waiting to hear my piece before they sent him off to meet Judge Rhadamanthos. I mounted the rostrum before the pyre. I had been rather nervous; but now the silence was so unlike grief, so like the theatre, that I felt quite at home.

While he lived, you would not have found me speaking praise of a man like Dionysios, whoever wrote it. But at a funeral it is proper to remember only the good; or one offends the gods below, and calls the angry ghost to vengeance. Dion's lines were quite honest, as far as they went. He gave him credit as a soldier, and defender of the city, and used most of the speech on that. He said also that, though entrusted with supreme power by the Syracusans (as he really had been, in the beginning) he had outraged no household in the city through incontinence or vice. People assured me, after, that this was no more than the truth, and was probably the secret of his long reign. As Hipparchos found in Athens, wronged kin and lovers are far more dangerous than demagogues; they will kill at the cost of their lives. The old man had learned from history; besides, he had been a demagogue himself.

I had worked hard over his son's little pieces in the Epitaph, to make them sound like something beside Dion's fine prose. The young man had to be kept sweet, to send for Plato.

At the close, I heard the deep murmur which is applause on such occasions. Then the victims were sacrificed; more offerings were flung; the kindred took their torches and kindled the pyre. At once huge rushing flames leaped up and hid the body, driving the crowd back with their heat. I stood with a scorched face, sweating in my tragic robe, watching Timaios' pretty pictures curl and blacken. Then everyone went home. I remembered my father's poor simple burial, and how we had sat round afterwards thinking 'What next?'

In due course I was paid, very handsomely. Dion had booked me a passage on a ship sailing next day. I had said goodbye to all my friends, except Menekrates who was coming to see me off. I felt as good as gone, when a palace messenger came, saying that Dionysios wished to see me.

This time all the gates opened for me easily; but, once inside the palace, I was led by a different way. Presently we came to a door without pretensions; the office of some functionary, I supposed. My usher knocked, and opened. There was a pleasant smell of wood and paint, like a carpenter's shop. Which is just what it was; and at the bench sat Dionysios the Younger, with a toy chariot before him, and a tiny brush in his hand, painting on scroll-work. This time he had really done me honour. He had let me into his sanctuary.

'I was very pleased, Nikeratos,' he said, 'with your speaking of the Epitaph. I have sent to Timaios' workshop for a copy of his Siege of Motya, one of his paintings for the pyre. You may have it, in memory of the day.'

He waved his brush at it. It was on an easel against the wall; more garish than ever, seen close to, and too large to ship home without a great deal of trouble. I thanked him as if he had fulfilled my dearest wish. Dion had been quite right. It was like giving sweets to an eager child.

He invited me to go up and inspect the brushwork, which I did. But the table beside it drew my eye; I could not keep from looking. It was full of small toys, chariots and horses, carts and asses and mules, a war-galley fully rigged; all painted-up Sicilian style, and perfect as real things shrunk by magic. One longed to touch. All these years, when his father had been watching him like a mousing cat for some twitch of dangerous capacity, he had indulged himself with doing one thing well.

Since he would hardly have asked me here if he did not want it noticed, I praised the fineness of the work. I was curious to hear what he would say. I got more than I bargained for. He jumped up and came over to the table. He must have talked for at least an hour. He told me what woods he used, and how, and why; he showed me his gouges, chisels and glue, and his lava-dust for smoothing; he pointed out the racing chariots, and the processional. His face grew lively, firm and keen; he looked a different man. Suddenly I pictured him in some nice clean shop in a good street, advising a client about the design of a chair or bed-head, successful, esteemed, content; a happy craftsman, doing the one thing he had in him.

Neither of us, I thought, is perfect casting for a philosophic king. I'm the lucky one; I need not try.

He asked me which of the models I liked best. It was hard to choose; but I pointed out a state chariot with gilded wreaths, which must have cost him most trouble. 'Take it,' he said. 'It's yours. Not many people notice the finer points. I gave one not unlike it to my son, but he broke it within the day; small children don't feel for fragile things.' The news that he was a father gave me such a start, I nearly dropped the chariot. Of course he was quite old enough, but it seemed absurd. 'I shall have less leisure for pastimes now,' he said, the sureness in his face changing to a weak conceit. 'Come back, Nikeratos, when the time of mourning is over, and give us a taste of your art. Then you can sample the pleasures Syracuse affords. Our girls deserve their reputation.' The greed in his eye showed something new, and none too pleasing. I remembered stories in the wine-shops.

Soon after I left, with the chariot in my hands. The last I saw of him, he was back at his work-bench, peering with his weak eyes at his little tools.

8

The following day I set sail for home, by way of Tarentum. Dion
sent for me again before I left, to give me a letter for Archytas, the
chief man of the city, and leader of the Pythagoreans there. It was
to urge him, Dion said, to join in persuading Plato, his guest-
friend of long standing. I undertook to deliver it without fail.
Something in Dion's face assured me it was a forceful letter; and
told me, too, that there lived on within the statesman, general
and scholar a beautiful lordly boy who was not used to hearing
'no'.

I had been lucky with weather on the outward journey. The
homeward trip looked like being just as good. I hate even now to
talk of it. Whenever I cross a gangplank it comes back to me. I
have turned down good engagements, time and again, because it
meant a crossing in the bad season.

Not to give you at length my shipwreck story, we capsized
outside Tarentum, in a gale that blew down off the hills. Before
this happened, I had felt so sick I thought I would welcome
death; however, I found myself swimming. I was almost spent
when some men who had found the ship's boat floating free,
hauled me on board it. In the harbour mouth, that capsized too.

I half-remember coming to on the wharf, feeling worse than dead, cold all through to the core, tilted head-down to run out the water. I don't know who did that for me. I went off again, and woke in a bed, with a young man sitting by me, who, after saying I was among friends, went out to fetch a greybeard. There were heated stones wrapped in cloth warming the bed, and sweet herbs boiling somewhere. It turned out, when I was able to understand, that I was being tended by these same Pythagoreans whose leader I had come to see. It is their rule to succour the distressed, as an offering to Zeus the Merciful.

I had a bad chest, and fever, and nearly went my father's way. I remember little of it, except some of the dreams. They played soft music to restore my body's harmony, and dosed me with sweet hot syrup. The alembic's blue steam danced all day before my eyes like a snake to the charmer's flute. I sweated, or shivered, and they raised me on high pillows to let me breathe. Once I woke from a dream to see my own body propped in the bed, myself looking down upon it. A priest stood praying that I might be reborn as a philosopher. Then I dreamed I was beside some tomb or grave, holding a skull in my hand. It was clean, and I knew this was a play. Some flashes still come back to me; I was the son of a mur-dered king whose shade had cried me to avenge him; yet I was not Orestes. It would be nonsense, I suppose, like most dreams, if I could recall the whole.

When first I came to myself, the young man who was nursing me showed me my money-belt with my gold; I was lucky it had not drowned me. I had only lost my silver, about a tenth of the whole. I asked at once after my letters; he said they were safe, but had had to be dried. They fed me on broths and pottages, meat being forbidden them; they will not kill, saying one should be as just to sensible beasts as to men. But my strength returned on their food. When next I asked for my letter-bag, the young man begged my pardon. I had had no such thing when I was saved; but he had feared to distress me and bring my fever back again. I thanked him for his kindness and said he had done right. Presently he asked me why I was weeping; what precious thing had I lost? It was not that, I answered; but now I would have to do the letters' work myself, and I was too tired.

When I could sit by myself, and felt a little more like a man, I asked to see Archytas. They said his work and his meditations took up most of his day, but they would ask him. He came within the hour: a man of about fifty, with deep-set eyes, lean, wiry and active. He was a man much trusted by the Tarentines; though no one was supposed to hold supreme command for two years running, they had kept voting him in for seven, never doubting his good faith. I could believe it; he had a calm that filled the room.

He sat by me, heard me out, and thanked me with great courtesy, saying we would talk when I was stronger. I slept well that night, feeling half my burden lifted.

When I could walk with the help of the young man's shoulder (I scarcely noticed he was handsome, which shows you how weak I was) they brought me to Archytas' house. He was in his study, a large white room, all shelves and tables, with books, and dried plants, and geometers' figures – cubes, prisms, cones and so on – carved in wood. There were pieces of complex tackle with ropes and levers; he was a great inventor, and some improved hoist he had devised was used all over Tarentum. There were also lyres and flutes and tuning-rods, and a noble Apollo playing the kithara in a long straight robe.

Having asked how I was, he questioned me closely about affairs in Syracuse. Dionysios, he said, had often made war in southern Italy, but through Dion's good offices had never attacked Tarentum; what kind of man was his son? I told him all I had seen myself; then repeated, as near as I could remember after all this, what Dion had said to me, and why he wanted Plato there.

At the end he said, 'You have caught the very tone and pitch of Dion's voice. You must have heard him with great attention.'

'I did, sir. But also I am an actor; one falls into it without thinking.'

'Indeed?' he said, looking at me with curiosity. 'Your ear must be very true.' He picked up his lyre, and struck some notes for me to sound; but soon said I looked tired and should be in bed. 'Rest,' he said, 'and fear nothing. I will give you a letter for Plato, recommending you as a man who has my confidence. I daresay, too, he will remember you himself. He seldom forgets a face.'

'And you'll ask him,' I said, 'to go to Sicily?' He smiled. I expect I sounded, as Homer says, like a child who drags at her mother's skirt and whines to be carried.

'Indeed I shall. You have been Dion's living letter; paper and ink could not have pleaded with such power. No doubt you and he have been linked in your former lives, in love, or kinship; or he gave you true teaching, or your life, or some great benefit for which your soul is still grateful. These ties can be many times renewed, in many births. You are both souls, no doubt, in the series of Apollo. Eat well of pure food; hear the proper music to wake and sleep; take your physic; pray to Apollo and Asklepios. The future is only with the god. Rest in his hand.'

All this I did. My strength increased, and in the mirror I saw my face less gaunt. I had dreaded the voyage home, but now was content to let what would be, be. Archytas, who was weather-wise from much observing the heavens, kept me back from the first ship I would have taken; when I sailed, the passage was as good as summer.

Whereas the first part of the voyage had nearly killed me, the second did me no good. None the less, when I got to Athens, having been kept up half the night with my friends calling to learn what had become of me, I could not face the long walk to the Academy, but hired a riding-ass.

Plato's private rooms looked out upon scythed grass and rose-trees. An old decent slave-woman opened; I did not trouble her with my name, but said I came from Archytas. She came back and led me in.

The study was light and sparely furnished, with few but perfect ornaments. 'Like Dion's' I thought, then saw it must be the other way about. In the window was a great table full of a scholar's litter: cubes, cylinders and spheres; a model of the planets' courses; music-rolls; books; compasses; and a writing-board with a scroll taped out across it, before which Plato sat, copying in ink from a wax tablet.

As the slave left, he got up, and gazing at my face with his deep overhung eyes, said slowly, 'You are the actor, the tragedian of Delphi. Nikeratos. It was you whom Dion meant.' These last words puzzled me. 'You look ill,' he said. 'Be seated.' I told him my business, and what had delayed me in it, and gave him Archytas' letter. He took it in his hands, seemed about to open it, then called the old housekeeper instead and told her to make me a posset to warm me, since the wind was cold. Still he did not break the seal, but asked me about the shipwreck, and my health. Then, like a man making up his mind to something, he excused himself, and read.

When he had done, he said, 'Archytas tells me here that Dion saw you in Syracuse, and told you the substance of his letter. Now all is clear to me. I have heard from him since, you understand; a formal letter, supporting an invitation from his kinsman Dionysios. The postscript said, "I recommend to you Nikeratos, who as you may know is back in Athens. He has done good work here." I had seen no one of the name, and could not tell what he meant.'

Nowadays, when well-known artists are sent openly upon state embassies, this would seem slow in a man of Plato's position. But at that time, that practice was just starting; coming about almost by chance, since actors must travel, and meet all classes, and no one thinks anything of it. It was all undercover business at first, like this of mine. I had never supposed I would be Plato's notion of an envoy.

'Sir,' I said, 'I won't trouble you with Dion's words; you know him and how he speaks. This was the substance. In the letter I carried, as in the formal one, he urged you to come to Syracuse. But he added that it should be soon, while young Dionysios' mind is still pliable. As Dion told me, his private message was his estimate of this young man. And he wanted me to tell you I had audience twice at Ortygia, if you would like to hear about it. He seemed to think it would confirm what he had written.'

Just then the housekeeper scratched on the door, bringing my posset. He assured me it would do me good; he had had the recipe from a priest in Egypt, who had nursed him through a fever there. It tasted odd, and rather nasty; but it was warming and I sipped it up. While I had it, he went back to the letter. Once, while I was looking out of the window as I drank and thinking my own thoughts, I felt him looking at me, and turned. I had been prepared, I suppose, because it was important business, to find him making sure of me, weighing me up. But he was thinking; thinking through me, you might say. He looked away, from courtesy; but for a moment I had felt him, as it seemed, going right through to whatever appeared to him the causes of my being, as if I were a cube or a star. Not for my sake, but for something beyond. He was suffering, and perplexed in mind, and had to break the surface somewhere. I happened to be there, opposite. All that I knew in an instant; it is only finding words that's slow. I finished my drink, and thanked him.

Suddenly he smiled; the same smile, I daresay, which had conquered Axiothea. 'Well,' he said, 'I can interpret Dion's postscript now: "Trust Nikeratos, as I do." Tell me then, about your meeting with him, how he was looking, and all he said. We shall agree, I think, in giving him precedence over Dionysios.'

Once or twice he interrupted me, to ask if Dion seemed in good health, and what his house was like. Of course he had never been back to Sicily in all these years, but it seemed odd to be telling him. In due course I came to Dionysios, the Eulogy and the toy chariots. He questioned me closely, and often beyond what I knew: what had Dionysios read, did he study geometry or music? I said I did not know, but Dion considered he had had no education. It had seemed to me that he longed to be valued, but was not much concerned whether it was fairly earned or not.

I looked at his face; and this time it held no enigma, I found in it something I could understand myself. It was just the face of a good professional, measuring a piece of work and feeling the call of the god.

I went on talking; ad-libbing, really, till he felt ready to speak. While I talked of Dion, and his feelings were engaged, his face had been a courteous mask; now, as I have said, it was open to a man like me. He was tempted, it was a great role, worth taking; but he was an old hand who had played, so to speak, Sophokles in Boeotia, and been hit with half an onion. He could remember the Athens the old men talk of: war, defeat, despair; tyranny, rebellion; revenge, injustice, hope gone sick. As I spoke and he sank into himself. I could see the weights going into the balance, this side and that.

He looked at the table, with its tablets and open scroll, just as I have seen a man look at a favourite dog he had to leave behind. Then he said, trying to throw it away, 'Well, Nikeratos, you have endured a good deal, but not for nothing. I daresay I shall go to Sicily.'

It was plain he wanted no speeches, so I just said it would be happy news for Dion, who had set great hopes on it.

He said rather drily, 'Too many are doing that. My art, unlike yours, does better without spectators.' He paused and added, 'But one does not want to end by finding one has been only a thing of words.'

As it happened, I was not long ignorant of his meaning. I had scarcely left his garden-close after taking leave of him, when Axiothea and two young men ran out from the olive-trees where they had clearly been waiting. After the briefest greeting she said, 'You have seen him? Did he say anything? Will he go?'

My surprise at their knowing seemed to amaze them. Nothing else, they said, was talked of here. Didn't I know the invitation had been public? In short, Dionysios had not just sent letters by an envoy, but – as I suppose I might have expected – a kind of embassy to the Academy. All was now clear: Plato's calm, his lack of eagerness for Archytas' letter. I had supposed I brought him news. All this time, he had had a crowd of philosophers, students of law and civics, sophists and geometers and historians, his young men and no doubt many of their fathers, all breathing down his neck, to learn if he would go and prove his theories by demonstration. I suppose most of what I had told him of Dionysios, too, he had picked up already here and there. I admired his courtesy. Maybe I had shed some new glimmer of light upon the work ahead; but mostly I had just loaded on him the Tarentine philosophers, pushing like all the rest.

Certainly, I thought, Dion means to have his way. But I suppose that's what makes a king.

9

After this, I was busy for some time with my own affairs. When the choregoi drew for protagonists at the Dionysia, I was picked quite early, and cast as Orpheus in a play of that name by Eucharmos. It was a good acting role, very pathetic; my music was done off-stage by a concert kitharist, but I sang myself. The play was well received; I was told later, on good authority, that I was in the running for the crown and did not lose by many votes. It went to Aristodemos, who had done a big bravura part as Ajax; perhaps a little florid, but, I don't deny, sound on the whole.

If I do not dwell on this time, it's not from pique that I missed the crown; I was lucky to get so near it. But I started a little love affair, of the sort that is well enough if you don't let it take hold. If he had been anyone else's choice, I should have known just what to advise. But getting deep in, I started to deceive myself, finding all that I wished to see, and calling the rest youthful heedlessness. So, when my Alkibiades of the Agora left me for a well-off fool with a racehorse and a house in the Kerameikos, I could not sweeten it with the thought that I had lost my peace for something worth my pains. I had known well enough, but would not know, for the sake of his laughing eyebrows and golden bloom.

Even so, once I could have taken it lightly. I could not now. I was at war with myself. All the while, when I was wasting hours in guessing where he was; planning the next supper, which had always some bitterness in the cup; brooding on a word or look – in a word, fishing for moonshine – the mask of Apollo looked at me with empty eyes. Once he gives you knowledge, you can't unknow it; if you try he makes you suffer. I was haunted by those scornful eyeholes, and by a youth whom only my mind's eye had seen, climbing the slopes of Etna with the snow-light on his upturned face. He had stolen my joy in my old contentments, by showing me what men can be.

With such thoughts, I took a walk one day to the Academy in the warm green of spring. I did not seek Axiothea; she might have heard things, and would not understand. But I happened to notice in the garden the dour-faced Xenokrates who I knew would neither question nor detain me; so I asked when Plato intended going to Syracuse. He raised his brows. Plato had been gone, he said, above a month.

Had all that time slipped by? Since the Dionysia, I thought, every day wasted. Suddenly I felt the need to shake it all off, as a wet dog shakes off water. Here in Athens, I would be meeting at every turn the youth, or his new lover, or friends who had seen my folly. The very air felt stale.

Next day, therefore, I did a round of the foreign consulates, to learn what cities were planning plays. It was not an Isthmian or Pythian year, and too early for Olympia. I hoped I had finished with small-town theatres, and was therefore passing by the Megarian proxenos' office, when I met Eupolis, coming out. I greeted him and said I was thinking of a tour. But he was already not the man he had been before he lost his teeth and spoiled his voice. He had been drinking though it was not mid-morning; and, without taking the trouble to wrap it in civility, said he wondered I did not try Sicily again, if I had had such a success there as I claimed.

'As for that,' I said, 'I don't claim even to have trodden a stage in Sicily. All I did was speak Dionysios' epitaph. But since you ask, it's true I've been thinking of going back there. I daresay that's what I shall do.'

I walked on, amazed at myself, thinking, 'Now I shall have to go, or he'll put it all over Athens. I, who swore never to set foot in a ship again. What fate made him cross my path? And why did I speak to him? He would have passed me by.' Then I went home, to think. The mask hung on the wall, straight-faced in the bright light of noon. But when I turned my back, I felt it smiling.

At least, by now, it was sailing weather. The Sicilian consul greeted me warmly, offered me wine, and said he had been expecting my enquiry. 'Not,' he said, 'that I have any special commission. But with youth at the helm, as the saying is, the crew will all be singing. Syracuse today is a gay city, very gay. I don't think it would be possible for an artist like yourself to lose by going just now. I shall announce you by letter, mentioning your success as Orpheus. Such poetry, such pathos; we were all in tears.' I thanked him, but could have done without it; I knew I had overworked the pathos, feeling sorry for myself just then. At all events, I left committed; he was writing by a ship which left that day. It had all been as if a hand in my back were shoving me.

All the same, remembering young Dionysios' fitfulness, I did not mean to put all my eggs under one hen, but called on the consuls of Leontini, Akragas, Gela and Tauromenion, telling them of my visit, and anything else it would do me good for them to know.

The question was whether to try and form a company. But Anaxis had joined a tour going to Ionia; Hermippos was back in comedy; and I was short of capital, having spent too many of those beautiful gold staters they mint in Syracuse, on human gold as lovely and as quick to slip away. I thought I would chance Menekrates' being free, and willing. Though I had never seen his work, he had seemed well thought of; and one can learn much from an artist's way of talking.

Some nights later, when all was done but my goodbyes, at the time of lamplighting came a knock upon my door. There he stood, sure of his welcome, in all the insolence of his beauty and my past surrenders, waiting to see me reel with joy. He had quarrelled, he said, with the new friend; after all there was no one like me. I suppose he had asked too much; rich men get the measure of that sooner than poor ones. For a moment Eupolis, the consuls, the westbound passage, seemed never to have been. It would do next year. Then, when I thought I had eyes only for him, I felt other eyes upon me. In the lamplight, which flickered in the draught from the open door, the mask was watching.

Beside those eyes of shadow, the blue ones looked shallow as glass. I found my voice. He should have told me, I said, that he was coming; I had promised to dine out with friends. He stayed awhile, not believing that I meant it; then made to go, certain I would call him back. In the street outside I heard his feet pause, and go away.

I had a perfect passage to Syracuse. Halcyons could have nested on the sea. At Tarentum I called on my kind hosts with some gifts to show my gratitude; then on Archytas, in case he wanted any letters taken to Plato. When I went in he did not know me, properly dressed and with something on my bones under the skin. I had put on my soberest robe; but an actor going to Sicily is bound to look frivolous in the study of a Pythagorean, and he gazed doubtfully at first. Presently, finding me the same man still, he talked more freely. He would be glad, he said, to write to Plato, from whom they had heard quite lately. The letter had been brought by a court courier, to whom he could have entrusted nothing private; but he had seemed cheerful and hopeful. He had asked for some of Pythagoras' treatises on geometry, and Archytas' own works; for plane and solid figures, and instruments. All these had been already sent. He spoke too of Dionysios' eagerness to improve his mind, which he had infected his whole court with; this was why Plato's own equipment was not enough to go round. 'If the gods please,' he had ended, 'this is the beginning of new things for Syracuse.'

'Plato knows how to be discreet,' Archytas said, 'but is incapable of falsehood. You can picture, therefore, our rejoicing. One must be happy to see Zeus' work done anywhere on earth. But our city lives in the shadow of Ortygia's sails; the health of Syracuse is ours.'

He added that this good news had followed hard on bad; for not long before, rumours had been pouring across the straits about young Dionysios' dissipations and debaucheries. Archytas, a veteran of many wars and not one to call three cups of wine an orgy, sounded quite impressed.

The young man had sobered up, however, in time to give Plato a state welcome. A gilded chariot had been sent down to the harbour for him. But this had been as nothing, it was said, to the effect of Plato's presence. Archytas added that if on my way home I would report to him how matters stood, I could expect his gratitude; and, as he hinted civilly, some solid token of it.

When I asked if he had any word for Dion, he said at once that he was anxious to get a letter to him by someone of discretion. This was state business, a serious matter, and I showed him I understood it. Now I was sure of seeing Dion, I would have put to sea in another Tarentine gale, if nothing else would get me there.

In fact, however, we had a good passage and sailed straight into harbour. As I made for Menekrates' lodging, I saw Syracuse was itself again. The streets were loud and jostling; the shops had everything a ship can bring from the shores of Ocean; in the gutters bony children scuffled like rats for bits of garbage, while the painted mule-carriages threw dust on them, and the carriage folk held flowers to their noses against the smell. When a Gaulish or Iberian or Nubian mercenary came in sight, the stall-holders would hide their choicest things before he passed.

The sun was just declining. Menekrates, still drowsy from his siesta, was shaving when I arrived. He jumped and cut himself; we had to clamber about finding cobweb to stop the blood. I felt I had never been away.

It was a thousand pities, he said, that I had missed these last few months, especially to get shipwrecked instead. I told him that at Tarentum I had heard wild stories; but no doubt they had gained in the passing-on.

'Not possible,' he said. 'Lost, more likely. Well, at least there was work for artists.'

'I never thought young Dionysios had it in him.'

'My dear Niko, even he would hardly ask flute-girls and rope-dancers to his father's funeral. He did observe the month of mourning decently. I daresay it took him as long as that to believe the old man was really dead. Even then, it looked for a while as if Dion would step smoothly in and become another father.' Then he seemed to catch himself up, and changed the subject. When, however, I asked him for news of Dion, he answered that he was well, and, lest the Carthaginians should grow too bold with the news of old Dionysios' death, he had made the city a gift of thirty triremes.

'*Thirty!*' I exclaimed. 'The richest man in Athens would cry murder if he were tax-assessed at more than one.'

'Well, he gave thirty. Our rich men are very rich, believe me.

Didn't you sail past the patrol?' He pushed it off too briskly; again I felt words unsaid.

'What is it?' I asked. 'You have heard something. I wish you would tell me, and not beat about.'

'Didn't you stop at the barber's tavern on your way?'

'No; it was calm enough to shave on board. What news would I have heard there?'

'Why,' he answered, making a business of giving me a drink, sweetmeats, and so on, 'the story of young Dionysios. To put first things first, it began when Philistos was recalled.' This name meant nothing to me. He said, 'He's still a great name here, though I was a lad when he was banished; Captain of Ortygia, he was before; as rich as King Midas; gave parties that made history. So did his love affairs. Old Dionysios' mother was one of his mistresses, but the Archon was only just in power, and turned a blind eye because he was too big to quarrel with. Later on, though, he married into Dionysios' family without his leave, and that was another story. That looked ambitious. He was whisked straight off into a trireme bound for Italy, to honeymoon in exile. There he stayed till this year, when we had the amnesty.'

'So,' I said, 'there have been reforms, then?'

'Oh, yes. As I was saying, Dion did wonders in the first couple of months, getting people out of the Quarries who had been in for years, or recalling exiles. When Philistos applied, I suppose he advised consent as a matter of principle. It can hardly have been Dionysios' doing; he was too young to have known the man. At all events, he came. They say he's spent his leisure writing history, as all these broke generals do, so no doubt he's kept himself informed. He's still very game for his age; he'd hardly set his house in order before he gave a party, quite up to the former ones, so people say who remember. Dion left early. But young Dionysios stayed. The party broke up two mornings later.'

'And that was the beginning?'

'Well, he always stole a little entertainment behind his father's back. No, I think it first came home to him, then, that he was the Archon and could do just what he liked.'

My mind returned to my second audience at Ortygia, and his face when he spoke of the pleasures of Syracuse. As Menekrates said, it was the mourning that had kept me from taking notice.

'It might have been worse,' he went on. 'It might have been blood he had a taste for. But while living like a mouse in his father's wainscot, he hadn't much chance of making enemies. He called for no heads but maidenheads. All he fancied was a party that would last for ever, without his father roaring in to demand quiet for his writing, and pack everyone home. So the next banquet was at the Palace. I heard a good deal about it from a girl I know who dances with a snake. Remarkable what she has taught it; you must see her act. But she left on the third day of the party; by then they were looking for something fresh. When the host wants novelty, and can pay, with the place so full too of hetairas and acrobats and so on, one thing leads to another. After a week or so, there was no tale coming out of Ortygia so far-fetched that someone couldn't cap it. There has always been a backdoor traffic between the Citadel and Carthage; the old man used it when he chose; Philistos knew of it. Now, instead of secret treaties, the exchange or death of hostages, and so on, it came in useful for summoning jugglers, fire-swallowers, knife-dancers, or experts in never mind what.

'From time to time the party would come out for fresh air; first into the streets of Ortygia, later, sometimes, through all the gates into the town. Pretty soon when the torches were seen weaving along, wives and sons and daughters were bundled behind locked doors; the revellers seemed to think they conferred a favour on anyone they ravished; no one was expected to pull a long face and spoil the fun. Anyone on business was shown the door at once. Soldiers and ephors ran the city; the bribery rate doubled overnight, when they knew no one was watching them.'

I asked, 'What did Dion do?'

'Looked in at the party, so my friend told me, to try and get sense out of someone. Of course Dionysios refused to delegate, and only tried to make him drink. That was while she was there; next time he came, I expect everyone was deadout on the floor, or busy on the couches. So he bided his time, and waited for his philosopher friend from Athens; and not in vain ... Well, at least no artist starved. Between parties, a play nearly every week; we don't keep them for the high feasts as you do in Athens. I can live half a year on what I've made. A good thing, for the grasshoppers' summer is over.' He gave me a glance under his brows, as if in hope he had said enough.

'All summers end,' I answered. 'I'd not heard of this when I set out; I was only hoping for something at the festivals.'

He stood silent, biting his lips, his dark brows pulled together. There was now no mistaking it; he looked bitter. I was getting on edge, and told him sharply to come out with it, whatever it was.

'I wish,' he said, 'you'd stopped at the tavern and heard it there.' He walked past me into the high-walled courtyard. It was green now with vine-shade, and the gourd dangled great yellow flowers. It gave his face the tint of bronze that has lain under the sea. He came back in again and I thought, 'Now it is coming.'

'Who wants to bring a friend bad news? The truth is, Niko, your Dion and his sophist want to make an end of the theatre. Finish it, root it up. That's all.'

I said, 'What? Impossible,' while feeling the shock that only truth can give. 'But the festivals are sacred.'

'So sacred that the theatre is unworthy of them. Or so the word goes round.' The hot dark anger of Sicily set his face in a frowning mask; then he overcame it, and put his hand on my shoulder. 'I'm sorry, Niko. One would think I was blaming you for it. Maybe one shouldn't believe all one hears. This I do know, though. Artists were everywhere in Ortygia, giving recitals, asked to supper, paid in gold. Now, overnight as it were, since this Plato came, nobody, no matter how distinguished. And what's more, for thirty years at least, there's been a play on the Archon's nameday. One of his own, if he had one ready, but always something. This month, the new Ruler's day came round. Nothing, not even a party. Just sacrifices and hymns.'

The shadows had lengthened in the courtyard. Its green light had got cold-looking, like light before rain. I thought of Delphi, of the painted wine-cup with Eros in it, the talk by lamplight. I could remember thinking what a high-class supper I had been asked to, all conversation instead of jugglers and flute-girls, a real gentlemen's symposium. I had no more expected this to come of it, than at a fencing-class one expects to be run through.

'Don't you think,' I said, 'that Dionysios is just lying up with a crapula? Has your cousin Theoros heard anything? After a debauch like that, there must be some palace stomachs needing physic.'

'I saw him yesterday in the street. He waited, so I walked away. If Theoros wants to give me news, I can guess what kind it will be. No, Niko, no crapula lasts so long. It's this philosophy. Everyone says so.'

We were looking at each other with faces of disaster, when I remembered what this meant. Dion had won the victory he, and the Academy, had been praying for. I ought to have been rejoicing.

Trying to bring all this to terms, I said, 'But surely, then, he must have given the city proper laws, and called a free Assembly?

Even if the theatre stops for a time, and artists have to tour, you are citizens too, so wouldn't the good outweigh the bad?'

'If that happened, it might. There were rumours at first, when we had the amnesty. But nothing came of them. I tell you, Niko, I don't mean to sit here eating up my savings. I must get upon the road, as soon as I find a man to tour with. I could make up a company of nobodies tomorrow and play lead, but I'd far rather do second to a good protagonist. More credit, more pleasure, and the money about the same.'

'I'm ashamed to ask,' I said, 'whether I would be good enough.'

He flashed his white teeth and grasped my hand, saying, 'I hadn't the face to ask outright.' I told him I had come here in the hope of it; we laughed, and at once found all our prospects looking brighter.

'I tell you what,' I said. 'Tomorrow I'll present myself to Dionysios. He told me to, next time I came, so I'll take him at his word. I'll learn what I can, and while I'm there I'll try to see Dion too. If I do, I'll ask him straight out about the theatre, then at least we'll know where we stand.' In spite of everything, I was wondering whether he might have some business for me.

We then turned to planning out our tour, on the usual terms; I would put up two-thirds of the expenses, including the hire of the third actor and extra (which I could afford, now I had not their fares to pay from Athens) and split the profits the same way. Then we went to drink to it at the barber's tavern. It was half-empty; the few men there were drinking almost in silence, or getting quarrelsome. We walked home still pretty well sober. He was in better spirits than I; the tour was fixed up, and he was a man for living from day to day. It was I who lay awake. I felt both my heart and mind being torn in two.

Next day I set out early, knowing how long it took to get through all the gates. This time I had no pass; besides, I might find the guards all drunk or dicing. But discipline seemed still fairly good. The assets of a mercenary captain, and his future, are in his men, and he will do his best not to let them spoil.

The guards had been changed at the causeway gatehouse. Instead of the Gauls there were some Italians, who spoke a dialect strange to me: dark, curly-haired men in polished armour, with straight-sided shields and heavy six-foot throwing spears. Their drill was much smarter than the Gauls' and their Greek less barbarous. They looked as proud as the Spartans but more at home; Spartans hate crossing water. These troops seemed as tough, and more professional. They asked my business (I had hoped for someone who knew my face) and then for tokens of my errand. Since Archytas' letter to Dion was confidential, I showed the one to Plato, which I thought should serve my turn, seeing he was the Ruler's guest.

The Captain read the name; at once his black brows knitted above his haughty nose, and his nostrils curled as if the paper stank. 'Plato!' he said for his men to hear. There was a general growl, and a clank as they shook their iron-shod javelins. The Captain handed the letter back as a housewife picks up a dead rat. 'Well, Greekling, if you get a quiet word with Plato, just tell him this from the Roman cohort.' He drew the edge of his hand across his throat. His men supplied the sound.

They let me through. But the news was passed on along with me, that I was going to Plato; and from each lot of guards I got, allowing for race and custom, much the same message. Even a Greek, who conducted me through the royal gardens, said, 'If you've come from his precious school to fetch him home, you can drink your way through every guardhouse from here to the Euryalos. Only let me know.'

He was a big hairy Boeotian, but I felt more at home with him than with the foreigners; so I asked what Plato had been up to, to be so much hated. At home, I added, he had the name of a quiet man.

'Let him keep quiet at home, then, or someone will quieten him for good. He was brought here to corrupt the Archon and make him fit for nothing; and you can guess who hopes to gain from *that*. Disband the hired troops – oh, yes, that's Plato's counsel – and the city left as a gift for his friend Dion. I wish the old man were back. He'd have nailed his head and his four quarters to the gatehouses, long before this.'

I made no answer. The long night had brought no peace to the war within me. We were getting near the Palace. The Boeotian stopped, to have his say. 'Have you seen these Syracusans on Assembly Day? They've not shifted for themselves these forty years. How long do you see them keeping off the Carthaginians, without us trained men?' He spat into the grass, saying, 'Tell Plato that from me.'

We went through the outer court, and a columned porch, to a court within. 'Wait here,' he said.

I waited just inside the porch, and looked about. It was a green shady place, with flowering creepers trained above, and a big square fountain-pool in the centre, maybe fifty feet wide. This had been drained, and the tiles scattered with clean sand. On the marble edge, a number of well-dressed men were sitting, and seemed, at first glance, to be fishing in the sand. Then I saw that the rods they held were really pointers; they were drawing geometric figures, with letters and numbers beside them. A slave was going about with a rake, to clean off finished work, and sand, to start again on.

When I had got over the oddness of this spectacle, I noticed something else; one side of the court was much busier than the other. I soon saw the cause. The fountain made a little island, a bronze palm-trunk twined with a snake upon a base of serpentine;

and on the slab sat Plato and Dionysios. It was the courtiers at my end, behind their backs, who were taking it easy. I saw two of them do a lewd drawing and quickly sweep it over.

Plato was turned a little my way. He was talking; sitting with his massive brow and heavy shoulders leaned rather forward, as if with their own weight; I remembered the pose. His hands were on his knees; sometimes he would lift one in a gesture so spare, but clear, that an actor could not have bettered it. Dionysios came further round, so that I partly saw his face. His lips were parted, and his countenance changed like a field of barley in a breeze, to show he was following every word.

My guard walked about looking for a chamberlain, passing on his way a couple of Gauls at the further door. The sight of them reminded me what a change this was. Nobody had searched me.

Dionysios beckoned my escort, who told his errand and presently came to fetch me. I scrambled across the balustrade, picked my way over the sand, side-stepped a diagram (Plato's I suppose) they had been discussing, and made my bow.

Dionysios had changed greatly. Of course last time he had been in mourning, unshaven and with cropped hair; but it was more than that. His skin looked clearer, he fidgeted less; he seemed better-favoured, like a plain girl pleased with her marriage. Plato was watching him; not as I had once seen him look at Dion, close and proud; still, there was a kind of affection in his face, like a mother's when her child is learning to walk.

'Well, Nikeratos,' Dionysios began, but then at once turned round. 'Here, Plato, is a man you know, though without, I daresay, knowing his face. This is Nikeratos, the tragedian of Athens, who was protagonist in my father's play.'

Plato greeted me with courtesy, but as a stranger. It did not offend me; I guessed the cause, and replied suitably. He complimented my performance, and congratulated me on my crown. He did, at least, seem to hear and see me; Dionysios, from first to last, talked through me at Plato, not slightingly, but as if nobody else were real to him.

'And what brings you to Syracuse?' he asked me.

Good, I thought; now we shall see. 'Just the business of my calling, sir. I have come to work.'

He looked pleased with this answer. 'Well, Nikeratos,' he said, going back to his opening line, 'so you have lately been in Athens at the Dionysia; and I suppose, after your success at the Lenaia, you were given a leading role?'

I told him yes; he enquired the name of the poet, the theme of the play, how it had been received; things that anyone might ask. But as he went on, I began to recognise that special tone I had observed at the Academy, when they played the game of questions, leading someone on till they scored a point. Being new and half-baked at it, he sounded rather silly. With the side of my eye I glanced at Plato. He was a man who would not have fidgeted if he had sat down on an anthill; but his patience was starting to show.

'So you enacted Orpheus. Did the play treat of his descent into the underworld to ransom his wife; or of his death at the hands of the maenads?'

'The second,' I said. 'Though he relates the first in a soliloquy.'

He brightened. I must have given him the right feed-line.

'Orpheus was the son of Apollo, as we are told. Is it possible that being god-begotten he should have failed to calm the maenads with his song, inspired as he was by the divinity?'

'I don't know,' I said. 'But some audiences don't want the best, and let you know it.'

'Tut,' he said, brushing this off. 'How will men think of the gods, if their sons are shown in error, or defeated?'

'Perhaps, sir, that they took after their mothers' side.'

Plato's eye flickered, like an old war-horse's when he hears the trumpet. But he kept quiet, and left it to the colt, who as I saw was looking put out. I should have held my tongue, as Anaxis would have told me.

'In any case,' he said, 'you imitated the passions of Orpheus in his desires and fears, hopes and despair; and the audience was pleased with you?'

'I think so. They gave the usual signs.'

'And I expect you are also skilled in imitating women, whether old and in sorrow, or young and in love?'

'Yes, I can do that.' I wondered how long he could keep this up, in any hope of making me look more foolish than himself. I recalled the quick smooth give-and-take at the Academy, and the humour, of the sort you get when people are really serious. So did Plato, I suppose.

'And you can imitate, too, brawling drunkards, scolding wives or thieving slaves?'

'A comedian would do it better.'

'Then you think such parts unworthy of you?'

'No; my skill is different.'

'You mean,' he said, his nose pointing like a game-dog's, 'that you find no kind of person too base to imitate?'

'That depends on how the author uses baseness.'

I could see I had cut his cue, whatever that should have been, and it had annoyed him. He came pretty close to asking me how I dared to argue, but then remembered the principles of debate. He peeped round at Plato, partly for approval, but partly in hope that the champion would ride into the battle, and spear me through.

Plato did not notice this appeal, and I saw why. A man was coming along the colonnade which ran round the empty pool. He seemed about Plato's age, and held himself like one who has been somebody all his life. His red weathered soldier's face was getting pouchy with good living, but his light blue eyes were still bright and hard; they had an air of having seen everything worth notice, and knowing what to think. He was well-dressed for Sicily, meaning very florid by our standards, but within the bounds of breeding there; covered with clasps of malachite and heavy gold, even to his sandals. He came along by the balustrade, limping a little, from a stiff joint or some old wound, eyeing each man and acknowledging greetings, sometimes warmly, sometimes not; one felt none of it was without meaning.

Plato had noticed him. Dionysios not yet. When he passed two men drawing in the sand, he said something, straight-faced, which made them grin, and followed it with a mock reproof. Plato, clearly, was meant to see. Then he swept along till he was level with Dionysios, to whom he bowed deeply.

The young man said, 'Good day, Philistos,' and their eyes met. Philistos paused a moment. His face was that of a man who sees his superior, a nice inexperienced boy, making a fool of himself, but blames rather the man who should know better, yet leads him on. The glance was eloquent of respect, discretion, and quiet irony; with a touch of patronage to make it sting.

Dionysios looked in two minds whether to call him over. He refrained, however. There was a moment when Philistos seemed to ask himself whether anything he could say would open his poor friend's eyes; then, as if deciding the time was not yet ripe, he gravely withdrew. He remained, though, at the far end of the court, watching the geometrists.

Dionysios looked after him, then back to me. He had been put off, and was now stuck. I would have given him his line, if I had only known what it was.

'But,' said Plato, 'we were talking, I think, about the nature of the actor's skill.'

He was not joining the debate, just making himself felt, like a protagonist who enters upstage and, though silent, at once commands the scene. That was his quality; it cut down Philistos at once to a rich old gentleman, rather overdressed and overfed, who is getting set in his ways and sniffs at everything beyond him. Dionysios revived. He was ready now to dash on and finish the scene.

'Well, Nikeratos, in spite of all your varied skills, I would rather hear from you always that dignity and seemliness with which you spoke the Eulogy. Shall I tell you why?' I saw Plato stir, but his pupil was off by now, showing his paces. 'All things here below are only imitations of the pure forms God knows; good if they approach the likeness, bad if they fail. So, when you enact men and their qualities, you are imitating an imitation, isn't that so?'

'So it would seem,' I said. I was anxious to keep him going, and get it over.

'Then, if you imitate the worse rather than the good in men, however well you do it, you are giving, really, the worst imitation, the least like the true model. Doesn't that follow?'

I had not met Axiothea and her friends for nothing; one must keep the rules. 'Yes,' I said. 'It would follow on the first.'

'But, Dionysios, are we not forgetting how recently Nikeratos joined us?' Plato's clear voice came in like a silver knife slicing an apple. 'You and I have come step by step to the concept of divine originals; but he in his courtesy conceded the premise without demonstration. There is a saying that one should not press a generous man too far. At present we may thank him for the pleasure his art has given us; later, when he has followed all the argument, we may win him to our conclusions.'

Dionysios looked clashed, as well he might. He took it, though, as pupil from master. The lord of the fleet of Syracuse, of the gates and the catapults and the quarried prison, sulked like a chidden boy. He shot me a look. I saw not the anger of a tyrant put down before a travelling actor, but just a pique, because Plato had not taken his side.

I was trying to think of some civility which would get me off, when at the end of the colonnade I saw Dion enter.

I can't tell you how I felt. It was wind against tide. There he stood, the same man as always, without a mean thought in his soul; a man who, if he had pledged protection to a suppliant, would have stood to it till death, though it were for a thrall on a peasant farm. Yet this same man wanted to take away, not just the bread out of my mouth, not just the reputation I had worked for all my life, but, as it seemed to me, the soul out of my body.

As he came on, he passed Philistos. I saw it was a greeting of open enemies. They measured one another, like men who do it daily as the fortunes of conflict shift. A child could have picked the better man. Philistos went out sneering; Dion did not look back. I saw a glow on him of victory and hope. He saluted Dionysios. But before that, his eyes had sought Plato's from far off, and the young man had not missed it.

When he noticed me, Dion did not show surprise. He must have known I was coming. His greeting was formal, but I knew he wanted to see me after. When, therefore, I was dismissed the presence, I made my way to his house. Waiting in the anteroom, I had a good while to think, but found no answer. It needs a sophist, I thought, for that.

At last he came. Keeping his distance before the servant, he went in, then sent for me; but, once we were alone, greeted me even more kindly than before. He shone with happiness. I had thought he would be ill at ease before me; but no. Among his great affairs, he had not even remembered.

I gave him his own letter, and the one for Plato. He put down my constraint, I think, to bad news I brought, for he read

Archytas' letter standing; then, reassured, offered me wine. The cup was Italian, the painting touched up with white, like his gift at Delphi. Memories crowded me: the crane, Meidias' death-cry, the battle of Phigaleia, my father as Cassandra, the great theatre at Syracuse where Aischylos put on *The Persians*, Menekrates saying, 'It's all one under the mask.' The cup shook in my hand. As one learns to do, I steadied it. He had been putting back the jug, and had noticed nothing.

Raising his cup, he said, 'To the fortunes of Syracuse. A glorious dawn, Zeus prosper it.'

I held myself in, and answered slowly, 'Shall we offer the prayer of Hippolytos, "Grant me to end life's race as I began"?'

'Choose,' he said smiling, 'some prayer of better omen, for, as I remember, that one the gods rejected.'

'I see you know your Euripides. Well then, a toast to purified Syracuse. Down with all riff-raff; hired troops, spies, gluttons and drunkards, whores, and artists.' I lifted the cup, and threw it down on the marble floor.

I had not known I would do this. The wine made a great red star, and spattered both our robes. A piece of the cup lay at my feet; a crowned goddess, in the Italian style.

He stood stock-still; amazed, then angry. Sicilians of his rank don't know such things can happen to them. Well, I thought, he is talking to an Athenian now, and must make the best of it.

'Nikeratos,' he said, 'I am sorry to see you so forget yourself.'

'Forget?' I answered. 'No, by Apollo, I have remembered what I am. I am a citizen of no rank; I don't understand philosophy; when you were studying, I was playing stand-ins and extras, picking up my trade which you want to take away. But whatever I am, or you choose to call me, one thing I know: I am a servant of the god, and though I honour you and love you, I will obey the god, rather than you.'

He had listened unmoving; but at these words he started, as if he knew them. I waited, but he did not speak.

'You have been godlike to me.' If I had let myself, I could have wept. 'But beside the god you are just a man. Farewell. I daresay we shan't meet again.' I paused at the door, but there was nothing to stay for, so I only said, 'I am sorry I broke the winecup.'

'Nikeratos. Come back ... I beg of you.' The words came out stiffly. His tongue was strange to them. It was that made me turn.

'Come, sit down,' he said. We sat by his desk. It was covered with letters and petitions such as are sent to men in power. There were sheets too of geometric figures and a diagram of the stars.

'My friend,' he said, 'Archytas tells me that you almost lost your life upon my business. I have grieved you, which I cannot help; but I did it thoughtlessly, and for that I ask your pardon.'

'If the thing is true,' I answered, 'does it matter how you say it? Is it true, or not?'

'This is hard,' he said, and leaned his brow on his open hand. 'Plato could say this better than I; but it rightly falls on me, the man whom you feel betrays you ... What did you mean, Nikeratos, when you said you served the god? Not just that you perform the sacrifices to Dionysos and Apollo, and respect their precinct; but something more?'

'Surely,' I said, 'you don't need yourself to be an artist, to understand me. It means not setting oneself above one's poet, nor being false to the truth one knows of men. When one can see that the audience wants the easy thing, or the thing just in fashion, and even the judges can't be trusted not to want it too, for whom does one stay honest? Only for the god.'

'You hear him speak, and obey him. But could you have heard so clearly, if you had not learned your art from boyhood?'

'No, I think not. Or not so soon.'

'Suppose you had been badly trained, and always heard bad work praised above good.'

'A great misfortune. But if an artist is anything, sooner or later he thinks for himself.'

'But others not? Bad teaching spoils them past remedy?'

'Yes, but they are men the theatre can do without.'

'You mean they can take up some other calling. So they can. But, Nikeratos, all men have to live, either well or badly, as they are taught. If enough are taught badly, the bad will get rid of the good. And you, whether you choose or not, are a teacher. Young boys, and simple men, don't go to the theatre to judge of verse; they go to see gods and kings and heroes, to enter the world you make, to steep their minds and souls in it. Can you deny this?'

'But,' I said, 'one plays for men of sense.'

'You keep faith with your art, Nikeratos. You will not offend the god with anything unworthy, even though men would reward you for it. But your power stops there. You cannot re-write your play, though the poet may be doing the very thing you would scorn to do.'

'That is his business. I am an actor.'

'But you both serve the god. Can his god say one thing, and yours another?'

'I am an actor. He and I must each judge for ourselves.'

'Truly? Yet you have to enter his mind. Have you never once felt you were entering a fake world, or an evil one?'

I could not lie to him, and replied, 'Yes, once or twice. Even with Euripides, in his *Orestes*. Orestes has been wronged, but nothing can excuse his wickedness. Yet one is supposed to play him for sympathy.'

'Did you do so?'

'I was third actor then. I should have to try, I suppose, if I were drawn for it.'

175

'Because that is the law of the theatre?'

'Yes.'

'But, my dear Nikeratos, that is why we want to change it.'

'I understood,' I said, 'that you wanted to destroy it.'

'No, not so.' He looked at me with kindness, as if I were a decent soldier he had beaten in war. 'Plato believes, as I do, that an artist such as you, who can portray nobility, has his place in the good city. In some such way as this: that the parts of base, or passionate, or unstable men should be related in narration, while only the good man, who is a fit example, or the gods speaking true doctrine, should be honoured by the actor's imitation. In such a way, nothing evil would strike deep into the hearers' minds.'

I gazed at him, solemn as an owl. If, having begun to laugh, I could not stop, which seemed likely, he would despise me for instability. I told myself this, to sober up. Not that I feared his displeasure now; as I had said, he was just a man. But the man was dear to me.

'You mean,' I said, 'that in the *Hippolytos*, for instance, where Phaedra reveals her guilty love, and where Theseus curses his son in ignorance, all that would be narrated? Only Hippolytos would speak?'

'Yes, just so. And we could not admit of evil being caused by Aphrodite, who is a god, to a just man.'

'No, I suppose not. And Achilles must not weep for Patroklos nor tear his clothes because that is a failure in self-command?'

'No, indeed.'

'But do you think,' I asked at length, 'that *any* of it would strike deep into the hearers' minds? You don't think it might be dull?'

He looked at me, patient, not angry. 'As wholesome food is, after those Sicilian banquets that have made us the scorn of Hellas. Believe me, our Syracusan cooks are artists too, in their way. Yet you would not lose your figure, health and looks to please

176

one of them, would you, even if he were a friend? And is not the soul worth more?'

'Of course it is. But ... ' It was no use, I thought, against a trained wrestler of the Academy. I had learned my art by asking how, rather than why.

'Only look, Nikeratos,' he said, his fine face lit with eagerness, 'at the world around us. Look what men as they are have brought it to. War, tyranny, revenge, anarchy, injustice everywhere. Somewhere, somewhere one must begin.'

At these words, my feet seemed to feel firm ground. I said, 'That is true. Then why, seeing Dionysios is eating out of Plato's hand, doesn't he seize his chance, and get the Syracusans a proper constitution? Soon it will be too late; even I can see that. Why is the city as full of mercenaries as ever? The tyranny goes on, while you all scratch circles in the sand—' His face reminded me, if my own sense had not, that I was speaking to the First Minister. I said, 'I go too far. But we were talking about justice.'

'We were,' he said after a pause, 'so I will tell you why. You have been very sick this year. When the fever had left you, could you get up at once, and go about your business? Or did you need an arm to lean on? Well, Syracuse has been sick for almost forty years. A whole generation, reared in sickness ... even to the highest.'

'And so,' I said, 'you must begin with the child at nurse, with the schoolboy at the theatre. And Dionysios; he must begin with mathematics.'

He clenched his hand on the desk, as if begging the gods for patience. 'Nikeratos, don't make me angry. Don't treat me like a child, and Plato like a fool. He was learning politics at first hand before I was born; and so was I, before you were. If you think you know your own business best, give us some credit for knowing ours.'

177

I was ashamed, and begged his pardon. He only put up with me out of gratitude, and because I had shown him my heart.

'Try to see you are not in Athens now. This is Sicily. Beyond the River Halys are the lands of Carthage. The enemy stands with his foot in the door, pushing as soon as our shoulder slackens. What use is it to pay off the mercenaries, and pull down the walls of Ortygia, and set the people by the ears with a new regime, before we have made a man to lead them? They are better off as they are than as slaves in Africa, or nailed on crosses, or spitted over fires, and they have always known it. Dionysios has no root of greatness' (he had forgotten in his deep earnestness even to drop his voice); 'he cannot lead men nor make them love him. But he can still save Syracuse, if he can only be taught to think.'

'Yes,' I said. 'All this is true, if you had time. How long do you think you have?'

He began to answer, then asked sharply what I meant.

'Only what you have surely seen yourself; that Dionysios is working at his geometry not because he likes it, but because he is in love.'

'In love?' He frowned to himself, looking for a joke. Like many good men, he had not much sense of humour. Plato had far more.

'You are not serious,' he said. 'Plato could be his father.'

'True indeed. He should know himself better. He is in love all the same. Youth worships the mask of love; that is his Eros, a powerful god. Didn't you once know him?'

'No. Our play was real.'

'How the gods loved you. Do you think all men have such fortune? That poor little man in the palace has had to be his own poet. His father wrote plays, he lives them. He has got right into his part, too; don't you see what it is? A young aristocrat, brilliant, dissolute, charming, reckless, called to the good life by a philosophic lover?'

178

For once he laughed aloud. 'Alkibiades! Come, this is a serious matter.'

'It is to him. He is rather short of beauty and charm, but, as he sees it, he can still improve upon his model, that bright falling star. He will be true to Sokrates' teaching, and deserve his love.'

'You cannot mean this. Plato's conduct has been in every way correct.'

'How not? Yet the young man's devotion touches him, and he is kind. After all, Sokrates mastered his desires; do you think Dionysios wants to know the difference? All he wants is to be the beloved disciple, to know that he comes first. If something seems to stand in his way, will he prefer to blame Plato's coldness, or an old rival who won't stand out of the light?'

'My dear Nikeratos! This is not one of your tragedies.' He was brisk, yet not quite at ease.

'Maybe not,' I said, 'but it's theatre all the same. I don't know much of politics, as people are always telling me; but at least an actor knows jealousy when he sees it. You should watch his eyes.'

He paused, biting his lip. 'That is nothing new. I was proving myself among men, fighting battles, leading embassies, while his father kept him shut up like a woman.' He did not add, though he must have known it, that it was he who had Alkibiades' lifelong beauty. 'Envy is natural.'

'Well, this is one thing more. You can load so much on a donkey, then he won't go. How long do you count on? A generation? From what I saw today, I'd not lay two obols on it to last a year.'

He gazed at me, only half his mind on the matter. He was wondering, as I could tell, how it had come to pass that I could take such liberties. A just man, he blamed himself and would not punish me. Maybe he still liked me a little; it was time to go, while this held good. But there was something I had forgotten to mention.

'I think,' I said, 'that it would be as well if Plato's friends warned him not to walk alone about Ortygia. The soldiers want to cut his throat.'

'What? Who told you this?'

'They did. I heard it at every gatehouse. They all say he's working to get them turned off.'

Aroused at last, he struck the desk with his hand and cursed as if he were in the field. 'The young fool! He will talk – like a barber, a bawd, a midwife. He leaks like a cracked water-jar.'

No need to ask whom he meant. 'Then Plato didn't advise it?'

'Plato has fought in war! Of course he counsels it, but as the goal, not the means. When the new laws are established; when the citizens are trained in public business, content, and loyal; when the ruined cities, which the Carthaginians wasted, are re-settled and could fight beside us. Who but a madman would strip the city now?'

'Now I understand. Dionysios proclaimed his good intentions? He's always wanting to be crowned before the race.'

'You may as well know, Nikeratos, what it seems has got known all over Ortygia. Not long ago was his name-day, and the usual sacrifices were offered. The priest made the accustomed prayer, composed in his father's lifetime, to the appropriate gods that they might preserve the Archon in his power. In the middle of the prayer, he flung up his hand and cried, "No! Don't invoke a curse on us!" Then he looked at Plato, expecting praise.'

I forget what I said. Anything would do, except what I was thinking: 'Why, in the name of every god, do you keep this mountebank playing lead, instead of taking the role yourself?'

I might not, as he had told me, know much about affairs. But I was not such a fool as to suppose that if I said this aloud, I could enter his door again. If I could think of it, so could he; there must have been times when he could think of nothing else but that, and his honour; and as fiercely as he had thrust aside temptation, so he would thrust me. So I covered my thought; but it burned within like a banked-down fire. From these unspoken words till I took my leave, there is no more of our talk that I remember.

10

I enjoyed my tour with Menekrates. We worked well together, though I had been warned of him, behind his back, as a man who would not give. Theatre in Syracuse is full of malice. Maybe he did not like being put upon, having had plenty of that at home, but as I never tried it I cannot say. After running through a few scenes with him I knew that he was sound, so chose plays with strong second roles, and never had to regret it.

It was at his suggestion that we put into our repertoire a modern comedy by Alexis. He is such an innovator, tragedians might as well play him as old-style comedians. Not only has he got away from all the topical satire and scolding which stale as quickly as cheap wine; he has even dared to put away that poor old prop the phallos, too tired these many years to pleasure the goddess Thalia much. Alexis has real men and women in real scrapes; natural masks for the juveniles and the sympathetic characters, and, between the jokes, much kindness of mankind. Menekrates said he liked to think, when he took off his mask, that maybe someone in front had gone home less ready to beat his children. This was about as near as he got to talking about his boyhood. It was a pity, I thought, that he and Dion would never understand each other.

We had both started young and poor and slept hungry in old straw; we laughed over it together, sharing our pleasure in good food at clean inns. Often we improved even on this; for Sicilians are theatre-mad, and lords with land to the horizon would not only ask us to supper, but put us up. The back-stage gossip of Athens or Corinth was all they asked; if one felt like giving an excerpt from some success not yet on tour, then nothing was too good for one. As for the peasants, they would walk all night to see a play, when the grind of their lives would let them. At Leontini, Tauromenion, Akragas and Gela, even in the little towns, the audiences were splendid and took all the finer points. The skies were blue, the fruit-trees blossomed, thyme and sage scented the hills; and we had, as Menekrates had foretold, no competition. The leading men of Syracuse feared to lose status by doing local tours, and were holding out in the city for better times; then, when they did not come, going off to Italy. Our own third actor and extra were much better men than we should have got when things were easy. We made good money, and lingered in the pleasant places.

No one we met believed for a moment that theatre could stop in Syracuse. People laughed or shrugged, saying young Dionysios had run through a dozen crackpot whims already; we should get back to find him learning the kithara. Hadn't we seen for ourselves that all Sicilians had theatre in their blood? At this the company would all cheer up, and I myself along with them; then I would think of Dion, trying to shift from its foundations a forty-year load of tyranny, and would be at odds with myself, not knowing what to feel.

We were playing Heloros, which is about twenty miles south of Syracuse, when we heard of bandits in the hills. By now we were carrying a good deal of silver, from smaller towns which could not give us bankers' letters. I showed the company the accounts; it was agreed I should go over to the city and get the surplus takings safely banked.

I did this business without trouble, and went to look about me. The theatre tavern I avoided; by now it would be a desert of old men and embittered failures; so I chose a wine-shop where the gentlemen resorted, which had a cool shady courtyard with a vine. I had hardly sat down and given my order, when a voice cried, 'Niko! What are you doing here?' It was Speusippos, Plato's nephew.

He came over to my table; as usual well-dressed and barbered; yet I thought at once that he was not as young as I had supposed, the wrong side of thirty. Lines showed in his face, and his mouth looked drawn.

I offered him a drink – which he refused, saying he had just been drinking with some Syracusans – and asked how long he had been in Syracuse. He said he had come out shortly after Plato, who was in need of help, with his work and correspondence, from someone he could trust.

I had always liked Speusippos. In spite of his temper, he was not the man to pick a quarrel, or drag it on. Though he was agreed to have one of the best minds at the Academy, and was an expert in the growth and properties of plants, he studied also girls and horses and the theatre, and found no trouble in talking with common men. I would have been pleased to see him, but for his look of having had bad news.

He asked about the tour; I told him, since Plato had better know, how rooted the theatre was in Sicily. He nodded, but I saw this was the least of his troubles. So I asked outright whether Dionysios was making good progress.

He ran his hands through his dark hair, upsetting the barber's curls. 'Progress! You met him, I believe. The progress a boy makes with his book, while someone is showing him a cockfight.'

I looked round; I had been long enough for that in Sicily. But he was no fool; the near tables were empty. 'Philistos?' I asked.

'You know the man?' He had sharpened, as if eager for any scrap of knowledge about a dangerous enemy. I said I had barely seen him, but had heard things before I left.

'You'll hear more now. And mostly praise. Can you believe it, Niko? That venal, greedy old lecher, who did as much as anyone to set up the tyranny. Now they call him a sound statesman, because he wants the city kept in chains; and a good fellow because he wants to make the man whose slaves they are, the slave of his own appetites.'

'Well,' I said as one Athenian to another, 'they were bred up without justice, like bats without light. It must hurt their eyes.'

'We all come from the light, Niko. The soul can remember, or forget.' For all his easy manners, he was Academy through and through.

'How much,' I asked, 'does Dionysios' soul remember?'

He gave a short laugh, then answered seriously. 'Enough to open his eyes. If that were all.'

'He won't work for it,' I said, 'and wants to blame someone else?'

'You must know him well.'

'No, I've known actors like him. Yet Plato is still in favour?'

'He won't hear of his leaving. Of course all Greece would know, and say the son had followed the father. But I don't think it's only that.'

'Nor I. So he loves him still?'

He looked down his high-bred nose. As a youth he must have been striking. Perhaps he had had some share in Plato's love. 'You may call it that; or you can say he would like to be Plato's best

student, without working. Of course he would like to be Philistos'
best student, too. He has rolled by this time in enough logic for
some to stick; he knows when two propositions exclude each
other, but . . .'

'But he feels,' I said, 'right down in his soul, that logic should
make an exception just for him.'

He propped his chin in his palm and looked at me. 'You are
mocking us,' he said.

'What am I to do that? A phantom in a mask, a voice of illusion.'

'You too, Niko, even you.'

A harsh Sicilian sunbeam stabbed down through the vine,
picking out the lines of thought and pleasure in his face, deepened by weariness. He had meant it; in his trouble even I had
power to cast him down.

'Forgive me,' I said. '"He who mocks sorrow shall weep alone."
But if you think me sour, talk to some Syracusan actors, and I'll
seem like honey.'

'It is your life,' he said wearily. 'I know it. But somewhere the
surgeon's knife must cut, or the patient dies.'

'Artists are few among many; that I understand. But bear this
in mind, Speusippos: while you, sitting in front, are watching our
illusion, we are looking at reality. While you see four men, we see
fifteen thousand. Twenty years I've played to them. One learns a
little.'

He said harshly, 'What do you mean? That they won't forego
the theatre? Or something more?'

'Well, both. What is it you Academics say of Plato? Like his
master Sokrates, he won't sell his teaching, he'll choose his audience. Does he think he can do that here? He must make do with
what comes, just like an actor.'

'Plato was born among great affairs, and has lived with them
ever since.'

186

Here's another, I thought, who loves him still. I said, 'Once at the Dionysia, someone in the skene-room fell down deathly sick, and they fetched a doctor. The good man came running, took the wrong door in his haste, and found himself up stage centre, standing next to Medea. Hasn't Plato seen yet where he is?'

He fetched a deep sigh. 'Oh, Niko. I think I will have that drink you offered me.'

I called the boy. When we were alone again, he said, 'What do you think I was doing here before you came? I'm all day about the city, scraping acquaintance, joining hetairas' evening parties, talking to bathmen and barbers, to learn the temper of the people. It's the best I can do for Plato; that, and staying away from the Palace. The Archon thought we were too close; he was getting to hate me nearly as much as Dion.'

'Hate!' I said, shocked. 'Has it come to that?'

'Hush,' he said, as the boy came with the wine. Then, 'On your life, Niko, keep that quiet. Every day that doesn't bring it out in daylight is something gained. So far it's only slights, coldness and pinpricks. If it comes into the open, what can Plato do? Honour, truth, the pieties of friendship, are his very soul. To put it as low as you can, he is a gentleman. He can't be neutral. It would be the end of this whole great mission.'

'Nearly two months ago,' I said, 'I tried to tell Dion this.'

'It is hard,' he said slowly, 'for a lover of truth, who lives in a corrupted polis, not to become rather unbending. He has seen too much base compromise; any accommodation scratches his integrity. With his looks, he must have come young to that.' He frowned into his cup, and drained it. I lifted the flask from its bed of snow, and poured again.

'At the Academy,' he said, 'we think that truth, being man's highest good, should be sought like joy, not endured as children take a purge. From that faith comes all philosophy . . . Don't look so anxious, Niko, I won't engage you in elenchos; I mean it's no shame to make persuasion pleasing – if you want clear water, don't tease the squid. Plato is forever saying that to Xenokrates – a kind man, if he would own it to himself – who charmed you so by likening actors to whores. "Sacrifice to the Graces", Plato says; I told him once I'd build them an altar in the garden. Well, not long ago I heard him say it again; but to someone else.'

'You mean Dion?' The blood stirred round my heart. I slammed my cup down on the table. '*He* need not sacrifice. He has the graces of a king. Why should he use a courtier's? Do you know what I think, Speusippos? If it comes to an open break, so much the better. Then he will be free to take his rights.'

Speusippos' face changed. He laid his hand over mine; it looked affectionate, but his nails dented my flesh. I took their message and was silent. He leaned forward and dropped his voice discreetly, but not quite enough. 'Of course, my dear, if they quarrel you shall be the first to know. That is, if you really want to court this boy? But I warn you, he's spoilt; as mercenary as he's pretty, and tells more lies than a Cretan.'

I had heard, while he spoke, the benches scrape close by, and thanked him with my eyes. 'You're jealous,' I said, 'because he went home with me after the party. A charming lad. I can't think why you call him mercenary. When he asked me for my ring, it was only as a keepsake.'

When I returned from the city to our inn at Heloros, the company crowded round me, asking the news from Syracuse. I told them I could not see much change. All their faces fell; I asked myself why I was hiding news which would have made them happy. They were fellow artists, and friends. The third actor, Philanthos, a promising young man who should have been playing second in better times, had stopped at every shrine of Dionysos along the road, and made some little offering.

I had affronted Dion to his face (with such difference of rank one can scarcely speak of quarrelling); yet had been ready almost to fly at Speusippos for his sake. If Menekrates and the others, elated by my news, went drinking to his speedy downfall, no doubt I would also fly at them, which they did not deserve.

Trying to understand myself, I thought how often I had sat before the mask of some hero king – say, Theseus in *Oidipos at Kolonos* – to feel my way into his greatness. As Plato said (from what I could make out of it) before there can be imitation, the original must exist. Can one hate the Form whose essence one has tried to enter? But having found the nature of my problem, I was no nearer solving it.

We played one or two more engagements, and a return visit to Leontini. Having seen us in Alexis' comedy, they now offered us a chorus, to put on *Hippolytos* at a public festival. I played, as the protagonist always does, Phaedra and Theseus; Menekrates was a good Hippolytos, moving in the death scene; and we had an excellent house. The party which followed went on till dawn; the hotter it gets in Sicily, the more they turn night into day. We were all offered hospitality, my own host being a retired captain of Dionysios' mercenaries, one Rupilius; a Roman, but quite civilised in his manners; he had been given some land here, by way of pension.

It was past noon the day after the party, and I was still in bed, playing with a breakfast of melon chilled in snow and pale cold wine from the slopes of Etna, when my host scratched at the door. Begging my pardon for waking me so early, he held out a letter. It had come from Syracuse by fast courier; the man had changed horses, and was waiting for my answer.

I put down my cup on the marble side-table, and took the letter. It was sealed with a crest which I could not make out, the shutters having been closed against the noonday glare; but I could think of only one. He needs me, I thought; in some trouble he has turned to me. He trusts me still.

If my host had been Greek, he would have been dawdling by me, in hope of learning all about the letter; but Romans are too proud to show curiosity, which they think undignified, and he had withdrawn. I jumped out of bed in the dim room, opened the shutters, and stood naked in the sun to read. The strong light dazzled me; it had been a real Sicilian party. I blinked and tried again.

'Dionysios son of Dionysios, to Nikeratos of Athens. Joy to you. When you spoke our late father's Epitaph, we expressed the wish to see you in classic tragedy, when the mourning time had passed. Cares of state, and our course of studies, caused us to defer it. These studies being now complete and ourselves at leisure, the City Theatre will present, on the ninth day of Kameios, the *Bacchae* of Euripides, with yourself as protagonist. You may choose your own supporting actors. A not unworthy chorus is already training. Philistos is choregos. Farewell.'

I read it twice. Something stirred in the courtyard; it was the courier's fresh horse, waiting to take my answer back.

I closed the shutters, and threw myself on the tumbled bed. The room smelled of melon-rind and wine and sweat. The flask was still three parts full; I reached for it, but put it back. It would not help me think.

Syracusans use the Dorian calendar; I tried to think which month Kameios was. It must be the coming one, our Metageitnion. The ninth was fifteen days ahead, barely time for rehearsals.

Why, I thought, did I ever come back to Sicily? I had my work, my friends, my life at home; I knew where I was, there. Out of a thousand actors minding their own business, why must it fall on me to be grasped by both hands and pulled in half? When did I speak the bad luck word? What god have I offended?

Not Dionysos; here he was, through his mortal namesake,

inviting me to play himself in one of the greatest bravura roles of classic tragedy; no deity of the machine, but the king-pin of the action. I thought of young Philanthos, lingering by all those altars with his pinch of incense or bunch of grapes. Who says the gods don't regard men's offerings? After a command performance, he could step into second roles at once. As for Menekrates, he would do a first-rate King Pentheus – his Hippolytos had shown me that – and be made for life. His family would offer him the chair of honour, and Theoros stand up for him.

Dionysos blesses his faithful servants. So much for Dionysos.

I lay a long time, while the flies buzzed round the melon rind, my arms behind my head, watching a gekko on a beam. At last I got up, and opened the mask-box on the table. This time I had brought it with me.

I propped the mask upright on the pillow, and lay before it, naked in the oven-hot Sicilian afternoon, my chin cupped in my hands. It gazed back at me; not empty-eyed as in those months at Athens, but secret, Delphic, dark. It answered nothing, only asked. 'Are you not Nikeratos, son of Artemidoros, who said to a man he loved and honoured, "I will choose the god, rather than you"? Choose me then, if you can find me. The courier is waiting, and so am I.'

'Phoibos,' I answered, 'they call you Longsight. You can see what this means. This is Philistos' triumph-song. Dion is out of power. Standing before your image I said I would not fail him. Must I sing for Philistos now?'

The mask looked formal and holy, as in a temple. 'Truly, friendship is sacred. Guest-friendship above all.'

'You mean Menekrates. My lord, I know; I am bound to both. What shall I do?'

'Most men count the cost.'

'To my fortunes? Little either way. If I play, I shall have a fine role with a handsome fee, and my company will love me. If not, I can go back to Athens and say I refused the tyrant. Everyone will admire me, and someone will give me an important lead, to reward my constancy, and because a well-liked protagonist helps a play to win. Someone else will pay: Dion, or Menekrates, as the case may be.'

'Which loses most?'

'Each loses something dear.'

'Are you a god, to measure loss with loss?'

'Apollo,' I said, 'we are starting to talk in stichomythia. This is not a play.'

'You say truly. Well? Are you asking me to help you choose between your friends? You said you would choose me.'

He had stared me out. I laid my face on my folded arms, but not to weep. I could do that later. The courier was still waiting. At last I said, 'It is my turn to ask you if I am a god.'

He answered in the voice of Speusippos, 'We all come from the light, Niko. The soul can remember, or forget.'

'Dion remembers, or so he and Plato claim. Justice, and the good life.'

'They remember their share.' A sun-glint through the shutters struck the pillow near him; the reflected light changed his face; he seemed to smile. 'And you? What do you remember?'

There came before my eyes, seen through those very eyeholes, the theatre at Phigaleia. I felt on my head the hot gold wig, smelling of Meidias; the lyre in my hand, my youth beating like wings in me, and words sounding out across the empty battlefield. I said aloud,

> The gods wear many faces,
> And many fates fulfil
> To work their will . . .

Far off in the mountains a shepherd's pipe was sounding. Now Phigaleia was gone; I heard Athenian flutes receding, the singers dying away beyond the parodos, the stillness left in the heart.

'Well?' said the god impatiently. 'So you remember the tag of *The Bacchae*. I should suppose as much. No more?'

He was going to tell me, so I waited. 'It seems to me, Nikeratos, that when last you sat in front to see this play, you said something to the youth beside you. He was not attending, since it was not for his knowledge of Euripides that you had sought him out; but I, as it happened, overheard. Don't you remember? "To my mind, Phrynon, one cannot go everywhere with Euripides. He is sometimes impassioned over dead things, the war, the oligarchs and demagogues of his day, or that old scandal when the Spartans bribed the Pythia; then he gets angry himself, instead of leaving justice to the nature of things, which after all is tragedy. The old scores are settled, the scar on the play remains like the mark of an old rotted goat-tether on a living tree. With the *Troiades* he rose above it; but with the *Bacchae* he digs down far below, to some deep rift in the soul where our griefs begin. Take that play anywhere, even to men unborn who worship other gods or none, and it will teach them to know themselves."'

There was a silence. He waited a little longer, then said in a voice as cool as water, 'Do you deny those words?'

I answered, 'No, my lord.'

'Goodbye, Nikeratos,' said the mask, making its eyeholes blank. 'The oracle is over.'

II

I called on Philistos as soon as I got back. He was genial, brisk and business-like, had clearly done choregos countless times, and knew what he was about. The secret of my work for Dion must have been well kept, for it was a sponsor's interview like any other. He was very correct, knowing what was due to his rank and to my standing; he would not nag or fuss, or try to fuss, or try to teach me my work. If he had been a stranger in a strange city, I should have gone home well satisfied. As it was, I thought how easy he must have found it to undermine Dion with his one weapon the other lacked, the knack of pleasing useful men whom he did not care two straws for.

The company was treating me like the eldest son's wife who at last has borne a boy. While I was thinking the matter over at Heloros, the news of the courier had got to all of them. Menekrates told me the other two had almost gone on their knees to him to intercede with me, but knowing me best he had more sense. When I told them I would play, they looked like men reprieved from the Quarries. I had to go drinking with them, or we should never have been at ease again.

One thing rode my mind, that I must get to Dion; not to

excuse myself, for I had broken no pledge to him, indeed declared I would do this very thing I was doing; but to say I was sorry to cross him even for the god I served, and was still at his service in any other way. But I had never used his name to get through the gates; if he had private work for me, it was the last thing I ought to do. I could have gone on there from Philistos, who also lived in Ortygia, but he gave me the feeling that spies surrounded him, and I feared he might have me followed.

I was wretched over this matter for two nights and a day; then I was summoned to go and see Dionysios.

This, as before, might serve my turn. I must own that I was full, too, of curiosity. He was a man who could put on three masks in a day, believing each to be his face, and I longed to know the latest one.

The gatehouse guards all seemed to be in better humour. The Roman officer had remembered me, and asked if I had come looking for Plato, not angrily, but as a man jokes with a boy. When I showed him Dionysios' letter, he became very correct. Once more I noticed how his men's obedience was without servility; how well they kept their panoplies; and the air they had, as if they not only thought themselves the best, but expected the world to know it.

I was led in through the searching-room, where I was well gone over. The eunuch even ran his fat fingers through my crotch. But the robe he gave me was handsomer than before; I had gone up a class, it seemed.

The room of state had been altered. From the quick look I had time for, I should think nearly everything good of the old man's had been bundled out, and the places filled (for the room seemed fuller than ever) with modern art. The Zeuxis had gone; the statues were all gesturing like orators, or, if female, wrapping their arms round their privates. One Aphrodite looked as shy as if she had just been through the searching-room. Luckily, before I started to laugh I saw Dionysios waiting.

He was sitting at the marble desk (it would need a crane to shift that) in an ivory chair which, this time, he quite succeeded in filling. He was dressed up to the height of Syracusan fashion, and a bit beyond. His hair had been camomiled, curled, and dusted with powdered gold; his robe, which seemed all border, was bordered with purple embroidery. I wondered if I could get at his chamber-groom and offer for his castoffs; you could have played Rhadamanthos in this one. Close up it almost knocked you down; so did his scent, which was drenched on like an old hetaira's. He had painted his face with Athlete's Tan and carmine, and touched up his eyes with kohl. I was surprised to find he wore all this stuff as if he were used to it, till I remembered Menekrates' stories. Of course, it had been put away when Plato came. I daresay I was the only man in Syracuse whom it could still surprise.

He was cordial, but had nothing much to say to me; it seemed he was just giving me an audience by way of favour. Presently, as he talked about past productions in the city, praising this artist or that, I saw why I was there: to spread the news that the theatre ban was over.

I wondered how Plato had been chased out of Syracuse this time, and pictured the dejection at the Academy. I must bring home some gift for Axiothea, to cheer her up.

'Only today,' said Dionysios, digging in the sweet-bowl that stood between us, 'Plato was telling me how you were ship-wrecked going home last time. I had not known of it.'

I related the tale, my mind busy elsewhere. So Plato still cast his spell. What? I thought. Will the bird he's whistled to his hand neither sing for him nor fly away? Else why this naughty costume? But then, all the world knows how Akibiades used to slip the leash, and come coaxing back to Sokrates, showing his radiant grace for password.

'And I suppose,' he said, 'you lost that painting I gave you of the Siege of Motya?'

'Alas, sir, yes.' He looked as downcast as a child, so to please him I said, 'A loss to me and Athens. But I grieved even more for the model chariot; not just for the giver's sake, but because I never saw, in that line of work, craftsmanship to equal it.'

I hoped to see his face light up as it had before; but he just looked gracious, and sent to summon his steward. The man came with his keys; he said, 'Go to that old workroom of mine and fetch a model chariot.' When it came, he turned it over once or twice in his hands (I saw he still bit his nails) and said, 'Well, here is one loss I can make good to you. State business gives me no time for toys.' There was dust on it. I am ashamed to confess such folly, but I felt near weeping.

No one troubled with me when I left, so I made for Dion's house, thinking, as I went, what Dionysios had said about his state business. He had sounded full of consequence. Having met Philistos, I could see him flattering the young man, as an expert charioteer coaching a rich young blood will let him think he is driving. Dionysios was the very one for it. I don't suppose Dion had ever stooped to such pretences. It was not in him.

His house, when I got there, was well-kept as ever, nothing shabby or run-down. Yet I felt a change, a loss of life and movement in the air around. As I reached the door I saw this was more than idle fancy. Before it had stood open, now it was shut.

I knocked, and sent in my name. While I stood waiting, a young boy of seven or eight, a handsome child, slipped round the corner of the house for a peep at me. One saw the likeness at once. He was curious, I suppose, having heard my name, but dodged back when he was seen. Soon came the servant to say his master was at his studies and could see no one. No word of my coming some other time.

I walked through Ortygia, sick at heart. I had thought he would forgive me; himself he had done what he thought right, sorry it hurt me, but never turning back. This was the same. I would never have shut my door to him. But to me, man's life is a tree with twisted roots. To a political philosopher, it must be like a diagram of Pythagoras.

Soon after I met Speusippos in the street. I hardly dared greet him; but he crossed over, and invited me to drink with him. I took courage, therefore, to ask if Dion was very angry with me.

'Angry?' he said. 'Not that I know of. Why should you think so?'

When I told him, he said the play had not been announced yet; I could see that it was news to him, and news of no great importance. He spoke kindly however. 'Don't lose your sleep over it. If Dion knows of it, which I doubt, he can see you must work to eat. Give him credit for being just. You know, I take it, that Dionysios stopped the plays of his own accord? Neither Plato nor Dion urged it; *they* are here to get law instead of tyranny. But Dionysios found it in the *Republic*; a thing he could do at once, without trouble. You know him, like a child with new clothes.'

'Still,' I said, 'Plato wrote it.'

'Yes ... You know, Niko, at the Academy we aim to provide the world with statesmen. Already now cities are coming to us to draw up their constitutions. But like shoemakers, we cut to measure. The *Republic* is, shall I say, a discussion of principles, not a working code. Between you and me, I think the purpose of those passages was to startle our poets into responsibility. Half of them today have the souls of whores: give me my drachma, never-mind who gets my pox. Plato is a man who would not add a grain to the weight of the world's evil, for a golden crown. When no more like him are left, men will devour each other and perish from off the earth. That's why Dion defended him to you, just as I do.'

'Well then,' I said, 'if it's not on account of the play, why does Dion shut his door to me?'

'I doubt you were singled out. He has refused himself to a good many people lately. He found if he tried to advance anyone's interests, just the opposite happened. That was Dionysios' way of making himself felt, without an open quarrel. He won't, if he can help it, force Plato into taking sides; he might learn what he has no wish to know. So he pricks in ways like these. Dion found he did his friends no good by taking notice of them. That's why he shuts his door.'

'I am sorry for it. But with me, I'm afraid he must be really angry. If not, knowing I would think so he would have sent a letter.'

Speusippos drew his black brows together, and shook his head. 'No, Niko. You think so, because it is what you would do yourself. Dion is proud. Till you know that, you do not know him.'

I remembered his desk, piled with petitions and state papers. How should a man like him beg pardon of a man like me, for being no longer even a trusted servant? The thought freed me from bitterness.

Since the year of my father's death, when I had come on as an extra, I had never been in the *Bacchae*. While a second actor, I had once been offered my father's roles, but had turned them down, more, I suppose, from superstition than from piety, for no doubt he would have thought me foolish. Now, as protagonist, I would play the god, with one short double as Tiresias the Prophet. Menekrates, as Pentheus and Queen Agave, was keen and shaping well.

It is a play about a mystery, and a mystery in itself. Ask any actor what he thinks Euripides meant by it, and he will tell you something different. Myself, I have played in it now some seven times, and still don't claim to know more than what one man makes of it, on one day. It is even possible, I suppose, that it was written to show that the gods are not. If so, someone crept up behind the poet, and breathed down his neck when he wasn't looking. One thing I take it we may agree upon: the god of the *Bacchae* is not supposed to be like men.

There are first-class maskmakers in Syracuse, and of course we had the best. The Dionysos was most beautiful, a delicate blond face, almost feminine, as the play describes him, but with slant eyes, darkly drawn round like a leopard's. It seemed to me just right. Menekrates was very pleased with the Agave, and the Pentheus was nearly finished.

Philistos gave no trouble. He looked in now and again at rehearsals, sat quietly in front, would come behind to say it was going well, and ask if we were satisfied with the machines, for there are a good many effects, with the earthquakes and so on. Of course such things are better done at Syracuse than anywhere in the world, but he was anxious it seemed to be cordial, and even asked the cast to a drinking-party. The others went, which I did not hold against them. I begged off with the excuse that I had had a feverish flux on tour (a common complaint in Sicily, where there is much bad water) and the doctor had me under orders. He could hardly press me, if he wanted the play to go on, so I was left in peace. I was doing this role to serve the god, not as Philistos' sycophant.

During the half-month of rehearsals, I made it my business to visit small wine-shops in poor streets, and find out what the people were saying. I reckoned in this way to cover ground Speusippos would miss; for he could never look like anything but a gentleman; while I, if I choose, can look like a soldier or an arti-

san, not by dressing up but just in small ways of sitting and standing and slicking down my hair. As a rule I said I was a
skene-painter from Corinth. The accent is very easy.

From being so much in Ortygia among the soldiers and servants
of the Archon, I had begun to think Dion had not a friend left in
the city. I now learned otherwise. The working folk, with one
accord, had blamed the theatre ban on Plato; a foreign sophist, of
whom they only knew he was Dionysios' latest fad, which in itself
was enough to damn him. Dion, they were all sure, would do
nothing so impious or so odd. Dion was a great gentleman. When
the old Archon died, and he had got the young cub at heel, it had
been an age of gold while it lasted. People could bring their wrongs
to judgement, even against the rich; taxes had been fairly levied,
and the worst extortioners had gone to the Quarries. The mercenaries had been made to behave themselves in the town, instead
of acting like conquerors. And so on. Everyone, they said, had had
hopes of his doing great things for the city; but it seemed, when it
came to the push, he was too much the gentleman.

I could not make out just what it was they thought he would
do, without help from them. Subvert the mercenaries, I suppose,
and form a conspiracy and seize Ortygia; but nobody seemed to
have a notion how such things are really done. Used as I was at
home to being told I was a fool at politics, here any Athenian,
even I, seemed as expert as a man among children. However careless we may be, there are some things we take for granted grown
men will do for themselves. All this they had forgotten.

They talked of Dion as if of a god, whose mind they did not
expect to know. But even the gods have oracles, and priests who
will take them messages from common folk. Dion had no such
thing. I suppose, in Sicily, it was to be expected.

I sought out Speusippos with my findings. He was glad of the
information, saying he had most success himself with the

middle-class citizens, with whom, he said, the friends of Philistos were daily making headway. They did not attack Dion direct, knowing how he was respected; it was through Plato they slipped their poison in. 'In the time of our fathers,' they were saying, 'the Athenians sent out two armies and a battle-fleet to conquer Syracuse. None got home alive but a few wretched fugitives from the mountain brush, or slaves on the run. But now, Athens sends just one sophist with a silken tongue, and look what *he* has achieved. He has got the Archon wound up in his web; soon he will suck him dry and hand over the power to Dion, who, as all the world knows, has been his fancy-boy.'

Speusippos said that the men of culture, who had read Plato for themselves or spoken with those who had, were not so easily led; but even they were starting to believe what they were always being told, that the reforms would be hurried breakneck in, and cause civil chaos. Dion's most solid support, he said, lay among men whom I had seen nothing of and he not much; the ancient aristocracy of Syracuse, whose fathers had fought the older tyrant. Their rising had been brief, but savage; Dionysios' revenge no less so; they, or their widows, had passed on the blood-feud to their sons, and it smouldered still.

All this he told me, and much more that I forgot, for I was now in *The Bacchae* up to my neck. I recall, though, his saying there was talk of a Carthaginian embassy coming about a peace treaty. In the old Archon's day, Speusippos said, their envoys had always been seen by Dion; they trusted his word, and his manners were such as they admire, commanding, spare of words, and stern, for he knew their ways. Now he was getting anxious lest Dionysios should try to handle it himself. He would be no match for them; at best they would get the profit of the bargain, at worst he might lose his head and provoke them into war; they might be all too ready once they had seen his quality. Dion was doing his best, therefore, to keep their chief men ignorant of his fall from power.

I said I hoped he would succeed; wondering in my heart whether he would come to see me act, and whether, if I did well enough, it would change his heart to me and open his door again. I feared this was not his play; he might only see it as one more folk-tale of Olympians behaving worse than men. But one cannot take this deity with the head; that, I suppose, is what the play is about. I must do it as I felt it, and leave the rest to the god.

Stratokles, old Dionysios' chorus-trainer, had stayed on in the city to put on dithyrambs, so was here at need. He was good at his work, and not above taking some direction from the protagonist, which is important in this play. Everything went so well that, lest some god should be getting jealous, we were almost relieved when the maskmaker told Menekrates his Pentheus mask had been spoiled by some apprentice spilling paint on it, and would not be ready till the day.

'At the worst,' he said, 'I can wear the second mask from the Hippolytos.' (There are three; the happy, the angry and the dying.) 'Pentheus is an angry young man all through, it will be well enough at a pinch, and we can say that the luck-god has had his sacrifice.'

'Amen,' I said.

Plays start at dawn in Sicily, for the heat of the day comes soon. The theatre of Syracuse faces south-west, built into the slopes of Achradina. Behind these the sun comes up; one begins in the dusk of their shadow, till presently the long sun-shafts strike the stage.

That day there was a glowing sky, with great wings of flame from the hidden east almost to the zenith. But when we opened, the wings were folded still; we had a subtle and sombre glow, dusky-red, bronze and purple. Seeing this light, spellbound and louring, which Euripides himself might have written in, Menekrates and I looked at each other, neither daring to say, 'A lucky omen!'

They doused the cressets which had lit the audience to their seats. I pulled down my mask as the flutes began.

Dionysos opens alone. I have a bit of business I always use, when the play starts early in half light. I cross to Semele's altar, where, as the dramatist directs, the fire is sinking; then, picking up a torch which lies there, I kindle it, lift it, and gaze around. I do the whole opening speech like this, walking here and there, looking at the royal house I shall destroy. The god must not seem like a mortal man plotting malice. He is curious, smelling out the ground; a stalking panther from the upland forests who snuffs at the walls of men, softly prowling, innocent of what he is.

I like this quiet start. Then when I raise my voice to call on the Phrygian Maenads, everyone jumps, which is good. In they come dancing, with their pipes and drums and cymbals, shattering the hush and stealth. There were young satyrs with them, doing a torch-dance.

Coming off, I found Menekrates dressed, with the Hippolytos mask pushed up; his new one had not come. I said it was hard, the masks being so good, that only he should have an old one. 'I'd rather, now,' he said. 'I'm played-in with this. I was only afraid the other would come by a panting messenger while I was lacing my boots. I know these eminent artists; one daren't offend them, the choregos always takes their side because he'll need them again. I should have had to wear it, with barely a glance in the mirror. One can't do oneself justice.' Grateful he took it so well, I went to do my change for the seer Tiresias.

When I went on, I found the sky growing blue. The highlands were in sun, and the dewy chill was lifting. This is right, when mortals take the place of gods.

One can work up Tiresias if one likes; some leading men do; but I had rather give this scene to King Kadmos, that old trimmer who will dance on the hills with god or mountebank, no questions asked, if it gives him status. I just did a straight man for his laughs. It helps the play; for bigoted and stiff-necked as Pentheus is, one must point up his integrity. That is the tragedy's core.

Tiresias has a blind-man mask; one sees through slits between the eyelids. Turning my empty gaze upon the house, I perceived the play had taken.

Menekrates started his shouting off, denouncing the Bacchae and their rites. Just at his entrance-cue, the first sunbeams struck the stage, one falling on the very door, all ready. I thought, 'Some god loves us today.'

Into the light stepped Menekrates, a big upstage entrance with supporting extras. The bullion and gilt jewels of his costume flashed, the crimson glowed. And he had got his new mask. It must have come at the very last, while I did my change. Enough to unsettle any artist; but he was sound and would keep his head.

Then I started to hear the audience. There was a pause; a buzzing; an angry mutter; a laugh. Good masks get their best effects with distance. I peered through my blind-man slits, which are less good than proper eye-holes, trying to see what was amiss, while Menekrates came on in the mask of Pentheus. A good character mask; a harsh proud face, for an enemy of laughter and the joyous god. What, then, was wrong with it? Then I saw.

It was a portrait mask, such as they use in comedy, only less crude; a caricature, but a subtle one, toned-down to the tragic style. It was the face of Dion.

I stood rooted, wooden as a post, while Menekrates went into his long entrance speech. I recalled the delays, the mask-maker's excuses; then its coming at the very last, after I was on stage and would not see. And just as a man will stare at a spear in his flesh, as if asking what it is, till suddenly the pain begins, so it broke upon me that Dion must be out in front there, in the seats of honour, getting this full in the face. What could he suppose, but that I knew?

He had thought the worse of me, no doubt, only for playing; and now, how much would he think Philistos and his master had paid me to make this worth my while? A nothing in a mask, a seller of illusions, a poets' whore, whose life is spent in the public show of those passions the philosopher lives to master; a stroller from town to town, without a household; such men are easily bought.

My stomach heaved. For a moment I thought I would throw up on stage. By now Menekrates was half-way through his speech.

> *They tell me that a stranger out of Lydia*
> *Has come to Thebes . . .*

Dionysos, in whose mask I would soon be entering. I thought of that opening speech by torchlight, promising vengeance on the man who forbade my worship. Dionysos, god of the theatre. A perfect buildup – for this.

As when I was a naked child on a Trojan shield, I longed for an earthquake to swallow up the skene. But that came later. I was a god, I would be giving the cue for it. I could have sat down, at that, and laughed until I cried.

> *Just let me get him here within my walls;*
> *He'll swing his thyrsos no longer, nor toss his head . . .*

Menekrates came forward, gesturing threats. Poison was everywhere. I thought, What does *he* know?

The mask came late. But one always finds time to stand back

and look. Perhaps he would not; did not want to confuse his interpretation, and would rather just clap it on. But, I thought, what is Dion to him, to offend a powerful sponsor for, except that he is my friend? If he saw, he'll never own it; who would?

He lives in Syracuse; what free Athenian dare reproach him? So there will be this between us.

Ha, this is your work, Tiresias . . .

He had crossed down towards me. At the end of this tirade came my cue, for a speech about twice as long. I could not remember a line of it.

*You are greedy for burnt-offerings, you scent
New fees for divination . . .*

I should be reacting to all this. Already he felt my numbness and was losing force. I was giving him nothing. My hand came up for the affronted seer, and tapped my staff on the stage.

Well might Tiresias be angry. I thought of that vain young fool in Ortygia, sitting like a clerk at his great, wicked father's desk; of jolly Philistos with his gentlemanly manners, the fat old spider shaking his web; and of Dion out in front, keeping a philosopher's straight face (the good man bears pleasure and pain with an equal mind) in the hour of fallen fortune, bitten even by the stray he had fed from his own dish. There had been no time till now for anger.

One is finished, if one loses one's temper on stage; so it was lucky I had learned young to master it. If, at nineteen, you have had to keep going when you find the inside of your mask has been smeared with turd, you never really forget it. Poor Meidias had never, right till the end of the tour, given up such attempts to

207

make me lose my lines. So, now, I grasped the weapon that had served me when I had no other. I was here to honour the god, in the precinct where if a man meets face to face his own father's murderer, still he must hold his hand. One seldom thinks of these sacred laws; one seldom needs to; but they are bone of one's bone. I could only fight within them. These people had tried to take the play from me, and turn it into a third-rate satire. If it cost my last breath, I would take it back.

I went into my speech on cue, living from line to line; once I saw Menekrates' eyes blinking within his eyeholes, and wondered how much I had just cut. Luckily it's the dullest speech in the play. I shook my staff or rather held up my hand which was skaking of itself; but Tiresias is very old, and angry. It was a ham performance; at all events it warmed Menekrates up again, and I did get his cue-line right.

When I exited with young Philanthos, who was doing Kadmos, we were hardly off before he lifted his mask and gaped at me, so full of words they jammed his mouth. I raised my hand, saying, 'No. We will get through this performance first. And nothing to Menekrates either.'

In my dressing-room I had just started to strip when Menekrates came straight in from his exit. 'What happened, Niko? What was the matter with the audience? Do you know you cut twenty lines, and ad-libbed half the rest? This mask has wretched eyeholes, too.'

I did not say, 'You need not act to me, my friend.' It might well be the truth. Even with good eyeholes, one can't see much more than straight forward; to see sideways one must turn one's head. Anything might have happened, for all he knew, beyond his sight-line, to cause the stir.

'My dear,' I said, 'leave it till after. It's politics; but let's keep to our own business while we are doing it. If you do find out, don't

208

be upset; the play's the thing. When I'm dressed, I shall sit with my mask awhile.'

Some actors swear by this rite, and it is much beloved by wall-painters and sculptors. For myself, I get my masks home beforehand (or I make trouble) and consider them there in quiet, with no witness but the god. Yet it is a good tradition of the theatre, that an artist who sits before his mask should be left in peace. It gives one the chance to compose oneself, if anything has put one out. I could hear my dresser at the door, turning people away in whispers. The voices of the chorus-boys rose and fell, down in the orchestra, as the dance brought them near or far. Chin on fist I sat, looking at the leopard eyes of bland fair Dionysos, thinking about the immortal hunter and his prey.

My call came; I was led by the guards before angry virtuous Pentheus. The god is disguised as a human youth; but all have felt divinity somewhere about him, except the King; to whom he gives soft answers, speaking truth darkly, smiling.

The audience had quietened now; but I could feel them on edge, rustling like mice in the wainscot. I must get hold of them now or never, for this passage is the axis of the play.

Pentheus denounces the god as a juggling charlatan, crops his long hair (the wig is a trick one) then orders him to give up his thyrsos. He, however, stands still. 'Take it yourself,' he says quietly. 'This belongs to Dionysos.'

This line I spoke with its meaning; and Menekrates, who was a sensitive actor, played back to me, holding off a moment and pausing, before he snatched angrily at the wand. I turned to the maenad chorus, and made the gesture which says, 'It is accomplished.' There was a hush, fraught, as I meant, with fear.

The thyrsos is the madness of the gods, which the man must choose for himself. Thus each fulfils his nature.

The god came kindly at first to Thebes, saying, 'Bring me all that wildness in your hearts; I understand it, it is my kingdom. My gift is the lesser madness which will rest your souls and save you from the greater. Know yourselves, as my brother Apollo tells you. You have need of me.' The Theban women answered, 'How dare you? Would you make wild beasts of us? We have laws and live in the city. You insult us; go away.' That's why they have the madness of the god without his blessing, and run on the mountains tearing wolves with their nails.

Then comes Pentheus, saying, 'You dirty foreigner, debaucher of decent ladies, don't try your tricks on *me*. I am master of myself; don't deny it, or I shall be angry. I am pure; I can't rest for thinking of those women's lecheries in the woods. To prison with you, out of my sight. Let me hear no more of you.'

It is from the man's own soul that the god with the smiling mask will draw his power, enchanting Pentheus with the hubris in his own secret heart. Once drunk on this sweet poison, he will know himself the one sane, righteous man in a wicked world. He has refused the little madness, to choose the great.

Yet the god warns him, as gods do before they strike. One can play it mockingly; indeed I had rehearsed it so. But suddenly, now, it seemed to me the mortal veil should be lifted here, for the man to see if he would. The line *You know not your own life, nor what you are*, I spoke softly, pitching it at the echo-chamber. It was a lucky try. I nearly frightened myself.

Menekrates played back, recoiling. I had asked a good deal of him, changing the tone like this, but he had caught it. Well, I thought, when one sits with one's mask one calls the god. I must take what he sends.

When we went off, the audience shouted and stamped, as people do after tension; another gift of Dionysos, I daresay. There was no such release for me. I did not lift my mask, though the sweat was pouring down my face. Menekrates put his hand on my shoulder, saying, 'Niko, this is a great interpretation. This is truly Euripides, I am sure.' He has found out, I thought, if he didn't know before. I loved him for his kindness, but could do with nobody just then. I said, 'We shall do, my dear,' and went away.

The chorus were lamenting their gracious leader in his chains. In my dressing-room I could not rest, but paced about. The sun was well up now; on stage the mask helped shade one's eyes, but one felt the heat. I wondered where Dion was sitting. The one thing I dreaded like death was that someone might come and tell me.

It was time to command the earthquake. I was so wrought-up, I felt a shiver, like a sailor when someone whistles at sea. Well, let it come, I thought, as I ran backstage to the sounding-board and made a noise like doom. The effects were tremendous; they can do anything at Syracuse, thunder far and near, whole columns falling, lightning that nearly blinds you.

Out steps the god, delicately, from his broken prison, a human youth again, chaffing the maenads for their fright, while the fire-effects smoke up behind him. Pentheus comes on enraged, his captive free, his roof on fire, his herdsmen in flight from the mountain maenads. He has learned nothing. He curses the smiling god, and orders his army to fetch the women. Even then Dionysos gives him one more warning. 'Don't fight the gods; it would be better to offer sacrifice. If you ask it of me, I will bring the women home in peace.' But Pentheus knows best; no smooth-tongued Lydian shall trick him. He calls for his armour. He is like the mouse that runs about before the crouching cat. And now the paw comes down.

Pentheus has had his run. Now the god will play with him. Yet it is not Dionysos who by himself has devised the game like a cruel child. It takes two to play. The god is that which is. If we will not know him, it is we who make the ironies the Immortals laugh at.

When the scene was done, we stood listening to that great chorus which stops one's breath each time – the beauty before the horror. Menekrates said, 'Niko; we don't do this next scene for laughs?'

'No,' I said. 'But someone will laugh in any case. They have to. Never mind it.' I had played myself in, and knew where I was going.

We were coming to the scene where the god leads forth King Pentheus in a woman's robe. Softly his wits have been charmed away; now, obedient as the bird to the swaying snake, he goes to spy, as he thinks, upon the maenads, who will tear him piecemeal. Dionysos walks around him like a tiring-maid, patting his hair and dress, stealing even dignity from his dreadful death; while the insensate man giggles at the joke, or boasts that his strength can uproot the mountains.

Euripides wrote this play in Macedon; where, if this did not get some laughs, it would much surprise me. But wherever you play it, and whatever the interpretation, one hears it somewhere; from someone on edge, or from one of those you are sure to find among so many thousands, who would laugh still more if the lynching were done on stage.

This, I thought as I walked on with raised arm to summon Pentheus, is the scene our sponsor and his lord have so much looked forward to. We shall see.

This was what the mask of Dion had been made for. Mockery like this is a crucifixion, meant not just to hurt but to kill. Even in comedy it can finish a man; a few score know him, the whole city knows the lie. It was so with Sokrates, they say.

As soon as Pentheus entered, the catcalls and laughter started. One can always tell a claque, they react too soon. Others – democrats, or those who just wanted to hear the play – hissed and shushed them. I had been prepared for all this. Presently they did me the honour of attending.

Much as I had asked from Menekrates, now he gave me more. Whether he read my thoughts, which can happen when the god consents; whether he was making his own answer to what had been put on him, I do not know. Both, I daresay.

Pentheus has refused the god's offered good, and now has got the evil. The god is more wicked, now, than ever the man dreamed at first; and it is the victim's fate to trust him.

This scene can be done in many ways. One can make Pentheus a loud-mouthed tyrant burlesquing his own pride, with Dionysos all wit and charm. One can direct the sympathy this way or that. This time, Menekrates needed no telling; he could not have matched my purpose better if we had rehearsed for weeks. In the previous scene, he had built up Pentheus' sincerity, his striving for order, and fear of the excess which makes men less than men. Now he showed a man better than his fate, a king in ruins; wrecked through a noble hubris, the belief that man can be as perfect as the gods.

When rehearsing with the chorus, I had arranged in this scene for them to sway forward when I raised my arm, like hounds when the huntsman lifts the quarry. They were intelligent boys; when I heightened my gestures, they worked it up. I heard one or two women scream in front. By this time everyone pitied Pentheus, and felt horror of the mocking, cruel god. But of course the claque kept on; they had been paid to. So at the peak of the action, the pack as it were just closing in, I made one more gesture, wider and higher, bringing in these people, as if they too were my servants. The audience took it, and so did they. There was quite a hush.

'I bring the young man to a great contest,' says Dionysos as he goes. But the worst of mine was over. I had given the Messenger's great narration of the death to young Philanthos, to give him his chance, though the protagonist often takes it. He was glad; but not half as glad as I felt now. Pentheus was out of the play;

Menekrates now changed masks for the crazed Queen Agave toss-ing her dead son's head. I left him to dress in peace for this testing role. He was good; though not better, I think, than my father was.

He played the Recognition; the audience groaned and wept; I appeared upon the god-walk dressed up for my epiphany, to pro-nounce everyone's doom; and the play was done. The chorus sang the famous tag, the flutes receded; we came forward mask in hand to take our bows. When applause is noisy at Syracuse, the echo-chamber picks it up, and it goes right through one's head. Mine was aching already.

I lay down (the first man's room there has every luxury) and let my dresser sponge. He talked away, as they do, and I was glad of it. My mind was filled with darkness. I had done my best, for Dion, and the god, and my own honour; but one can't enact a living man's death without horror, when one cares for him. What he himself must feel, I could only try not to think of. I had borne enough.

Menekrates came in, a towel flung round him, his dark body gleaming with sweat. 'Niko. What can I say? That cursed mask came with the call-boy. What could I do?'

'Do?' I said. 'I never had such support from another artist in all my life. I was coming to say so. Has the sponsor come behind?'

'Not that I know.' He dipped his towel in the basin and rubbed it through his hair. 'But I've not been out looking.'

'I doubt he'll come carrying garlands. But that's the theatre.'

As I spoke the door opened, and the usual crowd came in, poets and gentlemen and courtesans and merchants and young bloods, with their attendant sycophants; and nosing among them, like rats when the cargo shifts, Government informers, and spies of various factions, mentioning the mask and asking clever questions. Menekrates and I kept saying 'Thank you, thank you,' and looking stupid. As long as we kept quiet, nothing could be charged against Menekrates. The protagonist directs; they were not to know how we had rehearsed it. As for the choregos, there was still no sign of him.

At last they all went. I was alone, putting on my street clothes, when someone came to the door. It was Speusippos.

There was only one man I had dreaded more to see. He looked worn and ill. I greeted him, and waited to suffer what must be. He was a man who could make his anger bite.

'Niko; I saw the crowd leaving, and thought you would be here.' Then he saw my blank face, and said with tired courtesy, 'I am sorry to have missed the play. I have been with Plato. I was passing, and stopped to tell you. Dion has been exiled.'

No other man, I suppose, is so full of himself as an actor just off stage. For a moment I thought he was blaming me for it. I expect no one to credit this, except another actor.

'Come,' said Speusippos, 'it could be worse, he is not dead. We shall see him in Athens.' He looked about; I told him my dresser had gone. 'You know how it's been, like dry brush waiting a spark. It happened through the Carthaginians.'

I gaped as if hearing of this race for the first time. I don't know how he kept his patience.

'I told you, he's been in touch with their envoys; he's the only man they are used to treating with, or fear in war. He was sure they would push forward if they knew he was out of power. He wrote to the envoys, men he knew, asking them to let him see their terms first in private. Someone played him false, and gave his letter to Dionysios.'

I said nothing. One needed to know no more.

'I daresay his vanity was hurt,' Speusippos said impatiently. 'But it was Philistos persuaded him that it was treason. We knew nothing of this. On the contrary, Dionysios made Dion a great show of friendship, said he regretted their late estrangement, and persuaded him to an evening stroll by the water-stairs, to talk things over. Our authority for the rest is Dionysios himself, who, as you may suppose has never stopped talking since. He spent hours with Plato, trying to justify himself. I had to leave, it was so disgusting. He wept, laid his head in Plato's lap ... I thought that I should vomit.'

'But where is Dion?'

'Gone. During the seaside walk, it seems Dionysios suddenly pulled out the letter and faced him with it. He says Dion could give no proper explanation. No doubt he gave one which stuck in Dionysios' craw; it's the truth that vexes. In any case, everything was arranged beforehand, the ship at anchor, the boat at hand. I daresay it was done in less time than I've taken to tell you. You can imagine what Plato has been suffering, not knowing what orders had really been given, and whether Dion hadn't in fact been dropped overboard with a stone tied to his feet. But of course he guessed our fears; as soon as he was in Italy, he sent a courier over. He is safe enough. But the cause, Niko – the cause!'

I had no time yet for the cause. I said, 'A courier? From Italy? Then how long has he been gone?'

'Since yesterday. Of course it has been kept from the people. That's why he was sent off so quietly.'

We talked on, I suppose. He went. I stood in the empty dressing-room, hearing the shouts of the cleaners who were sweeping down the benches, calling across the theatre. No echo of us, no footfall left. So short a time since I had wrestled with the god, with twenty thousand people, with Dion, with Philistos, with my own soul. Dion had been gone, knowing nothing of it. Philistos had not stayed away in anger; he had serious business. I sat like a grain of sand in a scraped-out bowl, listening to the grasshoppers on the hillside.

Someone coughed hoarsely. An old man stood in the doorway.

I thought he had come to clean, and told him I was just going. He paused, and shuffled his feet. I saw he had a basket with him; he had been selling figs, or sesame-cakes, or some such thing. He cleared his rusty throat again. 'Pardon me, sir. But when I was a chorus-boy, I heard Kallippides in that role. He was the best of my young day, not a doubt of that. But to my mind, you put more into it.'

After he too had gone, Menekrates came hurrying. 'Niko, I waited, I thought your Athenian friend was with you. What's the matter?'

I should be starting to laugh soon. I answered,

'In vain man's expectation;
    God brings the unthought to be,
    As here we see.

But never mind. I have had an oracle from Dionysos.' Menekrates looked at the lynx-eyed mask on its stand. 'Won't it wait till we feel stronger?'

'No, my dear, it won't wait. Never keep a god waiting. He said, "Get drunk."'

217

12

Next day, Philistos sent for me to be paid. I had lain awake half the night, thinking what I would say to him. I kept improving it, till I wished I had written the best parts down. Then I slept; and in the morning I saw I could forget all I had thought of. Menekrates' home and kin were in Syracuse. Dion, in exile, might need a messenger who was not suspect, and could come or go.

Philistos received me in his business-room. His desk was heaped with state papers, just like Dion's before. His red pouchy face, with hard little eyes in smiling folds of flesh, made me queasy, like pork when one is seasick. He greeted me as someone he had discreetly shared a joke with. As I knew, he had not been at the play, but he commended my performance. His Egyptian accountant came at his hand-clap, with a big heavy leather bag. I waited for it to be opened, but Philistos just pushed it over. It had the silver talent mark.

In recent years, I had been paid as much for one performance; once, indeed, a rival sponsor offered me even a little more to go sick and not to play. But in those days it was a sum beyond belief. No actor got such money. I paused to make sure there was no mistake. I have never been so glad in my life that a fee was big.

'Thank you,' I said, 'on behalf of the company, and myself.'

'My dear Nikeratos,' he answered, breezy as a sailor, 'your company is provided for. This is your own fee.'

This saved me the trouble of doing sums. I pushed the bag back again. 'Will you offer it, please, at the temple of Dionysos, for some dedication in my name?'

He went on smiling, but not with his little eyes. 'Have you some reason?' he said, and watched me.

'Yes, I have. I was not satisfied with my performance.'

'Everyone agrees you performed outstandingly.' He did not say it in compliment, but with hard suspicion. Having pretended he had seen me, he could hardly now go back on it.

'I think not. Conditions were against me. You have a very well-equipped theatre here; but I prefer to play where poet and artist are taken seriously.'

'What do you mean?' he said, in a voice which did not ask, but threatened.

'Portrait masks are for comedy. In tragedy they distract the audience. To spring such tricks on actors in performance is to treat us like clowns at a fair. What is this money for – my reputation? Thank you, but I'm afraid it is not enough.'

He spluttered, then forced a laugh and held forth about the vanity of artists; quite believing, now, that this was all, and, of course, that I would take it in the end. With some trouble I undeceived him, and left him admiring my self-importance. It had never struck me this might impress him, but of course he was just the man. I could see, when I left, that my consequence had been raised with him.

I would have liked to leave at once. Just as when the old Archon died, the streets were full of muttering groups; the citizens in their factions, foreigners with their kind. Now and then soldiers would go past: a great Gaul staring haughtily over people's heads, a swaggering Nubian shouting to another across the street in their unknown tongue; or a group of Romans swinging along in step together, taking everyone's size in the self-sufficient way these people have, as if wondering when they would get orders to clear the street. The mercenaries were making their good spirits known. What the citizens thought, they were not telling.

No man has less taste than I for getting caught in foreign civil wars; yet I had thought that out of all those people I had heard praising Dion's justice, someone would strike a blow for him. But no. I was in Syracuse. They waited to see what would happen to them next; they had forgotten they could themselves make happenings.

Eager as I was to be gone, I lingered, to learn if Plato was leaving. Surely he would go; but if he were delayed, he would need Speusippos with him; and, parted from Dion without a moment's warning, he must have things to write, unfit for the Archon's courier. I knew where he was lodging, at the house of a Pythagorean up on Achradina. But it seemed unwise to be seen there; I was now a caller who would be noticed. So I hung about the wine-shops for Speusippos, thinking that if he wanted a word with me he would seek me there.

On the third day of this, I met by chance a most charming person, who came up to commend my performance in the theatre. Our talk lasted all bedtime, and one thing led to another; so it was morning when I got back to the house of Menekrates. He greeted me with the news that Plato had been murdered.

'The soldiers did it,' he said quite cheerfully. 'Everyone knows they've been spoiling for a chance. They said Dion was their best general, before this windbag turned his head. Why, Niko, what's the matter? I thought you couldn't bear the man.'

I said, 'This news will kill Dion. And I shall have to bring it.' This made enough sense for Menekrates. To tell the truth, I was surprised myself at what I felt. I had not understood a word of his lecture on the One; where I did know what he was saying, about the theatre, I had thought him dangerous, as men with half a truth can be. Yet, little by little, he had stamped his mark upon my mind, like some great actor beside whom one has played extra. I recalled how his eyes had said to me 'What are you?' and had seemed to know the answer. He was gone now, and the answer with him.

I was overcome with the guilt men feel, with reason or without, at such a time, because I had spent the night in pleasure. Presently I began to ask Menekrates who had told him, and where the body was; the bones ought to be sent to Athens, and Speusippos might be alive or dead. From the replies I got, I soon realised it was all street talk, nothing first hand. This gave me some hope, knowing what Syracuse is for rumour. So I went up to the house to see.

There was no sound of mourning. I knocked and asked for Plato, making up some errand. Without going inside, the slave answered at once that I should find him in Ortygia. He was now the Archon's guest.

He must have read my face (this was no doubt a house where people talked freely) for he added that the gentleman had come to no harm so far; I could count on that, for his nephew was here upstairs, packing up his books.

Before I had time to ask for him, Speusippos came running out. If he had looked strained before, he now looked ill. 'Niko! I knew that was your voice. Don't stand in the street, come in.'

He hurried me through the inner court, and upstairs to Plato's room, now in confusion and full of smoke. The floor was littered with open book-boxes and scrolls. In the middle was a charcoal brazier, where Speusippos had been burning papers. I coughed, and went over to the window. An actor has to be careful of his throat.

'A god sent you,' he said. 'Are you going back to Athens?'

'Yes or no; according to what help you need.'

He clasped my hands, then turned away, wiping his eyes and cursing the smoke. Any small kindness will move a man who is overwrought; but philosophers are not supposed to weep.

'What happened? Where's Plato? In the Quarries?'

'God forfend! No, what you heard at the door is true, he's an honoured guest – while it lasts, for he's a prisoner too, of course. Dionysios has given him a house in the Palace Park. No one leaves the inner citadel, by land or sea, without a pass. We were half-packed to go home, when a squad of Gauls brought the invitation ... I've just come from there. You should see the place. Bronzes, books, lyre-players, boy-slaves – as full of toys as a jackdaw's cage. It's as if some bandit had captured a chaste lady and were ashamed to rape her, so kept laying his loot at her feet and begging for a word of love. One could laugh. But how will it end?'

'In the end,' I said, 'he must let him go. Where Plato is, the world is watching; the learned world, at least. Think of the scandal. The second Dionysios is not the first.'

'But you know what he wants. He wants Plato to side with him against Dion. Before he will do that, Plato will sit in Ortygia till he dies. And it might come to that. He's past sixty, Niko; this climate doesn't suit him; he's not been well. Besides, Dionysios is as fitful as a woman. It needs only some open quarrel, or public slight; then the soldiers, or Philistos' faction, will take their chance.'

'I doubt it. It's not a chance I'd care to take, after seeing them together even once. I told you before, the poor antic is in love. And so vain; he wants to be in the histories as Plato's favourite pupil, not his murderer. Tell me, when did you last eat, or sleep?'

Luckily, soon after, his host sent a tray up with wine and cakes.

We got rid of the stinking brazier, and cleared two chairs. Books were piled on everything; Plato must have brought a small library along. Even then, as I remembered, he had written to Archytas asking for more.

Speusippos looked better for the food, and started scrambling about among the litter for things he wanted sent home. The books, to my relief, were going along to Plato; but muttering to himself or me, Speusippos picked out some notes for a lecture on the Nature of the Universe, which Plato wanted Xenokrates to give for him; a scheme for a future book, which he was afraid of losing in Syracuse; and a rare work of Pythagoras for the Academy library. After looking under everything in sight, he found a pack of papers with dead flowers pressed in it. I supposed it must be some old love-token, till he reminded me he was a botanist. 'If you can get them to the Academy uncrushed, I shall be much beholden to you. There is a lad who came to us this year from Stagyra, a promising boy, who helps me with my collection; he will look after them ... By the dog, I've been so harassed, it's put his name from my mind.' He clutched his brow, then remembered and wrote it down, Aristoteles. I promised to see to it.

All this concluded, he went to the door and window before taking from his girdle a little scroll. Softly he said, 'This is the thing, Niko. The rest could go by a courier. Not this. That's why I said a god had sent you.'

I took it. It had no superscription. He said, 'I see you understand.'

Now I was charged with the errand I had come to do, I did not stay much longer, either in that house or in Syracuse: just long enough to give my company a farewell party, and bid adieu to my friend of the night before. I do not name him; he is now the head of a very ancient house, and I have never been one to kiss and brag.

There were two letters in the scroll; the inner one for Dion, the outer for Archytas of Tarentum. I pondered the best hiding-place, in case I should be searched. Opening the mask-box, I said, 'My lord Apollo, two of your servants want help. If you value this man Plato as much as people say, you will look after his affairs. I leave this in your care.'

Just before the ship cast off, some of the Romans came aboard, and searched the ship, as they said, for treasonable matters. They never looked inside the mask, though they stared right at it. The god's face must have overawed them. I concluded therefore that he did take Plato seriously, and it should be borne in mind.

Though we had a fair wind to Tarentum, the rumour of Plato's murder had got there first. Ships cross almost daily between Messene and Rhegium, whence news spreads overland. Sighting a ship with the paintwork of Syracuse, every Pythagorean in Tarentum came to the dock to ask if the tale was true. Some knew me, so came to me first. In their relief they made as much of me as if I had saved his life myself.

I was taken straight to Archytas. Like a good host, and a true philosopher, he offered me refreshment before talking business, and sat quiet as a statue by one of his model machines, though I saw his toes twitch under his robe. I told him all I had heard from Speusippos, and gave him his letter from Plato. Then I asked whether Dion had passed this way, and where he was.

He said smiling, 'Two questions, my friend, with easy answers. Yes to the first. To the second: in the room next door.' Then he said with his soldier's dignity, 'Where else would Dion go?'

He questioned me a little longer. I was surprised Dion should have stayed outside till I remembered he had only just heard that Plato was not dead. Philosophers understand each other, as actors do; of course he had to be given time to compose himself.

Just then through the window I saw him pacing in the

orchard. He was tired of waiting, and had come out to show he was ready.

I found him on a marble seat under a plum-tree bowed with fruit. I remember the lime washed bark, the heavy-sweet scent of windfalls in the long grass, the wasps humming round their juicy caves.

He was haggard, and had lost more weight than one would think possible in so few days; but the good news had pushed his griefs aside, he was calm and smiling.

I told him all I knew, adding that I did not believe the Archon would ever give countenance to Plato's death. Rather, it seemed to me he had even some excuse, and perhaps a fair one, for taking him into the citadel, because of this danger from the troops. 'In the Ortygia, everyone is accountable. Dionysios may have other motives; he is more devious than he knows himself. But that will be one, I think.'

He said, 'I wish Plato were in better health,' and fell silent, his look of caring returning. Presently he said, 'You see me, Nikeratos, a man exiled for no crime; fallen from high estate, like the characters you portray.' He smiled slightly. 'It is said that while Sokrates was awaiting death, his wife lamented that it was the injustice of it she could not bear. He answered, "Why, my dear, you would not rather I had deserved it?" But if Plato should die in Syracuse, I shall admit that though men have been unjust to me, the gods have not . . . A man more precious than empires, both to us and to men still unborn; with who knows what wisdom yet undistilled in him. He is clear of all misjudgement, except his faith in me. He had not seen Syracuse for twenty years; Dionysios he had known only as a child who rode upon my shoulder. For no living man but me, would he have gone again to Sicily. And I sent for him – this is the irony the gods themselves must laugh at – for this very thing which has made and broken all: his charm

225

that can make discourse beautiful and catch the soul through the heart. Was Oidipos himself more blind?'

I said, 'You had only seen the son in the father's shadow.'

He shook his head, then looked at me. 'Nikeratos. Is it true, as I am told, that you refused a talent of silver from Philistos, because of a certain mask?'

'Yes. It was sent without my knowledge; I saw it first on stage.'

'Well, it is rightly said that there is good in every state of man. In misfortune, one can count one's friends.' Of course he had been new to exile and disgrace when this news had come, so it had touched him. Instead of shutting his door to me for ever, he had opened even his heart.

I wondered if he was in need, and how one could go about offering help to so proud a man. But he now told me he would be taking a house in Athens. From policy, or decency, or just because he could never have faced Plato else, Dionysios had had clothes and money put in the exile's boat, and not landed him at Rhegium like a castaway. He had been told, too, that his goods and household slaves would be sent him. This would enable him to live like a gentleman, by the standards of Athens; but one can't ship land abroad, and unless his yearly revenues came too, he would not be rich; or not as Sicily understands it.

His wife Arete, Dionysios' half-sister, had written confirming that his money and movables would follow; but it was clear, since he said nothing of it, that she was not coming to share his exile. He spoke of her, as it seemed to me, with pity rather than long-ing. It was said to be a state alliance, which had never warmed up in the marriage bed. I recalled his study, so like Plato's, a man's room well-kept by men.

'Dionysios will not harm her,' he said. 'But I am most anxious for my brother Megakles. He has never concerned himself with philosophy; but he is a man of honour, who would revenge an insult to our house, as Philistos knows very well. If he is wise, he must be in flight from Syracuse already, before he meets a knife in the dark. And above all, there is my son.'

I said that if Dionysios had been ashamed to offer the father violence, he would scarcely harm so young a lad, his own kindred too. Dion said, 'Not in his body, I daresay. But my wife will go back to her brother's house, and take him with her. I would wish him anywhere else on earth. He is restless; easily led; impatient of correction; he shows no bent to philosophy.'

'He must be young,' I said, 'for that?' I suppose a man of Dion's life and standards would expect a good deal from his son.

He was staying on a while, he said, at Tarentum, to await news of his brother and to enjoy the company of his friends. 'I had forgotten,' he said, 'that such peace as this existed.' His goods and servants would be shipped here; he would have a good deal of business; so he accepted my offer to take his letters to Athens. My ship was loading cargo, and would be there until next day.

I called next morning. He was sitting at his window which overlooked the orchard, listening to the chorus of the birds, late and sleepy with autumn. The air smelled of the turning year, and in the eaves a dove was cooing. He told me that yesterday, after I left, he had had good news. His brother Megakles had been hidden by family friends, as soon as they knew of Dion's exile. He had got a ship at Katana, which had just touched at Tarentum on its way to Corinth. He had sailed straight on there, where he had friends, but had called to tell Dion he was safe, and had managed to bring a good deal of money with him. They would meet again in Athens.

It was the seventh of the month, Apollo's day, and the Tarentines were offering a choral dance to the god. I had just time to hear it, before we sailed. The music was very fine; all strings though, for Pythagoreans think that flutes confuse the cosmic order (or some such matter) and disturb the soul. Young boys dressed in white, and crowned with bay-leaves, circled an altar of honey-coloured marble wreathed with a garland of gilded bronze. The lyre answered the kithara; a light breeze blew from the sea. The last sight I had of Dion, he was standing like a marble hero on the steps before the temple porch, tall and straight among tall straight columns, the cool autumn sunshine on his face. It seemed to me that once Plato was safe and free, he could even be happy.

On my voyage out, Archytas had promised to reward me, if I brought useful news from Syracuse. Among all my concerns this had slipped my mind; but he himself was not one to forget such things, and he made me a most handsome present, saying it was partly a good-tidings gift, no man having ever brought him better. What with this, and the profit from the tour, I might not be as rich as Philistos would have made me, but I would get along well enough.

Plato was in Syracuse all that winter.

Sometimes I surprised myself by the trouble I took to get news of him. Once it would just have been for Dion's sake, or perhaps Axiothea's. Even now, as was natural, I still resented him sometimes; but found I could not indulge it without feeling small. When I had seen him sitting with young Dionysios, seeing all through him, yet patient as a shepherd with a sickly lamb, and fearless of the wolves around, I had known the man was noble. The day stuck in my mind, when I had brought Dion's letter urging him to go. Actors are vain; it's true even of the best; but one does not feel one's talent, even when most pleased with it, as a burden one must bear in trust for other men. It was not pride in him; he knew. I thought of it often.

Megakles, Dion's brother, was living in Corinth, a city where Syracusans feel at home; but Dion himself had bought an estate near the Academy, beyond the olive groves. The house was just the proper size for someone of his rank in Athens; his Syracusan one would have looked hubristic. But with his beautiful things set up there, it seemed just the same. He asked me to supper once or twice, when he was entertaining poets and their friends; though not, of course, on his philosophic evenings.

Speusippos having stayed with Plato, the Academy was being run by Xenokrates, so, knowing what he thought of actors, I did not intrude. When news of Plato came in, Axiothea would send me a message to meet her in the olive grove, or by some hero-tomb in the Sacred Way. If the news was short, and would have gone into her note, we did not notice it. We had got fond of one another; though she liked the calm spare life of the Academy, she liked, too, to hear of the world outside, from someone who did not disapprove. She was setting into a strange archaic beauty; I have seen such faces in old shrines, there is an Artemis at Aigina very like her.

The Messene strait being so narrow, ships cross all winter in any but the worst of weather; so the Syracusan Pythagoreans could keep their brethren posted. They were in touch with Speusippos, who came and went somehow from Ortygia; no doubt Dionysios, who had always been jealous of him, would have been well pleased if he had slipped off. But he put up with the snubs and slights, which I could well imagine, to be with Plato and to link him with his friends.

At first the news was good; Dionysios was heaping him with honour, entertaining him, deferring to his advice. He had been able to realise Archytas' dearest wish, by recommending a peace treaty with the Tarentines, which was already signed.

Archytas' letters were full of this; Speusippos' own were a good deal franker. He made them cryptic with false names, and, for greater safety, addressed them to people outside the Academy, sometimes to me. When he got home, he was at pains to get them back and burn them, in case Plato ever saw them; but I kept this one. The device was his usual one, of someone gossiping about a fashionable hetaira.

Everyone is amazed at the conduct of young Damiskos. When first he courted Heliodora, he vowed no price would be too high. [The price meant accepting Plato's precepts.] Having now drawn back, one would think he might have more pride than to hang about her door and keep sending flowers. Lately she asked him why, if he still desired her friend-ship, he did not pay up like a man, since he could afford it. And his answer? That his friends had advised him her price would encumber his estate; he wanted to beat her down. How absurd, to someone of her fame and reputation! She is gener-ous in conversing with the youth, whose manners can do with polishing; but that he should presume to be jealous, is as vex-atious as it is laughable.

The other day there was an absurd, but painful scene. She was spending a quiet hour at her music, when he rushed in, and offered her the direction of his whole inheritance. A gift more to himself than her, for she would do it to his advantage. By now she knows him better than to be transported; she waited to hear more. Can you guess the rest? His condition was that she should shut her door to Dikaios, her friend of twenty years, and proclaim this coxcomb as her favourite. She behaved, as I need not tell you who know her, with the great-est dignity. He left, I think, ashamed. But the folly and the turmoil made her feel ill, and she made no more music that day. I am sorry to say that she is not well, and this did nothing to improve things.

A few days later, the fears this letter had raised were realised. Archytas wrote that Plato was very sick, perhaps to death; for so concerned was Dionysios, he had sent his own wife to nurse him.

Speusippos' code-letters ceased; nothing mattered but Plato's life, and he wrote openly to Xenokrates. Just when things looked worst, news stopped for nearly half a month, because the winter storms had cut off Tarentum from Korkyra.

Dion had made many friends in Athens. They called to express sympathy and ask for news; when he had company I did not like to trouble him. At first he seemed glad to see me; I was the only one who had been there, and could picture, nearly as well as he could, what was going on. He was too proud to show his feelings among his new acquaintance, as he had to me at Tarentum. After a while, even with me he grew withdrawn, and I left him in peace, asking news from Axiothea.

At last, a ship got through. Archytas wrote, enclosing back letters from Speusippos. Plato was on the mend. The Archon's wife had tended him like a daughter. Perhaps she had been sent to watch that no one poisoned him, or laid the pillow on his face. At all events, it did not seem Dionysios himself could have been better cared for.

It was with an easier mind, therefore, that I went into rehearsal for the Lenaia. I had been chosen early in the draw, and offered the lead in a new play by Aphareus, *Atalanta in Kalydon*.

I liked the play. It had fine acting roles, both for Atalanta and Meleager. His part was most tempting, with a lovely scene where he lies dying, while his stern mother Althaia burns the magic faggot that holds his life. I could have used in it all those effects which had made such a hit in *Orpheus*. The fact was that I could see more in

232

the Atalanta, which had much subtlety and truth, but did not want to own it. In a female lead, I would be measured against Theodoros.

He had been chosen at once by the sponsor who drew first pick, with such alacrity that there must be some perfect role for him; no knowing what, for new plays are well-kept secrets. Though still fairly young, he was at the height of his powers; if women, which the gods forbid, were allowed to play in tragedy, I am sure the best of them could not have spoken for her sex more movingly, or with more fire, than he. It would be wise to take Meleager, and make the best of it.

I was sitting at home with the play in my hands, wondering how to get the most from the death-scene, when I felt a pair of eyes staring at my back. Unwillingly I turned, knowing too well what I would see. The sun was westering; the mask stared out into full light, stern, radiant, without pity.

I went over, and looked reproachful. But he only laughed at me, in the dark behind his eyes. So I chose Atalanta, doubling it with Queen Althaia, and asked for Anaxis as Meleager. I was glad to offer him something, for he was then very dejected; he had lately risked half his savings in a tradeship to the Euxine, which had gone down. Land prices kept rising, the more he saved; this had been his last chance of buying back his father's land. Now he was back almost where he started. (Things have changed since then. He owns the family estate, and has bought the next-door farm, since he took up politics.)

I enjoyed rehearsals. Once I was played-in, I stopped wondering what Theodoros might be doing, and thought only what I would do. It was a part with plenty of light and shade; complex, spirited, harshly tragic, with a noble close.

At the Presentation, Theodoros and his company appeared with golden wreaths, showing they had a rich choregos, and the title of their play was given out: *Ariadne Forsaken*.

Well, I thought, there's the thing settled. He can't miss with that if he tries. The crown will have to have the judges' tears dried off it, before he puts it on.

I felt dashed for an hour or two; but it was only what I had expected, and losing to Theodoros, at least one lost to someone good. It was not like being beaten by modish tricks.

It was so-so weather on the day of the performance. We drew second turn to play, and Theodoros was on last. It was blowing, threatening rain, and clearing up by turns all day; I don't think it favoured any one play above the others.

Now I knew where the crown was going, I put it out of my mind, and just played for my own enjoyment, and for that of people, like Axiothea, whose judgement I respected. At the end, we were quite pleased with our reception. That's done, I thought, as I stripped and got dressed; now I'll watch Theodoros, and not give way to jealousy. It keeps one from learning, and one can't see such an artist every day.

As always, he was a pleasure when he only walked across the stage. Moreover, the play had clearly been written for him. If another sponsor had got him first, whoever they had drawn would have had to play Theodoros. But the poet had got the real one; and given him nothing to do but play himself. Every effect he had ever melted the theatre with, was written in for poor Ariadne. You would have thought he was a juggler in need of five balls and a stool to do his act, not an artist who wanted stimulus. He did his best to give it freshness, but it was like seasoning stale fish. All the same, he was such a delight to hear that I felt sure he must have won, until the herald gave out that I had.

So I had to get on my costume again, and be crowned, and make my bow; then back to the dressing-room, with the crowd about me. I was just combing my hair, when a voice behind cried,

'My dear! Superb! It killed me to miss the end, I was almost too late to dress.'

It was Theodoros. We had met once or twice at parties, but he was always surrounded, and I hardly knew him. He took me by the shoulders and kissed me on both cheeks. No one in the business had a bad word for Theodoros, and now I could see why.

'I sat there, my dear,' he said, 'quite hating you for having that lovely role and knowing what to do with it. But I had to give in like all the rest.'

I knew enough to be honoured by this foolery. His dignity could be freezing; he stood no nonsense from the richest of sponsors, nor, I believe, from kings. He kept this kind of thing for equals.

'May I come to your party? A married woman, dear, even though forsaken. A girl from the country needs a chaperone, among all these horrid men.'

So began our friendship, which lasted till his death. There was only one shadow on the day, one of those unlucky chances. Dion, while in Athens, attended all the sacred festivals, including those of Dionysos; he would have thought it uncouth to slight the customs of his hosts. But I had never thought for a moment he might come back-stage. This however, he did. The play had not offended his morals or his piety, and he had been struck, it seems, by my performance as old Althaia, when she repeats her vengeance after having destroyed her son. What with this and that, he decided to greet me; but by the time he made up his mind to it, the other gentlemen had gone; it was mostly actors and hetairas and old friends; and Theodoros, who had hated his own role, was burlesquing it, kneeling on a table for the Naxian shore, with words of his own invention. When Dion was seen in the doorway, the skene-room hushed like a class when the headmaster enters. Theodoros changed in a flash from a screaming whore to an ambassador, but still too late. Shocked as he must have been, Dion's courtesy never faltered, and he said his piece. For an instant our eyes met, his saying, 'How can you endure this life?' and mine, 'You might try to understand.' But I don't expect it was worse than his supposings, which had not prevented his former kindness. He soon forgave me, and greeted me as before.

From the Lenaia to the Dionysia never seems very long. I had a good role, but so this time did Theodoros; he won, and well deserved to win; and without him I might still have lost to Philemon. But I had been well received; I was now a leading man sponsors wanted, and felt well enough content. Soon after, a letter came to my house from Dion, speaking gracefully of my performance, then saying. 'You will I know share our rejoicing at the news of Plato's return. He is already in Tarentum, and sails for Athens with the first fair wind.'

It was not the return of spring sailing weather which had persuaded Dionysios to part with Plato. The cause was war.

Dion, from his knowledge of the Carthaginians, had tried to keep them ignorant of his fall from power; but the upshot was, they had learned he was an exile who could neither help nor harm them. Their envoys treated with Dionysios and Philistos; they distrusted the second, and despised the first. All winter they prepared for war; they attacked in spring.

Speusippos told me later the tale of those winter months. While Plato was sick, all Syracuse remarked that the Archon seemed more concerned than when his own father lay dying. But the danger past, Plato was barely on his feet again when once more he was worn out with scenes, always with this same demand to be first among his friends. Speusippos, who had had all he could stand and more, said it was like a young boy at school enamoured of another, but owned that the wretched fellow seemed really to be suffering.

A base man would have flattered him; a man of more common virtues put him quickly out of hope. But for Plato, who was used to young men loving him, this was the first step towards philosophy; he would have thought shame to reject it, just for his own peace of mind. Patiently and selflessly, he used that charm which Dion had remembered for twenty years, to make his jailer captive. Speusippos said it was like a dialogue between bird and fish, each calling from an element the other could not live in. To the one, the crown of love was excellence; to the other it was possession.

'His father has a good deal to answer for,' I said. 'As long as he lived, the poor wretch was never allowed an hour of self-esteem. Now he comes like a starving man to an elegant symposion, grabbing without manners. Put it down to poverty.'

'I don't suppose,' said Speusippos impatiently, 'he had half the troubles in his youth that Plato did. The war, the siege, the death of friends in battle and by the hands of friends; his kinsmen killed as tyrants, and execrated to this day – and then Sokrates, whom he loved and honoured above all men, murdered in form of law ... But never mind; the man who squeals gets all the pity. At all events, he kept telling Dionysios that the way to his regard led through philosophy; and Dionysios kept replying that Dion must be first disowned, else how should he know he was being advised to his own advantage? Philistos' faction had warned him he was just being softened to make way for Dion's usurpation. He wanted evidence of good faith.'

This startled even me. 'By the dog! How did Plato swallow such insults?'

'Insults are given by men. One doesn't strike a whining child when it tugs one's clothes.'

'Perhaps,' I said. 'But sometimes he has his wits about him.'

'Quite true. That's why Plato struggled all this while. But he is a child in his soul. A stepchild, rather.'

Even when the spring brought war, he was very unwilling to let Plato go. Speusippos had been desperate; for the Archon would have to show himself in the field; and, left alone in Ortygia among his enemies, Plato would have been lucky to live a week. He knew this, but kept his fortitude, and took care to show no dismay. Urging his long absence from the Academy, and his need for a change of climate, at last he prevailed on Dionysios to part with him; but only in exchange for a pledge, that if Dion were recalled from exile, he too would return to Syracuse. Thus for his friend's sake, with both eyes open, for the third time he put his life at risk.

I saw him soon after he got home, at a concert in the Odeion. He stooped more; he was sallow, and had lost a good deal of weight; his wrestler's shoulders looked bony, and deep lines were carved beside his mouth. But a fine head. Leanness showed up its structure. Hagnon said he would like to paint him, though he would be a better subject for bronze.

At the last he, and even Speusippos, had been sent off with a load of guest-gifts and every mark of honour. Plato, if he would have taken it, could have had a fortune in Sicilian gold, either for himself or for the Academy, of which it would have delighted Dionysios to be a patron; but endowments were never taken except from those who had embraced its precepts. Rather than give outsiders the power to interfere, Plato would have taught in the streets like Sokrates before him. None the less, one thing was clear: whereas Plato had left old Dionysios as a wronged man without obligations (except to revenge, if he had not been above it) he was bound now to the son by the sacred ties of guest-friendship, and I wondered what that would lead to later.

I had meant to arrange a tour that year. But I found I had so many offers that engagements kept me busy. I played at Ephesos and Miletos, and while there was asked to Pergamon. And at Delphi, at the Pythian Festival, by Apollo's favour I got the crown. As I bent my head for it, I heard from high up over the

Phaidriades the scream of an eagle; maybe the very one who had shouted 'Yaah!' at me as I dangled on the crane.

This was my last tour with Anaxis. We still got on pretty well; but he was a disappointed artist now, and the only thing which kept him from growing bitter was the hope of a career in politics. Since this was so, I did not try to dissuade him, and even let him practise orations on me, the sort of exercise they teach in the schools of rhetoric for making, as they so frankly put it, the worse cause sound like the better. This shows, I think, what I will do for my friends.

Once an actor gets known, he does a good deal of travelling; but in the next few years, Dion travelled at least as much as I.

One saw him at all great festivals; at Olympia, Delphi, Epidauros, Delos; always with a crowd about him, always some distinguished person's honoured guest. For this reason or that, he was everybody's hero. Most tyrants on seizing power start off by murdering the aristocracy; so conservatives are as tyranno-phobe as democrats, and Dion was all that they admired. His political aims had been moderate; his hands were clean; he had never stooped to use spies or knife-men, nor roused mobs to riot; all the gentry of Hellas praised his antique virtues. Even the Spartans gave him the freedom of their city, and they Dionysios' allies, because of his reverence for law and the sacred bonds of kinship. Yet he was beloved too by all the democrats, having opposed a tyrant and suffered exile. You could not go wrong anywhere if you praised Dion. I got almost ashamed to do it.

He bore fame as nobly as misfortune. He could wear his hon-ours without fear, being what he seemed, with nothing to hide that could help his enemies. Philosophers dedicated major works to him; poets brought him into heroic odes. His distin-guished presence, his great change of fortune greatly endured, his wealth (for his revenues came over every year, a vast sum by Attic reckoning), his links with the Academy, brought credit everywhere to the philosophic life. Living sparely himself, he could open both hands to others. His forecourt was crowded with petitioners; he was a liberal patron of the arts. I think it was the second year of his exile that Plato put on a choral ode in the contest at the Dionysia, making it known that Dion had financed it, as a gesture of thanks for Athenian hospitality. The costumes were splendid, green patterned with vine-sprays worked in gold, with a gold vine-wreath for the flautist. The music was in the Dorian mode, Plato and Dion being agreed, like all Pythagoreans, in thinking the Lydian too emotional. The good breeding with which they shared the public applause was much admired.

This was a good Dionysia too for me. I got the lead in a revival of Euripides' *Chrysippos*, the play it is said he wrote while he was courting Agathon. Doubling Chrysippos' lover Laios and the wicked stepmother, I got the prize, the first I had won at the greater festival. The sponsor gave a splendid party. I did not presume to ask Dion, his friends being all so distinguished now, but he looked in with Speusippos. The two were much in company; Axiothea confided to me that Plato favoured it, thinking it would loosen the proud shyness which often caused Dion to be misunderstood. Praise left him at a loss for answers, which made people think him cold, especially the democrats. But now he seemed more at ease than before, smiled oftener, and stayed at the party longer than I had expected. The truth is, I thought, he is an Athenian in his soul. Young Dionysios did him a good turn in the end. He thrives on exile.

One heard little from Sicily; few artists were going, because of the war, which dragged on some years. I could not learn that either side made much out of it. The Greeks lost no major cities, which they owed I think to Philistos; though a bad man, and getting old, he was a soldier and knew his trade.

These were good years for me. I could do the work I wanted. I had worked hard and gone short to make this beginning; for it is that, and not an end. But I had more than my work to live for.

I had bought a house near the Kephissos, just out of town; a pleasant place, not too fashionable, in reach of friends but not in the path of time-wasters. The garden ran to the river; birds sang in the willows, and at night one heard the stream. There were orchards and small vineyards between the houses; the road was quiet, so that passers-by drew a second glance. At sun-up, when I did my practice, there would often be someone loitering. Then it stopped, and I forgot it, till one day as I did change-of-pitch I found that I had an echo. I went on as if I had noticed nothing, and finished with a speech, then slipped quickly out at the back. Against the wall, where its corner had hidden him from my window, a boy was standing, softly running my last speech over, to fix it fresh in his mind. He had got every inflection and rise and fall, just so.

When I coughed, he jumped a foot and went white. Reassuring him as best I could, I asked him in. He was a big-boned lad, with high hollow cheekbones and grey eyes, and the auburn hair of the north. Though scarcely past the awkward age, he knew how to manage his big hands and feet, and kept his head up. I invited him to share my breakfast, which my man had just brought in, and asked how long he had wanted to be an actor. As red, now, as if scalded, he answered 'Since first I saw a play.' He would not tell me his given name, saying no Athenian could pronounce it. 'They call me Thettalos.'

'Well,' I said, 'you speak good Attic, which is right if you want to act.' Then, putting in the soft northerns's, 'When did you come from Thessaly?'

'That was my father,' he answered. 'I was born here myself; and we are citizens since last year.' But of course, while a metic, he had not been eligible for chorus work at the sacred festivals, so though now eighteen he was quite without experience, and had picked up all he knew from sitting in front, or in ways like this today. His father would do nothing to help; he had come south with little, in flight from one of his country's oppressive local lords, and worked hard till he owned a riding-school. He was waiting, none too patiently, for the boy to outgrow his nonsense.

'It seems,' I said, 'that you chose me to be your teacher. So why not have come to me, and asked for help?'

'I meant to,' he said, as if I should have understood. 'But I was waiting till I was better.'

At these words I refrained from singing a paean, or embracing him, but asked where he went to practise. He just walked, he said, till he found an empty field. 'Let me hear something,' I told him. 'Do what you like.'

I thought he would go straight into Electra or Antigone or Ajax, and tear himself to bits. But no. He gave me a speech for the third actor, young Troilos pleading to Achilles for his life. Not only did he know his limits, he turned them to account; he was the youth who would not see his manhood. There was no soft-ness, nothing pretty, but under the pathos a muted terror as he read the doom in Achilles' eyes. I could have sworn I saw the relentless figure standing over him; the placing of his gestures shaped it out of air. He would die with his scream unuttered, because he was a prince of Troy, and had despaired in time. When it was over, he sat back on his heels, a light sweat on his brow, and waited for me to speak.

I forget what I first said. For just then I saw his eyes look up past my shoulder, caught and held. I had no need to turn. I knew where the mask hung in its shrine. It was just as if a look had passed between them, of recognition, or of complicity.

They say that Daidalos, the first artificer, saw his apprentice would surpass him and threw him off the roof. In the soul of every artist the murderer's ghost lives on. Some make an honoured guest of him; some chain him, and bolt the door, but know that he is not dead. Well, I could not have been cruel to this boy. That was not in me. There are things, however, one can do and live on with the thought of it. One can say, 'You show great promise, but it's useless to start till you have more range. Come back when you are twenty.' That would have wasted his time and got him stale, and put back his career five years. But having seen him without the mask as he spoke for Troilos, I knew I could do better for myself than that: 'My dear boy, I think you have a future, when you have lived a little. What you need is to feel, to know the passions. Come back at sundown; we will have a little supper, and talk it over.' ... There are more ways of killing a bird than wringing its neck.

Once more he looked past me, and I saw that meeting of silent eyes. Though they only spoke to one another, they spoke to me. No good ever came, I thought, of robbing a god, and this one above all.

'Well, Thettalos,' I said, 'I think you have learned as much as you will manage from behind a wall. It's time you got up on a stage. Tell me what kind of man your father is, and I will do my best with him. There's not much time; I am taking a company to Epidauros a month from now, and I shall need an extra.'

This, then, is how the god acquired his servant Thettalos, an artist seldom surpassed; at his best, unequalled in our day. It was a few years yet, though, before he knew himself, coming to the art so late. He was uncertain; scared often of his own force. It was like training a nervous blood-horse.

Our play for the Epidaurian Festival was *Iphigeneia at Aulis*. From the first I let him understudy the third roles, which include the name-part; with only a little more technique, he would have been better than the man I had. At first I took him through the lines once or twice alone. Soon I thought better not. He played it all from the heart, knowing no other way; he was so eager, mulling half the day over everything I taught him; his eyes were flecked with green, and his chestnut brows met in fine down above them; in a word, he was starting to break my rest. But he was using himself so hard, and stretched so taut, that I dared not disturb him. Besides, he was both proud and honest; and his whole life, as he must see it, was in my power. I waited. Some god said to me that a time would come.

We made a hit at Epidauros. What with the festival, the beauty of the theatre, and his first appearance, he was quite drunk with joy; I was relieved that he kept his head. After the performance, I took him sightseeing. Going up to the portico of the Asklepieion, we met Dion coming out. He seldom missed these great occasions. Though men of note were pressing round him, he stopped and greeted me, spoke well of the production, and had a gracious word for Thettalos when I presented him. He, as soon as we were alone, said 'Who was that?' I told him Dion's story, adding, 'There goes the best man of our age.'

He followed my eyes, then broke out suddenly, 'Yes, and how he agrees with you.'

'My dear boy!' I said, quite startled, for though frank he was never impudent. 'What a thing to say. His modesty is proverbial.'

'And he knows that too.' He kicked a pebble, and swallowed a curse when it hurt his toe. I could see no cause for this sudden anger, which was quite unlike him; but took it he was over-wrought.

'You mistake him,' I said. 'He is shy by nature; but he is a man of too much pride to own it.'

'Why not? Who is he to be proud with you? You're just as great as he is. Why, the first time you spoke to me, I thought I should stifle before I could get my breath to answer you. Even now, if it weren't that I—' He broke off, red to the ears, almost swallowing his tongue backwards, and looking round like a thief for somewhere to run. I just put my hand behind his arm, and quietly walked him on. In silence we said everything.

So the god rewarded us. It may be that when I am dead, if he lives his span, he will hand on, to the young men coming after, small things I taught him. Since memories die with men, that's as near as one gets to immortality.

Success brought his father round; before long, he could leave home without discord, and live with me. Even before that, we were never long parted, and could do as we liked on tour. As I said, those were happy years.

Young as he was, he could manage everything except the heavies, and that came before long. He was, and I think will always be, one of those actors in whom feeling works like intellect, so clearly it forms its concepts. They have it straight from the god; they give reasons if you ask, but those came later. But he was greedy for technique; born knowing why, he had to know how before he could bring it forth; and his reverence for me was touching. He would come to the end of it soon, I thought; what then? Meantime we read The Myrmidons, talked half the night, and taught each other; for the thoughts he threw off while we walked, or ate, or lay in bed were full of careless wealth.

At about this time, Speusippos married a young wife, a niece of Plato's. He seemed contented, and praised her to me. I don't know how much she saw of him, between his work and his diversions. As for Dion, I met him often, as I had at Epidauros. I could never think without a smile of Thettalos' betraying jealousy; Dion had come as our god of luck, as the lad himself admitted; adding that no doubt he had been unjust, for what could he know of such a man? To me it seemed that Dion, though a king in exile, was still a king; he might lead no armies, but men would serve him with their minds, for by believing in him they could believe better in themselves.

As I said, the people round him were of many different kinds; gentlemen, soldiers, philosophers, politicians. He joined the best supper-clubs; and it was at one of these, I think, that he renewed his friendship with Kallippos, who had been his co-initiate at Eleusis. I myself had known the man rather longer; he was often about the theatre. One met him at all the sponsors' parties, and in the skene-room after the play. He had often paid me compliments, which would have pleased me more if he had not been just as ready with them after a bad performance. It gives me no joy to be praised at the expense of a better artist, by someone who does not know the difference or who thinks me too vain to be aware of it myself. After a while, I used to acknowledge his civility, and leave him, so to speak, hung up with the other masks.

His real interests were political; politics were the first things he looked for in a play. One that was only true to man's nature, bad and good, he found insipid. He was a sand-coloured man, with eyes like shallow sand-pools, which he would fix on one as if to say that he read one's soul. Knowing, as I did at home, what such a gaze is really like, I was hard-put to it sometimes not to laugh in his face. I don't know what he read in me; his readings of others were often out, but when this appeared, he put it down to dissimulation, a quality he saw everywhere.

I had a good deal of attention from Kallippos, because I had been in Sicily. Actors and hetairas, in different ways, hear about affairs if they have time to listen, and Kallippos knew it. Charissa the Delian, an old friend of mine, told me he never chose a girl for looks or erotic skill, but according to her clientele, which he took pains to learn beforehand.

Actors and whores, though he found them useful, were passing concerns for him. He had more serious business at the Academy, where he hung on the fringe, attending the lectures and discussions on political theory, but (as Axiothea told me when I asked her) finding no time for those upon philosophy, or the nature of the soul. Such being his interests, he was sure to seek out Dion; and though I was sorry to see him in the company of anyone so much beneath his quality, I could understand it. Kallippos took colour from his company, if it sufficiently impressed him. And he was a true hater of tyrants. In this he did not dissemble. He was a hater of many things, beginning I think with himself; but tyrants he had made a study of, and could tell you all their histories, right back to the Peisistratids and Periander. Dion, as I have said, had become for all Hellas the symbol of resistance to all tyranny. He was as a god, therefore, to Kallippos, who showed him a true face, whereas he only made use of men like me. Even fulsomeness, when the heart is in it, does not disgust the just man like sycophancy. I have no doubt, too, that the information Kallippos had picked up in the skeneroom or the stews, was believed by gentlemen and philosophers to be the fruit of insight and logic. As for his adulation, Dion was used to that. It met him everywhere.

Meantime, a year as third actor had been enough for Thettalos. Within three years of his joining me, I took him on as second; not just for love, but because I could have done no better. Often I felt like Arion; after the song, after the splendid dolphin swims up at call, comes the breathless searide, feeling the creature's power curbed by its tenderness, yet awaiting the moment when it knows only its own strength and the grace Apollo gave it, and with some great leap or dive is gone into the glassy green, leaving one to swim. He was obedient always. When he had talked me round to his own way of thinking, he would say how wonderful was our harmony, and so I am sure he saw it. When I insisted on my own interpretation, he supported me with all he had. His loyalty was perfect. But there is a curse on him who holds back the messengers of the gods. In the depth of night, the moon at the window would show me his face intent upon a dream; I would think, He will outgrow me and excel me, and leave me to love him still.

In the fifth year of Dion's exile, news came that the war in Sicily was over. It had dragged to a standstill, and ended in a draw. I think the Carthaginians, who are unloved by all their neighbours, had trouble at home in Africa. At all events they got tired, and there was a patched-up peace.

That same year, as soon as sailing weather opened up the sea roads, the Sicilian ambassador called at the Academy. He had a letter from Dionysios, entreating Plato to visit Syracuse.

As you may suppose, Plato asked at once whether Dion, then, had been recalled. The ambassador said that no doubt during Plato's visit there could be fruitful discussions of all such matters. On this Plato declined with thanks, and went back to his studies. As Speusippos said, he detested the very thought of Syracuse. He was now rising seventy, not an age when men lightly go on voyages, with their stale food, bad water, hard beds and the chance of storms. At that time of life a man must take some care of his body, to get the best from his mind.

The peace, though troublesome to Plato, was good news to theatre men, and many tours were being planned. For myself, I too had seen enough of Sicily, at least without Dion there. *The Bacchae* had been a bellyful which still lay heavy. So Thettalos and I went east; we played in Ephesos, Lesbos, Samos, Halikarnassos and Miletos, and toured the chief cities of Rhodes.

The old mask-box went with us. I never left it behind. But each time I hung it up upon the wall, it seemed that the face within was saying, 'Nikeratos, you have something of mine. I have been your friend; but do not tempt me.'

The grapes were trodden; winter came, we went by torchlight to bright rooms, then home to lie warm and discuss the party. The Lenaia came; then the Dionysia. It was one of the years I got the crown.

On a warm spring evening, two days after the feast, we sat on the grass by the river-bank, upon one cloak. A thrush swung and sang in the hanging willow. I said, 'Do you love me as before?'

He said, 'What? Niko, how can you ask me such a thing? What has made you doubt it?' I could not bear to see his look of guilt, so undeserved.

'My dear,' I said, 'I have never doubted less. You have good proof at the Dionysia. But there are proofs love dies of giving; it is better to keep hold of love. So you must join another company.'

His eyes were like a sick man's, who hears from the doctor what he already knew. He wanted to be angry; it crossed his face and he let it go. When he spoke, it was as if we had been talking of this an hour already. 'No, Niko, it's no use; I can't do it. How can I go? We should be forever parting, for half the year. Besides, it's too soon. It's not in reason I can be ready.' It was not with me he was contending; I might have known the god had been hounding him as well. 'It's you who can get the best from me. Who else would push me on as you've done? Wherever could I do better?'

'Henceforward, anywhere. You know it. Name me one other actor, one, for whom you would have underplayed as you did this time.'

'Now you're absurd,' he said, pulling up grass by the roots. 'In a contest, nobody steals from the protagonist. I should hope I know that. I am sure you never did so.'

'Not so as to get pointed at. But one shows what one could do. Come, my dear, you understand me.'

'Say I don't wish to. In the name of the god, Niko, what do you want to make of me? From you I have had everything. If at last I've something to give, don't you think I want to give it? Before I can even begin, you start saying no. You make me angry.' He did an angry gesture, to show he meant it. I had never loved him more.

'What was yours I have taken gladly. But the time has come, and you have seen it, when you are giving me what is *his*.' I had only to move my head towards the room behind us. We had shared that secret from early days. 'He will punish it,' I said. 'There is no escaping him.'

'He owes you something. Is he less grateful than a man?'

'He cannot change his nature, which can light or burn. We are scorched already, my dear. You have felt it too. All through rehearsals, through the contest, all through the victory-feast, you give and give, you behave perfectly. Then later your oil-flask is mislaid, and it enrages you. So it will be; and in two years we shall have nothing. Let us obey the god and keep his blessing. The time is now.'

This had come hard to both of us; having braved it, we were both in pain; but it was the pain of the cautery, not the poison; in our hearts we both knew it would be worth the cost. We disputed a little longer, both knowing the outcome now, but offering it as a mark of love; then talked of the past, sharing our memories. But the thing must be finished clean, so presently I said, 'Summer tours will be starting soon. You must be looking round.' To tease him I added, 'What about Theophanes? You'd have the heart to steal from him.'

He laughed; we were laughing easily now, as people do after strain. 'Theophanes would never let me in a mile of him. He likes his supports made of solid wood.'

'To be serious: Miron is getting no younger, and he feels his limits. He is looking for a second who can take more work. Of course all his plays will have some big oldish role, for him; but you will get some very good parts which are past him now. He's a man of the old tradition; but you'll fare no worse in the end from knowing how Kallippides did it in the ninety-third Olympiad or Kleomachos in the hundredth. He is quite well-liked, if you can put up with his superstition and eternal omens.'

'I don't mind other men's omens,' he said. 'I watch my own.'

'His greatest virtue in my eyes is that he only likes young girls.'

'I don't mind his likes. I know my own.' He added softly, 'I'm not one to go drinking vinegar after wine.'

So we talked, and slept, and next day he signed his contract. They were soon rehearsing; he would come home full of talk; we were happy like autumn grasshoppers, living from day to day. Then Miron fixed up a tour to Delos and the Cyclades; of a sudden they had sailed, and his absence lay everywhere, like a fall of snow.

I ought to have found a new second before he left. I had known this, but kept putting off. With every day of missing him, I grew harder to please. I turned down a good offer from Macedon, and drifted, passing the time. It could not go on; I made up a short-term company, and went to Corinth for the Isthmia. Work made me more like myself; when the games were over, I stayed with old friends awhile, and went back to Athens resolved to get my life in order.

Theodoros exclaimed that I was getting dreadfully thin, and gave a party for me, at which he produced all the handsome youths he could think of who were free just then. Though they went as free as they came, I was grateful for the kindly thought, and sorry to disappoint him by leaving with Speusippos. But he had let me know he had things to tell me, which would not do in a crowd.

As soon as we were alone, but for his link-boy walking ahead, I asked his news. He said, 'The Academy's by the ears. No one knows how it will end. Dionysios has written again for Plato.'

'Does it matter? He wrote last year, and Plato told him to go and play with it, or whatever philosophers say instead.' I had got rather drunk at the party.

Speusippos, who had sobered quickly, said, 'I think, this time, he may have to go.'

'What? You mean Dion's exile is rescinded?' Lately my mind had often turned to him. He was the man, after my father, who had taught me honour. Perhaps, I thought, it was he who had pointed out my way.

'No,' said Speusippos; and closed his mouth.

'But that was Plato's condition. So he can stay at home.'

'It is not so simple.' Nor, it seemed to me, was his trouble, whatever that might be; he looked like a man with warring thoughts. 'To begin with, Dionysios has turned back to philosophy.'

'My dear Speusippos! It's ten days to Syracuse with a good wind. By then he will have turned on his other side.'

'No, he's had a year at it, really studying. He's been writing to Plato and even making sense. So Plato has answered, and at a good deal of trouble too. The mind is there; it's just character makes it balk like a half-broke horse. That's what teases Plato; the thought that if the beast could be trained, he'd run.'

'Well, but since he got so frisky on the rein, he may study better alone.'

'So it began to seem. But it was you, I think, who said he always wants to be crowned before the race?'

'Don't tell me,' I cried, 'that he's calling himself an Academician?' My laughter stopped when I saw Speusippos was not even smiling. Maybe, I thought, he had drunk himself sad, as some men do.

'That is the least of it. Being a special case, he's got his hands on something no other student of Plato's owns; a written scheme of his oral teaching.' He saw my surprise, and said patiently, 'Plato believes in the spark that kindles mind from mind. If your brand won't burn, you carry it back to the hearth again. But he had to send it to Dionysios, since he couldn't come and his fire kept smoking. By now it amounts to a thesis, almost. So, instead of using in quiet such disciplines as make the mind's eye to see, he invites a philosophic concourse, and poses as a finished product of the school.'

'Plato must be angry. But, surely, not angry enough to get him out to Syracuse?' There was a pause. 'Who are these hangers-on?'

'Kyrenians, mostly, from the school of Aristippos. Like him, they equate the good with pleasure, but define their terms less carefully. And he himself wasn't careful enough. He was Plato's fellow-guest with old Dionysios; unlike Plato, he did very well out of it.'

'Does the son deserve better company? Why can't he leave Plato be? No, I can guess the answer. These are just rivals, flaunted to make the real love jealous. One could laugh, or cry.'

'I wish it may end in laughter.'

The moon had set, and a watch-dog howled in the dark. I thought of the cold bed at home. Whatever bad news he was holding back, I could do without it. But as one always does, I asked.

'Dionysios is resolved to get Plato there. Persuasion having failed, he turns, like every tyrant at the pinch, to power. His last letter invited Plato to confer with him, for the settlement of Dion's estates in Sicily. As I suppose you know, the income from them has reached him every year. If Plato goes, everything can be arranged to Dion's liking. If not, not; in other words, confiscation.'

'So that's it,' I said. 'The wretched little blackmailer! He should know better the men he has to deal with.' Speusippos was silent. I thought, as we walked on, of Dion's splendid progresses, how he had held court at Delphi, Delos, and Olympia, a beacon to every lover of justice. Of course spies must have brought word of all this to Syracuse, and one could picture Dionysios' jealousy. The wonder was, I thought, that he had not sunk to this meanness sooner.

'Well,' I said presently, 'it's good that Dion has always lived like a philosopher. With what he has, he'll be as well-off I daresay as you or I. His wife and son can't come to harm, being the Archon's kin; and though he'll miss his travels, at the Academy he'll have all he truly values; Plato, his books, his friends.'

In the flickering torchlight, I saw Speusippos look at me, then look ahead. Still he said nothing.

'Don't think I make light of it,' I said. 'Of course it will come harder to a man of rank, especially a Syracusan. But we know the man, and his love of honour. The greater the sacrifice, the higher his tribute to friendship and philosophy. That's how Dion will see it. Depend on it, he will never let Plato go.'

When still Speusippos did not answer, I began to be anxious, lest in some way I had offended him; but before I could ask him if this was so, he said drily, 'You are mistaken. He has been urging it.'

I got him to repeat this. When one sees two moons in the sky, one assumes it's the wine, not that they are there. Having heard it again, I said, 'Why? I don't understand.'

'Ask a god why, who can read men's souls.'

'But,' I said, labouring it over, 'even before Dion's exile, Syracuse was not safe for Plato. Philistos' faction hated him; the soldiers openly wanted his blood. Then he was kept there all winter against his will; he was sick; and he was younger then. As it was, he lost a year of work, at an age when every year counts. How *can* Dion ask him to go back there?'

'We must be just,' said Speusippos, appealing to himself. 'It is not simply the money. Dion hopes Plato will procure his recall.'

I asked, 'Does Dion himself say this?'

'Certainly. He said it to me.'

'How can he hope so for a moment? Dionysios was ready to believe the worst of him without any cause but jealousy. And now, for years, all Greece has been praising the Great Exile, every word of it at Dionysios' expense, every word a stab to his pride. He must detest the very name of Dion. Besides, they couldn't dare have him back; he is the hero of all the democrats in Sicily. Dionysios does not even offer it to get Plato there, for which he would offer nearly anything. Can Dion dream he would be recalled?'

'It is man's nature to believe what he greatly wishes.'

'That's true. But is it the nature of philosophy?'

He stopped still in the street. The link-boy paused at the corner, missed us, and came running back to make sure we were still on our feet. Speusippos waved him on. 'So, Niko, you were listening all the time. And back it comes, just when I run to you for comfort.'

'I am sorry,' I said. 'What do I know of philosophy? All that sticks in my mind is that Plato is his friend.'

Speusippos said, 'Yes, you have your own elenchos. I should have feared the logic of your heart.'

Now both of us were silent. We walked on through the dark, following the bobbing torch; presently we reached the turn of the road before my house, and the boy ran ahead to light my door. We lingered; both thinking, I suppose, that there must be something cheerful to part upon, if we could lay hold of it in time.

I said, 'One thing I can't believe is that Dion would do this only for the money. He has had all the luxuries of Syracuse at call, just for clapping his hands, and has gone without from choice. Look at his style of living.'

'I am sure he has no wish to change it. But there is one danger to a rich man in simple tastes: they enable him to be generous. Of course he has asked for no return; he would abhor the thought of buying sycophants. But, the world being what it is, there is a crowd about him, not all disinterested I'm afraid. It has given him great consequence, without his having anything to be ashamed of. Now he is used to it. As you know, he has his pride.'

We had come to the house. For form's sake I asked him in; he thanked me and said he must be early at work tomorrow. We dawdled towards the porch, still seeking the hopeful word.

'I can't forget,' I said, 'how nobly he used to speak of Plato, that first year of his exile. Of course, you were still in Syracuse ... There is a book of Plato's I read once – yes, truly, I read the whole of it. It was a supper-party where they made speeches in praise of love. I daresay you know it?'

'Yes,' said Speusippos. 'Yes, I have read the *Symposium* once or twice. I re-read it yesterday.'

'I just meant that Plato has lived up to it.'

'I see. I misunderstood. I thought perhaps you knew for whom it was first written.'

Our eyes met. I exclaimed, 'This must be a passing mood with Dion. Good actors have days when they can do nothing right; no doubt good men do, too. Now he knows how Plato feels, he will remember himself and think no more of such a thing. I daresay we are troubling ourselves over very little.'

Dawn was breaking. Birds sang in the willows, the same who had wakened me when the house was warm within. In the grey light, I saw Speusippos' face creased like a monkey's who has bitten a sour fig. He said, 'I see I must tell you everything. As early as last year, Dion wanted Plato to accept the Archon's invitation. Since he refused, nothing has been quite the same between them. Then, when this latest summons came, Dion called to discuss it, walked out in anger, and has not been near Plato since. Plato has written, I know. But there has been no answer.'

A cloud had caught the hidden sun, and glowed pink above us. Looking up to the High City, I saw the gilded ornaments on the temple roofs glitter in the first shafts of day. Before the house stood the lad with the torch waiting for leave to quench it. Something stirred in my memory; a shudder like a cold finger rippled up my backbone. I began to speak, and ceased.

'What?' said Speusippos, roused from his thoughts.

'No, nothing,' I answered. 'I forgot you missed the play.'

15

In early summer, Thettalos got back from his tour. I had awaited this with more pain than hope. Days are long for the young, the past is soon crowded out. But like a homing kingfisher, he came flashing straight back to his bough beside the stream.

All the spoils of his voyage, the theatres, cities, triumphs and troubles, his many scrapes (he was adventurous, more than wild) he flung before me. He talked half the night, about the plays they had done, how Miron had directed them, and how he could have done it better. He was just at the age when one must let out one's new thoughts, or burst. Now he was free to tell them all. When he jumped out of bed at midnight to show me how he would have done an upstage entrance if Miron had let him, I saw beyond the open door the mask smiling down on us, amused and kind.

We went everywhere together, a joy to those who wished us well, a grief to the backbiters whose meat is broken friendship, and who had been busy when he left.

One day, when we were sitting with friends in the scent-shop, I slipped away to Sisyphos the goldsmith's to order a ring for him as an anniversary gift; a sardonyx, carved with Eros on a dolphin. While Sisyphos did his sketches, I idled round the shop, and heard some merchant ask if it was true a ship was in from Syracuse. Someone said yes, but not a trader. This was a state trireme, sent by the Archon to fetch Plato the philosopher.

I had been taken up with my own happiness. This news so shook me that I dropped all my morning business, fetched Thettalos from the scent-shop, and told him I must go out to the Academy. Though he knew nothing of Plato but what I had told him, he was quite concerned.

'Yes, do go,' he said. 'I'll walk with you. It is wicked to treat the poor old man like this. I suppose he'll listen to no one but Dion (whom you know I never took to) and his philosophic friends. But one should at least take notice. We owe him a happy evening.' He was remembering a supper for two at home, when we had read the *Symposium* together. I said that Plato would have enough to do without my troubling him, and I would just ask for news.

'I would like, some day, Niko, to talk theatre with that man. I doubt all his notions are as silly as you think. It's time they stopped turning every play on the gods. Half the modern writers don't believe in them; the rest think like you and me, that they are somewhere or everywhere, but in any case not sitting in gold chairs on Mount Olympos, feuding and meddling like a brood of Macedonian royalty, ready to chop down any virtuous man who forgets to flatter or bribe them.'

Though myself not much above thirty, I often found the talk of the new generation standing my hair on end. At his age we whispered such thoughts; in my father's day they were a hemlock matter. Yet Plato had said something not unlike it; and he was seventy.

Among the olives of the Academy we greeted Axiothea, but did not linger, since she was not alone. She seldom was, now that Plato had accepted another girl. Lasthenia of Mantinea wore

260

women's dress, feeling, I suppose, that this suited her soul; she was small and slim, with a kind of serious liveliness. They walked with their heads together, their hands sketching the argument to and fro. It had been a good day for Axiothea, that brought her here. For the woman whose mind and body both need men, there is the life of the hetaira; it was not for her. She would have starved and turned sour, if Plato had not been above convention. I was glad for her, and wished her joy.

When we reached our destination, Thettalos, who had much delicacy about serious things, said he did not know Speusippos well enough to intrude on him just now, and went to stroll in the gardens.

At Speusippos' door, I could hear a girl inside crying and pummelling her breast, and wailing, for the hundredth time by the sound of it, 'I may never see you again!' Not having the face to knock during this scene, I walked off into the grove. I had heard what I came to know; but, longing to know more, persuaded myself I might be of help if I came back later.

Presently I was aware of two men ahead of me on the path between the trees. It was Plato, with Dion. I stopped, meaning to turn back; but just then Plato caught sight of someone beyond (no doubt he was full of business) and went over there, leaving Dion to wait.

He sat down on a shady bench. I could easily have got off unseen. But without pausing even to wonder at myself, I walked straight up to him.

It was impossible I could be welcome, and indeed he returned my greeting less coldly than I expected; perhaps I seemed a good omen, a harbinger of Sicily. At any time up till now, I would have walked on without presuming further. But I sat down beside him.

I conversed, I forget of what; of course nothing to the purpose. I could see Plato deep in talk; he would be some time yet. Dion was quite civil. I could feel him thinking that when Plato came back, I had manners enough to go; meantime, what with one thing and another, it was his duty to put up with me. My awe, I suppose, had first begun to spill away in Syracuse, with the wine from his broken cup. Since then, too, I had advanced in my calling; and, which perhaps made the more difference, also in love.

Awe was gone; yet I had come to recover something. The noble beauty of this face was like a splendid mask I had long been used to live with. I studied it now again. So many men of his age (he must now be rising fifty) have faces getting fat, or loose, or drawn with petty cares, or bitter. But his outlines had kept their shape; if his skin had aged, it was a healthy weathering. A royal face; one of those classic masks made of good hardwood that carves like stone.

I forget how we came to talk of Delphi; but I recalled *The Myrmidons*, and how seldom it was done in Athens. Whichever of us it was who referred to Homer, it was I – as I am not likely to forget – who said, 'Aischylos has departed from him here and there. Take Patroklos, for instance. In the *Iliad*, his father reminds him he is the elder of the friends; while Aischylos makes him the youth beloved. But in any case,' I went on, following my thought, if you can call it that, 'I suppose he would still be a man in the flower of his strength, when Achilles sent him into battle.'

It was not till these words were out of my mind that I perceived what I had been saying. If you ask how such stupidity is possible in a man able to get about and earn his bread, I can only suppose that my soul borrowed my tongue before I knew it. Had it been my own reflection, it was bad enough. But an actor's memory is like a jackdaw's nest; it came from Plato's *Symposium*.

Even before Dion's face went dark and cold as a winter mountain, I knew what I'd done, and had lost the look of innocence. To have begged his pardon would have made it ten times worse;

nor indeed did I feel the wish. I can't remember with what form of words he let me know he was not at leisure. He could not have wished me gone more heartily than I did.

One must be prepared sometimes to make an exit when one is upset. Thinking only of my back, I started at running into Thettalos, who made me sit down and tell him what was the matter. At the end he said, 'Nonsense. You could have said much more than that. Only wait till you are seventy, and see if I treat you as he does Plato.'

Laughing did me good, but it was not till next day that I felt fit to call on Speusippos.

I found him in his garden, talking with the old Persian slave who tended it, and with the young man Aristoteles to whom he had consigned his specimens before. The place was full of small shelters for delicate plants; rock-terraces, windscreens and potting-sheds. Seeing him busy, I would have withdrawn, but he said he would be glad of a break, and was only fidgeting there from restlessness. 'I must remember,' he said, 'to enfranchise old Oitanes in my will, in case I don't come home. It would break his heart to lose the garden; it would be too much to be sold himself as well.'

He called for cooled wine, and conferred a moment with the young Aristoteles, a dapper youth with thin legs and small, keen eyes. Presently he came back to sit with me against the shady wall of the house, under the vine-trellis. Sweet herbs stood in pots around. 'I can leave it all to him,' he said. 'He never forgets any-thing. One of our most gifted men, but not at home with first principles. How, how, how; he will probe into that forever; he can't see that for Plato the use of how is to find the why. Why, Niko, is man? And why does man ask why? When we know that, we have all truth in our fingers. Without, a lifetime of how leads where? Maybe to designing a catapult like old Dionysios', which can lob a stone two stades from the walk, and kill a man – a mystery of God which we can bring ourselves to destroy because we have never defined it ... But why run on? What can I do for you, Niko?

I told him I had heard he was sailing with Plato, and had just come to say goodbye. 'You have no notion,' he said, tilting back his head with a sigh against the wall, 'what has gone on since last we talked; and before that, for I kept things back; you were defining my own thoughts to me faster than I could bear ... Oh, yes, of course you're wondering how Plato was induced to go. The only wonder is he held out so long. He's had barely a day of peace – do you know Dionysios has written, over the last few months, to every friend of consequence he has in Athens, urging them to push him on; saying as a rule, that when in Syracuse he proposed reforms, which can only be carried out under his direction. He should know what that's worth; but you can suppose how he's felt, with half Athens saying he has power to reform the tyranny, but prefers his ease at home, or is afraid to test his theories. Besides all that, Dionysios has been pressing the Tarentines, and has written to Archytas hinting that the treaty may be denounced if he doesn't get Plato there. Archytas is trusted like the father of the city; how can he risk the people's safety for one friend's, when it must seem to him the friend might even do good by going? Of course the Archon's Kyrenian guests have written too, praising their host's progress in philosophy, and his devotion to Plato's doctrines; which means without doubt that he's been expounding half-baked versions which Plato would die to hear.' He paused for breath, while his servant set up the wine-table.

'Poor Plato,' I said. 'Like the poet when some barnstormer butchers his best lines.'

When the man had gone, he said, 'All Dion's friends have

written too. And there are more of them than all the rest put together.'

I said nothing. He broke off a sprig of basil, and turned it in his hand, peering into the little flowers.

'Dion is my guest-friend of long standing. In any case one owes him justice. He has a son growing up in the Archon's house. There is his wife ... ' He was some time silent before saying, 'There is another threat Dion does not know of. Plato promised not to tell; those were the only terms on which he could hope to avert it.' Next moment he was distressed at having said even so much, and made me promise to be secret.

I asked when they were sailing; with good weather, he said, in two days' time. 'God knows, Niko, when we shall get home, if ever. Before my wife I laugh at it; poor girl, she's pregnant, and hardly more than a child herself. I feel cruel to go, but it would be worse forsaking Plato. I wonder how long before you and I sit here again.' He looked round the garden, his eye dwelling here and there. 'Will you be playing in Syracuse? It would be good to see you.'

When the ship sailed, I went to see it off, since half Athens was doing the same. It was like a scene in the theatre.

Plato and Dion behaved perfectly; no doubt their goodbyes were already said. They exchanged a ceremonial kiss, like two kings in tragedy. I saw Axiothea and her friend shedding open tears, and the eyes of the Academy men were not much drier. They might have been watching Sokrates drink the hemlock. But Dion kept his countenance. His noble bearing so much impressed the audience, I kept expecting applause.

Months passed. It drew near autumn, and no news of Plato's return. I saw Axiothea seldom, both of us having a good deal to fill our time. Thettalos had been doing short tours, coming home between, and it was natural when I had the right offers for me to do the same. These were brief, happy fasts, on which I worked well.

When sailing weather was clearly ending, I went out of my way to ask Axiothea where Plato was. She said, in Syracuse; Dionysios had persuaded him to winter there, and complete the settlement of Dion's property.

'Again?' I said. 'No, that's too much!'

Little Lasthenia, sharp as a brown bird, added, 'I hope he'll get proper thanks for it.'

Axiothea looked at us sadly. She had always worshipped Dion; but if she felt a loss, she had still the Cause. It looked simpler to her than to me; she had never been in Sicily.

Winter passed; spring came. At the Dionysia, Philemon, a most distinguished artist, bargained with Miron to release Thettalos for the contest. Their play was *Herakles in Lydia*; Thettalos did Omphale and Iolaos, changing masks with great virtuosity, and most striking in the former role. I could see the pleasure he got from working under an up-to-date protagonist, though old Miron's discipline had done him good. I myself was doing *Theseus in the Underworld*, and would gladly have had him for Pirithoos and Persephone; but one can't have a bird without a broken eggshell. It was one of Theodoros' prize years; we came back from his party tired and happy, not reminding ourselves that roads and seas were opening, and we would soon be parting again.

Presently, after our seeing a good deal of each other in early summer, Miron got an offer to go to Macedon, and then on north to Byzantion. Knowing from the past that I should find it harder when alone to make any plans, I shook myself like a dog and began to stir about.

Only four days later, when they had barely begun rehearsing, Thettalos came home at noon. He had resigned from Miron's company.

266

'Not another day. I knew I couldn't last our rehearsals, so I played fair by the old monster and gave him time to replace me. Oh, no, Niko, I have to come up for air. O Agamemnon, lord of men, boom, boom, ototoi, ototoi, right hand up, left hand out. I feel like some image shut up in a temple strongroom, with the dust settling thicker every day.'

'By the dog!' I cried. 'I could clip you over the head. You stupid boy, why didn't you tell me you didn't mean to go north? Now I have signed up to go to Sicily.'

'Sicily?' He looked up with his mouth full; he was devouring barley-cake and raisins and cheese like a schoolboy back from the wrestling class.

'Yes; signed, sealed and witnessed. I shall be two months away, or more.'

'Have you got a second?'

'What time have I had? If you had only—'

'Dearest of men! I always longed to see Syracuse.'

I started; then subdued my heart, as one covers a cage to stop a bird from singing. 'Don't tempt me, my dear. You know as well as I do that you'll never rest, now, till you're creating your own play. It can't be long; two years, or three; meantime you're too sensible not to take direction, but will resent whoever you have to take it from. Don't let me be the one.'

'Truly, Niko, I swear, it will be Elysium to work for you. I've been living like someone flat on a frieze: I shall talk my mind out, seeing it's you; that I can't help; but I'll never cross you. All Miron taught me was to know how good you are.'

'It would never do,' I said, trying to sound resolute.

'Fate intends it. Look how I left him, the very day.'

'You've picked up his superstition, if nothing else.'

He came and sank down beside my chair. He had filled out his boyish hollows; his stride, like a young lion's had both weight and

267

grace. He was born to play heroes, though not in Miron's style. He flung his arm across my knees, and went into Patroklos' speech from *Myrmidons*, putting in all the grace-notes. *False to the sacred honour of our bed, O, most unthankful for those many kisses* . . . Please, Niko, take me to Sicily.'

'Well,' I said, 'now, if you grumble, you've put yourself in the wrong beforehand. I was holding out for that.'

He called me a monster and embraced me. Within the month we sailed.

Since it would be easy to find third and extra men in Sicily, we sailed alone. Good weather, and showing him the sights, made it a pleasure trip. At Tarentum, I did not omit paying Archytas my respects, in case he had letters for Plato. He thanked me, and said he had just sent a messenger. Though courteous he was not talkative, and seemed to me an unhappy man. He had sent a leading Pythagorean in Dionysios' trireme, to help persuade Plato; if he had had a hard choice, between his people and his friend, and was concerned for the outcome, he had my sympathy, but there was no reason why he should confide in me. He told me Plato and Speusippos were both reported in good health, and in favour with Dionysios. He forgot to ask how Dion was.

The Syracusan consul had of course announced our arrival; but I was amazed to find, when we made port, how many people turned out. Thettalos exclaimed that I must have made the hit of a generation, last time I came. But I soon learned the secret. When I had pushed back at Philistos his silver talent, I had supposed it would go straight into his treasury. As I now found out, he had done precisely as I asked. He had commissioned a life-sized bronze of the god, with a gold vine-crown, riding a gilded leopard. Of course, his own name was on the plinth as well as mine; he had the right, as choregos. I don't know if he did it for that, or because with all his vices he was too pious to rob a god. At all events, there it stood, in the sanctuary by the theatre; the citizens now supposed I was the richest actor in Greece.

One informant was Menekrates, who met the ship, sumptuously dressed, and looking just what he was, a successful actor-manager who plays all the big Sicilian cities, visiting Italy once a year. Last time he stayed with me in Athens, I had seen he was doing well; he must have been rising ever since. He carried us off, not to the lodging in the Lower Town, but to a great new house above the theatre, with a fountain-court paved in black-and-white mosaics, and a carved marble balcony facing the sea. Two pretty gold-skinned children came running out to meet him; from which I guessed, before I saw her, that he had got one of those blonde wives so much prized in Sicily.

I had never been there so late in summer; the streets were griddle-hot and dusty, the hills parched brown; but his court-yard, piped from a spring above, was fresh and green, and his thick walls were cool. We supped lying on cushions of Persian stuff, with two men and a boy to wait. Nothing was too good for us. It was his way of saying I had turned his luck, that day at Leontini.

We talked theatre at first. A big drama festival was coming on the feast of Arethusa, the local river-goddess. I had been met on the dock with a message from the tragic poet Chairemon, on a visit here from Athens, asking me to see him before I made any plans. In Sicily it's catch-as-catch-can for artists; no draw like ours at home.

It was not till the slaves had cleared and left us with the wine, that I mentioned Plato. I had noticed our host had grown more careful in his talk. He had more to lose.

'Plato?' he said. 'I've enough to keep me busy without running after sophists, especially when they're as meddlesome as that old man. If we get through to the festival without a riot here, and

269

looting in the streets, we can thank the gods rather than him. I'm thinking of sending Glyke and the children into the country.'

Startled by all this, I said it was inconceivable that a man like Plato would be conspiring against his host. 'No doubt,' he answered. 'But with the advice he gives, he'll hardly need to. What the Archon's just done – and everyone blames Plato for it – is to put his veterans on half-pay. Don't go near Ortygia. I tell you, there'll be trouble.'

I could believe him. Old Dionysios had had an excellent name with soldiers of fortune everywhere, if with no one else, because he rewarded long service. The country round was full of paid-off men settled on land he had given them, often enough at the citizens' expense. They made a useful reserve, and encouraged recruiting. Menekrates said, 'He was one to skin a flayed ox, as the saying is. But everyone knew where the money went; on power. Every few years, when the Carthaginians came, we got the good of that whether he cared or not. But the young one, who's pretty near as greedy, spends on his pleasures. While he's idling, we get twenty extortioners where we had one before. Believe me, he can't afford to sting his garrison. Let's say no more; it's hearsay only, and least known's best. But Plato must know too much, or too little, to give such counsel.'

'If he ever gave it. I'd lay a year's takings against. We heard all this last time, put about by Philistos. It was just a tale.'

Thettalos, who had maintained a modest quiet but could not forbear supporting me, said all Athens knew that Plato had come out about his friend Dion's property, and to try for his recall.

'Recall?' said Menekrates, staring. 'If Dion wants to come home, he'll have to recall himself, not wait to be invited. Then, who knows ... But that's dangerous talk. We've travelled; we've seen in other cities what comes of *that*.' He walked over to the doorway, to make sure the slaves had gone to bed. Coming back, he said, 'As for the property, God reward all true friends, but in Plato's case I don't know who else will. Dion's land was all sold up this spring. There was some talk of putting it in trust for his son, young Hipparinos; but where's the odds? It would go the same way as if Dionysios spent it.'

I remembered Dion's words at Tarentum. 'How old is the boy?'

'I suppose about fourteen. He's a favourite with his uncle the Archon, who's fond of saying he won't grow up a spoil-sport like his dad. He comes to all the parties. I was at one myself not long ago, after a *Madness of Herakles* that took well. Plato was there too. A handsome lad; they say, not unlike Dion when he was that age. But the Academy won't see *him*; his education's well in hand. The liveliest of the girls was sent over to his supper-couch, but I couldn't see he had much to learn. His hand was down her dress all through the first course, and up it all through the second. Old Plato did try, at the start, to get a word with him, but the boy laughed in his face. Even his uncle had to remind him he was speaking to a guest, though he couldn't keep from smiling.'

Thettalos gave me one of his looks when Menekrates' back was turned. He had sparkling eyes; sometimes one could see it even through a mask.

'Where is Plato staying?' I asked. 'His nephew is a friend of mine, and I'd like to see him.'

'Plato himself has that house in the Palace garden he had before; it's the Archon's chief guest-house. But I don't think the nephew's staying there. Maybe he wasn't asked very heartily. I heard he was with religious folk, Pythagoreans. I'll enquire tomorrow. Thettalos, dear boy, your cup; you're drinking nothing. I'll show you our theatre, while Niko's hunting sophists. The acoustics are first-class, but you need to know them.'

Next morning I went to the house where Speusippos and Plato had stayed before. For fear of missing him, I was there before sun-up. When the slave reported him still in bed, I said I would wait till he woke. This was not long; while I sat on the rim of the courtyard fountain, two smiths came in with a great new bolt for the outer door. They said, as they clattered, that they were sorry to rouse the master, but they were pushed with orders like this. One must blame the times.

The din soon woke Speusippos, who looked out to see what it was. A pretty tousled girl, clutching her dress, appeared behind him; he had not counted on early rising today. Having urged her to go home quickly and not loiter in the streets, he turned and saw me. 'Niko!' he said, and laughed shortly as he caught my eye. 'I heard you were in Syracuse. Have you been waiting long?'

I said I was sorry his night had been cut short so rudely. 'No,' he said, 'it's as well I woke. I must see Plato in Ortygia; it's better to go early, while the streets are quiet. They seem to be expecting trouble. Come in while I finish dressing.'

His host greeted us going in; a silver-haired old man shrunk with age, but upright and with a skin like a baby's. In Speusippos' room, with the tumbled bed still warm with the scent of the girl, he said, 'I don't think he saw her leave. Not that I've ever deceived him; he knows I follow the philosophy rather than the regimen, which, let us admit, has picked up much superstition since the founder's time. He'd say, I suppose, that I've set myself back two or three rebirths with last night's work. "The body is the tomb of the soul." Well, I was on edge, which my soul was taking no good from; besides which, I've learned from her more than she ever set out to teach, as I'll tell you sometime. I must go; will you walk along with me?'

As we headed for Ortygia, I remembered Menekrates warning me not to go near the place. But I was ashamed to be less bold than a philosopher, not to speak of forsaking a friend. So far, only one thing was to be noticed about the streets, that they were empty.

I asked how Plato was, and if his mission had prospered. He made the gesture of a man so weary of his troubles that he can hardly bear to talk of them. 'Plato's as well,' he said, 'as he's likely to be after wasting a year for nothing, or worse than that. I suppose you've heard. All Dion's property has been sold up, a hundred talents' worth or more; and Dionysios has ceased even to pretend that he'll get a drachma.'

I exclaimed suitably. There seemed nothing to say.

You think Plato should have foreseen it. Of course he did. But with all these protestations, appeals, and guarantees, he couldn't be certain. Short of that, he didn't think he should hold back.'

'When my bad day comes, God send me such a friend.'

'He's always been the same. At Sokrates' trial, neither his kin nor his friends could keep him from getting up to testify. When the court laughed him down because of his youth, which I daresay saved his life, he fell so sick with grief, they doubted he'd outlive Sokrates. May he keep his luck. I tell you, I begin to wonder.'

'What? But the Archon . . .'

'Every day it's worse. How not, unless the man had really changed? Plato came here for Dion's sake. That was the bait. Merely by taking it, he had Dionysios jealous even before he'd sailed. Every word he's spoken for Dion has been oil on fire. Every friend of Dion's he takes notice of is a mark against him. It can't stretch much more without breaking. Each time I come here, I'm cold with fear of what I'll find.'

I don't know what he thought his own life would be worth with Plato gone. He did not speak of it, but strode on, a thin quick harassed man, towards Ortygia. I could hardly keep up.

We got over the causeway and through the gates without any trouble. The reason was simple. No guards were there. They had shut the big gates, but left the posterns open.

At the last of them, Speusippos said, as if we had been strolling from the Agora to the Academy, 'Well, Niko, thanks for your company on the way.'

'Oh, no,' I said. 'What do you take me for? Come on.'

He was in too much haste to argue, and, with the hill, soon out of breath. Nikeratos, I thought, you are too big a fool to live, and so you may find. At the same time, I am inquisitive; there is no sense in putting up with the hardships of travel, unless one looks about.

We had got to the barrack quarter; the street, I think, of the Gauls. It was empty; no men off duty standing about, or dicing in doorsteps. The doors hung open. Soldiers have to be very over-wrought, to stop guarding their things from other soldiers. I was pointing this out to Speusippos, when we heard the yelling.

Someone up ahead had started a kind of paean. Never having heard any of these barbarians in action, I don't know whose it was; in any case, all the rest took up their own, in a cacophony I can't describe. Now and then some howl more piercing than the rest would catch the general ear, and they would come in on that with a wordless bellow all together.

I felt a weakness in my knees, like stagefright but worse. 'They're under the walls,' I said; 'you can hear. The gates must be shut. No use going further.'

There was a soldier coming down the street. I was all for get-ting out of the way, and so I think was Speusippos; then suddenly he started forward, exclaiming 'Herakleides!'

He was an officer, Sicilian Greek, dark and good-looking, with the dress and speech of a gentleman, and an easy, pleasant way. He had been so wrapped up in his own concerns as he came that he had not seen us till he was almost on us; but he did not look scared, nor ashamed like a man running away, and, as soon as he saw Speusippos, gave him an open steady look. Then he said, 'I'm off duty.'

'In the name of the gods,' said Speusippos. 'Listen.' He lifted his brows. 'What do you mean? I hear nothing.' Speusippos drew breath to speak, then waited. Herakleides shrugged his shoulders. 'Some of my best men are there. Men who got me off the field with a spearhead in me, when they might have left me to be cut and trimmed by the Carthaginians. I can't stop them; I can only give them an order they won't listen to, which won't help discipline tomorrow, and take their names. No names, no floggings. In their place, I'd be there too.' He went off downhill. I remember thinking what a simple, decent fellow he was, and how his men must love him.

Up above, the yelling got louder. Across the top of the street, a troop of Nubians went by towards the Palace. They were stamping as they went, and chanting in time with it; now and then they would give a whoop, and leap, tossing up their spears. I pulled Speusippos into a doorway. 'Come home,' I said. 'What can you do? Those walls there are ten feet thick; they'll never get in.'

'Not,' he answered, 'if the men inside want to keep them out.'

'It's with the gods,' I said, for want of any other comfort. 'Let's be gone from here.'

He took a few steps with me, then stopped. 'No. I'll wait. If they can get in, then so can I.' No doubt my face was an open book. He pressed my shoulder. 'My dear Niko, go back, you've come more than far enough. You've no call to stay; I have ... He would have died with Sokrates, and I've had more of my life than he'd had then. If it's his turn now, I can't leave him to die alone.'

One part of me applauded this; the rest was angry with him for catching me up in his choice. I said, 'No, I'll come with you to the walls, to see what is going on. If you want to get yourself killed inside, that's another thing.' And I turned up the street beside him.

Soon we got to the wide ring-road that circled the Palace wall.

We could hear the noise further along. As we walked that way, a squad of Romans ran past us shouting to each other. Presently we came to the great main gates, twenty feet high. There was a square before them; below, the Sacred Way cut down towards the causeway, lined with trees, statues and shrines. Filling the square were the soldiers. They had kept together more or less, Iberians with Iberians and so on; beyond this, they were a mob, and the most dangerous sort on earth, being both armed and used to violence. The one comfort was that, since the day was early, they were not drunk.

Now we were near, we could hear that they were shouting in their different uncouth accents, 'Dionysios!' When no one came, they threw up stones at the gatehouse. The Nubians were the best shots. There was a sculptured frieze above; they were aiming at the gods' heads, and had knocked half off already. To my surprise, the Gauls were absent.

There were cheers; all heads turned towards the Sacred Way. Here were the Gauls. Stripped naked for battle, with blue warpaint flourished all over them, they were hauling up the slope a huge beam, I should think a keel from one of the naval yards. The crowd rushed to help; the beam came up the square as if on wings. They lined up each side, while some expert started a heaving-chant. The gate was oak and iron, but I did not see it holding long.

They rammed it two or three times; the tongues of the hinges began to start. Speusippos watched in silence, no doubt composing himself with philosophy. The Gauls plodded back for another run-in.

A trumpet sounded above the gate. The yells died to muttering. The Gauls laid the ram down for a rest. A Greek voice called, 'Dionysios!'

An old man in armour appeared on the gate-tower. There was almost silence. It was Philistos.

He looked older than I remembered. His florid face had mottled, his eyes had sunk, his nose got sharper and bluer. At sight of him they growled, but listened. He might not be a loved commander; but he was there, standing in javelin-range. He had earned a hearing.

The upshot of his speech was that there had been a great misunderstanding. Ill-disposed persons had falsified the Archon's orders. He had been shocked to learn of their grievance. Not only were veterans' wages being maintained; they would be raised, from today.

There were cheers, of course; triumphant, but ironic. One could hear it in the voice of every race, though the note was different. Even with the Nubians, one could tell.

Philistos gazed down at them. He was a man I detested; but there was not much pleasure in watching an old general shoved out to give his troops this craven lie. He did it, I must own, with what dignity it allowed.

He limped stiffly down to the stair-rail. The Greek who had called before shouted again for Dionysios; this time it was an open jeer. But no one came.

The mob broke up, and went off in groups shouting and singing towards the wine-shops, leaving the ram in the street. The Gauls shouldered past us either side, but noticed us no more than dogs. The morning was getting warm, and the sweat ran down their war-paint. It did not blur; it must have been a kind of tattooing. They smelt like horses.

Speusippos and I were left in the empty square, by the ram with its frayed hammered nose. He had not got to die with Plato, nor I with him. I expected him to be looking as relieved as I. But he was standing with his mouth set in a hard, shrewd look that was new to me, gazing after the soldiers. He said, 'Dion should know of this.'

Nothing surprised me much by now. I said, 'Do you mean what I think?'

'I daresay,' he answered. Then, 'I was talking to that girl last night. She was twelve years old when some scout of Philistos' saw her, and hauled her off from home to amuse Dionysios. Her father objected; he went to the Quarries and was never seen again. Dionysios hadn't even decency enough to have her sent home after. She was put out like a stray cat, picked up by some Iberians, and passed around the barracks. Her own story's nothing to some she told me; but sharing a bed seems to bring it home. He can do anything he likes, to anyone, that one man alone. It's hard for the mind to grasp it.'

He was right; when one is not bred to it, one doesn't conceive it, it must be smelt and tasted. Like me, he was too young to remember it at home. For that matter, even the Thirty had at least to agree together. 'One man,' he said again.

'If you call him that. I doubt the troops do, now.'

'What was it old Dionysios said on his deathbed, Niko? "A city in chains of adamant." The chains are rotting. Dion should know.'

16

The soldiers rejoiced all night, at the expense of anyone they found at hand; then they went back on duty, and the city breathed again. I was scolded by Menekrates for going to Ortygia, and by Thettalos for not having taken him with me. At the mention of Herakleides, our host looked so nervous that, remembering his past hints, I added two and two. Though it was hard to think of so frank a soldier conspiring, yet it was certain that the mutiny had tested the troops' loyalty, and the Archon's strength. I wondered if Speusippos guessed.

Two days later, all being still calm, I went to call on Chairemon the tragic poet; taking with me Thettalos, whose work he would certainly know. After asking around (just like a poet, he had forgotten to say where he was staying) we learned he was in Ortygia, as a Palace guest.

'Good,' said Thettalos as we went. 'This time you can't leave me to bite my nails all morning, wondering if you're lying dead in a gutter. Lead me to the tyrant's lair.'

It was with no great delight that I approached Ortygia. If the gates were to be closed again, I had no fancy to be inside. However, I showed our passes for outer Ortygia (these were easily got from the Athenian embassy) and had them endorsed for the Palace citadel by the captain of the guard.

I had expected slackness at the guard-houses, after yesterday, but not what met us everywhere: restlessness, rumour, suspicion. At the Iberian gate two men were quarrelling. As the first blows were struck, an officer came up cursing; there was a dangerous moment before they obeyed. We went on, not envying him his employment, nor indeed much liking our own. 'Never mind,' said Thettalos. 'It's all in the business. One must study how men behave. Something can happen anywhere; pirates in the islands, satrap wars in Ionia; and in Macedon they're forever assassinating the king.'

Our one strict check was the last, into the Palace citadel. In the park, we found the groves full of men running about, light-armed Cretans going like beaters through the coverts, calling to one another. Some of them stopped us, but passed us through without saying whom they wanted.

In due course we found our way to the second-class guest-house where Chairemon had a room. All the other inmates – poets, envoys, minor philosophers and so on – were huddled in the courtyard muttering. When Chairemon recognised us they all ran up asking for news. 'What of?' I asked. 'If you mean the mutiny, it seems to be over.' Someone said, 'Then they've not caught him yet?' When I asked whom he meant, he said 'Herakleides.'

'I don't think so. The place is full of men searching. Why, what has he done?'

Of a sudden, everyone got careful; Chairemon said one could not be sure, one merely heard he was being searched for; if we would come to his room, he had a play he would like to talk about.

When the door was shut, he wrung our hands and thanked the gods for the sound of Attic speech. I thought he would burst into tears. 'Never again! I came with Karkinos; he's been before, and persuaded me to accept; the works of art, banquets, music and so on. Never, never again! Not that I'm concerned in this, not at all' (he looked round at the door). 'It's to know that anything can happen – really, anything. It's the thought, just the thought of it.'

I answered, 'Pythagoras said, "Accept in your mind that anything which can happen, can happen to you".' I had heard this aphorism at the Academy. He looked at me in appeal, as if I could make it otherwise. I saw Thettalos laughing to himself.

It seemed Herakleides had been accused of causing the mutiny, and gone missing. His friends had been pleading for him, including Plato, because he had belonged to Dion's party; and had got a safe-conduct for him from the Archon, to prepare his affairs for exile. Then today, on news that he had been seen, troops had been sent out to catch him. It was now supposed that the safe-conduct had been a trick, to delay his getting away.

'Maybe,' I said. 'Or Dionysios just changed his mind.'

'But, surely, Nikeratos, his honour . . . '

'There's only one judge of honour, in Syracuse.'

Chairemon blinked. I said, 'Never mind, there's still the theatre. If Troy hadn't fallen, where would we be today?' His eyes reproached my frivolity, but he consented to talk business.

He had a choregos for his new play, *Achilles Slays Thersites*, and wanted us to do it for the festival. Although he would read it aloud (why do so few poets read well?) it was a good piece of work. It started with the Amazon Penthesilea arriving as a Trojan ally. She challenges the Greeks; Achilles, still mourning for Patroklos, is brought the tale of her victories. Now he has resumed his place as champion of the Greeks, it is for him to meet her. They hail each other, she on the walls and he below, to exchange defiance. Love at first sight. But they are equal in pride and standing; each values honour more than life; they must fight to the death. Achilles wins. He enters from battle walking by the bier on which they bring her breathing her last. There is a lovely speech where he praises her valour to cheer her parting soul. She's gone. He kneels and weeps for her, bowed upon the bier. Thersites the mocker, who has been longing to hear that the great Achilles fell at last by a woman's hand, now has his say. What a mourner! he cries. You've only just done grieving for Patroklos; now it's this Amazon, and both of them died through you. Achilles gets up; Thersites takes fright and runs; off-stage sounds his death-cry as Achilles fells him with a blow. After a lively scene with Diomedes, who has to demand satisfaction for the blood because Thersites was his kinsman, Artemis appears to stop the fight and reconcile the heroes. Big choral procession, Penthesilea given to her Amazons for burial, to end the play. It is now well-known in Athens, but this was its first performance.

Achilles is for the protagonist, but there is a great deal of fat for the second too. Penthesilea dying is a dummy; he can play both her and Thersites. Chairemon had had the script copied, so that we could take it home; we walked off so full of it that we hardly noticed the Cretans still rummaging the boskage. Reading as we went, we missed our way, and found ourselves in a new part of the park, among houses which looked dangerously important. I pushed the script into my robe, saying, 'We must get back the way we came.'

'By all means,' said Thettalos, 'if you know which it is.'

There were three paths behind us, all much alike. Beyond a grove of pink oleanders one could glimpse the Palace roofs. 'We had better look through,' I said. 'If I see which side we are, I can steer by that.'

We pushed into the bushes. As I saw light, I also heard people talking, and stopped dead, gripping Thettalos' arm. One of the voices was Dionysios'.

Thettalos, who read my eyes, stood soundless. It was not a time to be found where one had no business, creeping up on the Archon. I recalled Pythagoras' saying, which I had quoted to Chairemon so lightly.

Thettalos had paled a little, but was already edging softly towards a gap in the leaves. One must study, as he said to me later, how men behave.

At first I could only hear Dionysios' voice, eloquent with self-pity. Now and again one of the men with him, some two or three, would say, 'Yes, indeed,' or 'Everyone can witness that', or 'How true!' They were coming towards us; as their words got clear, fear that they might discover us made me deaf. They paused, however, as they naturally would on coming to a thicket, and I allowed myself to breathe. Dionysios was saying, 'But no, a friend of Dion's can't do wrong for him. Anyone, a traitor who eats my salt and corrupts my soldiers, anyone before me.' He almost sobbed. He was half-drunk, but quite sincere.

Someone said, 'Birds of a feather, sir. You have been too generous to his insolence. The truth is – forgive me for my plain speaking – you don't value yourself enough. It feeds his pride.'

'When I think—' Dionysios was beginning; then he broke off. They were now walking away; I crept along to share Thettalos' peephole. There was the Archon with his friends; and crossing the lawn to them came three men, the oldest leading. Thettalos, who was watching entranced, mouthed a name at me with questioning brows. I nodded.

The two younger men stood silent, in attitudes of formal grief. Plato came forward. His shoulders and heavy head were stooping more than I remembered; his beard, which had had some grey in it, was nearly all white, though there was black still in his brows. His eyepits had deepened; from their caves gazed his eyes, piercingly grey. I could almost see Dionysios' gaze shifting, through the back of his head. However, encouraged no doubt by his admirers, he decided to put a face on it. 'Yes, Plato?' he said. 'What is it?'

'I am here,' said Plato, 'at the insistence of these friends of mine. They are afraid you may be taking some new action against Herakleides, in spite of the promise you made me yesterday. I believe he has been seen hereabouts.'

Dionysios' back jerked upright, giving at the same time a kind of wriggle. 'Promise?' he said, sounding indignant. He had tried, also, to sound surprised.

At this one of the other two rushed forward, flung himself on his knees before the Archon, and clasped his hand. He made some plea, broken by weeping. Dionysios allowed his hand to be cried on, drawing himself up and looking powerful. Perhaps for once he felt like his father. Plato stood watching this scene with distaste. After a while he stepped forward, and put his hand on the man's bowed shoulder. 'Courage, Theodotes,' he said. 'Dionysios would never dare break our agreement in such a way.'

Dionysios' pose collapsed. His hand having been let go before he could snatch it back, he folded his arms furiously. 'With you,' he said, 'I agreed to nothing. Nothing at all.'

As I said, Plato had aged. His stoop had settled into his bones; he would never draw himself straight again. None the less, at these words he grew alarming. Once, I remember, in some old country theatre, I came to the skene-room with a torch at night, and found myself face to face with a great old eagle-owl, hunched in his dark corner, his round eyes glaring into mine. I almost dropped the torch and burned down the building.

'By the gods, you did!' He thrust forward his beak; I could almost see the lifted feathers. The sycophants clucked; the friends looked panic-stricken. In case Dionysios had not got his meaning the first time, he added, 'You promised just what this man is begging for.' He turned his back on the Archon, and walked off.

There was a silence; then Dionysios told Herakleides' friends to get out of his sight. Next moment he was gone himself, I suppose to urge on the soldiers. The lawn was full of powerful emptiness, like a theatre after a play.

We scouted our way back to the public path before either of us spoke. Then Thettalos said, 'He called him a liar, in front of all those people.'

I said, 'And two of them Dion's friends.'

'Will he kill him?'

'I don't know.' I could feel myself trembling a little. 'His father would have done it. I don't suppose he knows himself what he means to do. It's with the gods.'

'A terrible old man! Niko, can't we try to get him away? It's like leaving Prometheus to be gnawed by rats. At least he deserves a vulture.'

'My dear, he has a dozen devoted friends in the city. The best thing for us is to find Speusippos and warn him. He may need it.'

Menekrates, when he heard our news, decided at once to send his wife and children out of town, to her father's place. She could take some valuables with her, in case rioting broke out. The house was in a turmoil of packing.

We called twice at the house where Speusippos was staying; but he was out, they could not say where. The rest of the day we spent going over Chairemon's script; but next morning, resolved that Speusippos should be found without more delay, we called again. The porter, who knew me well, said he and the master were both at the house of Archidemos, the philosopher, where Plato was a guest. We stared. He went on carefully, 'I understand, sir, the Archon needed the guest-house. So he asked him to stay with friends.'

We looked at each other with relief. 'So Plato is well,' I said, 'and staying with friends of his own?' He answered yes. 'And your master and Speusippos are both there too?'

'That I can't say, sir. But that was where they were going.'

No doubt he was keeping things back, but we felt satisfied, and walked off in relief, remarking that Plato must be even more glad to go than Dionysios to see the back of him. As Thettalos said, it was the end of a famous friendship, but at least he could go home. I thought of Dion, and how he would take the news.

Our minds now at rest about Plato, we settled down to get a cast and begin rehearsals. There was no chorus, only musical interludes, which would be looked after by a music-master. Chairemon was a very modern author. The third actor I had in mind was free, and brought me a friend to audition for the fourth, who had a few lines; I took him on. The extras were easy. Chairemon had found a reasonable choregos; he was said to be mean by Sicilian standards, and therefore pleased to have Athenian actors, who don't demand bullion trimmings over everything, and real gold crowns. I am a little too vain to hide in a heap of ornaments, so we suited well.

We had been rehearsing two or three days when on the way home I said to Thettalos, 'My dear, I said nothing before the others; but whatever are you doing with Thersites?'

He met my eye in a way I knew, which meant he was going to try and talk me round. 'Don't you think it would be new, and in the spirit of the times, to play him for sympathy?'

'What times? The play is about the Trojan war.'

'Well, but it's true Achilles did kill Patroklos, or cause his death. In Homer, the first thing you hear of Thersites is that he stood up to Agamemnon when he was in the wrong. Who else did?'

'Achilles. Diomedes, Chryses. Odysseus.'

'Well, Thersites spoke for the common people.'

'No, my dear, just for the mean ones. He is the voice of envy, which hates great good worse than great evil. In this Chairemon has followed Homer. Penthesilea is the part to play for sympathy; Thersites offers you contrast.'

'It's in the modern spirit,' he said. 'It's anti-oligarchical. Let us show the common man rebelling; they can do with that in Syracuse.'

'God help the Syracusans, if they recognise themselves in Thersites. They have forgotten greatness; all the more reason to remind them of it. Achilles' anger lasted a few days of his life, but scarcely a dramatist has stepped outside them. It is quite bold of Chairemon to show him at his best; why be afraid of it?'

'O Zeus!' he said. 'I believe you think I want to steal the scene. Do you think that?'

'No, indeed. I know you. You want to create what your mind has seen. I could do an Achilles to that Thersites; full of nothing but his own importance, indulging his own grief because it's his, and killing Thersites just for showing him up. It's not in the lines, but one could put it there. Who knows? The audience might eat it.'

'Well, then, why not?'

'I suppose because men could be more than they are. Why show them only how to be less?'

'One should show them true to life.'

'How not? But whose? Truth is to reckon on Achilles as well as Thersites, and Plato as well as Dionysios. There is truth even in Patroklos, who couldn't pass by a wounded man, and whom the slave-girls wept for because he never spoke them an unkind word. The world is not Thersites', unless we give it him.'

'Dear Niko, I didn't mean to put you out. Don't think of it again. You are directing, and I promised to be good. I just thought it would freshen the theme a little.'

As he walked on, I wondered how much of what I'd said I had picked up from the men of the Academy, even while rejecting their views.

Menekrates' house had settled down into a place for men. His wife had never worked, so the steward ran it as well as ever. After a few days, one of the servant-girls looked sleek, and had a new necklace; and Menekrates sang in the bath. His wife, a well-born girl, was inclined to bully him.

We were working hard on the play, but there was something just amiss with it. Thettalos was doing Thersites just as I said; but it was overdone, the character had lost all humanity. I could see he was not doing it on purpose; he was above such pettiness; it was only that the life had gone out of the part for him. I must simply leave him to settle down.

There was a rota for rehearsals in the theatre; the rest of the time we hired a room in the usual way. Some days went by before our theatre turn. We were still working without masks, so I could see with the tail of my eye; as I did my last exit, someone in front jumped up and made for the parodos. I waited. It was Speusippos.

'My dear friend,' I said, 'what is it?' He looked unshaven, even unwashed; his robe was dragged about him, and soiled along the border, as if he had trailed it in the dust.

'Niko. Can I speak to you alone?'

'Of course. Not in the dressing-room, everyone comes in there. Let us try the shrine of Dionysos.' I thought how gladly I had assumed that all was well with him, so that my work should not be disturbed. At least, if he could sit in the theatre he could not be on the run.

The sanctuary was empty, but for an old slave sweeping down. We sat on the plinth of a votive statue; it was my gilt panther bearing the god, bought from Philistos' fee.

'I was here all yesterday,' he said wiping his brow. 'Then I found a man with a list, who told me when you would be coming ... The guards won't let me into Ortygia any longer. I don't know what to do.'

'Ortygia?' I stared in surprise. 'I should have thought that would be the last place where you'd want to go. You're both well out of it.'

'No. Plato is still there.'

'But,' I said, as shocked as bewildered, 'they said when I called that he was staying with a friend.'

'He is the guest of Archidemos, yes. But the house is in Ortygia.'

I remembered the porter's reticence. Syracuse, as always, was full of spies.

'A few days ago,' Speusippos started to explain, 'Plato gave great offence to Dionysios . . .'

'Yes, yes, I know. Never mind how; what happened next?'

'Next day, he sent a message that the ladies of the household needed the guest-house for retreat and purification, before the Arethusa feast. An open lie, but at least a formal slight, better than a dagger in the dark. Or so we thought. Plato said it showed that the man had not surrendered all his soul to evil. The message said that a mutual friend, Archidemos, would gladly put him up till further notice; owing to the uncertain times, the Archon didn't wish him to leave Ortygia.'

'Can this host be trusted?'

'Certainly, for anything he can control. He's kin both to Dion and Dionysios; a Pythagorean, who has never touched politics. He reveres Plato deeply. I've been visiting every day, till now. Oh, yes, Archidemos is safe, but he's been anxious all along. With this feeling among the soldiers, anything can happen. And now they won't let me in.' He picked up the dusty border of his robe, and tugged it through his fingers.

'On whose authority?'

'I should think their own. Each day I've been insulted as soon as I was recognised; yesterday a Gaul took my pass to look at, and wouldn't give it back. They were all laughing. I think they hoped

I'd lose my temper; I saw it just in time to hold back. I appealed to a Roman officer who was passing – they're a little less barbarous than the Gauls – but he said that in his opinion I was being done a favour. I daren't think what he meant.'

'Are the troops still mutinous, then?'

'No, their demands have all been met. But the long-service men, who led the riot, have revived that old lie about Plato wanting them turned off. They feel sure he advised the pay-cut; I am told it's all over Ortygia.'

'Philistos,' I said. This followed the scene upon the gatehouse as night follows the day. 'Well, as we saw, the soldiers can't get into the Palace citadel as they choose.'

'You fool!' In the impatience of his trouble, he looked as if he could have struck me. 'Archidemos' house isn't in the Palace citadel. It's in outer Ortygia, where all the soldiers are quartered. The barracks are less than a stade away.'

I laid my hand on his knee and cursed Dionysios, neither likely to help much. 'At least they can hardly attack the house of the Archon's kinsman.'

'Unless there's another mutiny, when anything can be done. Or they can break in after dark; bribe a servant to poison him ... Niko. Have you a pass for Ortygia?'

'Yes, so has Thettalos. But you can't use a borrowed one; they know you. You would just end in the Quarries.'

'Of course. It's a great deal to ask, from you especially; I know your feelings about Plato's theory of art; but as a man ... I've no one else. Do you think you could go in, and see how things are with him?'

I thought, It means cancelling a rehearsal, and then, I suppose it will be dangerous. 'Certainly,' I said. 'I'll go tomorrow, one can't get in after dark.' Then I said, 'Well, I could try.' It would save time; and then we could still rehearse.

When I got back, Thettalos was pacing about in his best clothes. 'Wherever did you go? Have you forgotten the party at Xenophila's?'

'My dear, that well-named lady must do without me. A subsequent engagement. Give her my regrets.'

He had the truth from me within moments, and asked how I had dared think of going alone. I did not withstand him. Though, as I often told him, he had not enough sense to stay out of trouble, when in it he had great resource.

'Anything that happens,' he said, 'shall happen to us both. I suppose I must change my clothes ... No, you must change yours. Why do people like us walk about at night? Of course, to parties.'

I had a bath and a scented rub-down, and dressed myself to the teeth. Thettalos went out, coming back with a big straw-lined basket from which poked the necks of wine jars. 'I don't think,' he said, 'we need be above buying popularity.'

About sundown we reached the first gatehouse, and showed our pass to the Iberians, saying simply, 'We are going to the party.' Everyone at once knew which. They added that we should not find the drink run out.

'I told you so,' said Thettalos to me. 'But you would load us up like pack-mules. These lads are right. Who'll help us lighten the weight?'

We got in this way through all five gatehouses. Luckily the Gauls were off duty; they can drink like camels, and we would never have got away with a jar in hand, which I rightly guessed that we would need.

By the time we were in Ortygia it was almost dark. A link-boy came touting us; we hesitated, then took him on. It would show us up, but looked more natural for party guests. I had been at pains to learn the way to Archidemos' house, to avoid asking; but the boy led us easily, it was his trade to know the streets. We skirted the barrack quarter without mishap; it had been wise to dress well, like the friends of someone important. He had just told us the house was round this corner, when he peered ahead, stopped and drew back. We did the same.

It was a good street; all one saw of the houses was high court-yard walls, broken with thick doors and a lodge or two. Outside one doorway, a little way down, was a knot of soldiers. They were loafing about, keeping rather quiet; a child could see (and this one had done so) that they were up to no good.

'This is serious,' I said. 'Not like the gatehouses.'

The boy, pressed flat to the wall, said quickly that if the gentlemen did not mind the dirt, he could take us round to the back. We girded our robes, and followed him through alleys just wide enough for a laden donkey, where hens darted squawking from before our feet. Presently he turned and said, 'This way, sirs.' This alley was cart-width, and fairly clean. Further on a little fire was burning, with five men sitting round it; slaves, I assumed, till we got a little nearer. Then we saw they were soldiers.

The torch wavered; I started to draw back; then Thettalos said softly, 'Too late, don't stop.' He strode on, pushing the boy impatiently aside, towards the fire. The back-gate of a house, no doubt the one we sought, was just beside it. The soldiers stared; a Gaul, a Roman and three Greeks. Even sitting, one could see the Gaul was gigantic. His moustaches almost brushed his chest.

Thettalos said, 'Can any of you gentlemen tell us the way to Diotimos' house? This son of fifty fathers swore he knew the street, and now he's lost us.' One of the Greeks looked up. Thettalos said swiftly, 'Diotimos, son of Lykon, the Kyrenian.'

'Never heard *of him*.' They offered us others of the name, all of whom we rejected. I said it was clear we had been hoaxed; this was what came to wine-shop friendships. I was about to add that we were strangers in those parts, when I saw the way they were eyeing our clothes and rings, and noticed that the boy, though still unpaid, had run away. So I told them, with a good deal of self-importance, who we were; adding that the mud had ruined my new robe, which I had meant to wear next day for my audience with the Archon.

They exchanged doubtful looks. My accent had shown I was from Athens. One of the Greeks, who must have been sometimes in the theatre, peered up. 'If you're the actor, let's hear a speech.'

'By all means,' I said. 'But first, since we've lost our party, would you care to help out with this?' I offered the basket with the last of the wine-jars. 'To Hades with Diotimos, I'd sooner drink with honest men.'

This line was well received. It was a big amphora, and of course the wine was neat. No one complained of the lack of water. I thought the Gaul would never stop pouring it down. When next they demanded a recital, it was merely for diversion. 'I will give you,' I said, 'The Death of Ajax, if someone will lend me a sword.'

There was a flash of metal; then the Gaul seemed to jump right at me. The other four grabbed him back; this I could not see well, because Thettalos had thrown himself in between. Bawling with laughter, the Greeks explained that the Gaul, not having followed the dialogue, had thought they were about to cut our throats, and meant to help. It was all over in moments. Thettalos looked like a man who has done the natural thing, and thinks no more about it.

The Gaul begged my pardon, but added that no other man should have his sword. I bore up under this news (the weapon was about three feet long) and took a Greek one. As I walked off to acting distance, it came to me that I had never handled a real sword before. With its greasy hand-grip, old blood in the crevice of the tang, hacked blade and razor-bright edge, it was quite unlike a stage prop.

Needless to say, I gave them Polymachos' version of the death, known to all actors as the Barnstormer's Delight. Besides being just their mark, it has that passage where Ajax calls the gods to witness his wounds, and so on, endured in the cause of the Greeks, because of whose ingratitude he is going to run himself through. The soldiers all looked like veterans; the Roman was fairly seamed with war-scars. It was, without doubt, the most shameful performance of my life – I dared not look at Thettalos – but I could not complain of the house. They twice stopped the speech with cheering. At the end, since there was nowhere to go off, I had to kill myself on stage; which, having been brought up in the decencies of the theatre, I had no notion how to do. I contrived it by turning my back, fearing to the last that I would slice a finger off. As I lay in the dust, loudly acclaimed, I felt myself being lifted in enormous hands. The Gaul thought I had really done it.

I was now everyone's darling. Returning the sword with thanks, and plied with wine, I said they must be guarding some man of high rank, no doubt, to be posted here all night – a love-visit, maybe?

This brought me more than I bargained for. It is a kind of wit I can do without. Athenians, used to the good-natured phallic humour we all enjoy at the Lenaia, have no notion how nasty such jokes can be when cruelty informs them. I kept thinking that these were just five men out of thousands in Syracuse alone, all much the same. They were some time accounting for Plato's attachment to Dion's cause; going on to add that it was a pity, when they caught him, he would have to be finished off quickly before his rich friends got wind of it. They recounted, like men who sigh for the good old days, how he might have been dealt with in the old Archon's reign. There had been that Phyton, the general who had wasted everyone's time by holding out for months at the siege of Rhegium, till everyone inside was skin and bone, the women not worth having nor the men worth selling. Phyton had been hung all day from the top of a siege-tower, where the news was shouted up to him that they had just drowned his son. This he took as good news, which spoiled the joke; but when he was taken down, they whipped him through the streets, where each man could suit his fancy. At this the Roman, who had not said much till now, remarked that he had been there, and had seen no sport in it; the man was a good soldier, and bore it, one could only say, as if he had been a Roman. He himself and his mates had decided to put a stop to it by rushing the punishment squad and getting Phyton away. But they had done too much shouting first, so the squad had settled the matter by throwing him in the sea to find his son. There was some argument about this; but the Roman remained obstinate.

The Gaul, who had been getting a speech ready for some time in what Greek he knew, now said he had once seen Plato with his own eyes. It seemed none of the rest had done Palace duty. Pressed to tell more, he brooded awhile, and said, 'He looked like an Arch-Druid.' The Roman, interpreting, said Druids were a kind of holy warlock among the Gauls; they could call thunder, lightning, mist and wind, wither men away with a curse, and fly at will through the air. The Gaul confirmed all this, and began to look askance at the wall which hid such a person. One of the Greeks, however, pointed out that if Plato could fly through the air at will, by now he would be doing it.

'Sooner or later,' another said, 'he'll come out upon his feet. We're staying till the midnight watch; then five more of the lads are coming.'

I looked at Thettalos, as if I had just made up my mind to something, as indeed I had. 'Do you know,' I said, 'what I think?'

'No?' he answered, on cue.

'We've had a pleasant party. What harm have these lads ever done us, that we should go off without telling them the truth?'

'You're right,' said Thettalos. 'Just what I was thinking myself. You tell them, Niko.'

They all leaned forward. 'In my calling,' I said, 'one hears things. But if it ever gets known that I was the man you had it from ...' I shuddered. They vowed discretion, slicing their hands across their throats. 'Very well, then,' I said, playing up the suspense, 'I'll take the risk. I don't like to see brave men made catspaws of by those they've spilled their blood for.'

I now had a breathless audience. All this last week, the army must have been seething with rumour. I went on, 'I've had it from someone whose name, by the gods, I dare not tell you, that Plato's lodged where he is, to tempt you men into doing just what you plan to do. I was even told, though I don't know the rights of it, that he never advised the pay-cut; it was put about to set you on. From what I heard, they want him out of the way on account of Herakleides, but no one wants to answer for the deed. So, if it's done for them, to prove how clean their own hands are, they'll make an example of the killers, beside which Phyton's end will look like a pleasure-party. I don't know; I'm a stranger here. But when you men struck out for your rights the other day, you seemed to think the wrong man was put up then to be shot at. Well, that's all I heard. We've drunk together; so I give it you for what it's worth.'

There followed a gabble of which I understood about one word in three. They discussed it in the idiom of Ortygia, the mixed argot of the foreign troops, thick with the terms of their trade. It seemed I made sense to them. Indeed, when I thought about it, it made sense even to me. It would be just Dionysios' style.

I had spoken vaguely of Herakleides, not knowing if they favoured him. It seemed they did; so I said it was known all over the Inner Citadel that Plato had quarrelled with the Archon on his behalf. I did not say I had witnessed it, which would have made them sure I must be lying.

Presently the Greeks named some friends they thought should hear of this, and got up, followed by the Roman. The Gaul, however, had rolled into the shelter of the wall, with his cloak about him. When called, to my dismay he stayed where he was; he must have decided to watch alone. I could have cried with vexation, after all that work. Then the Roman went and pulled his arm. He turned on his back, and gave a great snore like a boar's grunting. He was dead drunk. The others shrugged, and went off.

We walked the other way till they had turned the corner. We could still hear them going off down the alleys. 'And now,' said Thettalos, 'how are we going to get in?'

'I shall be surprised, with things as they are, if no one is watching this gate inside.'

I tapped. There was no answer, but I could hear breathing. I announced my name, adding that we were friends of Speusippos, sent to bring him news of Plato. A stealthy voice was heard, asking me to repeat my name. I did so. It said, 'Can you prove who you are, sir?'

'By the dog!' I answered, 'didn't you hear me outside just now? I made noise enough.' Thettalos started laughing. I said with what restraint I could, 'Fetch your master Archidemos, and I will recite him some Euripides if he insists. But hurry, in the name of Zeus. There may be more soldiers coming soon.'

There was an iron-barred squint in the gate; a different eye appeared in it. The fire still gave some light. I heard the bolts being drawn. Archidemos was there beside his porter. He was an elderly man, tall, rather severe (perhaps just from hiding his fear) with the plain good dress of these rich Pythagoreans, and a family look of Dion. He apologised for our being kept outside; the gate was double-barred up again. We declined refreshment, pleading our haste, and paused only for a slave to wash our feet, which were filthy, before going in to Plato.

He was sitting at a table, with a writing-stand in front of him, working on the wax. I remember noticing he had just rubbed out about half a frame; but it showed the man was a professional, that he was trying to work at all.

He knew me at once; so I wondered, while I was presenting Thettalos, why his face showed so much dread, till he asked after Speusippos. Then it came to me that when he had failed to pay his daily visit, they had all supposed him murdered. I said he was well, and warned Plato of the danger he was in himself.

He heard me without much change of countenance, his face just setting a little more into its lines. 'Thank you,' he said when I had done, 'for confirming a warning I had yesterday. Some seamen came here, for no reason but that they were fellow Athenians, and, like sailors everywhere, democrats to whom an autarchy is odious. They had heard some tavern talk among the mercenaries, and advised me not to go out. But this guard, I believe, is new. It seems I have God to thank that Speusippos was turned away.'

Sir,' I said, 'we've got rid of the men out there, or so I hope, at least till midnight. I've been thinking that since actors move about more easily than most men, and with luck one can always appeal to the Delphic Edict, it might be worth your while to take the risk of coming with us now, before things get worse. I don't suppose any of the gatehouse guards would know you by sight.' I added, with apology, 'I'm afraid, sir, we are supposed to have been to a party, and we would all have to go back as if that were true.'

Before even the words were out of my mouth I knew it was no use; but I had never thought he would be amused. I could see his courtesy holding it in. 'My dear Nikeratos, you speak like a true friend and fellow-citizen; also a brave man. I am not less grateful to you both than if I had taken your offer, and owed you my life; pray believe this. But as you see, I am an old man, set in my ways, and without the skill for which you are so widely honoured. I don't think I could sustain the role of an old Pappasilenos, reeling home in a vine-wreath, before so shrewd an audience. I should be unmasked before long, and either end my life in a way not much to the credit of philosophy, or survive to delight the comic poets, and make my friends, both here and in Athens, ashamed to go out of doors. That would be a certain gain for tyranny; my death here, perhaps not.'

He had been looking at me; now his glance was caught by Thettalos; who all this while had been sitting, perfectly still, on a cross-legged stool with a woollen cushion, himself forgotten, all ears and eyes.

As I've said, he had never been a pretty boy; nor was he now what people today call handsome. He had the northern face, with strong cheekbones; his nose and chin were too boldly carved to please a modern sculptor. Yet if I could tolerate the notion of any actor playing without a mask, it would be Thettalos. I suppose by now I was in danger of getting used to him. Now, seeing through another's eyes, I thought, That is beauty.

You could not say Plato's face softened; it was more like a lamp touched by the taper, as he turned that way. I felt power flow out, and that charm which, as Dion said, had made and undone his cause. 'Does my choice surprise you? No, I see that you have understood. I must have been about your age, or a little more, when an old friend of mine in Athens was accused of changing the gods' worship, and corrupting the minds of us young men. He was put on trial for his life; the best man, I may say, whom I ever knew. We – all his friends – were present, in the hope of doing something for him.'

Thettalos listened with deep attention; I who knew him, could see him taking part of the sense from the voice, and storing it away.

'I had hoped to be called in evidence for the defence, since my witness was relevant to the charge; or at least, if we could not get remission, to have the sentence commuted to a fine. But he would not appeal for this. When he saw it meant disowning the truth he lived by, he replied in words something like these: "It would be strange, Athenians, if I who stood my ground in the line of battle, facing death at my commander's order, should desert the station where God posted me, from fear of death, or any fear. For what death is, we do not know; and no man can tell whether this which is feared as the greatest evil, may not really be the greatest good. But injustice, and disobedience to our betters, of whom God is best of all: these I know to be dishonour. So, if you say to me, 'This time we will let you go, on one condition, that you do not ask such questions any more', then I shall answer, 'Men of Athens, I honour you and love you. But I shall obey God, rather than you.'"'

He must have seen me move, for he turned to me, saying, 'You have heard these words?'

'Yes,' I said, seeing Dion's face above the broken wine-cup. 'Yes, indeed.'

He spoke some while with Thettalos, who told me after that he would remember it all his life. He was amazed my mind could have wandered; but it had concerns of its own. Soon I remembered that time was passing; whether with Plato or without him, we must be away. As I waited for a chance to say this, I recall Thettalos saying (for he had talked as well as listened) 'And yet, sir, men's souls put me in mind of scattered seeds, which may fall in cracks of the earth, or at a stream's edge, or where a stone rolls over them, so that each has to find its own path to the light and rain. Can one seed know it for another?'

Plato cast a look of longing at him; not for his body, though he had found that pleasing, but because he had to let him go with their dialogue scarcely begun. 'You are standing,' he said, 'at the very threshold of philosophy. What do we know, and what only guess? We know that without sun the shoot will not grow green, and without water it will die; just as we know that numbers cannot lie to us, but have the constancy of God. These things we can prove. Where proof ends, knowledge ends. Beyond, we must test each step, learning never to love opinion more than truth; never forgetting that men see as much truth as their souls are fit to see; always, till we pass through death and go forth to know ourselves, ready to go back to the start and look at all our premises, and begin again.'

I said it was time to be on our way, and asked if there were not some service we could do him. 'Indeed there is,' he said. 'You can tell Speusippos how I am placed, and ask him to send word to Archytas at Tarentum, or go himself if he can. Dionysios guaranteed my safety to Archytas, who can therefore ask formally for my release. If that is refused, Dionysios will have to answer for me to Archytas or anyone else whom it may concern. Even to himself; a thing which in his case should never be overlooked. If you will do this, I and my friends will be much beholden to you.'

The back-door guard was still absent. On the way to the gate-houses, we picked up some draggled wreaths shed by homebound revellers, and put them on. We were let through, in return for a good account of the party at each gate. When we were past the last and had turned the corner, Thettalos stopped, threw his wreath in the gutter, and dragged the back of his hand across his brows.

'Well,' I said to him, 'some of them wanted to rescue Phyton. I shall sleep better tonight for knowing that.'

'Niko, take those filthy twigs off your head, you don't know what you look like.' He removed my wreath, and stroked down my hair with his hand. 'Well, you have won, you monster; I shall have to reconsider Thersites.'

He was a great success. Whether the troops would have recognised themselves I am not sure, but the audience left them in no doubt. Chairemon, terribly put out, said it would have been as much as any judge's life was worth to give the play a prize; and we thought it better to leave the city before dawn next day.

While finishing our tour in other towns, we heard three pieces of news. The first was that Herakleides had kept ahead of Dionysios' search-party, and crossed the border into the Carthaginian province, to take ship for Italy; the second, that a state galley had come from Tarentum to ask for Plato, and that the Archon had let him sail. The third was that Dionysios had declared he could endure no longer to have his sister Arete joined in marriage to an exiled traitor who was his open enemy. Without her consent, in his authority as hierophant, he had pronounced her divorce from Dion, and had given her hand to a certain Timokrates, his favourite drinking companion.

17

It was now some weeks past midsummer. We were in the west, in
an Olympic year; it would be stupid to linger in Sicily when we
could take in the Games on our homeward way.

I had had to miss the last festival, and Thettalos had never
been at all; his father had believed in attending to business, not
jaunting about. I was nearly as eager as he; at my last visit, eight
years before, I had been little older than he was now. One's life
takes long strides, between Olympics.

I still knew my way about, well enough to buy stores at Elis and
hire a pack-mule, which costs less than being skinned by the
traders on the spot. We bought our own tent; if one sells it later
it's as cheap as hiring and much cleaner. There is a bank at Elis
where one can leave spare cash before going on. All the great festivals are holy to Hermes the Light-Fingered.

Having thus saved time and temper, we got on ahead of the
crowds, in time to pitch our tent in a cypress-grove with good
shade, so that we would not come back tired at evening to lie in
a bake-oven. On the best sites near the Altis, which are bespoken
by important visitors far ahead, servants were already putting up
pavilions, ready for when their masters came. The athletes who

for two months had been training here, were still walking about, like men with the place to themselves; thick hulking wrestlers, lean runners, broken-nosed boxers; and some most lovely boys, their proportions not yet spoiled, like the men's, with lopsided exercise for one event.

The crowds were coming. Every road had a dust-cloud ten feet high for as far as one could see. The first market was opening, for food, cook-pots and oil, blankets and tent-ropes, fire-grids and knives. Next day, when visitors are settled in, is the time for fairings, such as ribbons, gilt strigils, charms; cheap vases; painted figures of well-known actors in character (the comics sell best, but I found one or two of me). Last appear costly goods for rich connoisseurs: winecups with beautiful athletes drawn in the bowls, embroideries, small marbles, inlaid armour, books in fine calligraphy, goldwork from Macedon. There were women answering to all these classes, at prices to match. They had to keep the far side of the river, but one could see their tents, from straw lean-to's up to silk, skirting the banks, all ready for the athletes when they broke training, and the visitors loose from their wives.

Soon the quiet grove round our tent was a mass of squatters, putting up bivouacs, making cook-fires, or just spreading out the beds they would sleep on in the open. We hired a lad to guard our pitch, and went off sightseeing. In the Altis we met, of all people, Theodoros without a roof for his head. He had been invited months before by a well-off Athenian sponsor; this man, as appeared later, had been taken suddenly ill, too late to get word to Theodoros, who was then in Corinth, and now looked in vain for his host's pavilion. Of course, once his plight was known he would have had a score of offers, and we were flattered at his choosing to take pot-luck with us. He was a perfect companion for the feast, knowing who everyone was and what they had all been doing; no city in Greece held many secrets from Theodoros. At bedtime, when we were sitting round our fire, he did us his party tricks; he could imitate any animal or any thing with a sound. When he did his most famous turn, the creaking windlass, all the campers in hearing, who had to fetch water from the river, started up and began looking for the well. To explain would have brought us a crowd of hundreds; we had to smother our laughter and leave them searching.

Next morning was the formal opening of the Games; the air rang with trumpet-calls from the heralds' contest; presently the winner, who would give out all the victories, sounded for the Dedication. We saluted Zeus and Pelops from a distance; the crowd round the Great Altar was as thick as porridge, and as hot.

By now the sleepy valley was like a city, and all the sideshows were on. In the recital hall some political philosopher, from the school I think of Isokrates, was delivering an endless lecture, instructing the world's leaders how to conduct their state affairs for their own good and that of Greece. All the envoys, sophists and politicians were there; the hall was packed and they were standing in the stoa, even out in the sun. Theodoros pointed out to us the secret agents, who, indifferent to what the expert insisted should be done, were moving among his auditors to learn what was really happening. We noticed too a knot of bright-haired Macedonians, loaded with massive jewellery (I admit they can wear it, and it is exquisitely made), all listening just like Greeks. Though they make wildly enthusiastic theatre audiences (every actor has a stock of stories about Pella), this sophistication surprised me. Theodoros, however, said he noticed a change each time he went there; they were getting more and more involved with the southern states; not, he added, that it would come to much until one of their kings could contrive to stay alive for two Olympiads running. It was remarkable, he said, that the role was still so much sought after. He wondered how the lecturer would shape in it.

We walked on, visiting a booth of dancing dwarfs, a concert in the Mixolydian mode for double-flute, aulos and kithara; a diviner who foretold the winner of the stade-race by casting pebbles (the morrow proved him wrong), and even, briefly, some lawyer's exposition of how he could win his client's case when justice, law, public opinion and all the evidence were on the other side. Then we walked back the way we came. In all this time, the political philosopher had only just stopped talking. The street crowd had dispersed, and the audience was coming out, discussing as keenly as if all these words might engender some real event.

I was saying this to Theodoros, when at the far end of the street I saw someone coming, whose walk I knew at a glance. It was Plato. Speusippos was with him, Xenokrates, and a group of friends and well-wishers. I was glad to see him back where he belonged, among people fit for him; and pointed him out to the others. Thettalos remarked that he was looking better, but that Syracuse had left its mark. Theodoros, who had been watching intently, said, 'From the people greeting him, it seems he has only just arrived.'

'Yes,' I answered. 'He'll have come straight from Tarentum.'

'Then, my dears, let us wait where we are, for unless I'm wrong we shall see a memorable bit of theatre. In a moment he will meet with Dion.'

'Are you sure?' For some reason I wished to doubt it. 'There were none of his men working on the pavilions.'

'Niko, my dear, you don't suppose Dion has to bring his own tent like common people? He'll be at the state hostel, the Leonideion, with the other lions. Look, here he comes now.'

He came out into the sunlight, with a train about him, among them Herakleides and his Athenian friend, Kallippos. They were conversing, and well out in the street before they noticed anything. Plato saw Dion first. He slowed down; those with him all fell silent. As he came on, people round them became aware. He must have felt it; but he had had practice lately in keeping his thoughts to himself, if he had needed it. I saw, or fancied, a searching in his face; either of the man down the street, or the man within.

Now Dion had noticed the stares. He scanned the street; stopped dead; strode forward. Thettalos' hand closed round my wrist.

They met. Dion clasped Plato's hands, took his arm, and drew him aside. The gesture was explicit, dismissing both their retinues; all fell back, and stood looking after them as they walked our way. I saw Kallippos pour out words to Herakleides. I don't know what they were looking for; as for me, I had seen what I had seen: the perfect seemliness with which Dion had greeted Plato and asked after his health, and his impatience showing behind it like fire round a furnace door. It was something to be got through, before he could ask for news.

Of all places on earth, I should think none offers less privacy than Olympia in Games Week. One can't even relieve nature in the presence of fewer than a dozen; one would need to walk a mile into the country, to find oneself alone. Dion was a Council guest; Plato no doubt was sharing a tent with friends. Neither was one for creeping into a corner. What Plato had to tell Dion, he told him in the Street of Victors, upon the marble seat under the statue of Diagoras the Runner. Standing between two plinths near by, we saw it all.

I daresay Dion must have heard something about the selling-up of his properties; but I think he must have supposed the capital still intact, if Dionysios could be got to send it. In any case, I could tell the truth had taken him by surprise. One could guess just how it was going; Plato leading in with the loss of the money, as the least of the evils; Dion swallowing that without too wry a face, his calm just setting hard; then asking after his son. I knew that from Plato's pause. He told, I suppose, as much truth as he had to. Dion swallowed; his mouth clenched; this touched him closer. Plato offered some consolation; I don't know how much he heard of it. He was watching Plato's face, which told him something unguessed was still to come. I could tell just the moment when he cut him short to ask.

Plato did not keep him waiting. After that, there was silence. It seemed to spread from Dion all along the street. It was like one of those great mute build-ups in Aischylos, for Achilles or for Niobe. But no big speech followed. Dion just clenched his fist and brought it quite slowly down upon his knee. His face said all the rest. Looking round, I saw Kallippos grasp Herakleides' arm; Speusippos turned to Xenokrates, triumph in his eyes. Dion saw it too; a man used to living in public, who had said the thing he meant; no going back now. Then, as if pulled against his will, he turned again to Plato.

Plato said something, a handful of words, and slowly shook his head. For a moment he seemed quite alone, like a man watching a ship out of sight. Somewhere she may make port; but not the harbour he faced the storm for. He commends her to heaven, and turns away.

When they had gone, Theodoros, who, without knowing what we knew, had known well what he was looking for, said, 'Did you see their faces? There will be war.'

I said that it seemed so to me. We talked; but Thettalos was quiet. At last he turned to me and said, 'Did he love his wife? You said not.'

'That was my guess. But he would hardly tell me.'

308

'In any case,' said Theodoros, 'think of the affront. Could there be a greater?'

Looking at me again, Thettalos said, 'Well, not to him.'

I understood him. I remembered Speusippos' little flute-girl, whose father had died in the Quarries, one of thousands in those long years. I had seen, just now, her story and his anger still burning in Speusippos' face. I thought of Plato, thrown to the wolves of Ortygia, scraping out barely with his life. Through all these things, Dion had remembered the maxims of Pythagoras and the teachings of the Academy. But there is a limit to what the just man can bear.

We walked on towards the temple. I lifted my eyes. There on the west gable stood Apollo, stern and beautiful among the Lapiths, shedding victory from his lifted arm.

I thought, Perhaps it is impossible for a philosopher to be a king; at any rate, to be both at once. Perhaps that is only for the god. There at his side stand Theseus and Pirithoos, the heroes who will win his battle. We are weary of ourselves, and have dreamed a king. If now the gods have sent us one, let us not ask him to be more than mortal.

18

It was a year before Dion was ready. The talk about Olympia would have died down, but for the rumours that ran underground like the shoots of the aloe, always coming up somewhere new. Greece was scattered with Syracusan exiles; father and son, the tyranny had lasted nearly half a century. These people were being sounded; I can confess, after so long, that I did some of this work myself. Sometimes I carried a letter to someone of importance, sometimes just took the feeling of the exiles in the place. I did not often see Dion; usually Speusippos took my reports. The Academy was in very deep.

Plato I never saw, except by chance as I came and went. He would greet me, but never ask my business. He had told everyone where he stood. Dion had been wronged; he had the right to claim satisfaction, their friends the right to support him. Plato would neither blame nor praise. Himself, he believed about civil violence what his hard youth had taught. Besides this, he was Dionysios' guest-friend, with all its religious duties. When people reminded him of the days in outer Ortygia, he would answer that Dionysios had done nothing to him, though he had power to take his life and had been angry with him; the sanctities of their bond still stood inviolate. He was old; he could not bear arms, even if he had had the right. Therefore (though often urged to it, I believe) he would not make war with his tongue or pen, which he thought a coward's compromise. If ever the two kinsmen could be reconciled, his duty would be to mediate, being bound to both.

Corinth, the mother-city, had more Syracusan exiles than any other place. It costs a good deal to live there; so it was mostly the exiled aristocrats who had been settling there over the years. With these I did not deal; Dion's brother Megakles did that, being one of themselves. He was Dion-and-water, you might say: good-looking, dignified, soldierly, fairly tall, but everything scaled-down. I doubt if the wrongs of Syracuse had ever irked him much, while he suffered none himself; but he was a Sicilian noble, well-bred and brave, and eager for revenge. I minded my own business; but from what I knew of the exiles, whose children were growing up Corinthians, I did not think they would be rushing to leave this pleasant city and take arms against the greatest power in Hellas.

Thettalos agreed; but was less concerned than I. He came and went, trying his hand at whatever he felt he could grow by; he was now wanted as a second by good leading men, and his range was stretching with each new role. We understood each other. I knew pretty well, by now, what kind of actor I was, and how to use it; he was still learning to know himself (I daresay there was more to know); as this or that choice crossed his path he was restless and moody, all ups and downs. Neither of us could have borne for long to work together; owning this frankly, and taking the weather as it came, we escaped shipwreck and found new shores. He came back from Delos, where he had made a hit, swearing nothing had gone right with him, and demanding to work with me, if only for one production. 'You taught me how, Niko; now you remind me to ask why. Perhaps it's these philosophers you can't keep away from.'

Just now, as I have explained, one could learn a good deal at the Academy besides philosophy; for instance, that Dion was hiring soldiers. With all his Sicilian losses, he was still richer than I had guessed till now. Most of the exiles had failed him; he did not get firm pledges from more than thirty. The rest had suffered too much before they got away, or feared for their kin in Syracuse, or liked their comforts, or simply did not think the venture had any chance. So the landless, banished Dion hired spearmen like a king. They were taken on in the Peloponnese, marched west, and ferried over to Zakynthos, where they were trained by Megakles. Only he and the captains knew what they were to do. Zakynthos is a quiet island, very rustic; I don't think there is even a theatre. Not much leaked out from there.

None the less, by next year's sailing weather, something was known in Syracuse. No doubt the exiles had talked. Greece was as full as ever of Dionysios' agents; which meant Philistos'. The latest fugitives, friends of Herakleides, went straight to him and Dion, and said that the old man now ruled Syracuse in all but name. They added that he could have had that too if he had tried; he had at least the virtue of loyalty. Since Plato left, Dionysios had thrown himself back into dissipation, and was seldom sober enough for any serious business. As the drink gained on him he got grosser in his pleasures; Philemon, who had lately appeared at the theatre there, assured me that the very hetairas, when the Archon asked them to supper, drew for the short straw because no one wanted to go. His son Apollokrates, now a growing youth, despised him openly, preferring the company of the mercenary captains. But young Hipparinos was still to be seen at every party, his uncle's favourite, very much at home.

Speusippos supported the war without reserve. The little flute-girl, whose sleepy face I remembered, had kept him awake to some purpose. Afterwards he had met some of her friends; and, in the end, people had talked to him who, because he had been received by the Archon, had fought shy of him before. The more he heard, the angrier he grew; but also the more hopeful. Dion's exile had made him a legend among the people. He would come again, like some ancient hero-king, to lead them all to freedom. If no one would sail with him, let him come alone, and he would have an army from the moment his foot touched land.

Some of the younger men from the Academy were already setting their affairs in order, to be ready for the call. Axiothea confided to me her grief that she could not be one of them. 'I must have done wrong,' she said, 'in my last life on earth, and this is the punishment I chose when my eyes were opened. So I ought to bear it patiently, and hope for better next time. But oh, it is hard.'

Speusippos himself would not be going. Plato, now trying to make good a lost year of work, could not have spared him; besides, he too had been, even if uneasily, the Archon's guest; he ranked next to Plato at the Academy, and it would have been almost like Plato going himself. But some of their most distinguished men were putting their books aside and polishing their armour. One of them, Miltas of Thessaly, came from a long line of seers in Apollo's service; it was he who chose the day when Dion sailed; just after the god's feast-day. Dion arrived at Zakynthos in time to perform a sacrifice of dedication.

He reviewed his troops the day before, and told them what the war was. They were shocked; they were professionals, and knew the defences of Syracuse. They started to shout; but Dion had not commanded troops all those years for nothing. He got them quiet; told them the prospects of success, with no words wasted; and had them cheering for him at the end.

On Apollo's day, he arranged a splendid ceremony, every vessel made of gold; then he feasted his men, all eight hundred, in the race-track. Such wealth he had left, after hiring, keeping and training them. The display did its work; they were certain he could not spend like this unless he were sure of support in Sicily.

Word of all this came back to Athens, then and later, as the Academy men sent news. To tell it whole, however: on the very night before they sailed, when everyone was happy, singing by moonlight round the fires, the full moon started to wane and to change her colour, and presently was in eclipse. The men were appalled. No omen, they said, could be worse for any army; this very same sign had come to the Athenians before Syracuse in the Great War. The whole force had perished off the earth, and even that had been only the beginning of evils.

Here Dion, who could have explained the matter by its rational laws, showed himself a shrewd commander. He called on Miltas to read the signs. That wise man proclaimed that the moon must stand for the brightest and biggest power on earth, as in the heavens; here was the empire of Dionysios being quenched before their eyes to give them heart. No omen could be better.

The men were cheered. One thing Dion and his brother took care to keep from them; Herakleides, who had promised to raise a fleet of ships with men to sail and fight it, had not arrived at Zakynthos.

During the year of preparation, a coolness had begun between him and Dion. As exiles working together they had had to see more of each other than at home. Herakleides had an offhand hail-fellow way, which was part both of himself and of his politics; he made it a touchstone of goodwill to be met on his own terms. This Dion would not do; at first because it went against his grain, later because he grew to distrust the man. Now Herakleides sent excuses; whether good or not I don't know, nor I daresay did Dion either. At all events, he put his faith in the god, and set sail with what he had.

There were three good-sized freighters in the little fleet, with two war-triremes for escort. As well as his men's own arms, he carried shields and weapons for two thousand men. At the heel of Italy, the fleet of Syracuse, under Philistos, was waiting to cut him off.

He got word of this in time; and now truly he threw all into Apollo's hand. Instead of hanging back in the hope of Philistos' going away, he left the coastwise route which every sane ship-master follows, and struck out across open sea. I turn queasy even to think of it.

Apollo blessed him. They made Sicily in twelve days with a fair wind all the way. Their landfall was the South Cape, which was a bare thirty miles from Syracuse; this seemed tempting the god a little far. They stood out again; and as if to punish their doubt, ran into a storm which blew them across to Africa, and nearly ran them aground. They laboured with oars off a lee shore; were becalmed off Great Syrtis Heads, and said their prayers. A breeze from the forgiving god cradled them back to Sicily; they landed at Minoa, in the Carthaginian province.

The troops of the guard-post all turned out, thinking the war had started up again. For this Dion was prepared. He had warned his men that their lives would depend on their steadiness; they had the advantage of numbers, and must push back these men without bloodshed; then he could treat with the commander. They locked shields, and took the strongpoint without killing a man. Dion sounded for a parley. Up came the Captain; and turned out to be a man he knew. Dion had taken his surrender in some old campaign and treated him with honour. As soon as he was assured they were not marching against the power of Carthage, he came to terms. Dion gave up the strongpoint;

Synalos quartered his soldiers and gave them stores. Anywhere in Sicily Dion's word was good. If he threw out Philistos and his master, no Carthaginian would complain; if, as rumour had it, he meant to disarm Ortygia and disperse her mercenaries, they would object still less.

Dion's men were in camp at Minoa when news came of the god's greatest favour yet, a bounty almost past belief. Not only was Philistos still away watching the door of the empty stable; Dionysios himself had sailed from Syracuse, with eighty of the ships that were left, all filled with troops.

Don't ask me why. Perhaps he thought Dion would put in at Tarentum, and he could kill two birds with one stone; I don't suppose he had forgiven Archytas for demanding Plato. Or maybe he just wanted to be in at the death. Whichever it was, I am sure he did it on impulse after being left to his own devices. I should think Philistos could have killed him.

Dion's men were so struck with this run of luck that they declined the rest he offered them to get over the sea-trip, and begged him to push on while the stars were good. I don't know what they would have said if they had known the whole story of Apollo's care for Dion. He had just worked him a miracle.

Dionysios, when he sailed, had left as regent his favourite Timokrates, the husband of Dion's wife. This man, at the news of the landing sent a fast courier to Italy with letters to him and to Philistos. The man landed at Rhegium, and took the quick inland road towards Kaulonia, where the Archon had his ships. There he met someone he knew, who had been at a sacrifice and brought back a gift of meat. Since the courier could not stay to share it, the friend gave him a cut to eat when he had time. Knowing the business urgent, he pushed on long after dark; when he had to rest, the hills were desolate, with no shelter but a wood beside the road. Too tired to cook, he supped on a crust, and slept with his letter-wallet by his head. He awoke to find it gone, with the meat which had been tied to it. His panic search showed him no trace of human thieves; only the marks of wolf-pads, and a dragging trail between. All morning he searched the wild country round about, hoping that when the wolf had eaten it would have dropped the bag; but it must have taken it to its lair, for its young to chew on. No one, it seems, had told him what the message said; he was there to do as he was told. He could only confess, you may suppose with what result. So he did just what I would have done in his shoes, ran away up to Italy and changed his name. Long after, he told the story. The wolf, as everyone knows, is a creature of Apollo.

Dion meantime with his eight hundred set out for Syracuse, leaving his spare arms with Synalos, who agreed to send them on.

They were needed soon. They were hardly across the Halys into Greek lands, when men started coming in: cavalry from Akragas, hoplites from Gela (which old Dionysios had let the Carthaginians sack, when it served his turn); more from Kamarina. As soon as they got to the country around Syracuse, the peasants came down from the hills; serfs of the great landowners, the little russet Sikels who were there before the Hellenes; poor Greek small-holders, ruined by the taxes which had bought old Dionysios' catapults and young Dionysios' girls. Load after load the spare arms were issued. It was as if a god had come down to lead them.

All who were there are in agreement that Dion never sank, in all this time, below his role. It was as if he had been rehearsing for it all his life. He was now at an age when he might have sat to a sculptor rather for Zeus than for Apollo. In the years at the Academy he had grown his beard; now it had a short soldier's trim. He was a hard-muscled, noble Zeus, fit to throw thunderbolts, a Zeus for Pheidias; the grizzle in his hair only gave him dignity. He was saviour, hero, father; if he kept his distance it was only fitting.

Timokrates, his despatches bringing no help, was trying to put Syracuse upon defence with the few men left him, and had to call in reservists to man the walls. These were mostly land-pensioned veterans of the old Archon's wars, from Leontini. He put these on the city ramparts, keeping his regulars to hold Ortygia. Dion, whose last recruits had come from inside Syracuse itself, heard of these dispositions, and staged a feint advance on Leontini, now stripped of all its men. Young boys came racing up to the Syracusan walls to warn their fathers, who opened the gates and quick-marched for home, not reckoning they owned young Dionysios anything. After dark Dion marched straight on to Syracuse. Daybreak found him at the river Anapos, a mile away.

Before he went on, he sacrificed to Apollo Helios. He had now got five thousand men behind him. He looked so godlike to them, bay-crowned, lifting his hands to the sun, that they all broke sprays from the trees and wreathed themselves for victory. Nor was their over-confidence punished; let us call it prophecy.

When the Leontinians deserted, Timokrates sent orders to close all the gates into Ortygia. But before he could get back there himself, the Syracusans were rushing out through the city to welcome Dion. If he showed himself he would be lynched; and outside was the man he had done a wrong to, which demands the extremest vengeance everywhere. He grabbed the first horse he could find, wrapped his cloak round his face, and got away. To justify himself, he galloped about describing the vast might of Dion's forces, and making him sound invincible; so that those who from prudence had held back before, now flocked to join him. All the veterans of Leontini, finding their homes and women safe, joined to a man.

Syracuse was free. Before Dion had set foot inside, the tyranny was broken. Every man could speak his mind, and do as he chose. They chose first of all to hunt down Philistos' band of informers. All over the streets, these people, and people who looked rather like them or were their kin, or whom someone denounced for private vengeance, were chased or run down at home or dragged from the temples they had fled to, and battered to death by the crowd.

Dion marched up to the walls, and they opened the great gates for him. He had put on his parade armour, inlaid with gold. On his right marched his brother, on his left Kallippos the Athenian. Herakleides and his ships had still not arrived.

The chief men of the city came out clothed in white. As they went up the Sacred Way, flowers and wreaths and ribbons showered on them from the house-roofs. People set up altars and sacrificed in thanksgiving as Dion passed by. Treading in laurel and myrtle, rose-wreaths and blood, he went on to the great sundial of Dionysios which stands opposite Ortygia, and from its dial addressed the citizens. With the favour of the gods, he said, he had brought them liberty. It was theirs, if they would only help him to defend it.

At once they wanted to give him and Megakles the office of military dictator the Archons had held before. He thanked them; would not take advantage of men so unused to freedom; and proposed a council of twenty, from the returned exiles and such loyal friends as Kallippos. This being carried with acclaim, he marched on the last strongpoint that still held out, the great fortress of Euryalos. Its garrison had barred themselves in for safety rather than offence; they surrendered, on condition they either joined Dion or left the city. The garrison of Ortygia could do nothing but watch all this from the gatehouses, and be thankful for the gates. In the Captain's lodging of Euryalos were the great bronze keys of the Quarries. Among cheers that must have been audible on the slopes of Etna, Dion turned the locks to free the captives.

Now only Ortygia still held out. That was impregnable; but Dion had a siege-wall built on the land side of its neck, to seal it fast. He got his new recruits armed and drilled and set up his command in the Euryalos. Seven days later Dionysios, who had had the news at last, sailed up with his ships into Ortygia dockyard.

If Herakleides and the promised fleet had come, they might have stopped him. As it was, Dion's men could do nothing but look on. Dionysios could bring in everything he needed; soon Philistos came too, with a second fleet. Ortygia would be a long business. But meantime, Syracuse was free.

With the forces he had, Dionysios could have landed along the coast and attacked by land; but he stayed in Ortygia, hoping, as it turned out later, to agree with Dion privately, as one gentleman with another. As the Archon saw it, the rabble had just been the engine of Dion's private war, and need not be considered. Having known Plato, he should have known Dion better than this. He sent back the envoys, saying he would read nothing that could not be laid before the people. Public proposals came, for remission of taxes, talks and so forth. The Syracusans laughed, and Dion sent word that if Dionysios would abdicate, he would treat with him for his safe-conduct. Short of that, he could save his breath.

After a while, Dionysios offered to consider this, on terms to be agreed, and asked for envoys. Some leading citizens went; the gatehouse guards were seen idling, calling out to the people that they would soon be out of work. At sunset the talks were still going on; the envoys would stay overnight. However, all seemed settled; the troops on the Syracusan siege-wall took a lazy watch, as the enemy was doing. Work on the wall, a rough makeshift meant to be reinforced, had stopped. At midnight the five gates of Ortygia opened; the garrison rushed out upon the siege-wall and its sleepy men.

The yelling Nubians, their faces daubed like white skulls; the naked, painted, seven-foot Gauls, drunk on raw wine; the steady iron-hard Romans, rushed on citizens unused to fend for themselves, new to arms and half awake. They broke and fled screaming. That would have been the end but for Dion's regulars, who did not wait for the trumpet but got to the wall as soon as he. His voice drowned by the din, he just showed himself in the vanguard and led them on. A fine thundering Zeus, with a javelin like a lightning-bolt, he rallied the line till his shield was stuck full of broken points and his corselet dented all over. Even when a spear went through his right hand, he got on a horse and rode about to encourage the Syracusans, getting some back to fight. By now he had brought up the men from the Achradina; the enemy was contained in the streets nearest the causeway; under this new onslaught they broke and fled, many being trapped below the wall. On Dion's side only seventy-five were killed; partly because his regulars fought so well, partly because the Syracusans had not stayed to fight at all. They were very grateful, and voted the troops extra pay of a hundred minas; the men spent part of it on a golden wreath for Dion.

Next day the envoys were sent home. Dionysios, though he broke the truce, had not sunk to killing them; perhaps, after all, Plato's visit had not been for nothing.

The next embassy from Ortygia was addressed to Dion in person. He received it publicly; and was handed letters from his wife and mother. These he read in a steady voice aloud to the people; they were sad, but innocent of intrigue. At the end, one more letter came out; this he was begged to read in private, since it was from his son. He must have been tempted for many reasons; but he broke the seal. The letter inside was not from Hipparinos at all, but from the Archon. It is in the archives of the Academy; I read it once. People say now it was a clever bit of policy, but to me it reads just like the man; all feeling, petulance, self-pity and unreasonable hopes. It dwelt on Dion's years of faithful service to both the Archons; reproached him with unjust resentment; swore his kindred, wife and mother should suffer for it if he kept it up; begged him not to throw holy Syracuse to a senseless mob, who would bring her down in chaos and then blame him for it; and, as a flourish at the end, offered to accept him as the Archon, if he would maintain the autarchic rule. I daresay Philistos added that.

Dion disdained to write back, and sent a short soldier's answer. But the letter had not been in vain. The people knew he had had these offers; surely they must tempt him? It was argued in the wine-shops; Dion's men just laughed, or hit out if they were fighting-drunk. By now they loved him like a father.

It was now that at last Herakleides arrived in Syracuse, with twenty triremes and fifteen thousand men.

He had held back a long time. If his heart had been in helping, he would have come, like Dion, with what he had. The triremes alone, without the troop-freighters, might have kept Dionysios out of Ortygia. One can hardly doubt he meant to find Dion in trouble, rescue the enterprise and take command. What he wanted after that, whether it was for the people or himself, he is not here to tell us.

In any case, he found Dion an honoured victor, adored by his troops and respected by the citizens. Something had to be done, if Herakleides was not to be just the slow-belly who gets there after the feast. He had still much in his favour; his exile spoke for his stand against the tyrant; and he had his cheery, hearty way. No one could miss the contrast. If Dion at fifty had not learned ease with people yet, I suppose he showed a kind of sense in not straining at it, like an actor forcing his limits.

All these parleys with Ortygia having ended nowhere, the land war was getting static; but some of Dionysios' war-triremes decided to join the Syracusans, so that Herakleides now commanded sixty ships. One day he got word that Philistos was sailing up towards the straits. Now was his chance of glory. The fleets engaged; Philistos was hemmed in; when they took his galley, the old man was lying on the poop, with his sword stuck into his belly. Being nearly eighty, he had not had strength enough to do a clean job, and was still alive. Herakleides, who always knew how to please the people, gave them him to play with.

You may say he knew what he deserved, which was why he had tried to kill himself. He had been the right arm of the tyranny, father and son, since it began. But you could say of him too that he remained faithful to the son, from whom he could have taken everything, though the father had had him exiled on mere suspicion. That he should have put on arms at all, at his age, when he might have sailed off with a sack of gold to die in bed at ease, might have earned him some grudging honour. No matter; it was the death of Phyton all over again, though there was no tyrant now to order it, just the free citizens of Syracuse. A siege-tower they lacked; in any case, they were too impatient to wait a day. He was stripped naked, and haltered. Because of his wound he could not be got to walk about the streets; but he was dragged along, and every man did what pleased him. At last, when it could be seen he was senseless and would give no more sport, they hacked his head off, and gave his trunk to the boys for what it was worth. They tied it by one leg, lamed in battle fifty years before, and pulled it about till they got tired, when they threw it on a dung-heap. By the time Dion got the news, the man was dead.

I have been told, by Timonides of the Academy who sailed with him, that Dion shut himself up alone all night. It had always been his faith that honour begets honour. He had sweated and bled to free these people; they had had a share of his soul. Small wonder if while Herakleides went drinking with the captains, everyone's hero, he did not join the feast. Long ago at Delphi, when they killed Meidias, I had seen he did not understand. He did not know a crowd. He had not learned, even yet, what most men are who have had to eat dirt for two generations. He was not content to pity them, and be angry with those who had debased them; he had wanted to persuade himself that freedom would ennoble them. When they had forsaken him in battle, he had forgiven them; he was a soldier, and did not expect too much from half-trained men. I think it was this killing that first seared his mind. Such people, he began to think, could not know their own good; if left to fend for themselves, they would suffer worse than under the tyranny, and sink even lower: for he believed what Sokrates had taught Plato, and Plato him, that it is better to suffer evil than to do it.

Autumn was closing the open seaways, though ships still crossed the straits to Italy, as they do in good weather all the year. There were no more sea-fights; but Herakleides now equalled Dion in public esteem. He was pleasant to everyone, and made no secret of his belief that Syracuse should be governed just like Athens, by popular assembly and the general vote. As long, however, as Dionysios still sat in Ortygia, the need of a commander was clear to everyone. Herakleides was content at present to intrigue for an equal share in the command.

I don't know what Dionysios did when he learned of Philistos' death, and knew he had now got to conduct the war himself; I suppose he got drunk. What's certain is that before long he sent to Dion, offering the surrender of Ortygia: the Palace, the castle, the ships, his standing army and five months' full pay for it, in exchange for his own safe-conduct into Italy, and a yearly revenue from his private estates.

Dion must have been tempted by now to make his own terms out of hand. However, he had pledged his honour to lay all tenders before the people, and for him this settled the matter. With one voice the people said no. They had tasted blood with Philistos; how much sweeter would his master's be! Dionysios must be at his last gasp, to make this offer; they were resolved to have him alive. In vain Dion told them that all they had been fighting for was theirs to take if they chose. They only thought (and said) 'There is a man who has not suffered.' Sicily is a land where revenge is prized. Some said he must have had a better offer than before, to let the tyrant off scot-free; but then the man was his kin. None of these rumours was opposed by Herakleides. Perhaps he believed them; it is easy to think the worst of a man one hates. The envoys were sent home empty; the siege went on. Herakleides spent more and more time ashore, busy with his politics. And one misty dawn in early autumn, when the lookouts of the fleet were taking it easy, Dionysios boarded a ship, cast off with a little squadron that carried all his treasures, and sailed away. By the time the news broke, he was in Italy.

When this reached Athens, nothing else was talked of all over the City. The greatest tyranny in Hellas had been broken, and by a man trained in Athens; almost an Athenian, you might say. At the Academy, grey-haired philosophers ran about like schoolboys. Axiothea and her friend both kissed me in the olive grove. They told me, what was not yet known in the streets, that Ortygia still held out without its lord, who had left the young Apollokrates in command. This passed even my notion of the man; if his son was like him, the war was as good as won, and we agreed we might as well rejoice now as later. We recalled that not very long ago a shooting star had crossed the heavens, so brilliant that it had been seen from a dozen cities, and had turned the night into day.

A number of people gave parties in honour of the event, among them Thettalos and I. Theodoros told us a splendid story. He had lately played in Macedon before the new King, Philip, a man who he predicted would be harder to kill than those before. It seemed that when the bright star appeared, this hill-king thought it had been sent in his own honour, because he had won some battle and a chariot-race, and then his wife had had a son. He and his whole court had drunk all through the night upon it. Then, only a few weeks later, had come the great news from Syracuse. So having laughed at the barbarian's pretences we thought no more of him, and drank to the freedom of all Greeks.

19

'Oh, Nikeratos!' said Axiothea (she was the first I told). 'Are you really going to Sicily? Dear friend that you are, I could almost hate you. Where will you be playing? Not, surely, in Syracuse, with the siege still on?'

'Nowhere, that I know. For once I'm travelling for pleasure. Why not, while I've got my strength?'

'Strength? After that lion-like Diomedes? I am ashamed of you. Is Thettalos going too?'

'No, he's in Ionia. He's a partner now, and won't be free for some weeks. This I am doing just for myself. I saw this enterprise begin; I'd like to be there when it is crowned.'

These words, once spoken, displeased me. When a tragic actor talks of crowns – especially when he has just won one – he talks of tragedy. I had only just dodged the bad-luck-word; I am care-ful of such things, and it was unlike me.

I asked her what fresh news there was. Timonides still wrote to Speusippos; but he, between his research, his Academy business, and keeping up the archives of the campaign, was too busy now to get about much, and I seldom met him. She answered that he had had a letter last week and there seemed no great change.

Then she added, 'But we don't see all the despatches now. They used to be read aloud. Of course, there must be less to tell. It seems the man Herakleides (you know, he was never one of *ours*) is still giving trouble. Did you ever meet him?'

'For a moment, once. I thought him a good simple soldier, which he is not. He should have been an actor. But I wouldn't want him in my company. He'd hide your mask and do a brilliant impromptu while you looked for it.'

'Did you hear what he did to get back in the citizens' favour, after he let Dionysios get away? He proposed at the Assembly that all Syracusan land should be divided equally.'

'What, now?' I said. 'With the war still on? I don't believe it.'

'It's true. I saw that part of the letter.'

'In Sicily! No one would give up a yard of onion-patch without a fight. There would have been a riot; then a sortie from Ortygia, and Dionysios back at home.'

'Herakleides must have known that, I suppose, as well as Dion. But it was Dion who had to say no.'

We were sitting on a marble seat, by the statue of the hero Akademos. His shadow fell far beyond us in the evening sunlight; a long thin helmet-crest, a spear stretching ten cubits over the grass.

After a while she said, 'We always heard all the letters ... They say Dion has changed.'

'I doubt it. Stopped trying to change, more likely.'

'Plato has changed,' she said.

'Yes; there I can believe you.'

'When he was young, you know, he travelled, like Solon and Herodotos. He studied in Egypt. He doesn't see barbarism everywhere outside Hellas, as most men do. Not even always in Macedon. But he's always taught that one must legislate for any polis according to how many of its men can think. Once he believed there would be a good many, if they could be chosen out freely from rich and poor alike, and trained together. He still prefers merit to birth; but now he thinks such men are fewer, not enough to bring it about, or to keep it working. That is all.'

'All? It seems a good deal to me.'

She sighed. 'He has been there, I've not. Well, you are going, Nikeratos. How I envy you.'

I had arranged to sail in about half a month. Speusippos gave me a pile of letters for Dion. He said that Herakleides and Theodotes (that very kinsman who had entreated Plato to beard Dionysios for him) were writing to all kinds of leading people in Greece, making mischief about Dion, and he must be warned.

Plato wrote too. Long after, when it was in the archives, I learned what a troubled letter I had carried; starting with good wishes and good hopes; reminding Dion that the eyes of the world were on Syracuse, on him, and through him on the Academy; warning him that rumour was running everywhere about strife between him and Herakleides, which was endangering the cause; and adding that hearsay was all he knew, it was so long since Dion had written to him. The end, as near as I remember, went like this: 'Take care; it is going about that you are not as gracious as you might be. Don't forget that to achieve anything you must conciliate people. Intolerance keeps a lonely house.'

I had the roughest sea-crossing to Tarentum since the one when I was wrecked there. With a first-rate pilot and good crew, we just weathered it. I was deathly frightened; but there were people on board who knew who I was. If I had ever doubted how much vanity there is in most men's courage, I knew it then.

I crossed the straits at Rhegium and went on by road, not wanting to run through the war-fleets off Ortygia. Most of the city's traffic was going the same way. I hired a good riding-mule, for the look of it, since I was known thereabouts; it was a long ride, and I was tired by the time I got to Leontini. The city seemed empty of its men, who I was told had all gone to fight for Dion. When I asked the boys about my old host, the Roman captain Aulus Rupilius, they said he was here, burying his father. I called to pay my respects and make an offering; they pressed me to stay the night, and although I would not intrude on a house of mourning, a friend put me up instead; Rupilius saying he would be glad of my company next day, when he rode back to Syracuse.

We set out early together. He was in no deep distress (the old man had long been failing and witless) and seemed fretting to get on, concerned more for the future than the past. When I asked what the matter was, he would only say he had heard everything was not what it ought to be in Syracuse. I noticed he was in armour and wore his sword. He jogged along, a broad grey-bearded man with a boxer's nose, red-faced, and sweating as the sun warmed up his corselet, brooding, with half an ear for what I said.

I wondered if he had been turned against Dion by Herakleides' faction. It was lucky I kept this to myself. As soon as Dion's name came up, he shamed me with an encomium that took us over several stades of road. Ah, there was a man with the ancient virtues! Nothing for himself, everything for the common weal. Courage and strategy in war; the endurance of a man twenty years younger; a general who never slept softer or drier than his men, nor ate while they were hungry; a man with 'gravitas' (a Roman word, which I think means dignity of soul); incorruptible in office, flawless in personal honour. He might lack the arts by which base men flatter foolish ones; but he was never at a loss for the right order in a tight place, or a cheerful word to the men. In a word (it slipped out in spite of him, civil man as he was) Dion was wasted on Greeks. He should have been a Roman.

Plainly, this was the praise of indignation. But I could not learn

330

the cause, so resolved was the man that only good should be spread through him.

Wherever there was a sea-view it showed us warships. I asked how the siege went, and found him hopeful. Apollokrates, a lad of about sixteen, could hardly be more than a token leader, a hostage to the garrison for their flitted lord. The blockade was tight and they must be pinched for most things. 'Everything,' he said, 'favours the Syracusans, except themselves. They remind me of the people in that play you did here: resolved to drive out the gods.'

'You are making me anxious. How long before we reach the city?'

'It depends on whether we can get remounts. Nowadays one can't be sure. If not, we shall hardly do it by nightfall.'

'Never mind,' I answered. 'It's a pleasant ride up here. A pretty road. This next rise should show us the sea.'

'Be quiet,' he said.

Romans, like Spartans, don't see the need for wasting words. He held up his hand, and reined in. I heard, as he had done, the battle-noises from on ahead.

'What can it be?' I asked. 'That's nearer than Syracuse.'

'It's at the river-crossing down there. Dionysios may have landed troops. Keep in cover, till we see.'

We rode up the nearest hill, tied up our mounts below the sky-line, and finished on foot. All the while the sound got nearer: two fighting forces, one lot quite out of hand, yelling cat-calls and abuse (the sound told that, even from here) the other strangely silent, except sometimes for the sharp sound of an order.

We were just below the crest; Rupilius, panting and grunting in his armour, had paused to breathe. Suddenly he grabbed my arm so that I nearly cried out. Then I, too, knew the commander's voice.

331

Clambering so fast we grazed ourselves, we made the summit. Then we forgot to take cover; just stood backed to a rock, and stared.

Below was the river, widening in the flat land between hills and sea. A regiment had started to ford it, in good order, going north towards Leontini: a file of men plodding through the rocks and thigh-high water, keeping their equipment dry, while the main body covered their rear. The other army, if one could use the word for what looked more like a mob, was trying to harry them. Some of these were armed like soldiers, some with whatever people snatch up in a brawl; others were hurling stones. There were also a few light horse skirmishing about and waving spears, as if getting ready to attack the column, if they could make up their minds to it. No one seemed to be leading them, unless it was from behind. The other leader, however, was clear in sight, encouraging the rearguard. I could hear the crack of a stone against his shield. It was Dion.

Rupilius clutched my arm, hitting the bruise he had made before. 'Ours!' he said. 'I must go. I must go down.'

'Wait,' I begged, 'till you tell me what is happening.' I could not think why trained soldiers should fall back before such a force; Dion above all.

Rupilius craned forward. Dion had now formed up his men, of whom only a few were yet in the river, in six-rank line of battle. The enemy, at once less eager, milled awhile; however, someone yelled out a paean, and they made a ragged charge. Dion's men stood firm. At first they just shouted and clashed their arms. This daunted some of the attackers, but most came on. The foremost of these Dion's troops struck down with blows of their shields or spear-butts; when they fell stunned, the rest backed into a huddle. There was no pursuit; the line just waited on the defence, while Dion signalled for the crossing of the river to continue.

About another fifty had got over, when the stunned men started to stir and help each other up. At this the others took heart again, and shouted war-cries. Somewhere I even heard an order.

Dion halted the crossing, and again dressed his lines. But this time (I could tell from his loud shout) he gave the word to charge.

His men ran forward, keeping a steady, solid shield-line. They hit the others like a wave that breaks hard and heavy in one piece. Now men were really falling, most of them the enemy's. It was soon over; they ran like rabbits; those who were caught could be seen making the ritual gestures of surrender, kneeling before the soldiers to touch their beards or knees. Some of Dion's men, whose blood was up, started off in a pursuit; but he called them off, and they came back like good hunting-dogs, lugging a few more captives with them.

All this while, Rupilius had been rooted where he stood, knowing he could not be in time to join the action. Now he started scrambling about again and saying he must go. 'Get your horse, then,' I said, 'which you will surely need, and I'll come with you.'

He just stopped himself from telling me I would only be in the way. As we climbed down to our mounts I could hear him, when he thought I was out of earshot, calling down curses upon treacherous, envious, cowardly, thankless Greeks.

When we reached the ford, Dion's men had finished crossing; they were looking after each other's wounds, and pushing the prisoners into the middle. Dion had ridden up to these, and was sitting on his horse in silence, looking down at them.

I said to Rupilius, 'By the dog! Those look like Syracusans.'

Rupilius just leaned over and spat in the dust; when he kicked his horse's flank, I followed him.

As he got near, his mates in the column started calling. I could make nothing of it, but abuse of the Syracusans, as if this would speak for itself; and that they were marching to Leontini. At this Rupilius, without waiting for more, dashed over to Dion, threw himself from his horse before him, and looking like a dog that has swum from Piraeus to Salamis and found its master, said, 'Sir, Aulus Rupilius, back for duty.'

'You are welcome, Rupilius,' Dion answered. 'Though it seems neither of us has any more duties here.'

Before I could hear more, I was surrounded by soldiers, asking me if I was a Syracusan, as they might have asked some snake if it was the poisonous kind. I told them who I was; soldiers are friendly to actors, unless there is some good reason why not, and when they knew I was not even a Sicilian, they all started to talk at once. Piecing it out as best I could, I gathered that Herakleides (whose name no one uttered without a curse) had again brought up at Assembly the shareout of the land. Dion had again opposed it, as inopportune; the people, worked up beforehand, had then voted him out of his office as commander in chief. This angered his troops, who cheered for him and booed the new generals chosen instead. At this, Herakleides had moved that these men were a private army, kept at the city's expense to further Dion's aims and set him up as a tyrant; he proposed that their pay (which was five months overdue) should not be met from the treasury. This was carried by acclamation.

'And so,' said someone, 'we told them what they and their Archon were welcome to do with each other, and took the General away out of the muck. And lucky to get him.'

Others broke in, saying Herakleides' faction had offered to make them citizens – what a gift! – and even pay them, if they would leave Dion's service. Those rats could keep their filthy silver. They themselves would go anywhere – Egypt, Persia, Gaul or Babylon – to fight under Dion. They would go to North Africa and found a colony. And so on. They were half out of their minds with anger.

'But,' I said, 'you had left; so why this battle?'

Curses followed, of which it was hard to make sense. 'The General took it too cool, they must have thought he was soft.' 'The demagogues meant to get him.' ' . . . Snapping at our heels like pi-dogs after a beggar.' ' . . . before we were out of the city. We just turned and rattled our spears against our shields, and they all fell down and wet themselves.' 'Dion wouldn't let us lay a hand on them.' 'Driving him like a scapegoat into the hills, the sons of whores.' 'I suppose their mothers laughed at them, so they came out to try again.' 'Stay and watch what we do to those we've got.' They jerked thumbs at the captives, who were wailing and stretching out their hands. The soldiers shouted to them, promising them horrors.

Dion was still there, looking down at them, a tall man on a tall horse. He looked no older than when I'd seen him in Athens; younger, I think; tanned, lean and active, with the quickness of a man long at war: bronze man, bronze horse, like a victory statue. Like a statue, too, he was there to be looked at if one wished, not to reply. His face told me he had ceased to put himself out for anyone; no sense in it, nothing gained; he would tell his thoughts when and where he chose, if he chose at all. He saw me, and moved his head in greeting, without asking why I was there. He had business of his own to mind.

Rupilius was still up by his bridle, fidgeting for another word with him. 'Sir, as long as you're in Leontini, my house is yours. My guest-room is nice and cool, Nikeratos here will tell you . . . '

Another officer said, 'You're late in the day, Aulus. Do you suppose no one's thought yet of bidding the General to his hearth? He's promised me that honour.'

The Greeks, who made up the greater part of the army, grunted their approval. They could not compete, being from the main-land: Argives chiefly, the stocky men who win the wrestling at so many games; with a sprinkling of Corinthians, and tough Arcadian mountaineers.

'Thank you, Rupilius,' said Dion. 'Silence in the ranks. I will see those envoys.'

Two men were coming from the distant rout of Syracusans, waving green branches. Dion sent no one to conduct them, just set his horse and let them come up. The soldiers leaned on their spears, silent as ordered, like dogs called back from a cat-chase. You could almost see them twitch.

The envoys sidled up, while the troops did all they could, by scowling and slyly fingering their swords, to keep them scared. With glum servility, they asked leave to remove their dead; thus conceding, by the law of arms, the mastery of the field.

'Take them,' said Dion.

They waited; but that was all. Dion's horse shifted impatiently; its rider ceased to attend. They coughed, and asked if he would graciously declare the captives' ransom.

There was another pause, while the soldiers growled in under-tones, and Dion looked the envoys over, as he had done the prisoners. Presently he pointed to a pile of shields, which his men had collected from those dropped in flight. 'I have heard,' he said, 'that not long before Dionysios was expelled from the outer city, he stripped the citizens of their arms, for fear of their rising against him. But you came armed, I see. Who armed you?'

They shuffled with their feet. I looked at the shields; they were Corinth work, one knows it anywhere. The soldiers gave a roar of anger. Then I understood him.

'Silence,' he said again; then, 'go, and take those men with you.' He pointed to the prisoners, who had been craning in anguish to hear the outcome. 'I am a Syracusan. I do not hold fellow-countrymen to ransom. And I have no other use for them. Take them away.'

It was not till envoys and freed men were wading back through the river, and I saw him at leisure, that I ventured up with my bag of letters. He thanked me, courteously but shortly, and gave it to one of his officers to look after. I said, 'Here is one more, sir, which I thought you would want by itself.' And I gave him Plato's.

He took it, thanking me. As I saw, he was on the point of putting it with the others; then he noticed me looking, and perhaps it brought things back. At all events, he opened and read it. It was short, as I had known from its thinness. There was no change in his face.

'Thank you, Nikeratos,' he said. 'I am obliged to you. There is no answer.'

337

20

I nearly rode straight back to Messene, to take ship for home. Leontini must be crowded three to a bed; and I sickened at the thought of Syracuse. However, I had come a long way. Everyone in Athens would ask for news, and I should look a fool to have run off. Besides, I had written to Menekrates that I was coming; he could be trusted at least to have minded his own business, and I would not need to break bread with one of Dion's enemies.

At his door, however, the porter told me he was on tour in Italy; my letter had missed him and lay unread on his table; his wife and sons were at her father's. Wishing once more I had not come, and now travel weary, I walked round the New Town to find an inn. The porter had expected him home shortly; I would stay awhile in the hope of seeing him. It was windy weather, and I had had enough of the sea.

The city was fuller than ever of party warfare, the leaders chosen in Dion's place having each his faction; they had united briefly in an interest common to them all. I was told that Dion, while they were stoning him out of the city, had pointed towards Ortygia, whose ramparts were crowded with watching men. But no one heeded him.

Having found a quiet clean inn, I went to bed early. But I had had enough to keep me wakeful; and, when almost off, was disturbed by someone in the next room weeping. I listened for some time, to see if anyone came to comfort her; but she seemed quite alone. It was no affair of mine, whether she was some woman of the house or a hetaira; she must be one or the other, to be by herself here. If she had been noisy, I might have thought less about it; but the way she smothered the sound disturbed me, and I could not rest. People were still about; I found a servant and asked who had the room. A young man, he replied, from Athens.

I went back upstairs. I could have sworn it was a woman; a man's weeping is harsher as a rule; but it explained the wish to hide it. I hesitated no longer, but took my lamp and scratched at the door. The sobbing went on, unheedingly. I tried the latch, and finding it give went quietly in.

All I could see upon the bed was dark hair and a cradling arm. Disturbed by the light, however, my neighbour started up with a gasp, clutching the sheet. Dishevelled, with drenched eyes and features blotched by many tears, the face made me stare, it was so like one I knew. 'Forgive me,' I said, 'but I am an Athenian, Nikeratos the tragic actor. They say you come from my city. You are in trouble; can I help?'

'Niko! Oh, Niko!'

I walked over to the bed. I could scarcely believe my eyes; but they were right.

'Axiothea! In the name of all the gods, what are you doing here?'

She looked as glad to see me as a friendless child its mother; and more like that than anything else I sat down and took her in my arms. I had guessed the truth already, before she poured it out. All her men friends were with Dion; she had thought how the world was being changed while she sat at home like a housewife;

had quarrelled with Lasthenia who had thought it madness, and slipped away. The voyage had been wretched for her; though often taken for a youth she had never tried to sustain the role, or thought what it would be like on shipboard. Nobody shaves at sea; they had taken her for a eunuch, which she had had to confirm and bear the sailors' jokes. Then, when at last after a bad crossing she got to Syracuse, it had been just in time to see Dion driven out like a dog.

Shaken already by the voyage, she found everything scared her: the soldiers, the beggars, the young drunks coming from the wine-shops, the agents who canvassed her for their factions, the pimps offering her girls or boys. Every moment she expected to be caught out and stoned by the crowd. She had meant to join her Academy friends who were with Dion, hoping they would admire her boldness; in this wilderness beyond the olive-groves, they seemed just men among men, who would despise her folly, and find her a burden they were ashamed of. Now in any case they had left for Leontini. She was quite alone.

I told her what I had seen, and that Dion was safe. 'I saw him at Assembly,' she said. 'He has changed, Niko. But who can wonder, among such people?'

'He was born among them. I suppose, in Syracuse, it is hardly his fault he did not know them. If he had, he might have done no better, just given up beforehand. As it is, he and the people are like figures in a tragedy, who come together meaning well, but are born to work each other's ruin. Neither is without good; but they are fated never to find it in one another. Dion has more virtue; but he has suffered less. Only a god could judge justly here.'

'Is there justice,' she said, 'anywhere under the sun?'

'Come, dry your eyes,' I said. 'You've read too much, my dear, before looking about you. You can take the word of a man who has been poor: goodness is there, and with the world what it is, that's proof enough to my mind that the gods exist; I don't see how else you can account for it. But goodness is like money; a city only has so much; you have to start small and build up the capital. It's no use to overspend the assets, then when the bank goes broke to get bitter and believe in nothing.'

'Now you are here, dear Niko,' she said smiling, 'I can believe.'

'That's better. You never called me that before. Smile again! Here we both are in Syracuse, with time on our hands, and who knows when you'll travel so far again? You can't hide in a hole till you sail home. So wash your face in cold water, get some rest; I want my boy friend to do me credit; and tomorrow we'll see the town. Knock on my wall if anyone tries that door; why didn't you lock it?'

'The bolt is warped; I was afraid to complain, in case the landlord looked too hard.'

'Well, now you can leave such things to me. Sleep well.'

Next morning I got her out of doors, and we spent some days seeing Syracuse. She had always been a slender girl, without much bosom; the journey had left her far too thin for her sex; but quite interesting for a youth, as some of our acquaintance showed us. If she blushed, I explained that she had been reared by a pro-Spartan father in the strictest decorum. She never spoke before her elders. When we were alone again, neither could help laughing. To keep up the joke, I bought her the latest fashion in keepsakes, a brooch with a flying Eros; and we went everywhere hand in hand, to warn off rivals. Apollodoros was the name she went under.

I showed her the theatre and its machines (the caretaker was most obliging) and my gold leopard in the shrine. Then we went down to the water-front, whence we viewed Ortygia and its catapults; a use for mathematics which surprised her, as it would have done Pythagoras I daresay. Dion's siege-wall was still unfinished;

they had not touched it since he left. One end was still rough piles, brush and timber. The garrison inside had raised the flanking-walls of the first gatehouse to overlook it. I showed her, under the water-stairs of Ortygia, where the spring of Arethusa comes up fresh into the sea. 'They'll never lack water,' I said, 'but it seems certain they're short of food. It can't last much longer.'

'And Herakleides will take the credit. Is that his fleet coming in?'

We watched awhile. 'What are they about,' I said, 'sailing so close into Ortygia? They must be in catapult range.' Just then they struck sail and started rowing. I said, 'Those are the enemy's.'

A patrol-ship in the harbour was making for shore like a scalded cat. People started shouting and running and crowding to the waterfront. I put my arm round Axiothea in case we were pushed apart. 'Don't be afraid,' I said, 'they've no time for us. Herakleides has blundered again. That's a supply fleet for the garrison.'

Cheers sounded across the water as the ships moored by the water-stairs. Unloading started at once. The garrison would eat well for some time to come.

As this thought got home to the crowd, there was a furious rush towards the galley-slips. After much noise and milling, prows thrust out into the harbour, and oars were seen.

'What use is that?' I said. 'Except to save Herakleides' face.'

The ships rowed full-speed across the harbour. The freighters kept on off-loading, but the escort triremes came smartly about. It was a brisk engagement, in which the catapults could not be fired for fear of hitting their own side. The end of it was that the Syracusans sank two or three of the warships, and captured four which (without their men, who dived off in time) were towed home in triumph. The freighters, all safe, went on unloading.

It could be seen that not only supplies were going ashore, but soldiers. Before long the guard of the outer gate-house yelled across to the Syracusans on their wall that the great Campanian captain, Nypsios of Neapolis, had brought his troops; they had better rejoice while they still could. These men were silenced rather sharply by an officer; but in any case, the Syracusans were taking their advice.

I never saw such another public orgy. They were dancing in all the streets, to the piping of flute-girls from the brothels, while they still had legs to dance; the wine flowed like streams in spring. Herakleides was carried about the city like the image of a god; the very oarsmen were fêted from house to house until they dropped dead drunk where they were. One would have thought Dionysios and his whole navy had been sunk, and Ortygia stormed. By my guess, they were ashamed in their souls of the way they had treated Dion, and scared, too, to be without him. Now they could love themselves again, and it went to their heads.

I soon took Axiothea back to the inn, after two roaring-drunk men had tried to grab her off me. As we took to our heels, they bawled out asking who I was to keep all the pretty boys to myself – an oligarch? One of Dion's set?

If it had looked ugly in the streets, it looked worse from the inn roof at nightfall. They now had bonfires to light the revel. The sentries up on the siege-wall could be seen with a wineskin big enough for a satyr-play; between swigs, they bawled abuse at the enemy on their rampart; who stood listening, quiet as judges in a theatre.

Downstairs, the din nearly burst one's ears, the women louder than the men. No one had mended Axiothea's door, so I made her come in with me. She was worn out by now; we seemed like old companions, and when I got her settled on my bed, saying (which was true) that I would not sleep in any case, she made nothing of it. She lay decorously, wrapped in her robe; as by

343

degrees the people drank themselves quiet, she grew drowsy and closed her eyes.

I was getting tired myself, and wondering whether she would notice if I lay down beside her, when suddenly the night was split by a most frightful yelling. I nearly swallowed my heart. I don't think I doubted for a moment what it was. Flinging open the window-shutters I leaned out. The night sky was clear, showing me the top of the siege-wall swarming with men. Bodies were falling, ladders waved about as the storming party lowered them over. From the sound, they must have been all over the wall before the sentries woke.

It is the nightmare of every touring actor that he may be caught in some town during a sack. All through my career, by using my head, I had managed to avoid it. Now, without even the excuse of a good role or big contest, here I was. If I had had my wits about me, I should have taken the road before sunset with Axiothea. Never, in my worst dreams, had I seen myself with a woman on my hands at such a time.

She had been slow to stir, having heard so much noise all day; but now she was sitting up and saying 'What is it?' I said, 'A sortie from Ortygia. I'm afraid they have forced the siege-wall, and you know what that means. My dear, you and I will have to look out for ourselves. Go and get your travelling shoes. Is that your money-bag? Tie it round your middle; don't bring anything else. We'll try the roofs. One can get trapped in a place like this.'

She was quickly back. The noise was getting closer at a speed that frightened me, but should hardly have surprised me after what I'd seen all evening. Suddenly a great sheet of flame roared up from the cross-wall; the Syracusans had fired the timber end. As usual they were too late; the enemy were through and the blaze just lit them on their way.

The roof-stairs were outside. We ran down through the inn,

where the half-sobered were stumbling about over drunken bodies. The floors were slimy with vomit, and in the clean night air outside the stink clung to our shoes. But it was soon overpowered by the smell of burning. Caught from floating sparks, or started by the raiders, fires were breaking out on house-roofs, and showed us the Ortygians pouring through the streets. Already women were shrieking. Axiothea's fingers, icy cold, closed round my wrist.

'We must keep ahead of the crowds,' I said, 'or we'll be trampled on. The roofs stretch a good way. Gird up your robe, you can't run like that.' Seeing her fumble I did it for her. We clambered along the roof-tops, hearing behind us the panic roar of the Syracusans and the Campanian battle-yells. Their officers were no longer troubling to keep them in hand. It was plain the town was theirs. Axiothea was behaving very well, keeping up without fuss. I remembered the girls' race at Olympia. When we paused for breath, she said, 'Where are we going?'

I had not known myself, but now answered at once, 'To the theatre.' There was a climb to the next roof. When we had hauled each other up, and seen the red glow getting brighter in the sky, I said, 'It's as good as anything; full of places to hide in. I can think better there what to do next.'

Our line of roofs running out, we had to take to the streets, and were caught up in a flying crowd making for the city gates; but we were still ahead of the thickest press. Wherever one could glimpse the outer walls above the houses, they were being overrun by the Ortygians. As we turned off into a side-street, I heard a frenzied din from the gate; we had been right not to think of trying it. Here was the theatre, just ahead, its tall gilt thyrsos catching the firelight. 'Come,' I said, 'we'll trust ourselves to Dionysos. I gave him a splendid present, apart from all the work I've done for him. Now he can do something for me.'

345

There was a temple of Apollo near the theatre, crowded to the doors with people taking sanctuary. Inside, the god's golden hair glittered by lamplight; I lifted my hand and invoked his blessing. But the temple was full of treasure and of women; I feared it might strain the Campanians' piety. Men don't dread the gods of the conquered like their own. It was Dionysos or nothing.

The theatre was quite empty. Like a sounding-bowl, its hollow curve magnified the roar and screeching of the sack. Back stage, it seemed pitch-dark at first, but soon we found the windows gave light enough. In the caretaker's room I poked about and found some food; there was even a wine-jar. We took them into the pro-tagonist's dressing-room. Neither of us was hungry, but we were glad of the wine. We must have been the only people in all Syracuse who needed any. I said, 'Stay here, don't wander about; I am going up on the god-walk, to see what is going on.'

I saw nothing, however, the high tiers of the theatre cutting off the view; there was just the din, and the glare. I lay down (an actor can't be on the god-walk without feeling twenty thousand eyes on him) to think awhile. I had forgotten, as we came, the splendours of the theatre, given by the older Dionysios for the glory of his plays. There were bronzes and gilded swags wherever you looked; it might not be the first place they thought of looting; but once inside, they would go through it end to end before they put a torch to it. Dionysos, I thought, won't you help your servant? And I remembered the last time I had been up here; it was in *The Bacchae*, appearing as the god to close the play.

I suppose one thought leads to another; but it was just as if he lit up my mind with a flash of lightning. I clambered down and groped my way over to Axiothea, my eyes unused to the dark again. Her hand reached out from the couch; I got up beside her. 'I had been thinking,' I said, 'what to do if they come here.' I felt her stiffen like wood; but she did not let out a sound. She was trying hard, poor girl, after Plato's precept, Be what you wish to seem.

'Remember,' I said, 'that these men are Campanians, up-country peasants from Italy. I don't suppose any of them has been in a real theatre; they've only just arrived. It is for us to put them in a proper fear of the god. Come with me, and I'll show you how.'

I led her out, among the levers and tackle and big wheels. I have never yet been in a play with special effects, without finding out how they work. In Syracuse especially, the machines are so famous it would have been unprofessional not to study them. I knew them all.

'This big one,' I said, 'is for the thunder. It is heavy, but you must pull it somehow, and keep pulling till you get the thunder-drum to turn; then pull twice more. Then wait, till you hear me shout, and do the same again. After that count up to ten, and pull this one here. This is for the earthquake.'

We went over this several times; then I looked about for the pulley of the sounding-board. It must be somewhere up in the dark. I tried this or that, in dread of releasing something that would get us noticed. At last it came down, and I got it fixed. 'We mustn't stir from here till morning,' I said, 'so as to be ready. How cold you are. Wait while I look for something warm.' There was an old door-curtain among the skene-flats. I pulled it round both our shoulders, and rubbed her hands in case they should be too numb to work. When some shriek more dreadful than the rest, and getting nearer, rose above the din, she crept closer and I took her in my arms. Her thin shoulders were touching, felt like this in the dark.

The sky was covered with fiery smoke which hid the stars; I lost count of how the night was passing. I thought of Thettalos, whom I might have to leave without farewell; she of Lasthenia,

347

who had begged her not to go. We talked of our lovers, for comfort, holding each other's hands. I kept to myself the thought that if the Campanians were coming here, it had better be before daybreak. It would be long odds against our fooling them in the light.

The night was rent by an outcry that made what had come before seem like a hush. A thousand women seemed to be shrieking at once, amid the death-cries of as many men. A child screamed on and on, shriller than a bird. They had got to the temple of Apollo. I wrapped the curtain round Axiothea's ears; she pushed out her head to say, 'Shall we try the thunder?' I answered, 'No. The acoustics only work inside. Poor souls; may the god avenge them.'

It took them a good while to go through the temple. After a time, we heard the wails of the women left alive, being dragged off to Ortygia. The child screamed on one note until, I suppose, it died. I looked over Axiothea's head at the sky behind the window, fancying every moment the first grey of dawn.

Then they came. I could hear their uncouth shouts as they went through the top entrance and found themselves on the upper tiers; bewildered at the strange-shaped precinct, then baying at the loot below. 'Let them come down further,' I whispered to Axiothea. 'Get them all well in, don't play to half a house. I'll make you a sign.' By now we could see in the night like cats. I gave her a kiss for luck.

The board at Syracuse has a secret, which you don't learn unless you are in the right play, one like *The Bacchae*, or one with a ghost. Turn it a little to the right, and it catches a shaft to the echo-chamber. The noise is dreadful; it is hard to believe a human mouth has made it, even though it's one's own. I waited, getting it placed just right. They were coming down the centre steps and scrambling over the seats, a hundred or so; by now looters straggled as they chose. When I saw no more were coming, I gave them still a little longer, to feel the space and quiet. Then I filled my chest, and yelled 'Iakchos! Iakchos!' praying the god in my heart for his gift of terror. He did not fail me. The sounding-board was unearthly; but when it came back from the echo-chamber, it was like all the Furies in full cry.

All the shouts ceased. I waited, it seemed for ever, wondering if the lever had stuck or she had pulled the wrong one. Then came the first peal of thunder, the great drum turning its stones. That sounds too into the echo-cave. It is loud enough by day, with a full house to tone it down. In the empty theatre, by night, it was beyond belief. Feet started scrambling. I yelled, holding it longer this time. Again the thunder. In the pause before the next effect, I heard them all clattering off like madmen. I doubt if even one stayed on for the earthquake.

I ran back to Axiothea, who stood clutching the earthquake lever as if frozen there, and picked her up in my arms. I remember carrying her over to our heap of curtain, hollowed like a dog's bed. We fell down clinging together, laughing silently, and kissing. I can't, though I have often tried, remember just how it happened; all I know is that we surprised ourselves and one another, yet there seemed nothing strange in it, and it did us good. All was still in the theatre; in a little while, as if the god had told us we were in his care, we slept, and did not wake till daybreak. When I had watched in dread for dawn, it cannot have been more than an hour past midnight; such are the illusions of fear.

Doves were cooing in the trees outside; there was still noise from the city, but broken now and further off. Axiothea stirred, and looked at me dazedly, wondering, as I could see, how much she had dreamed of it all; but having been a virgin in respect of men she could not be in doubt for long. I pushed back the hair from her brow and stroked her head, saying, 'Well, dear friend, we gave ourselves into the hand of Dionysos, and you know the sort of god he is. After all he did for us, we can't grudge him his little offering. Come, it's another day, and you are Apollodoros once again. You know, nothing that happens at a Dionysia needs to be remembered after.'

She shook her head a little, as if to clear it; then kissed me quickly, and started putting her clothes to rights. I went off to find the water-tap; her mouth had been as dry as mine.

We found the streets round about all quiet now. The Achradina still held out, and the soldiers had been called back to their work. We picked our way through smoke, ashes and blood. Of what we saw on our way, I have forgotten as much as I am able to; but not the temple of Apollo. It would have been better not to look in. An old priest, with a bandage round his head instead of a bay-wreath, wandered round among the corpses, crying like a child with his hands pressed over his mouth, the whole shrine one vast defilement and only he to cleanse it. Somewhere the dying moaned in corners. And on its plinth stood the statue of Apollo, the gold bow wrested from his hand, his head bald as an egg. The gold hair had been made like a wig, just fixed with pins. I don't know why this should have seemed the crown of horror; yet if ever to this day I see a bald young man in the street, my stomach turns.

A dead girl was lying on the threshold, in a pool of her blood; my eye was caught by her hair, which I felt I had seen dishevelled like this before. So I had; she was Speusippos' little flute-girl, whose wrongs had made up his mind to war. Much good it had brought her.

Axiothea stood beside me in the porch. I tried to pull her away, but she stood her ground. 'No. I have been concerned with making laws for men, and have only known the best of them. I've no right to hide from the worst.' She went forward, and took a long look. 'Now come,' I said, 'that's enough'; and dragged her to the steps by force. In the street she said, 'Plato and Dion have both been soldiers. I suppose they knew.'

'I'm told it is worse with Carthaginians. This will be just a common sack. Now let's talk of something else, before we fall into despair. Let's talk of the good men we have known; they are real too.'

Not to make a long tale of a tedious business, we got out of the city by the northern gate of the New Town, and started walking along the road to Leontini. We had what was left of the care-taker's food to keep us from hunger by the way. The road was not crowded. I suppose few citizens wanted to take refuge in a city filled with Dion's soldiers.

A man stood shouting by the road; a seaman, making his profit as someone does from every disaster, offering at a high price a pas-sage coastwise to Rhegium. Though it was certain the boat would be overloaded, we closed with this at once. Both of us longed for Athens like the babe for the breast.

We were just walking the last stretch of highway before the turning off to the shore, when the clatter of hooves sent everyone scattering. We looked after the six flying horsemen, wondering what news they carried. One had stared at me as he passed; I heard him call my name to another. Then they all pulled up and rode back.

They were Syracusans, so I waited. A man dismounted, who looked like a gentleman through the dirt and dust. 'I am Hellanikos,' he said, and told me who the others were. 'You are known to Dion. I beg you, in the name of Zeus the Merciful, ride with us to Leontini, and join us when we throw ourselves at his feet. The Achradina has fallen. He is our only hope.'

I could hardly credit my ears, even in Syracuse. Not wishing to insult over men in misery, I just said, 'You cannot suppose he will come. If he would, his men would not. My friend and I have just taken our sea-passages for home. I am sorry.'

'Niko,' said Axiothea, 'don't be a fool. Do as they ask; I'll see you in Athens.'

She had forced a boy's voice so well, it quite startled me. She pulled me aside. 'Go to him. If he is still Dion, he will come.'

'Impossible! What man upon earth ... ?'

'He despises vengeance; he says it is sharing in the evil. Isn't that what he told you at Delphi?'

'Nikeratos!' someone shouted. 'I beg of you. Time presses.'

'No, by Zeus! To leave you on the road like a stray dog ...'

'I came for the cause. Since I could not help, at least don't let me remember that I hindered it. I've learned how to manage on the ship; it will be nothing, after all this. Goodbye, Niko. You have made me a truer philosopher. Go with God.'

The men coughed and fidgeted, hiding, since they needed me, their contempt for the silly actor who could not get gone without kissing his fancy-boy. One of them, who had agreed to stand down because Dion did not know him, gave me his steaming horse. From the bend of the road I looked back at her; but she did not turn, walking with her thin shoulders held straight, down the path to the sea.

21

We got to Leontini at evenfall, when the men were strolling in the cool and sitting outside the taverns under the trees. At our noisy entrance they all came crowding. When we asked for Dion his own voice answered: he had been taking the air with Kallippos and his other friends.

We all dismounted and ran to him; while the onlookers stood on tables or climbed trees to see, we knelt in the pose of supplication. It is a thing one needs training to do with grace. One man almost fell over.

Hellanikos told the hideous tale without excuses; an old-time, decent small squire, eating dirt for what he had had no part in; a clever choice, for an envoy to Dion. Then each of us said something. His eyes moved from face to face in a kind of wonder; one could not tell what he thought. Not being a Syracusan, I spoke last. 'Sir,' I said, 'we come before a man more deeply wronged than Achilles, asking far more than Priam did. But the city is Syracuse, and the man is Dion.'

He gazed down, his face held stiff, swallowing and biting his lip. Then a hard sound came from his throat. I saw that he wept.

When he had mastered his voice, he said, 'This does not rest

353

with me alone. The men must judge for themselves. Is the crier here?'

The Assembly met in the theatre, as it does at Leontini. Last time I was in it, I had played lead. Now I was an extra; but there is no protagonist I have felt so honoured to support. Gladly I would have swept the stage for him.

Hellanikos did his speech again, this time to the soldiers, and we ad-libbed as best we could. Then Dion addressed them. 'I have called you here so that you can decide what you think best for you. For me, there is no choice. This is my country. I must go; and if I cannot save her, her ruins shall be my grave. But if you can find it in your hearts to help us, foolish and wretched as we are, you may to your eternal honour still save this unhappy city. If that is too much to ask, then farewell, and all my thanks. May the gods bless you for your past courage, and the kindness you have shown to me. If you speak of me after, say I did not stand by to see you wronged, nor forsake my fellow-citizens in disaster.'

I don't think he could have gone on; but the cheering drowned his voice. They yelled his name like a war-cry, then shouted, 'To Syracuse!' I suppose Hellanikos made a speech of thanks; I think he embraced Dion. I could scarcely see for tears.

They stayed only to eat and get their kit; that same night we saw them off on the thirty-mile march to Syracuse. As for me, having served Dionysos all my life, I never bore arms except upon a stage; and this was work for professionals, not walkers-on. But though the boatmen were still hawking passages to Italy, I did not sail. I had witnessed an act of magnanimity it would not be impious to call godlike; I felt a need to know the outcome. Great evil, or great good, seem the concern of every man; they touch our destiny.

This is what happened, as I heard it later from Rupilius. All day in Syracuse the raiders had been plundering, or storming the few street-barricades that held out. Herakleides and his officers dashed hither and thither, trying to order their scattered forces; but they could not overtake the wasted hours of drunkenness and panic. At nightfall, like wolves gorged with prey, the men of Ortygia went back over the causeway, to the women they had taken.

The Syracusans crept forth, and spent the night searching for kindred, or patching some shelter from the ruins. Daylight showed the city still their own. They shored up the cross-wall with half-charred timbers, and got it manned again. By noon, a rider brought news that Dion was on the way. Are you supposing they flocked to the temples to give thanks? This was Syracuse.

Herakleides took the news as his own death-warrant. As it was, the people were blaming him for the debauch rather than themselves; for his petty triumph he had lost the city. If Dion, whom he had driven out, marched in as saviour, what could he expect? Perhaps he thought of Philistos. Such men see in others what they know about themselves.

He and his friends rode among the distracted people, crying out that the danger from Ortygia was over; they would be mad to let in a tyrant they had expelled, with his own army, every man hot for vengeance. Fear was the air they breathed; tyranny they had grown up with; it all made sense to them. They despatched envoys to tell Dion he was not needed, and could go back.

The small gentry, whose forbears had fought the elder Dionysios and paid dear, witnessed in helpless horror the loss of their only hope, together with the rags of their self-respect. They knew why Dion had marched. Since the tyrant crushed their fathers they had kept themselves to themselves; the great estates went to his friends; but a little piece of land, a few rents coming in, had bought them schooling from mainland teachers; they had learned to wrestle by the rules, to sing the old skolions, even to remember honour.

They sent their own envoys, begging Dion's pardon for this last disgrace to Syracuse, praising his greatness of heart, and imploring him not to repent of it. It was madness to suppose that Nypsios' troops were sated yet, or could be contained again. Without Dion all would perish.

Both messages reached him near together, and he heeded both. He now ceased to force-march his men; but he still came on. I suppose by now nothing much could surprise him.

At sunset, to keep him out, Herakleides posted troops at the northern gate. But they were called to other business. With the fall of dark, Nypsios' men burst out from Ortygia and poured over the cross-wall like a river in spate. This time they had come to destroy the city.

By now, I suppose, Dionysios valued nothing but Ortygia. The city had rejected him; let it perish with its rabble, and if he got back he could re-people it more to his mind. Nypsios and his army must have brought despatches with them; their leaders must have had orders. Perhaps Dionysios now saw himself in the role of Herakles translated; except of course that the pyre was not for him.

Everything worth having had been looted; there was nothing left but to kill. They went through the city not like men but like Gorgons or unpitying Furies; cutting up the women, spitting children on spears or hurling them into burning houses; they brought fire wherever they went, and shot flame-arrows at the roofs too high to reach. In that night died Glyke, the wife of Menekrates, and his young sons with their golden skins. It seems she had come back to the city just before Herakleides' victory-feast, to prepare for her man's return. I have heard how they died, but have always denied to him that I knew anything, and as far as I know he has not learned it. May the gods keep him ignorant.

The roar of the fires; the incessant screams, like a single cry of the dying city; the crash of falling houses, sounded as if the gods had sent Death himself to end mankind. Into this Tartaros came Dion and his men, and were received like rescuing gods. How not? He was brave, generous, and noble; true as gold. No one remembered, that night, that it was he who had begun the war.

All night they fought among the smoke and flame and cinders and charred corpses; keeping discipline, holding their lines of communication open; threatened not only by the enemy but by falling walls and beams. Before morning the raiders were driven back. Those who were trapped under the cross-wall were killed where they were found. After that, they had to put out the fires.

All this Rupilius told me, when he was carted back with the wounded to Leontini. After fighting all night with a burned arm, he had got a leg-wound which went half through the tendon; the doctor forbade him to walk or stand. I repaid a little of his kindness by doing such business for him as was beyond the servants, or reading Greek to him; he only knew it by ear. Dion, he said, had been wounded too, but had fought on, bandaged with a rag torn from the clothes of a corpse, the usual dressing that night. As for Herakleides and his friends, they had been gone like ghosts by cockcrow; seeing the temper of the people, they had been wise.

News came in daily to Leontini. When victory was certain, the City Council came to me, offering me a chorus to put on *The Persians*, as a thank-offering to Apollo. I accepted, provided I could find some supporting players alive in Syracuse. I went on this business sooner than I had meant, when we got the news that Herakleides had come and given himself up to Dion, throwing himself upon his mercy.

Rupilius flatly disbelieved it; the teller was offended, and said he would demand an apology in three days' time, when Herakleides and Theodotes were to be tried by the Assembly. I calmed Rupilius by undertaking to be there.

I rode, therefore, from the cool of the hills across the hot dusty plain with its cactuses and aloes, down to Syracuse. Roofs had been patched, corpses and wreckage cleared away; but the place still stank of burning, fear and death. I wondered if they had destroyed the theatre in the second raid; but it was unharmed. There was a rumour that it was haunted at night by the vengeful god. At present it was full, since they were using it for Assembly. I was just in time to get a tenth-row seat.

Entering through the orchestra to roars of applause, Dion went up on stage with his brother and Kallippos. Then Herakleides and Theodotes were brought in under guard, with a cordon of soldiers round, to keep the crowd from lynching them. Theodotes had given up and looked like a corpse already; but Herakleides was still giving a performance. He stood upright, brave without defiance, a man whom fate had tricked into folly; who, if he must, would accept his doom without repining. More than ever I could imagine him an actor: talented, but making mischief everywhere and stealing from other artists, till no company would have him.

When the charge had been read, they were given leave to speak in their own defence. Herakleides came forward; I saw his mouth open, but the sound was lost in the howls of anger and shouts of 'Death!'

After some while of this, Dion stepped forward; the curses changed to cheers. He held up his hand for silence; they offered it like a garland. Instead of speaking, he led Herakleides forward.

Thus sponsored, Herakleides was listened to. He had got the fell of the house; it was his greatest gift. Wisely, he kept it short. Pointing towards Dion, he said this man's virtue had conquered all his former enmity; nothing was left to him, but to appeal to a generosity he had not deserved. In future, if there should be such a thing for him, he hoped he might learn to do so.

The audience jeered. Unlike Dion, they had heard Herakleides upon Dion in the past, and guessed what this was worth. Hellanikos, or some old-style squire just like him, jumped up and begged that the city might be delivered from this double-tongued snake. One or two others followed, pointing out that the man had harmed Syracuse more than Dionysios ever did. The shouts for his death redoubled. It was now clear that Dion was about to speak. At once the theatre was as quiet as at a tragedy.

'Fellow citizens,' he began, 'I am a soldier.' (Loud applause.) 'While I was young here, I trained like other officers in the use of arms, in strategy, and in the care of my troops.' (Cheers from the soldiers.) 'Then I was sent away; and rather than waste my life in idleness, I took up other studies. I went to the Academy of Athens, which teaches men to be truly men. Instead of Carthaginians, I learned to conquer anger and the lust for vengeance, not to lay down my arms before them or drop the shield of self-command. If we do good to those who have done us favours, where is the merit? The true contest is to do good for evil. Triumph in war is a passing thing; time changes every fortune; but to excel in mercy and injustice is to gain an unfading crown. This is the only victory I wish for over these men; and I believe that if you grant it me, it will enrich us all; for I think no human heart is so lost to the memory of that good our souls were born from long ago, that it cannot be reminded, and its eyes washed clear. Men sin from ignorance of the good; once shown it, they know their happiness. Let us show it now to these men, and I believe they will return it to us, many times over, in the coming years. If I have deserved any kindness from you, men of Syracuse, do not involve me in wrong, but let me go home free of it. Vengeance is for the gods alone.'

There was a long murmuring hush. I thought how if this had been a play, the applause would have stopped the show. It was magnificent; spoken with a whole heart, by a man whose voice and presence were equal to every word. And yet I sat here, dry-eyed in the tenth row; bearing my part in the troubled silence. It had not been so when he spoke, at Leontini. Was the fault in me? I still did not know, when next day I sat down by Rupilius to tell my story.

He listened at first with exclamations; then in silence, just like the Syracusans. At last he said, 'And they gave the pardon?'

'They did it for Dion. The men went off with their friends. Of course there were speeches first. I left before the end.'

He gave a long sigh. 'What is it?' I asked. I was asking myself as well, as I suppose he saw. 'Do you believe, Nikeratos,' he said, 'that Herakleides will keep his word?' I shook my head. 'Well? Then what's your question?'

'Perhaps Dion was right, even so. He was the victor in virtue.'

He leaned over, grunting from a twinge in his wounded leg, and patted my knee. 'Don't take offence,' he said, 'at my plain speaking. A friend to a friend. Dion is the best man I know. I'd die for him, and not wait to ask why. But at bottom, when all's said, he's a Greek. If he had been a Roman, he'd have known why he couldn't pardon Herakleides. In Rome, you'd not be asking yourself.'

All Romans are vain of their home customs, even if they can't make a living there and have to hire out their swords. I had got fond of Rupilius. When he saw I was not angry, he went on, 'You Greeks, I know, excel us Romans in all the gifts of Apollo. But in the gifts of Jupiter, Zeus I mean, you sometimes seem like children. It's each man for himself before the city, and each city for itself before Greece. You've come to harm from it often, and you will again. Dion I thought was different. He's never looked out for his life or anything he owned, if the people needed it. But now see what he's done. Because this man was his personal enemy, whom he wants to excel in virtue, he lets him loose on the Syracusans,

360

as if it weren't through him their streets were like a shambles the other day. If he doesn't mend his ways, which Dion, being a man and not a god, can't guarantee, mayn't it be so again? By Hercules, he could at least have insisted on exile! To a Roman's way of looking, he's helped himself to public property, as surely as if he'd put his hand in the treasury. Not that I hold it against him. He's a Greek; he thinks like a Greek; that's all. He's still the best general I ever served under. Perfection is for the gods alone. But the truth's the truth.'

I suppose it was knowing we both loved him still, that made us able to talk. I said, 'He has been like a god, Rupilius. It must be hard to come down. Our greatest sculptors leave some little bit unfinished, or rough, so as not to challenge the gods. Once one has been a god, one must be perfect, and seen to be perfect. I don't know how that seems to you, as a Roman. I'm a Greek. And it frightens me.'

22

At the next Assembly, when the dead were scarcely buried and the prisoners just ransomed from Ortygia, Herakleides proposed that Dion should be offered the title of Supreme Commander with full powers. It was the old office of the Archons. Dion neither agreed nor refused, but left it to the people. The gentry and middle citizens were for it; the commons, led by his friends, cheered Herakleides' bigness of heart, and voted him back into his rank of admiral, with equal status.

I was rehearsing for *The Persians*; but getting this news in the agora of Leontini, I brought it straight to Rupilius. 'Thundering Jupiter!' he groaned. 'The man's not fit to take a grain-fleet across the straits. How did Dion stop it?'

'How could he? He has forgiven Herakleides solemnly, in public; he has refused supreme power on principle. If he'd opposed it, he'd have looked suspect both ways.'

'And Herakleides knew it. Dion shouldn't have let him live.'

'He said to me once, "A state is the sum of its citizens. If they have all renounced their private virtue, how can they build a public good?" Surely it's true.'

362

'Well? What then?' He felt about for his stick; I put it in his hand.

'I don't know,' I said. 'Even Plato has gone home to think again. But he's old. He hasn't much time left.'

'Plato! Don't name that man to me.' He leaned politely over, to spit on the far side of the couch.

At the next Assembly, Herakleides brought up again the re-division of the land; reminding the people it had already been passed once, but not mentioning what had followed. It got a majority vote. Those against were the landowners, large and small, who were also the citizens trained in arms, bearing the brunt of the war. Dion, without wasting words on a formal speech, vetoed it as Supreme Commander of the land forces. The people went off grumbling, as poor men would anywhere on earth; and Herakleides' faction went among them murmuring 'Tyranny!'

Shortly after this I put on *The Persians*, sharing leads with Menekrates, who had said that he must work or lose his mind. He had dashed home from Italy, but happily too late to find the bodies of his family. So I paid off the man I had engaged, who did not like it but understood; it was little to do for an old friend. I played the Messenger and the Ghost; he did Queen Atossa and Xerxes. It was a bad production. I had not given my mind to it, and was off form myself; the chorus was a scratch one; Menekrates, though I think he saved his reason by purging his grief through this tale of old disasters, gave a poor performance, as actors do when playing from raw emotion instead of considered art. However, as always at these times, the audience was sure that, feeling what he portrayed, he must be superb, and received the play accordingly. He was in tears by the end – no matter, the action called for it – but from then he could eat and sleep again.

He left Syracuse soon after for Ionia, which was new to him, trying to forget. His house had been burned to the ground, but his money was still buried there in a place he had shown to nobody. I don't suppose the knowledge would have saved his wife, after she had told the soldiers; but they might have killed her more quickly. Since he knew nothing of this, he could find some relief in not being destitute. I myself stayed on a little longer, teaching Rupilius to write Greek. He would soon be on his feet again, but had come to count on me meanwhile; his daughters were married, and he had no sons living. It was a reason to give myself for staying on. I don't know if it was hope or fear that really held me.

Dionysios had settled down in Lokri, his mother's city, north up the coast from Rhegium. It was said he was rarely sober much after sun-up. But his captains were, and his fleet was troublesome. So Herakleides' navy sailed north to sweep the straits, and anchored at Messene.

The ships' fighting men were soldiers serving under their own officers in the usual way. They had scarcely made camp, when their commander sent despatches back, to warn Dion that Herakleides was working up the fleet to mutiny.

Its men had always served under him; he had won their favour by slack discipline; they did not know Dion like the troops. In Syracuse as elsewhere, the seamen are poorer than the citizen soldiers, who have their own panoplies to find. All sailors are democrats; but ours in Athens are used to public business, and have heard promises from too many demagogues to take them all on trust. These men had had less practice. Herakleides was telling them that whereas their old tyrant had been too sottish to do worse than neglect them, their new one was cold sober, and would never let them be.

The soldiers being loyal one and all to Dion, the whole expedition was almost in a state of war. Soldiers and sailors would wreck any wineshop where they met. The officers meantime were watching Herakleides like dogs around a foxhole. A doubtful messenger was pounced on; it turned out he was treating with Dionysios.

On this, they faced him with it, threatening to march back their men and accuse him, if he would not sail home. This he was forced to do; just at the time when Dionysios sent a mercenary army, Spartan officered, across to Sicily. They met no trouble from Herakleides' ships, and got ashore near Akragas.

Rupilius was hobbling about, by now, but could not have marched across his garden. I thought he would kill himself, when this news came in, trying to drill himself into fighting shape. I felt a fool running about after him, trying to make him rest, while he held himself back from asking what I knew about such things. The wound started to look angry, the doctor angrier still. He had put himself back instead of forward, and would have wept, I think, if Romans ever did.

Leontini is the sort of small town in which an Athenian feels mewed up; I soon found business to take me into Syracuse. The city looked dreadful, full of rat-ridden rubble with people squatting under wattle, hurdles or hides; the theatre tavern, in order to keep open, was selling raw wine to anyone who came by; there was not an actor to be seen. Still, it was where Dion was and things were happening. He was never seen, he just sent out orders; but the factions from Messene had come back here to breed. Street fights were three a day. There were always soldiers marching about to clear the streets; often the sailors met them, stoning them or trying to hold them up.

I met in the street Timonides of the Academy, that same man who wrote the history later, and who was now keeping Plato posted with the news. Though I hardly knew him, our being Athenians, here, made us greet like friends. He was a small wiry man, with a high bald head now covered by a helmet. He told me the force of Dionysios was digging-in, and Herakleides kept urging the army should march to meet it, though a child could see it would be madness as things were. As with the land-division, it was left to Dion to say no. Herakleides then accused him of dragging out the war, to prolong his time in power.

'But,' I said, edging him out from under a stoa with three broken columns, which looked like falling down, 'why isn't this man brought to trial? Not only has he broken solemn pledges made in public; he is now a traitor to the city three times over.'

'Not unless the citizens say so. If not, who can try him?'

Timonides was yellow from a recent fever, as thin as a wasp, and as tetchy. 'I have told Dion,' he burst out, 'all of us have told him, he put himself in this dilemma, when he pardoned the man at first. Moral logic, statesmanship, the commonsense of a country housewife – show me even one of them in it, I said to him, even one. But no, he freezes and taps the table. He is Dion and won't be less; and there an end ... Law – the assent of the citizens – justice; after the sack, when the man was tried, he had them all behind him. And now what's left for him? Only to say like old Dionysios, "To the Quarries, because I so command." Can you see it? He'd as soon tumble a whore in public. He's tied hand and foot; we all know it; he knows it; even more to the purpose, Herakleides knows it. What can we do? Just pray the fellow gets killed in battle. My dear Nikeratos, I pray it daily, to every god I think will listen.'

'What battle? Since you can't set out because of this?'

'Oh, we shall set out. Dion won't endure the imputations of cowardice and of tyranny.'

'*Cowardice?*' I said.

'Oh yes, yes. People forget. Don't you find in your calling that the crowd forgets?'

'It's a cold world you show me, Timonides,' I said.

'Well, that's nothing new. We must all do the thing we can ...

366

"Know yourself." "Nothing too much." There's truth in these old laws.' He had taken leave of me, when he turned back to say, 'He's a good man. One of the best of our time. If he could only question it, like Sokrates, then he would be great.'

Sure enough the expedition set out against Dionysios' troops; the fleet coastwise, the troops inland. They were gone some weeks with nothing settled either way. Rupilius began walking again; telling everyone, though it was now clear he would be lame for life, that he would soon be in the fields. Then came word that Dion, with all the cavalry, had come galloping on almost foundered horses back to the city; he shut the gates and manned the walls; the man who brought us the news had been kept inside till morning. Word had come to Dion, just in time, that Herakleides with the fleet was sailing back to seize Syracuse. He, finding himself forestalled, made a peaceful entry, pretending he had heard Dionysios' fleet was sighted. Everyone knew the truth; but no one could prove it.

The trouble was now bruited all over Greece. The Spartans in fact, with their ancient insolence, just as if they were still the masters of Hellas, sent over a general to take charge of Syracuse because its leaders could not agree. Herakleides got to him first with a pack of lies; but though a Spartan he had sense enough to look about for himself. Having done so, he declared for Dion. Herakleides had made so sure of the man, he had publicly welcomed his arbitration. So at the Spartan's instance, he had now to go into a temple and vow to mend his ways. This contented the Spartan, who went home. They are a simple, pious folk.

Soon after this, I heard from Thettalos, asking if I had gone mad to linger on in a cauldron of trouble like Sicily, by myself without work. Had I found a new lover, as he was starting to suppose? His letter was full of theatre news, neatly planned to make my feet itch for home. What indeed was I doing here, putting on plays at local festivals (I had just done *Niobe* at Katana) and watching great hopes withering? I wrote back that I was sailing as soon as I could, with unchanged heart. This was true; there had been a curly-haired, Roman-Greek lad for a while in Leontini; but nothing serious.

I had now been so long from Athens, I knew I must take care to come back on a good ship, looking like someone. So I let go the first I might have caught, because it carried hides. Some god must have guided me. It was wrecked off Lokri, with half its people drowned. And, just after I would have gone, Ortygia surrendered.

Since Herakleides was brought to heel, the blockade had been kept tight. The gatehouse guards had stopped singing. A deserter, who had swum across by night, revealed that they had eaten the elephant, though it was at least forty years old. Even then no one dared voice his hopes; till the envoy came from Apollokrates. He agreed to give up Ortygia with its standing army, navy, war-engines and all, in exchange for a safe-conduct covering five triremes, to take away his mother and sisters with their things. It seems Dionysios had left these ladies behind when he ran away. To do him justice, he may have feared being attacked at sea.

Anyone in Syracuse who had friends within reach of the city, sent them word to be there on the great day. Rupilius and I got early news, and went in overnight to be sure of good places near the sea. All at once the half-ruined city seemed to burst out with life. Porches hanging askew and propped with logs were now adorned with garlands; skinny children stuck flowers in their hair and danced in lines down the streets. All the hetairas put on their thinnest silk dresses, like nakedness but prettier, and drove shorewards in painted carriages, singing to the lyre. Boys hung on the palm-trees as thick as date-clusters. At every altar the priests were offering libations, and wreathing the statues of the gods.

It was a bright day with fair wind; light gleamed on the unfurling sails and flashed from the dripping oar-blades. Dion boarded the escort ship which saw off the last of the tyrants' line. The trumpets sounded from the walls, and the cheers rolled like surf along the shore. Old men stood weeping, young men danced, and threw each other in the air. The gates of Ortygia stood wide and unguarded, after fifty years.

Timonides, whom I saw before I sailed, told me that as Dion reached the Palace, his mother came out to meet him, leading his son by the hand. Behind them his wife, a woman with greying hair who must have seemed like a stranger, walked in tears. Since her second husband had fled before Dion, she had lived on in Ortygia, the wife of two men and of none. His mother, a noble old woman with the family's fine bones, and little more of her left, led forth this poor soul by the hand, asking if Dion wished to receive her as his kinswoman, which she was by right of birth; or as his wife, which in her heart she had always been. Dion behaved superbly. If one were writing a play to show him at his best, one might contrive some such a scene. He embraced and kissed her tenderly, committed the boy into her care, and had her led to his house with honour. Timonides, wiping his nose when he recalled it, said there was not a dry eye as far as you could look.

'How did young Hipparinos take it?'

'He looked frightened, and sullen. But he may simply have been overwhelmed by the occasion. He is only sixteen or so; plenty of time to correct his upbringing.'

'Of course,' I said. For the play must close here, with the victory procession, the wife restored, the hero at the height of honour, the chorus singing praises, the happy audience going home. I could sail back to Athens, the first with the good news. A long piece of my life, which sometimes had caught my very soul up, was ending in a paean of joy.

369

Next day, or the day after, I went to pay my respects to Dion, as everyone of consequence was doing. He saw us a dozen at a time; I had expected nothing else, so great was the press; my only wish was to wish him joy. He met us in a plain white robe, simple even for him. In the time of the factions, he had lost weight; but it just showed up the splendid bones of his face, now lit with his fulfilment. He was the saviour of his people; had avenged his exile, and his wife's wrongs; conquered a base enemy without once sinking into baseness. He was Dion, and never had been less.

He singled me out for a greeting, saying he had given me short thanks on the Leontini road. His kindness touched me; he had forgiven me my calling, in the fullness of his heart. The plain room was brimmed with happiness and triumph, like a beautiful krater filled with wine.

Some close friends stood round, who would stay when the rest had gone: Timonides, longing, I expect, to be off and write up his history; and Kallippos of Athens, the tyrant-hater, who had long been Dion's right-hand man. I wondered how he felt when he saw Ortygia empty. His pale eyes wandered, as if looking for something he had lost.

It was time to go. I took a last look at Dion, smiling among his friends; and there came into my mind the story of the old Olympic victor, who saw both of his sons crowned in one year. 'Die now!' the people cried to him, meaning that no moment of his life to come could equal this. I stood in the doorway, though my exit was already made, looking at his stern happy face; and a voice in my soul, which I could not silence, said 'Die now, Dion. Die!'

I brushed it from my mind – one must avoid words of ill omen – and went off to take my ship.

23

I was busy that year. I came back to hear what everyone else had been doing, while I was out of the way. Thettalos, as he confessed, had had an affair with a youth in Corinth. None the less we met again with joy, forgave each other, and talked two days without stopping. It is always so when we've been apart, and time does not change it.

Rumour had it that I had been on secret missions in Sicily, to keep me there so long. I held my peace and was praised for discretion. While I was away, Thettalos had got on the protagonists' list, and at the Dionysia for the first time we were in rival plays, he as Troilos, I as Ulysses. Each knew he would do his best and there would be no repining; we had outgrown such follies. I won, on a divided vote; his turn would be soon. At the feast, we got so taken up with talking about technique (he could at last direct, and it had been a striking production) that our friends had to drag us apart. I had nearly forgotten whose the party was.

We decided to tour as partners for a while, and went to Ephesos. Once in every few years, it is a joy to tour with Thettalos; after that, one needs a year or two to get one's breath. Between his work and his escapades, the days are full and there

371

is not much left of the night. In his art he pleases himself; in his adventures he always asks my advice, and is as grateful as if he took it.

Here and there we got news of Sicily; that Dion was still in power; that Dionysios had not tried to get back, though much detested in Lokri for his beastly drunkenness and debauching of the local girls. Both armies still served in Syracuse; Dion had packed off Nypsios' men but kept the rest. The city had never been so well defended since old Dionysios' day. Dion himself still lived by Pythagoras' chaste and simple rule.

I heard no more than this; perhaps because I did not ask. The play was over. The hero lives on in honour; the audience knows it; but the theatre is empty, and the sweepers have moved in. It is the time for memory.

Returning by way of Delos, we stayed for the feast of Apollo, and put on *The Hyperboreans*, whose setting is the island. It was during rehearsals, on one of those dazzling, scorching Delian days, that walking on the Lion Terrace by the lake to get the breeze, we met Chairemon the poet. He had taken care never to go back to Syracuse since he had been Dionysios' guest; but having then spent a whole month there, was reckoned an authority on its affairs. We now got once more the tale of his adventures, which everyone in Athens knew by heart, except for the touching-up added each time to prove his hatred of tyranny. At the end he said, 'Unhappy people! Ever since their cruelty to Nikias' men in our fathers' day, they seem under a curse.'

'But now the Erinyes have relented.'

'Do tell us,' said Thettalos, breaking in, 'is your new play ready?'

Chairemon never liked being interrupted, even with flattery. He turned back to me. 'That we wait to see. It seems that, but for the Palace orgies, everything goes on much the same.'

'Come,' I said, 'they are living now under law.'

'There is a constitutional council sitting. One can't expect a statute book overnight, of course. Meantime, military government still continues.'

'That could hardly be helped. Well, the people no longer have to pay for Dionysios' parties.'

'Taxes are still heavy, I hear. There are the troops to be maintained. *They* have nothing to complain of; strict discipline, but looked after; none of young Dionysios' meanness. And then, of course, all who helped Dion to power have been treated well. He was always generous, even in exile; but it's grown beyond what anyone could meet from a private purse. Well, he's supreme commander, he can do what he chooses. No one accuses him of spending on himself.'

'Herakleides has really kept those vows, then?'

'Herakleides!' He looked surprised, and pleased to be better informed. 'He can't choose, where he is now.'

'Niko,' said Thettalos, 'the flautist will be there waiting. You wanted that bit of recitative gone over.'

'What!' I cried. 'Herakleides dead? A blessing to everyone. The gods owed Dion that.'

Chairemon lifted his brows. 'The gods help him who helps himself. In that sense, you may be right.'

'Very true,' said Thettalos. 'You will have to excuse us, Chairemon. We—'

'No,' I said. 'Wait. Chairemon – how did he die?'

'He was stabbed to death in his house, by some gentlemen of ancient lineage who had been waiting a year for leave to do it. This was withheld, till he moved at Assembly that Ortygia be dismantled and its walls pulled down, as a den of tyranny fortified against the people. They, it seems, had expected this from the time it was surrendered; and Herakleides was getting increased support. It was thought unwise to try him publicly . . . Appalling, dreadful. But that is Sicily. One has ceased to expect Greek ethics there. One might as well be in Macedon.'

Thettalos, who had been drawing me off, stood quiet, with his hand on my arm. It is a mistake to think, as some people do, that he has no discretion.

'My dear Chairemon!' I said. 'The deed doesn't surprise me; but I'll believe that Dion gave it countenance when I see water run uphill.'

'I assure you, I had it from Damon the banker, who was there on business; a very sober man. Dion as good as owned to it in the funeral oration, but said it was necessary for the sake of the city.'

'What funeral oration?' I heard my own voice, sounding stupid. 'Who spoke it?'

'Dion, as I said. He gave him a state funeral, because of his past services, and made the speech himself . . . You are feeling the heat, Nikeratos. This is the fiercest sun in Greece. Let's go under the stoa.'

'We must get on,' said Thettalos, shoving me. 'A rehearsal call.' Chairemon said he would walk with us to the theatre. The streets were hotter than the terrace. Thettalos walked in the middle, to give me quiet. I heard Chairemon say to him, 'I daresay this self-sufficiency has grown on Dion since his son died. He has no other.'

I woke from my daze. 'Has he lost his son?'

'Say rather he never regained him. He had acquired all the tastes of his uncle, and did not like correction. It must have been a trial to Dion, both as a father and a public man. They say he was somewhat severe. One can't believe all one hears; it may not be true the boy threw himself off his father's roof. Very likely he was drunk, and stumbled.'

The skene-room seemed dark, after the brilliant light outside.

Thettalos had got rid of Chairemon at the door. 'My dear,' he said, 'I wish I'd told you in Samos. But it was the night before the performance when I heard; there was no sense in upsetting you; and then I kept thinking some better news would overtake it.'

'He did it for the city,' I said. 'Or so he saw it. How he must have suffered! But the oration, the state funeral ... Who could conceive such a thing?'

Thettalos said in his lovely voice, '*The God for his presumption struck him down, But then, relenting, raised him to the stars.* That's how I think he conceived it. Come, Niko, let's work, or you'll get no sleep tonight.'

I had been back some weeks in Athens, when I heard from Speusippos, asking me to see him at the Academy.

I had been keeping away, mostly because Axiothea was still so shy of me. The memory of our Dionysia confused her, and brought back too much else of that night. The look into the temple had been more than her soul could bear, and she had thrown herself into philosophy, trying to understand why the gods allowed it. She said it was better than the peace of ignorance, and no doubt she knew best. But it was a good while after this before we had our old ease together. Meantime, after having made sure I had not got her with child, I did not intrude. Lately, too, I had been afraid of getting any more news from Syracuse. This summons disturbed me, for Speusippos did not entertain at the Academy, and there was only one sort of business in which I would be of use.

'Niko,' he said as soon as we were alone, 'have you any engagements in Sicily?'

Once I would have answered yes, whether it was true or not. But I shook my head, and waited.

'Then,' he said, 'I can only beg you, if you are my friend, if you

375

love Dion, to make some pretext for going. None of us is expected there; a sudden visit would look strange, and might hasten the very thing we fear.' He picked up a letter from his table. Still I did not say that I would take it, but looked at him and waited. When he saw he would have to tell me more, he said, 'Plato asked me to keep it as secret as I could. This man, you understand, has been at the Academy; never really one of ourselves, but the world doesn't make such distinctions. The truth is, we have fears for Dion, even for his life. Not from known enemies, whom he can well deal with, but from a trusted friend.'

'Kallippos?'

'What?' he cried, almost jumping up in his chair. 'You knew?'

'Only now. I should have known. He is a man in love with hatred. He has lost Dionysios; where else can he look? I saw it in his face, if I had only understood it.'

'We have heard from friends at Tarentum. Someone who had been sounded came to warn them. He said he had first warned Dion himself; but Dion would not believe him. Now you see what I ask of you, and why.'

'Yes,' I said. 'I'll go. Dion deserves that much of his fellowmen.'

He looked at me with sadness; as I suppose I had looked at him. 'You have heard, then. Try, Niko, to think of him as a man trapped not by any baseness in his soul, but by its magnanimity.'

'I do. It comes easily to an actor. Tragedy is full of it.'

'He is accused of prolonging his own authority. This I am sure is unjust. Plato and I have sent out a draft constitution, the best that the city as it is will bear; Corinth has sent advisers too. But where there's justice, no one gets all he wants to everyone else's loss. Such things take time to agree on; there has been faction and distrust; Herakleides left his legacy.'

'What will Dion be, in the end?'

'A constitutional king.'

376

Even now the word sang in my ears like a great line in a play. I said, 'Surely it was ordained by heaven.'

'A king under law. He will have no powers of punishment; those are vested in the judges. There will be a Senate; and some form of consultation with the people, not yet determined.'

'That's where it rubs?'

'How not? ... Don't tell anyone in Syracuse, except Dion, that you come from us; for your own sake, as well as his.'

'I will take good care. I have known Kallippos a long time.'

'There is a great freight of human good,' he said, 'almost safe in harbour. You may yet save it for the world, Niko. Go with God.'

The year was turning mildly. The ship laboured through calm seas under oars. At evening the sky was pale red above a pale blue horizon; the ruddy hair of the Thracian rowers smouldered like embers. Their chantyman sang endlessly, an air like a breaking wave, mounting in a wail, crashing with the oar-stroke. We were three days late at Syracuse; but I lost the sense of passing time, in the space and quiet of the sea. At night I would look at the low stars turning, not knowing if I fell asleep late or soon. For the first time since boyhood, I had no wish to end the voyage.

Syracuse had been cleared of rubble and almost rebuilt. Everything seemed quiet. The same thin-legged, swag-bellied children were scavenging among the pi-dogs. Now, though, when a carriage passed they would sometimes chuck a stone after it. They would not have dared before.

I went to the theatre tavern, to account for my presence with the story I had prepared: I had been told that now things were settled down here, the theatre was not getting as much encouragement as it should; Athenian actors were concerned about it, and I had come to see, before any of us risked capital on the journey. I talked vaguely of looking out for talent. This brought the answers I needed. There were still plays at the greater festivals; but as the Commander never went, those who liked to stand well with him also stayed away. In Athens, choregos duties are a tax levy on rich men; in Syracuse they had just done it for the glory, or to please the Archons. Some could afford it no longer; others would not, without hope of gaining by it. Theatre was as good as dead; except that Kallippos the Athenian had lately sponsored *The Offering-Bearers*, which had pleased the people, and given a few artists work.

I thought it was just the play for him, all hate and vengeance. Then I was approached by a group of young actors, all eager to get out of Syracuse, and was busy till it was time to find an inn. My former one was still standing. They gave me the room that had been Axiothea's.

I had refused evening invitations, meaning to be up early, and was going to bed, when my host announced a visitor. It was Kallippos.

He was now a man of importance here; it would have been natural if he wanted to see me, to invite me to wait on him at his house. With some men, I should have thought this unassuming; with him I thought that he would take more care, if it were not near the time.

He was just as I had remembered him at home, when he came sniffing about backstage; except for a certain tautness, which he was trying to hide. He asked after my career, and I thought as usual that he was waiting for me to relate some harm that had been done me, so that he could be angry, and that for having no grievance he liked me less. However, this time he did not much care; he was hurrying through the civilities. To help him on, I told him how sorry I was for the artists of Syracuse in their hard times. It was sad, I said, to think they had done better under a tyranny than now with enlightened rule.

At once he began to feel his way with me. It was the only time I have been approached with such a purpose, and I hope the last. It was like some suitor who disgusts one, starting to stroke one on the supper-couch, beginning as if by chance. There however one can move aside; whereas I had to pretend to like it. He began with faint praise of Dion; going on to disappointment and faint excuses. I replied that all this confirmed what I'd heard; I did not say of whom. Then, casting off all disguise, he said it was certain Dion had brought war to the city, only to take the tyranny for himself. 'We of the Academy' (I could picture Speusippos white with anger) 'have been most bitterly deceived.'

I said this was terrible news; that if he wished, I would see Speusippos in Athens and tell him; or would he like me to carry a letter? I was anxious to see if this frightened him; if it did, his plans might not be too far advanced.

'I should welcome it,' he said. 'You, with your knowledge of Syracuse, would be believed. You have watched this man's career; you have seen the tyrant within the egg tap on the shell and crack it, and start to look about for food. You have seen the beginning ... are you staying with us long?'

He did not ask idly. I felt my hands grow cold and damp, for he had meant me to understand. His pale eyes waited. I knew, as if I saw through his clothes, that he had a knife on him, in case I showed he had said too much. Why did he think he could kill in the city and not answer for it? That told more than all.

I had now to act for my life; to seem well disposed, without seeing his purpose. He wanted me to justify him to the Academy. If I seemed to consent, he would be encouraged. I could think of nothing a man like me could say to him, which might persuade him to delay.

So I became full of my own affairs, which surprises no one in an actor. I told him about a play I had just read; how I would

379

direct it unless I changed my mind; what Syracusan actors I might take on, consulting him about each. I told him I had meant to call on Dion, on behalf of us artists, asking him for his patronage, but now could not make up my mind to it after what I'd heard; I must sleep on it and think again. He soon had enough of this, and got ready to go. To see him off smoothly, I commended his reviving that fine old play, *The Offering-Bearers*. He paused at the door with a meaning smile. 'It was a comfort, I think, to those who mourned for Herakleides. And it reminded them that the mourners for Agamemnon did more than weep.'

I scarcely closed my eyes all night. Knowing Dion always rose at dawn, I got up in the dark so as to lose no time. He had gone back, as I knew already, to his old house in Ortygia.

The gatehouses were still manned. The guards were civil, though, and only asked my business; one did not need a pass. No one had followed me there, I must have persuaded Kallippos he need not trouble.

Dion's house looked the same as ever, well-kept, simple and clean. This time no lively boy came peeping. I looked at the roof; on the side where the slope fell away, it was a long way down.

At the door the porter told me I had just missed the master. He had gone up to the Palace, to start the business of the day.

In the porch, between the red lions of Samian marble, a sturdy Argive with polished armour saluted and took my name. He led me in, though I had no need of it. I knew the way so well, my feet could have taken me by themselves.

The clothes-racks were gone from the searching-room. It was just an ante-chamber, with a few people waiting already, early though it was. I remembered the faces one had seen hereabouts in the old days: frightened, or insolent, or cunning; faces that watched each other, eager faces of flatterers. They were gone; but the new ones were not those of happy men. Worry, resentment, impatience, long-suffering duty, all these I saw. I did not see hope nor dedication. I did not see a smile, or love.

However, I had not long to look; almost at once a clerk came out to say the Commander would see me. I went in, hearing angry mutters from those who had come first. The gilt bronze grille stood open. I entered the room I had not seen for a dozen years.

All the gaudy trimmings had gone; it was almost bare; there was only one bit of furniture that I remembered. Dionysios couldn't take that off to Lokri; it would have sunk the ship. It stood in its place, on its bronze-winged sphinxes, solid as a tomb, just where it had been when its first owner sat at it to write *Hektor's Ransom*. Behind it, in a good plain chair of polished wood, was the master of Ortygia.

I would hardly have known him. His hair was almost white. He had never carried spare flesh, but his body had had the athlete's hard smoothness. He was lean now; the loose skin on his arms, dragged about his battle-scars. He might have been sixty; but he had shaved his beard, perhaps to try and look younger, as ageing leaders must if they can. Between his strong cheekbones and the fine arched brow above, the skin of the eyelids looked brown and creased, with blue shadows under; the inner ends of his eyebrows were drawn together in a fixed frown he no longer seemed to feel. His dark eyes looked at me with a kind of hunger – for what? For old years, for some simple comfort of man to man, for a message of good tidings? I don't know; he put the need aside, whatever it was, with an air of habit. He had been weak in sending for me first, and was angry with himself, but too just to turn it on me.

He stood up. I was from Athens, where citizens are not kept standing before seated men. It was the courtesy of a king to one who had been his host in exile. We were going, I suppose, through the formalities of greeting. I remember only his face. A king, I had said; he will be King at last; the gods ordained it. Well, now I

381

looked on it; the name was nothing, here was the thing. Always, when I had pictured it, I had seen him as on that day in Delphi long ago, when he came into the skene-room like the statue of a victor. I had seen his face like the antique masks of Apollo, which stamp on youth the wisdom and strength of manhood. Now I stood before a king – an old king weary of the burden, stained by the sins that power forces men's hands to when they dare not lay it down; bearing their shame with his other cares, in a stubborn fortitude; the familiar of loneliness, forgotten by hope.

The godlike mask was off; as with the lover of my boyhood, it was I who had put it on him for my own need. Who does not dream of clear water, when the springs are brack? But I had dreamed only, he had tried to bring the dream to be. Now he had all, which if he had sunk his soul to evil could have made him glad. Old Dionysios had had it and died content. He suffered because he had loved the good, and still longed after it. And I thought, I too am marked with my trade. Next time I play Theseus in the Underworld, I shall remember him.

'Sir,' I said, 'I've a letter from Speusippos; may I beg you to read it soon? Since I came here myself, I've learned that the warning in it is true. The man it names has approached me. He is planning an armed revolt, which is almost ready. He intends your death.'

He heard me steadily, without change of colour, nodded, and held out his hand for it. I think he would have asked me to sit while he read it, then remembered there was no other chair and went on standing himself. It was a fairly long letter, but he skimmed it quickly, looking for something; when he had found that, he laid it aside.

'It seems,' he said, 'that Speusippos told you what he had heard. It was only Kallippos you were warned of? No one else?'

'Only him. I knew him in Athens. He took less care with me than I expect he did at the Academy. He is a dangerous man.'

382

'Subtle, let us say, and capable.' He smiled at me; the smile of a king to a simple fellow who means well. 'Set your mind at rest, Nikeratos. If Kallippos is dangerous, it is only to my enemies. I shall give you a letter for Speusippos, if you will be good enough to carry it, which will reassure him.'

I was alarmed, rather than surprised by this. Men expect of others what they know of themselves, I thought. So I described to him all last night's talk, leaving nothing out, even what might insult or wound him. The thing had gone beyond delicacy.

'Yes, yes.' He sounded indulgent. I could hardly believe my ears. 'As I told you, he is a subtle man. For some time he has made it his business to test people in the city whose loyalty he feels doubt of. Of course he asked my leave; someone he tested might, as you and others have done, loyally report to me. I am sorry he so mistook you, Nikeratos. But now you understand and I hope are satisfied. Thank you none the less for your goodwill.'

I said something. I believe I even apologised. My whole body seemed one grief. All was gone, the bronze-hard honour, the pride of Achilles, pure as fire. There was just an old king, fallen to the sad needs of sick power, who had learned to use a man like Kallippos as a spy.

I said whatever I said, and waited for leave to go. Yet he kept me back, asking things about Athens, with that hunger in his face again. I had never known him talk for the sake of talking. He was alone, and would always be; perhaps even the memory of other days was something.

'You may assure Speusippos,' he said, 'that his fears are groundless. Even my own wife and mother were deceived, and I could not reassure them. Kallippos however did so, by taking the holy oath of Demeter in the sacred grove ... You must understand, Nikeratos, that Syracuse is not Athens.'

I thought of the road to Leontini and answered, 'No.'

'These people are my charge. Fickle, foolish, cowardly, abject as they are, my forbears helped to make them so. I must save them in spite of themselves, and give them time to grow before the Carthaginians make them slaves for ever. You do not know, Nikeratos, you who show kings and rulers at a simple crux of fate, the base means men require of those who would rescue them from their baseness. Do you know they have wanted me to pull down the monument of the elder Dionysios, the father of my wife; the man who for all his faults loved me more than his own son, for he trusted his life to me alone? Can they think I would buy their love so sordidly?'

'We must respect the dead,' I answered. 'They are helpless, as one day we shall be.'

'Helpless?' he said, staring at me out of his sunken eyes. 'You think so? You hold with Pythagoras that they sleep in Limbo, till they are brought before the judges to choose their own expiation? You don't believe in dead men's vengeance, the stuff of all your tragedies?'

'I don't know, sir,' I said. 'All actors are superstitious. But I think I would rather leave it to the gods. They know more of the truth.'

'You are right,' he said. 'That is the answer of philosophy ... I had a strange dream yesterday, if one can say one dreams when one is waking. I was reading in my study, when my eye was caught by some movement. I looked up; at the end of the room was an old woman with a broom, sweeping the floor. No servant would do so in my presence; as I looked in surprise, she turned towards me. She had a face, Nikeratos, like the masks of the Furies in *Eumenides*; more dreadful than I can describe. The mask was alive, with eyes like green-burning embers; and the snakes moved in her hair.'

I saw sweat on his brow. With almost any man I knew, I would have gone up and laid my arm across his shoulders; but of course I knew I could not. 'Sir,' I said, 'you have been spending yourself night and day for the city, without getting much thanks for it to ease your heart. You dozed, I expect, as you read, and dreamed of some fright in childhood. When those masks come on, I've heard of women miscarrying in the theatre. In my opinion, no young child should see the play at all.'

He smiled; chiefly from pride, but I saw in it too a certain kindness. He was about to dismiss me. Suddenly – I suppose it was his words of ill omen – I was possessed by the thought that I should never see him more. Like a fool I exclaimed, 'Sir; remember how happy you were at Athens. Everyone there honours your name. Why don't you come back to the Academy? Think what joy it would give to Plato.'

He drew himself up, if that was possible for a man who still held himself straight as a spear. His brows lifted; for a moment in the old worn face I saw the imperious youth I had glimpsed at Delphi. 'To Plato? To come running like a coward, with nothing achieved save to have changed tyranny for chaos, back to Plato who three times risked his life here for my cause and me? I had rather have died unborn, than return from battle a man who threw away his shield.'

'You speak like Dion, and I see it must be so. Forgive me, sir; but since Kallippos thinks you are in danger, don't people see you too easily? I had not much trouble in getting in; not like the old days.'

'The old days?' he said. 'I hope not; or why am I here? Better death before this day's sunset, than such a life.'

He said a few words more, promising me the letter for Speusippos if I would come back tomorrow; then wished me goodbye. I went away thinking, Well, then, after all I am sure of seeing him again.

I went about the town, saw one or two friends, and was told that a certain young actor, who I had been told had promise, had been seeking me. It seemed a pity not to see him; so in the evening I went to the theatre wineshop.

Through lack of custom, they were still serving all kinds of people; it was not the pleasant place it used to be. The long table at the bottom end was full of soldiers, young Greeks with their heads together, talking quietly. They looked strong young louts; when such men are quiet, one always suspects mischief. Just as I had been served my wine, a man got up from among them and went out. I recognised Kallippos. If the wretched fellows had been foolish, then, they would soon be sorry.

They went on talking in a huddle; they were in street dress, without their arms, so I supposed could not be up to much harm just now; yet they were neighbours I did not like, and I decided I would wait no longer. I had almost got up, when a man of about fifty, who had been sitting alone in a corner, crossed to my table. 'Nikeratos,' he said, 'I have been making up my mind whether to greet you, or if you would remember me after so long.'

He had a kind, gentle, failed-looking face, which must once have been handsome. I could not recall if we had met, but liking the look of him, I murmured something. He went on, 'No, of course you could not; you were just a boy, walking-on in your father's plays. But I would have known you anywhere ... Once, long ago, we met to read *The Myrmidons*.'

'Ariston!' I said, and grasped his hands. It was like meeting a stranger; I had forgotten our love like a dream; but all through these years I had cherished gratitude. It was his kindness I had remembered.

He told me he had been touring each time I came before. I don't think it was true; I think he had been out of work, and was afraid of seeming to trade upon the past. Never having heard his name in Syracuse, I had thought he must be dead; but it was just that he was not a very good actor. His robe was darned; he looked hungry, but had bought his own drink before he spoke to me. I suppose that now, when no one had work in the city, it had come easier.

I resolved at once that I would take care of him, get him to Athens, and find him something; but that must come later, for he was a man with self-respect. So we talked of the past, and so on; while at the long table the young soldiers muttered together, or laughed sharply; like boys up to something bad, which frightens them, but not enough to make them cry off.

Once I heard something, some phrase I can't bring back, which caught at my mind, so that for a moment I tried to listen. I think it was, 'He'll have gone to his house', which might have meant anyone in the city. I don't know why I noticed it. Yet I did, and my attention wandered from Ariston, just long enough for him to feel it, and me to know he did. This I could not bear. I was too well-dressed to afford it. I would not have hurt him for the world. It is true, too, that I would not think of myself as such a man. To each his own shape of pride.

So I turned my mind to him, and talked, and listened, and got him to take a good meal with me; and before we had finished, the young Greeks left all together.

We parted, arranging to meet again (I knew better than to ask where he was living) and I walked towards my inn in the dying sunset. In the south night falls quickly; red turns to purple as you look. Whether it was this brooding light; or words heard and not heeded stirring in my head; or whether some new note reached me through the city's noise, I cannot tell; but of a sudden my heart jumped, and I understood. I had heard the truth from Kallippos. It was to Dion he had lied.

I began to run through the streets towards Ortygia. People

stared at me; I ran as a child does from some bugbear he knows that only he can see. As the fading day sank to a murk in the west like blood, I knew I was running from the knowledge in my soul, that it was too late.

Already shouts came from Ortygia, passed along from gate-house to gatehouse. On the Palace roof stood a man with two torches, signalling his news against the darkening sky.

I did not run on, in the hope that my fears were folly, that the tumult had some other cause. I knew; and now fear was over, I did not even grieve. It was all that was left him, to die like a king in tragedy, treading upon purple to the axe behind the door. He was freed from his prison in Ortygia, in the only way he could be freed, before it closed on him for ever. I had no need to be told he had died with courage, fighting like a soldier against them all. I hoped, for as long as it was possible to hope in vain, that he had not fought alone.

I had no wish to stay on in Syracuse and speak his epitaph. There was no one here to write it; that was for the old man in Athens, who had written it, I suppose, already in his heart. As for me, Kallippos would not take time to look for me, a vain actor with a head for nothing but his roles. I would sail with Ariston, who had been kind when kindness or cruelty had power to shape my soul, and see he did not die hungry, or alone. That, I thought, is as much as most men can hope to bring away from the march of history, when all is said.

24

A dozen years have passed since then. I have never been back to Syracuse. They say grass grows in the streets there, and it has fewer people now than a country town in Attica. Tyranny has followed tyranny (that of Kallippos was so hateful that it only lasted a year) and for a time even Dionysios himself came back to rule over the desolation. At last Corinth the mother-city, taking pity on her wretched child, sent them a general, a good man it seems. He has got Dionysios out again; whether he can get rid of the Carthaginians, only God knows. Meantime, he has had faith enough in men to disarm Ortygia; the walls of that lair are rubble now.

Dionysios got off just with his life. He is no one any more; keeps a boys' school in Corinth, and goes shopping in the market for his own dinner. Last time I played there, he came behind to commend me. The gods did him a backhand favour, for he can't afford to drink himself into the grave, and is merely getting fat. He still thinks himself a good judge of the drama, and held forth for some time, till some more important citizen interrupted him.

Except in Corinth, which has an interest of its own, no one thinks much about Syracuse. It is a place where things happened once. Too much is going on now in Greece, with Philip of Macedon pushing south and meddling everywhere. No one has time for a backward island, full of squabbling bandits, with all its glories in the past. I suppose now and then there are a few hundred folk in that great theatre. All the good actors left years ago.

Greece has plenty of work for us. It is said that technique has never been so advanced, though it's long since I read a good new play. The great successes are all revivals, which we try to shed some new light on, or at least to present with a splendour worthy of the mighty dead.

Thettalos and I still share the house by the river, and tour as partners every few years. We have our own ways and our disagreements, but neither of us can conceive of being without the other. It is lucky I am the elder. There is a life in him which will demand its own span to work in, when I am gone, whether he likes or not.

We were together through most of this year's spring. He was crowned at the Dionysia, and gave a party which, like all his others, will be talked of through the year. Then he went touring north, to Pella. Nobody nowadays who wishes to be considered at all in theatre can leave Pella out for long. Actors are so esteemed there, we even send them on embassies.

Thettalos enjoyed his tour, and came back with some handsome presents as well as his fee. He told me he felt startled when, being presented to Queen Olympias, he found her wreathed with tame snakes, which stood up and hissed at him; she seemed to have stepped straight out of *The Bacchae*; but then Pella was never dull. 'Besides,' he said, sighing and shaking his head, 'I am in love. I have lost my heart for ever. I shall never be the same again.'

I was used to this declaration, and to pulling him out of whatever scrape it meant, and said I hoped this time she was not the wife of a general. I was quite relieved when he told me it was a boy, and asked if he had brought the fair one to Athens. He laughed immoderately, and said when he could get it out, 'No, I was afraid of his father.'

Macedon being as full as it is of powerful brigands, I praised his wisdom. He added, 'And still more of his mother, and more than all of him.' I raised my brows and waited. 'No,' he said. 'You'll be at Pella next month, and can see him for yourself.'

'Excellent. Tell me his name.'

'You will know when you see him. He will be there. He never misses a play.'

He would tell me no more, but said a little later, 'When you go up to Pella, why don't you put on *The Myrmidons?*'

'My dear,' I said, 'I think it is time I hung up the mask of Achilles. I've left fifty behind, though it is kind of you to forget.'

'Nonsense. You wear a young mask as well as ever. You know if you were making a fool of yourself I'd be the first to tell you. Do it while you can; you are a beautiful Achilles. Give them something to remember.'

I was touched, and pleased, for it was true he could not have lied about it. Then I said, 'But why *The Myrmidons?*'

'Well, it has not been done there for something like ten years; the young generation has never seen it.'

'Thettalos!' I said. 'I believe you are asking me to put on this whole production, simply to oblige your boy friend.'

'My ...?' He stared, laughed, then said, 'Alas, you flatter my hopes. But it is true he is anxious to see it. I would have done it myself, if I could have raised a script in Pella.'

'Couldn't he lend you his?'

'He's never had one. It is only that he has heard it follows the *Iliad*, most of which he knows by heart.'

'Well,' I said, 'that's something. Your last flame could not read.

I might really do it, if it's so long since they had it there; I should enjoy it myself.'

'Good. I promise you won't regret it. But let your third man fly on as Apollo. I can't spare you, dearest Niko. The crane-man drinks.'

'I've never done it, except that once in Delphi as an offering to the god.' I fell silent, thinking of the war there, the very sanctuary plundered of its gold. Nothing is sacred to our age.

In due course I took my company to Pella, which gave us its usual eager welcome. They are used however by now to actors going to bed early before the play, instead of drinking till dawn. The noise downstairs is something one must put up with.

King Philip has adorned King Archelaos' theatre; everything of the best. The crane-man was sober. Just before I went on, I touched, as I always do, the antique mask of Apollo. I no longer wear it; no one would understand it now; but I take it everywhere, thinking, like Lamprias' old friend, that it brings me luck. The god looked stern but serene. I thought he said to me, 'You must be good today; there are reasons. But don't fret; I will look after you.' I had been doubting myself before; but it left me as I went on, and I don't think I was ever better. At the end I thought, 'I must never do it again, for fear of tempting the gods.'

There was a crowd in the dressing-room. I was still in costume, with the dresser combing my mask, when there was a stir about the door, and the people parted, just like extras for a big upstage entrance.

A boy was standing there, of fourteen or so, with fire-gold hair lying loose on his brow and down his neck. All Macedonians have blue eyes; but not of a blue like that. Half a dozen other lads, about his age or rather older, were standing behind him. When I saw that none of them pushed in front, I guessed who he was.

He came in, sweeping his gaze about the room, and said, 'Where is Achilles?'

It is a big theatre; even from the front row, one is a good way off when one takes one's bow. I said, 'Here, my lord.'

He stood still, looking. His eyes were big, which made them look even bluer. I was sorry that so beautiful a boy should be disappointed; at his age, they always half expect the face to match the mask. I supposed him at a loss for words, till he came nearer and said quietly, 'That is most wonderful. There must be a god in your soul.'

I did not spoil it by telling him I was lucky to have kept my teeth. I said, 'I had a good father, sir, to start me off young, and I keep up my practice.'

'Then you've been an actor always, all your life?' When I assented he nodded his head as if this answer satisfied him, and said, 'And you always knew.' He asked me one or two questions about technique, which were far from foolish; I could see where he had talked with Thettalos. Presently he looked at the people standing round and said, 'You have leave to go.'

They bowed out. When the lads behind him started to follow, he reached out and caught one by the arm, saying 'No, you stay, Hephaistion.' The tall boy came back with a lightening of all his face, and stood close beside him. He said to me, 'The others are the Companions of the Prince; but we two are just Hephaistion and Alexander.'

'So it was,' I said smiling at them, 'in the tent of Achilles.'

He nodded; it was a thought he was used to. He came up and touched my flimsy stage armour to see how it was made. On his arm, half-covered by his big gold bracelet, was a thick scar one would have thought had been got in battle, if he had not been so young. His face was a little longer than the sculptors' canon; just enough to make the canon look insipid. His skin was clear, with

393

a ruddy, even tan; he was fresh, yet warm. A sweetness came from him; not bath-oil, but something of himself, like the scent of a summer meadow. I would have liked to draw him nearer, to feel the glow from him; but I would as soon have touched a flame, or a lion.

He noted that we had the place to ourselves, and said, 'I have something to tell you. You shall be the first to hear. One day, I shall make a sacrifice at Achilles' tomb. Hephaistion will do it for Patroklos. It is a vow we have made.'

Good news, I thought, if King Philip means to turn eastward. I said, 'That's in Persia, my lord.'

'Yes.' He looked serene, like Apollo among the Lapiths. 'When we are there, you shall come out and play The Myrmidons.'

I shook my head, saying, 'Even though it is soon, I shall be too old.'

He looked at me with his head a little sideways, as if reckoning the time. 'Perhaps,' he said. 'But I want to hear your voice on the plain of Troy. No one else will be the same, now. So if I ask you, you will come?'

As if he had bidden me to supper across the street, I answered, 'Yes, my lord. I will come.'

'I knew that you would. You understand these things. There is a question I have to ask you.'

Someone coughed in the doorway. A small, dapper, thin-legged man came in, with the beard of a philosopher. He looked at the boy with dissatisfaction, like a hen that has hatched an eagle-chick. The boy looked back, and then at me, as if saying, One must take men as they are, no sense in making a fuss. 'Nikeratos,' he said, 'let me present my tutor, Aristoteles. Or perhaps you have met in Athens?'

It was plain he did not recall it, and plainer still that he didn't like being presented to an actor. One could hardly blame him. I smoothed it over as best I could. He had left the Academy, so someone had told me, in displeasure when Speusippos became its head. I had not known he was here.

Setting this business briskly aside, the boy said to me, 'There is one thing in the *Iliad* I have never understood; I was hoping the play might explain it. Why didn't Achilles kill Agamemnon in the very beginning? Then Patroklos and the other heroes need not have died. Have *you* heard why it was?'

'Well, Athene counselled prudence. Agamemnon was the greater king. And he was supreme commander.'

'But what a general! He wasted his men's lives. He never really led them. He robbed his best officer, to cover a debt he owed himself, and had to beg his pardon. He started a rout with a stupid order, and then couldn't even get them in hand; he had to let Odysseus do it. Can you think of anything more disgraceful? Supreme commander! He couldn't have stopped a Thracian cattle-raid. I can't think why Achilles didn't kill him. He owed it to the Greeks. They knew him. They'd all have followed him, and finished off the war. No one but Agamemnon could have made it last ten years. They should have taken Troy between two winters.'

Aristoteles fidgeted, trying, I perceived, to get the prince away without telling him to come, in case he might say no and authority be lost. I could see the boy taking it in, not as boys do, but like a man measuring men. I think it amused him, too; but not enough to keep him long from his thought.

'If Achilles had taken Troy, I doubt he'd have sacked it; not if Patroklos was alive. (If they'd killed him – yes, then!) It was such a waste. The Trojans were fine, brave people; they could have made a great kingdom together. Think where Troy was. And all those ships, never used at all. He could have married one of Priam's daughters. *He* would never have stooped to enslave the royal ladies. I am sure of that.' He gazed out past me, seeing it all.

The shine from him almost scorched me. He said, speaking the verse well, *Sing, Goddess, the destroying anger of Achilles, Peleus' son, which brought great sorrows to the Greeks. Many the brave man's soul it sent to Hades, and flung the flesh of heroes for the gorging of dogs and kites* ... But it wasn't his anger. It was his not seeing at first what he had to do.'

With his long hair, cut as they show it in the archaic statues (Macedon is full of these old customs) and his ardent eyes bluer even than theirs, he was like some kouros in ancient legend, listening for the voice of a lover who is also a god. Aristoteles coughed; and the boy withdrew himself calmly from his vision. He said, 'But Achilles must have had some reason. It was so long ago; twelve generations of men, they say. I suppose the real reason has been forgotten.'

Aristoteles reached out discreetly and plucked Hephaistion's tunic. The young prince looked round, as if by chance, just in time to catch him at it. 'We must be going,' he said, like someone rewarding a dog that has done its trick. He remained, however, standing by me. I thought it was just to tease the man. Then he said, 'I have always tried, when I read the *Iliad*, to give a voice to Achilles, and have only heard my own. He will have your voice now. This is a great gift you have given me.'

As I was seeking some answer fit for this, he tugged off his arm his great heavy bracelet of Macedonian goldwork, a thrice-coiled snake with ruby eyes and delicately graven scales. He took my hand, and slid it up into place. There was a life in his touch that seemed to kindle all up my arm, with the warmed gold. 'This for remembrance,' he said. I thought he spoke of the gift, till he took me by both shoulders and kissed my mouth. Then he put his arm round Hephaistion's waist, and they went out together, the philosopher following behind.

*

This morning, having got back to Athens, I went out to the Academy. No one was about; I chose the quiet time, when everyone is working. The myrtle they planted on Plato's grave is getting thick and tall, and the marble begins to mellow.

The grove was green. But I saw in my mind the white slopes of Etna, the titan lava-rocks black on fields of snow; and the snow-light on those blue eyes, enrapt and listening.

He will wander through the world, like a flame, like a lion; seeking, never finding; never knowing (for he will look always forward, never back) that while he was still a child the thing he seeks slipped from the world, worn out and spent. Like a lion he will hunt for his proper food, and fasting make do with what he finds; like a lion he will be sometimes angry. Always he will be loved, never knowing the love he missed.

No one would fight for Dion, when he gave, as his own soul saw it, his very life for justice. But for this boy they will die, whether he is right or wrong; he need only gaze at them with that blue fire and say, 'My friends, I believe in you.' How many of us, like Thettalos, I suppose, and me, will follow this golden daimon, wherever he calls us to show him gods and heroes, kindling our art at his dreams and his dreams at our art, to Troy, to Babylon or the world's end, to leave our bones in barbarian cities? He need only call.

I thought how, before I went on at Pella, I had touched the mask for luck, and it seemed that the god had said to me, 'Speak for me, Nikeratos. Someone's soul is listening.' Someone's always is, I suppose, if one only knew. Plato never forgot it.

Sitting by the tomb, I took from my arm the golden bracelet. It seldom leaves me; most people put it down to conceit, but not Thettalos, though he laughs at me. The marble was warm with sun and dappled with shade. I laid the gold on it, as if it could speak, as if I laid a hand in a hand.

All tragedies deal with fated meetings; how else could there be a play? Fate deals its stroke; sorrow is purged, or turned to rejoicing; there is death, or triumph; there has been a meeting, and a change. No one will ever make a tragedy – and that is as well, for one could not bear it – whose grief is that the principals never met.

AUTHOR'S NOTE

Nikeratos is an invented character. The inscriptions which listed the victors in the Athenian dramatic festivals survive only in fragments, few of which relate to the years covered by the story; the name of the leading man in *The Ransoming of Hector* has not come down to us. Nor is it known who the actors were, or what they did, when the exiled oligarchs of Phigaleia stormed the the-atre. Both events are related by Diodorus Siculus; so is the story of the chorus man who brought Dionysios the news of his fatal victory of 368 B.C.

Thettalos and Theodoros are both named in the victors' lists, and there are literary references to their gifts and fame. I have inferred the character of Thettalos from a highly dangerous adventure he undertook on behalf of the young Alexander in 338 B.C., four years after this story closes. During one of the recur-rent Macedonian family feuds, Alexander, on purpose to foil his father's dynastic plans, wanted to arrange a marriage contract between himself and the satrap of Karia's daughter. Thettalos went on this secret mission, in which he succeeded until Philip found out. The King's arm was by then a long one, and he had Thettalos brought to him from Corinth in chains, apparently reprieving him later. It seems unlikely that Thettalos could have expected, in the circumstances, payment from the eighteen-year-old prince in proportion to the risks involved. That he took them is informative about both parties.

Theodoros was one of the Greek theatre's greatest stars. Like all other actors of the day he must have had to satisfy his audiences in male roles; but his fame rested on his tragic heroines. When he was playing Merope before Alexander of Pherai, that blood-thirsty brigand had to leave the theatre, ashamed to be seen in tears.

It is important to remember that the grimacing, flat-faced masks of Tragedy and Comedy which are a cliché of today's commercial art bear no relation to anything worn on the Greek stage. Masks covered the whole head and included a wig mounted upon cloth, the front only being rigid material. In Graeco-Roman times, as theatres grew more enormous and taste declined, tragic masks were grotesquely enlarged and stylised, while the actor was padded and raised on high pattens to give size and height. Since his neck could not be extended in proportion, the total effect got progressively uglier and more conventional. But in the fifth and fourth centuries masks followed the trend of sculpture, idealising or enhancing nature; from the few representations that survive, they seem to have had great subtlety, variety and often beauty. The mouths were not, as with late examples, opened in a vast dolorous gape, but parted as if in natural speech.

No part of Greek life has aroused more scholarly debate than the techniques of the theatre. Literary accounts are late and conflicting, contemporary references casual. In a novel one has to choose between rival theories on such matters as the use and form of the machines, and the height of the stage above the orchestra. (I have listed some books for those who would like to examine the evidence for themselves.) It is certain however that three men sustained all the speaking roles in every tragedy, the extra, if there was one, being almost or wholly mute; and that the actors somehow achieved the amazing versatility required. There is an anecdote about one who became so absorbed in doing his voice-exercises that he missed his cue to go on.

By the start of the third century, actors were highly organised in guilds centred on large cities, through which their tours were arranged. The fourth century must have been a period of transition, with a good deal more left to private enterprise; I have had to conjecture what arrangements actor-managers of the time may have made for themselves. Their use in diplomacy is well attested.

Throughout the whole classical period actors, though often dissolute in private life, were held in their work to be performing a religious rite in the service of Dionysos, or any god to whom the performance was dedicated. (For this reason they were exempt from military service.) Plato's concern about the content of plays should, in fairness, be seen not as a mere censorship of ideas, but more like the wish of an enlightened Christian to drop from the liturgy passages about the wicked gnashing their teeth in flames of eternal torment.

The deep political disillusion of the time expressed itself intellectually in a search for ideal systems, and historically in the phenomenon of Alexander. To understand it one has only to recall the long miseries of the Peloponnesian War, and to read the speeches of fourth-century politicians. The mean-minded, snobbish and dishonest personalities to which even Demosthenes sank in public controversy have to be read to be believed; and these were not published by enemies, but by the author himself after careful polishing.

For the story of Dion I have relied mainly on Plutarch, who had access to many sources now lost to us, including the accounts of Timonides and the History of Philistos. Upon Plato's second and third visits to Syracuse we have Plato himself. Nearly all scholars today now accept as authentic the third and the all-important seventh letter; the personal voice which sounds in both is highly persuasive.

Axiothea and Lasthenia are listed among Plato's pupils by Diogenes Laertius. He tells us nothing of their lives or characters, except that they continued at the Academy under Speusippos, after Plato's death, and that Axiothea 'is said to have worn men's clothes'.

Ten years after Dion's death in 354 B.C, the Syracusans appealed for help to Corinth against the renewed tyranny of Dionysios and the impending threat from Carthage. Timoleon was sent with a small force. Gifted with astuteness and luck as well as solid integrity, he was successful within a few years. Under his fatherly guidance the city enjoyed two decades of peace and prosperity before the cycle of demagogy and tyranny began again. The constitution of Timoleon seems to have been a limited democracy with a qualified franchise; in view of the grateful honours paid him during his life and after, it must have satisfied the citizens. In justice to Dion's failure one must remember that Timoleon was dealing with a different population. So decimated had the Syracusans become through war, privation and flight that one of his first measures was to invite, with their consent, new settlers to strengthen the city. He got about 60,000 (a figure for men only, not including their families) of whom many thousands came from Corinth and other stable polities. If the Syracusan lands could support so many, there can have been very few native Syracusans left.

No true parallel exists between this passage in Syracusan history and the affairs of any present-day state. Christianity and Islam have changed irrevocably the moral reflexes of the world.

The philosopher Herakleitos said with profound truth that you cannot step twice into the same river. The perpetual stream of human nature is formed into ever-changing shallows, eddies, falls and pools by the land over which it passes. Perhaps the only real value of history lies in considering this endlessly varied play between the essence and the accidents.

The short book-list below is not a bibliography, but gives the most important sources and works of reference for anyone interested in following up the subjects concerned.

HISTORY

Plutarch. Lives of Dion and Timoleon.
Plato. Letters. Republic. Symposium.
Diodorus Siculus. History, Books 15 and 16.
George Grote. History of Greece.

THE THEATRE

Margarete Bieber. THE HISTORY OF THE GREEK AND ROMAN THEATRE.
A. Pickard-Cambridge. THE DRAMATIC FESTIVALS OF ATHENS.
T. B. L. Webster. GREEK THEATRE PRODUCTION.
Demosthenes. Oration against Aeschines, ON THE EMBASSY. Aeschines. ORATIONS. ON THE EMBASSY. Reply to Demosthenes. (Aeschines was an ex-actor who took up a career in politics.)

Aeschylus' *The Myrmidons* has been lost to us, except for a few passages preserved as quotations in the works of other authors, some of which I have used. Out of a very large output by the three tragic poets, only a small fraction remains. Other authors, sufficiently valued in their day to have defeated these masters in dramatic contests, are now known only by name, their entire body of work having disappeared. Plays mentioned in the story are therefore often fictional.

Adult Dyslexia:
Assessment, Counselling and Training

David McLoughlin
Adult Dyslexia and Skills Development Centre, London

Gary Fitzgibbon
People at Work, London

and

Vivienne Young
The Employment Service, London

Consultant in Dyslexia: Professor Margaret Snowling,
University of Newcastle upon Tyne

Whurr Publishers
London

British Library Cataloguing in Publication Data
A catalogue record for this book is available from the
British Library.

ISBN 1-897635-35-4

Photoset by Stephen Cary
Printed and bound in the UK by Athenaeum Press Ltd,
Gateshead, Tyne & Wear

Preface

This book is written with the aim of improving the understanding of dyslexia as a condition that affects people throughout their lifespan. It is not addressed to any one particular professional group as it is intended to be of use to anyone who, in the course of his or her work, comes into contact with dyslexic people. We hope that it will be of interest to medical practitioners, therapists, teachers, trainers and personnel managers.

Each chapter could easily be the subject of a complete book. We have, however, opted for a comprehensive approach over a range of issues rather than for an in-depth coverage to produce a 'how to do it' manual. At the same time, we have brought our experience of educational and occupational psychology to what we consider to be an applied book. It is necessary to put any issue in context; as a result, in Chapter 1 we have described a theoretical model of dyslexia. Some readers may find this a little technical, but it is important to understand dyslexia for what it is before we can intervene appropriately. The remaining chapters are more practical: in Chapters 2 and 3, we describe assessment procedures including the role of psychological tests; in Chapter 4, the counselling needs of dyslexic individuals are placed in the context of a four-stage model and the behaviours that typify each stage are illustrated with case studies; Chapters 5–7 raise issues related to training, teaching and career development. These are addressed in a way that is intended to provide insights into, as well as understanding of, the world of the adult dyslexic.

Above all we have made a great effort to dispel the myth that dyslexia is a childhood condition which only affects reading, writing and spelling. We have demonstrated how dyslexia can have profound effects, both positive and negative, on individuals' personal and working lives.

David McLoughlin, Gary Fitzgibbon and Vivienne Young
August 1993

Dedications

For Jim, Mary, Robyn and James – DM.
For Alexa, Magali, Laurie, Joelle and Kirsten – GF.
For Anthony and Kathleen – VY.

Acknowledgements

Our thanks to Patricia Weller for her help with the preparation of the original manuscript; to Carol Leather and Patricia Stringer for their advice and enthusiastic support; to Margaret Snowling for her comments and suggestions; and, most of all, to our dyslexic clients and friends from whom we have learned so much.

David McLoughlin, Gary Fitzgibbon and Vivienne Young

Contents

Chapter 1
Introduction

The common understanding of developmental dyslexia is that it affects people's ability to learn to read, write and spell. It has been perceived as an educational problem. Descriptions of the condition and the publicity given to it focus on its implications for written language skills, particularly reading. Moreover, it is generally viewed as a childhood disorder.

The nature of the demands on dyslexics change as they get older, and even those who overcome childhood difficulties continue to experience problems in living, learning and working. There are also a large number of undiagnosed adult dyslexics who face problems of life adjustment without knowing that they are bright enough to achieve but are inefficient and ineffective when learning and applying knowledge (Ryan and Price, 1992).

Dyslexia continues throughout life; the constitutional difference that causes difficulties with reading, writing and spelling persists into adulthood. Adult dyslexia should be studied as a condition distinct from childhood dyslexia and adult dyslexics acknowledged as a distinct population with needs that are quite different from those of their younger counterparts. The research on childhood dyslexia is commendable but largely irrelevant for adult dyslexics. To paraphrase Patton and Polloway (1992): adult dyslexics are not simply children with a learning disability 'grown up'.

The conceptualisation of dyslexia as a childhood condition that affects reading, writing and spelling is too narrow. It distorts its true nature and engenders the false belief that dyslexia somehow disappears as the child becomes an adult.

The underlying philosophy of this book is that dealing with dyslexia can and should be a creative experience in that it is about finding solutions. So many adult dyslexics have achieved success in their working and personal lives that it must now be accepted that dyslexia is not an insurmountable barrier. Success, however, does not necessarily imply that the individual no longer has any of the difficulties that are part and

1

parcel of dyslexia. People continue to develop and the demands on their skills increase. Successful adult dyslexics could suddenly find themselves in a difficult situation. For example:

> John was a successful consultant gynaecologist who had, over the years, developed very impressive strategies for learning, remembering and generally organising a very demanding working life. John discovered that his dyslexia was still operating when he came to be interviewed for his consultant's post. The interview was very demanding because of his difficulties with short-term memory.

In some cases an adult dyslexic seeks advice because he or she has been quite successful. Success for dyslexics can often mean that the demands on them are very different from those placed on people who are not dyslexic: what might be a simple task for someone else can, for a dyslexic, require careful planning, thought and enormous effort. For example, a dyslexic employee in a meeting at work could lose the sense of a discussion that others find quite straightforward and could have difficulty taking minutes or putting forward an argument. Non-dyslexic colleagues follow the meeting simply by taking notes and, on the spot, scanning a document given to them, whilst the dyslexic person might need to tape-record the meeting, listen to it a second time and spend an evening reading the document to achieve the same level of understanding. The demands placed on dyslexic people, if they are to achieve success, are greater than the demands on people of similar intelligence and background who are not dyslexic. To achieve success, dyslexics must work harder than others and they must develop an understanding of their areas of weakness and ways of working to compensate for them.

That dyslexia does not present an intrinsic barrier to occupational success is clear from studies of dyslexic individuals who are highly successful. It is, however, common for dyslexic adults to be faced with emotional, psychological and social difficulties, which make success harder to achieve. Difficulties with literacy skills can be, and frequently are, overcome but an individual who has attended a school at which the teaching style and the attitude of the teachers was inappropriate for their needs, develops a low self-esteem, lack of confidence and frustration which lasts for a long time. Furthermore, the fundamental inefficiency in memory persists and in adulthood operates to make some basic (and some not so basic) skills more of a challenge than they are for non-dyslexics of the same level of intelligence.

Gerber, Ginsberg and Reiff (1992) have made a major contribution to understanding and helping dyslexic adults by studying those who have become successful. In contrast to research that has focused on why dyslexics fail, it has identified the factors that contribute to their success. The overriding factor is the extent to which dyslexics have been able to take control over their lives. Being able to do this involves internal decisions and external manifestations. The former include:

- a desire to succeed;
- becoming goal-oriented; and
- reframing, which means recognising that there is a difficulty, accepting it, understanding its effects and acting to overcome it.

The external manifestations are:

- being persistent;
- developing coping skills and strategies;
- using support networks; and
- being in an environment in which the person feels comfortable.

These findings are consistent with our clinical experience and the main results of Gerber et al.'s study underlie much of what is written in this book.

The reframing process is especially important. Dyslexic adults seeking assistance are at one of four levels of awareness, understanding and compensation and therefore fall into one of four groups:

1. Those who have not really been aware of their difficulties and have little understanding of them.
2. Those who are aware of their difficulties but do not understand, and have therefore not dealt with, them.
3. Those who have an awareness of their difficulties and have unconsciously developed compensatory strategies.
4. Those who are aware of and understand their difficulties and have consciously developed compensatory strategies, but who need to develop these further.

The purpose of the interventions described in this book, whether assessment, counselling, teaching or training, is to help the adult dyslexic to move through stage 4 and beyond.

A note on incidence

As a result of the lack of agreement on exactly how dyslexia should be defined estimates of the numbers of adult dyslexics vary considerably. American studies suggest that 2–25% of the population are dyslexic (Farnham-Diggory, 1978). If only those who are severely affected by the condition are counted then the lower figure for incidence is probably about 4%: Miles and Haslum (1986), for example, estimate that if only those who are, or have been, 'significantly handicapped' by the condition are counted the incidence is 2–4%. The estimates available are based entirely on the child population and therefore, because the condition in childhood is frequently undiagnosed, it is logical to conclude that the 4% underestimates the number of adult dyslexics in the population. It is therefore reasonable to conclude that at least 1 in 25 adults is dyslexic.

Some definitions of dyslexia

The obvious starting point in attempting to explain a phenomenon is to define it, but this is no easy task for dyslexia. In addressing this issue Wheeler and Watkins (1978) listed more than a dozen definitions, nearly all of which include reference to written language skills. Most of these are 'discrepancy' definitions, i.e. they focus on the difference between a person's potential (as measured by an intelligence test) and their performance in reading, writing and spelling. The following recent definition by Thomson and Watkins (1990, p. 3) is a good example:

> Developmental dyslexia is a severe difficulty with the written form of language independent of intellectual, cultural and emotional causation. It is characterised by the individuals' reading, writing and spelling attainments being well below the level expected, based on intelligence and chronological age. The difficulty is a cognitive one affecting those language skills associated with the written form, particularly visual, verbal coding, short-term memory, order perception and sequencing.

In the last 100 years numerous definitions have appeared, most of which include reference to reading, writing and spelling as important areas of weakness; however, some discrepancy definitions focus on reading alone. For example, Critchley (1964) defined dyslexia as

> a difficulty in learning to read, which is constitutional, often genetically determined and which is unassociated with general intellectual retardation, primary emotional instability, or gross physical defects. (p. 116)

It is wrong to assume that dyslexia relates only to reading. As Singleton (1991) has argued, writing and spelling are more likely to be affected than reading, particularly in the older dyslexic.

Given that most early definitions focused on literacy problems, it is not surprising to find that dyslexia is generally understood to be a reading and writing difficulty, or that discrepancy definitions have influenced the process of diagnosis. Nevertheless, the focus on literacy skills and the preoccupation with discrepancy definitions are both misguided.

The problem with discrepancy definitions generally is twofold:

1. They do not discriminate between dyslexics and other poor readers, the underlying areas of weakness being much the same (Stanovich, 1991; Siegel, 1992).
2. They cannot be applied to older dyslexics who have been able to compensate, by one means or other, and no longer have major

problems with literacy. According to a discrepancy definition, such adults would no longer be dyslexic, but clearly they continue to experience difficulties which stem from the inefficiency that was responsible for their slow acquisition of literacy skills during childhood. One might add that discrepancy definitions have resulted in a myth regarding early identification: as with the compensated adult, it is difficult to establish that a very young child is significantly behind in reading and spelling. However, if one does base identification on underlying inefficiencies, particularly when this is put in the context of other factors such as a positive family history, then it should be possible to identify dyslexia well before dyslexic people of all ages experience major learning problems.

A more useful approach has been to focus on the underlying cognitive processes and describe the characteristics of dyslexic people. Fundamentally, the view has been that dyslexia is a problem with short-term memory and an increasing amount of research has been devoted to such an explanation: Miles (1983a), for example, describes dyslexia as a syndrome characterised by a variety of symptoms such as problems with short-term memory tasks, left/right confusion, late achievement of developmental milestones and familial factors – most of the items in his Bangor Dyslexia Test (Miles, 1982) involve short-term memory. Further, a great deal of Miles's research has involved experiments to examine the difference in short-term memory skills between dyslexics and non-dyslexics, allowing him to conclude that

> Dyslexia should not be thought of simply as difficulty with reading or as difficulty with spelling but that the reading and spelling problems of a dyslexic person are part of a wider disability which shows itself whenever symbolic material has to be identified and named. (Miles, 1983a, p.98)

Further examples of this type of explanation are easy to find, for example, Vellutino (1987) and Chasty (1985) both argue that dyslexia is a problem with information processing and they identify deficits in short-term memory storage as being central to this interpretation.

Clinical experience suggests that descriptions of dyslexia that focus on deficits in information-processing capabilities are the most useful. Specifically, in the course of assessing, counselling and training adult dyslexics it has been noted that the most common weakness manifested by dyslexics is in short-term memory, as evidenced by their difficulty in work-related tasks and their performance on psychometric tests. In particular, administration of the Wechsler Adult Intelligence Scale – Revised (WAIS-R; Wechsler, 1981) to an adult dyslexic generally yields a pattern of test scores entirely consistent with what would be expected from someone who had a short-term memory deficit. The same pattern emerges when the Wechsler Intelligence Scale for Children – Revised (Wechsler, 1976) is administered to dyslexic children. Both dyslexic adults and children score less well than non-dyslexics on the subtests that place demands upon short-term memory – dyslexic children and adults have in common a weakness of short-term memory, and definition, diagnosis and programmes for improving performance should focus on that. Difficulties with literacy skills should be seen as just one symptom.

Characteristics of dyslexia

There is a general consensus on what constitute typical dyslexic characteristics and the controversy over definitions can be bypassed in favour of providing an explanation for these characteristics. This chapter presents a model to account for the following symptoms:

- dyslexics are often late in learning to read but in most cases are eventually successful;
- dyslexics have difficulty with naming tasks;
- dyslexics have some initial difficulty with detecting rhyme;
- dyslexics have difficulty with paired associate learning (i.e. associating a label with an object), particularly when this involves speech sounds;
- dyslexics are weak at memory span tasks such as recalling series of numbers presented aurally;
- dyslexics find mental arithmetic difficult;
- dyslexics have difficulty learning sequences such as the months of the year and multiplication tables;
- dyslexics are slow in learning material presented exclusively in verbal or written form;
- dyslexics remain poor at spelling.

All these characteristics can be shown to arise from a single cause – a specific memory deficit. How a failure in one component of human memory can account for the pattern of difficulties associated with dyslexia is described below.

Models of human memory

The problem of determining how we remember and why we forget has occupied the attention of philosophers and psychologists for hundreds of years. Plato compared the human mind to an aviary and specific memories to birds; information was remembered when one of the birds was caught and information was forgotten if the correct bird could not be seized. Plato's aviary analogy is a version of the *spatial metaphor*, according to which memories are treated as objects stored in specific locations of the mind and recall is a process of searching through these locations for a specific item of information. The spatial metaphor is inherently attractive and for centuries it dominated the way memory was conceptualised. It was eventually abandoned because it was unable to explain the emerging facts concerning how we remember and why we forget. The finding that contributed most to the demise of the spatial metaphor was the consistent observation that there are least two different types of memory: one that holds information of which we are consciously aware and one that holds information of which we are not consciously aware but which can be brought into consciousness.

William James (1890) first proposed the distinction between two types of memory, which he named primary and secondary memory. James argued that the function of primary memory is to hold information in consciousness for a short time after it is perceived and that secondary memory acts as a huge capacity store, containing information that was not in consciousness but which could be brought to consciousness. This broad distinction between primary and secondary memory has survived for over 100 years. Primary memory is now called short-term memory and secondary memory long-term memory. Current theories identify short-term memory as a store with very limited capacity that holds information for short periods of time; long-term memory is viewed as a store with almost infinite capacity that holds information for indefinitely long periods. The existence of these memory types is now universally acknowledged and human memory is one of the most researched (and arguably the best understood) of all cognitive processes.

In an attempt to account for the findings from experiments on memory, and for observations of the behaviour of people with various memory impairments, researchers have developed ever more complex models of human memory: short-term memory, in particular, has occupied a great deal of attention. To date the most promising is the *working memory model*, initially proposed by Baddeley and Hitch in 1974 and revised by Baddeley in 1986. This model conceptualises short-term memory as an active (or working) memory system made up of a number of subsystems. According to Baddeley there are three main components of working memory: a master system (the *central executive*) and two slave systems (the *sketch pad* and the *articulatory loop*).

The central executive system is thought to control exactly what we attend to, and in this way determines what information is processed further in one or other of the slave systems. The sketch pad is specialised for visual and spatial coding, and is thought to be particularly important for recalling information about the spatial relationships between objects. The articulatory loop is by far the most investigated and best-understood component of working memory. It is involved in many speech-related processes, including perception and production.

The articulatory loop is the system that operates in tasks where a sequence of steps or a list of items has to be recalled immediately. Psychologists test this ability using 'memory span tasks' which, for example, involve asking people to repeat increasingly lengthy series of numbers in the order in which they were presented. The person's memory span is the number of items in the longest list recalled without error.

The articulatory loop itself is made up of two interrelated subsystems: the *phonological store* (which is involved in speech perception) and the *articulatory control process* (which is linked to speech production). A deficit in either subsystem will result in difficulties with recall of phonological (i.e. speech-based) material. Such difficulties will be observed both with the recall of information heard or spoken and with the recall of phonological information from long-term memory. A deficit in the articulatory loop will also result in difficulties in recalling visually presented material. This is because, when seeing an object, people describe it quietly to themselves using words (a process called 'subvocal articulation'); this is the means by which information about something we see enters the phonological store. This implies that a deficit in the phonological store will have an adverse effect on the recall of both auditory and visually presented material.

Because so many everyday tasks involve recalling information about what has just been seen, read or heard, the articulatory loop must occupy a central role in a wide variety of tasks, most of which are taken for granted. Evidence from many studies indicates that a deficit in the articulatory loop affects the development of basic literacy skills and other tasks involving working memory. The precise nature of this proposed deficit is, as yet, unknown: a plausible speculation is that the storage capacity of the articulatory loop in a dyslexic person is smaller than it is for other people (Gathercole and Baddeley, 1990), which means that fewer items than normal can be stored. Thus the articulatory loop can be conceptualised as a continuous-tape loop and the deficit can be viewed as the tape being shorter, with the consequence that less information can be recorded. This deficit, which may be referred to as an inefficiency in working memory, is the key to understanding developmental dyslexia.

Support for this interpretation comes from a study by Jorm (1983), who demonstrated that when subvocal articulation is prevented there is no difference between poor and normal readers in terms of paired-associate learning using visual material. Thus, while there is evidence that dyslexics have difficulty with paired-associate learning, it would appear to be restricted to material involving, directly or indirectly, phonological memory. The dyslexic's problem with paired-associate learning is more likely to be an effect, not the cause, of inefficient working memory.

Inefficient working memory and reading skills

Reading is a complex and demanding skill that is dependent on a number of other subskills. Learning new words, reading words that have been learned and understanding sentences are the foundations for skilled reading. Studies attempting to identify the cause of poor reading have investigated a number of possible causes, including

- poor hearing acuity;
- impairment of auditory perceptual processes;
- deficits in articulation rate (i.e. slowness in structuring words or sentences);
- inability to store meaningful speech sounds in long-term memory;
- failure to use effectively the process of repeating words to oneself quietly as a means of understanding what is read.

Each of these factors has been investigated exhaustively but there is little evidence to support the contention that any of them result in the slow development of reading skills. The only factor that has been convincingly related to poor reading development is a deficit in phonological memory. Thus it has been suggested that inefficient working memory contributes to reading failure.

The effect of inefficient working memory in the development of reading is apparent from a study by Gathercole and Baddeley (1990) of a group of children who were slow or poor readers. The children all had severe difficulties in learning new words and particular difficulty with tasks involving learning names. Not surprisingly, these children all had less well developed vocabularies than others of the same age and intelligence and thus lacked knowledge and subskills essential to the development of reading ability.

To understand how inefficient working memory results in deficits in basic literacy skills it is important to examine the process by which new words are learned. An internal dictionary (a lexicon) is stored in long-term memory; it begins to develop very early and continues to develop throughout the lifespan. The precise process by which new words come to have a representation in the lexicon is complex and not fully understood but there is little doubt that it involves the conversion of strings of letters into meaningful sounds. This process, called phonological encoding, is dependent on the phonological store.

Gathercole and Baddeley (1990) argue that the contribution of phonological memory to the learning of words centres on the process of achieving a stable representation of the initial novel sound sequence in long-term memory. They consider that the sound is most likely to be temporarily represented in the phonological store just before the long-term memory representation is established. Thus, the success of the transfer of a new word into long-term memory is determined by the adequacy of the temporary memory representation. Because inefficient working memory disrupts the quality of the temporary memory representation, the obvious implication is that it will in turn disrupt the acquisition of vocabulary. The findings of Papagno, Valentine and Baddeley (1991) support this: they found that short-term phonological storage is important to long-term phonological learning and that people with inefficient working memory skills will rely, more than other people, on the meanings of words as opposed to their sounds. Dyslexics appear to favour the use of existing verbal–semantic associations rather than phonological codes.

The function of the lexicon is to give recognition to the words we read. Once a word is recognised the semantic system gives the word a meaning. When a word is encountered there is an unconscious search through the lexicon for it and, assuming that the word is one that has already been learned, it comes to have meaning. Normal readers retrieve phonological information from long-term memory as part of this search process but dyslexics, because they have difficulty with phonological information, develop the skill of retrieving semantic information instead. Clearly this strategy (of bypassing inefficient working memory) cannot be exploited when new words are being learned, which is why the early stages of learning to read are so demanding and onerous to dyslexics. However, as Colehart (1978) has pointed out, once the slow process of acquiring a reasonably large vocabulary is complete, single words can, with practice, eventually be identified using the semantic coding alone. Thus, although the identification of words usually involves the retrieval of phonological information from long-term memory, this is not an obligatory step in the identification process. Dyslexic people can, by learning to associate symbols with meaning, complete the identification without using phonological memory and thus overcome the disruptive effects of inefficient working memory.

It is important to emphasise that, although dyslexics have a preference for semantic coding (i.e. coding based on meaning), they do have access to the phonological codes and use them alongside the semantic codes. In the context of silent reading skilled dyslexic readers probably use semantic codes more than phonological codes. They may, for example rely on semantic coding when reading polysyllabic words, because the process of coding such words would place too heavy a demand on phonological memory. This explains why some adult dyslexics can read polysyllabic words silently but have great difficulty in pronouncing them. Reading aloud necessitates the production of meaningful speech sounds but this can only be achieved by using phonological short-term memory. The implication is that those with inefficient working memory will perform poorly when reading aloud.

Evidence to support the argument that dyslexic people who have become successful readers, sometimes referred to as *compensated dyslexics*, make heavy use of semantic codes comes from a study by Lefly and Pennington (1991), who investigated the performance of compensated dyslexic people and other adults on silent reading and reading aloud. It was found that the two groups could not be distinguished in terms of their silent reading behaviour but they could when reading aloud. The explanation for this is straightforward: compensated dyslexics use semantic coding in silent reading, bypassing the inefficient working memory and allowing them to read competently, but when reading aloud they are unable to use this strategy because speech sounds rely on the use of phonological memory, the consequence being that skilled reading cannot be maintained. Lefly and Pennington's study is important because, although it suggests that dyslexic people continue to experience problems with certain aspects of reading, it demonstrates how such difficulties can be overcome effectively.

There is no doubt that inefficient working memory continues to interfere with learning even after a dyslexic has acquired good reading skills. For example, compensated dyslexics continue to have difficulty with aspects of literacy such as the learning of new words. Unfamiliar words, by definition, do not have a representation in the lexicon and thus the method of recognising a word by focusing on meaning, rather than sounds, is not available. If the new word is to be learned, then the reader must create a phonological representation of it, which, for dyslexic people, is a laboriously slow process. This provides a partial explanation of the difficulty experienced by dyslexic people when they attempt to learn a foreign language, even when they have become skilled readers.

Generally speaking, when dyslexics are faced with tasks requiring new learning, they have more difficulty than non-dyslexic people, despite having had similar educational opportunities and being of the same intelligence. However, it is possible to make learning and skills acquisition easier by adopting appropriate learning styles and developing strategies for bypassing the effects of inefficient working memory. An appropriate learning style is one that uses as many sensory inputs as possible; this is called *multisensory learning* and is described in more detail later. Compensatory strategies are methods of processing information that allow individuals to achieve goals using alternative means: they range from the mundane to the ingenious.

- When encountering a new word, for example, it can be learned by looking up the meaning in a dictionary, using the meaning to draw an appropriate picture and putting this, together with the word, in a prominent place where it will be seen often.

- Another strategy would be to use the word frequently in conversations, letters or reports.
- Alternatively, the new word can simply be ignored.

The last of these might not be the most creative strategy but, because skilled readers are unlikely to come across new words often, it is a workable one that is unlikely to lead to many difficulties. However, beginning readers cannot use this particular strategy because most of the words they encounter are new.

An inefficiency in working memory clearly creates problems at the single-word reading level but reading involves other skills, including comprehension of text. Baddeley and Wilson (1988) demonstrated that inefficient working memory causes difficulties at this level. They argued that both spoken and written language comprehension involve processing phonologically encoded information to construct some form of mental model which determines what the reader or listener comprehends. If, for example, one hears someone say 'the object is a red sphere', a mental model of a red ball is constructed using images as well as sounds. When the information presented is relatively straightforward the model can be created as the text is read or heard. However, when the information is complex, or the rate of presentation rapid, the model can be created only if some of the information is held in a temporary buffer. If, for example, you hear someone say 'the object is made of plastic, it is red on the inside, yellow on the outside, cylindrical, about two inches long with a diameter of one inch. It is closed at one end and it has a handle' you might eventually form a model of a child's toy cup. Unlike the earlier example, however, the model for the toy cup required some information to be retained, specifically information about the material, colour, shape and dimensions, until other information (about the object being closed at one end and having a handle) was assimilated. The temporary buffer for holding such information is almost certainly the phonological memory store. Thus, in the process of language comprehension, the phonological store is a tool that is used in a flexible way. It is not an obligatory component of an automatic process but an optional element employed according to need. For a dyslexic person, when the phonological store is needed in its capacity as a buffer to hold information, language comprehension will be poor. Once again the adverse effect of this can be partly overcome by developing skills that allow greater use of semantic coding and reduce dependence on phonemic coding.

Item memory and serial order memory

When someone is given a list of words or numbers and is required to recall them in the order they were presented, at least two memory processes are involved: the capacity to hold individual pieces of information (*item memory*) is one and the other is the ability to preserve the order of the pieces of information (*serial order memory*). The two are closely related and impairment of one will usually affect the other: people who have poor item memory will, for example, have difficulty in remembering the order in which a series of items was presented because they are unable to remember the items. The memory span task (i.e. the immediate recall of a list of words or numbers in the order in which they were presented) is frequently used in diagnosing dyslexia. It is generally thought of as a measure of serial order memory but, almost certainly, taps both item memory and serial order memory. Thus, poor performance on the memory span task, known as the *digit span deficit*, could be the result of a deficit in either item memory or serial order memory.

The digit span deficit is a common symptom of dyslexia. It manifests itself in various everyday situations: difficulty in remembering telephone numbers is a typical example. It is also apparent in the way dyslexics deal with so-called automatic tasks such as reciting the months of the year and the alphabet. However, while many dyslexics have trouble with such tasks they have less difficulty with those that involve fewer items, for example reciting the days of the week. It can be concluded, therefore, that whilst serial order memory may be involved to some extent, the number of items to be recited is an important factor. When this is combined with the fact that dyslexics have a reduced item-memory capacity the logical, if somewhat speculative, conclusion is that the impairment in serial order recall is a secondary effect of a deficit in item memory. In other words, the disruption in serial order memory may be due to the dyslexic person's reduced capacity to hold items in phonological memory.

One might expect that, if the above argument is correct, the digit span deficit is restricted to situations in which items are presented verbally. However, people have a strong tendency to give visual stimuli verbal labels, which is probably what happens in memory span tasks involving visual presentation, i.e. dyslexic people unconsciously recode the visual stimulus into a verbal one. Thus inefficient working memory would result in a digit span deficit for visual as well as for verbal modes of presentation. This is supported by research, which reports that when the memory span deficit is observed with visually presented stimuli dyslexics appear to attempt to recode it into a verbal form; Torgesen and Houck (1980), for example, found that when dyslexics are given a memory span task involving visual items that cannot easily be given verbal labels, the digit span deficit is no longer observed. There is, therefore, a sound basis for arguing that a dyslexic's difficulty with serial order information is due to inefficient working memory.

Phonological confusion and rhyme detection

In a number of studies examining short-term memory researchers have found that words or letters with similar sounds (e.g. house, mouse) tend to be confused *less* by people who are dyslexic than they are by people who are not. Dyslexics do not appear to be as susceptible to this so-called phonological confusion effect. Most of these studies, however, have involved dyslexic children and there is at present little information on how susceptible adult dyslexics are to phonological confusion. What little evidence there is (e.g. Hall et al., 1983) suggests that as dyslexics improve their reading ability they become *more* susceptible to phonological confusions. This is consistent with the finding that dyslexic children have difficulty in recognising rhymes but do in time acquire this skill.

Both phonological confusion and the recognition of rhymes require the use of phonological information stored in long-term memory. If the phonological codes are not well established or are unavailable (which is true of dyslexic children) then similar-sounding words will not be identified as such. When the phonological information is established and available in long-term memory (the case for compensated dyslexic adults) similar-sounding words will be identified. Consequently, as a direct result of inefficient working memory, the recognition of rhymes and the phonological confusion effect will occur later for dyslexics than it will for others.

The persistence of poor spelling

One of the most persistent difficulties dyslexic people encounter is in spelling. This is more of a problem than reading because it is harder to produce a word from scratch than it is to recognise it when it is presented for reading (Miles, 1990). Most people find spelling more difficult than reading but the difficulty dyslexics have is that the use of phonological memory is essential to spelling and so the effects of inefficient working memory cannot be bypassed.

The issues in the psychology of spelling are ill defined (Kreiner and Goff, 1990); however, phonological awareness (the ability to divide words into their component sounds) is thought to be a very important in the development of spelling skills. Nevertheless, the precise way in which words are broken into sounds is the subject of some debate. A commonly held view is that spelling involves the matching of phonemes (the smallest units of sound) with graphemes (written symbols). A more recent perspective (Goswami, 1991) adds another dimension: it has been argued that syllables are broken down into units known as rimes and onsets, which are larger than phonemes. What seems certain is that the use of sounds is central to the development of spelling. It is a skill which involves accessing phonological information (whether phonemes, rimes or onsets), and this process is difficult for dyslexic people because of their inefficient working memory.

Problems with arithmetic

Arithmetic is particularly difficult for dyslexic people because, as well as demanding reading skills, it requires connection of words to symbols and an understanding of the processes that these symbols represent. Furthermore, arithmetic involves the ability to process certain items while storing other information for later processing. For example, consider the problem of finding how £180 should be shared equitably between three people, Imogen, Joyce and Fred, given that Fred worked for 3 hours, Joyce worked for 2 hours and Imogen worked for 1 hour. When an attempt to solve this problem is made, phonological information from long-term memory (e.g. how to work out ratios) must be stored in short-term memory together with other phonological information from the 'outside' (e.g. how many people and how much money). A mental operation needs to be performed (dividing 180 by 6) and the partial results (180/6 = 30) need to be stored while further calculations are made (3 × 30 and 2 × 30). We have, then, a situation in which phonological information must be temporarily stored until other information has been processed. Because inefficient working memory is a reduced capacity for storing phonological information dyslexic people will find such tasks difficult, unless they develop strategies for bypassing phonological memory, and consequently it is not surprising that dyslexic people are typically poor at arithmetic.

Difficulties with learning

In the earlier discussion of memory two systems of working memory were described: the sketch pad (working memory for objects seen) and the articulatory loop (working memory for sounds). There are also parallel working memory systems for taste, smell and movement; for example, working motor memory stores information about physical movements which have been, or are about to be, made. All these working memory systems feed into long-term memory and represent alternative ways of strengthening the memory trace in long-term memory. Hulme (1981) has shown that motor working memory can be used to supplement visual coding in short-term memory tasks: thus children will learn the alphabet faster if the letters are traced out with the fingers as well as being seen and recited.

People involved in teaching dyslexics are generally well aware that learning is enhanced if it involves seeing, hearing and doing – and this is supported by research. That the learning process is improved when information is presented in a variety of ways, tapping different sensory modes, is well documented: foreign-language learning, for example, is accelerated when the learner can speak, hear, see and take part in language-related activities. This process, because it involves more than one sense, is called *multisensory learning*. Multisensory learning maximises the chances of establishing new learning by using all available routes to the brain.

In practice, most learning is not multisensory: in schools, colleges and universities, for example, considerable emphasis is placed on reading, which places a heavy load on phonological memory. Traditional approaches to learning and teaching are the least useful for dyslexic people. Inefficient working memory is essentially a weakness in phonological memory and there is no evidence to suggest that this extends to other working memory systems. Thus it is not surprising to find that dyslexics benefit from teaching methods that utilise the other sense modalities. Once the emphasis on auditory memory is removed, they can compensate by making maximum use of the other pathways to learning and knowing.

Overview

Defining dyslexia is a difficult and sometimes controversial task. Some people prefer to avoid the word 'dyslexia' altogether, using instead terms such as 'learning disability' and 'specific learning difficulty'. There is, however, little doubt that there is a distinct identifiable group of individuals who can appropriately be described as 'dyslexic'. Many people in this group have become very successful and, given the academic and professional levels they have reached, describing them as 'disabled' or as having a difficulty in learning seems inappropriate. They may have needed to learn differently, but have done so very effectively. *Dyslexia* is the most appropriate term and is the one with which adult dyslexics themselves seem most comfortable.

The research literature on the types of problems experienced by older dyslexics is fairly sparse but there is no doubt that their difficulties are pervasive throughout their lives. Thomson (1984), for example, says that the dyslexics' difficulties will include the

> ...frustrated science, engineering or medical students unable to present their very able thinking in a written form; the referrals to psychiatric hospitals of men in the 30 to 40 age range group whose breakdowns are traced back to inabilities to read and write; and the high incidence of illiteracy amongst young offenders in penal establishments.

(page 20)

Although the manifestations of dyslexia alter during the lifespan as a result of learning, experience and the changing demands from the environment, the dearth of longitudinal follow-up studies limits our understanding regarding the prognosis for reading proficiency as well as the general effects of the condition on individuals over time (Frauenheim, 1978).

Clinical experience and research suggest that the most significant and pervasive problem dyslexics experience is in dealing with tasks that place demands upon working memory. Specifically, dyslexics have a reduced capability to deal with meaningful speech sounds in working memory, i.e. the deficit appears to be located in the phonological memory store. As described earlier, phonological working memory can be conceptualised as a continuous tape loop: when information is received it is recorded on this loop and once the loop is full no further information can be accepted without overwriting, and therefore losing, existing information. Thus everyone has a limit to the amount of phonological information they can hold in working memory space. Dyslexic people have a shorter loop and the impact of this is wide ranging.

We have suggested that the most significant symptoms of dyslexia can be explained on the basis of a weakness in phonological memory: 'inefficient working memory'. In particular, it has been demonstrated how inefficient working memory can account for the slow acquisition of reading skills and the persistence of poor spelling. These basic literacy difficulties have understandably occupied the attention of researchers, with the result that many people view dyslexia simply as a problem with reading, writing and spelling. There are, however, many adult dyslexics who are skilled readers and competent writers. Their dyslexia has not disappeared: they have not 'grown out of it' but have overcome many of the more obvious symptoms. Such people continue to experience difficulties, which are the direct and indirect result of an inefficiency in working memory.

The nature of the difficulties experienced by adult dyslexics is described in the rest of this book. They may be divided into two broad types: primary and secondary. The former are a direct consequence of inefficient working memory and include general working-memory difficulties such as forgetting sequences of instructions, an inability to keep track of what is said during a conversation, or following what is presented in a lecture. Secondary difficulties are behavioural, social and emotional. For example, because of their memory and information-processing difficulty, dyslexics may understand poorly non-verbal information such as facial expressions, which is an important factor in interpersonal skills (Kronick, 1983; Creasey and Jarvis, 1987). Further, they may experience feelings of frustration, lack of confidence and have low self-esteem as a result of years of academic failure and perhaps occupational failure after school (Hoffman et al., 1987). Lenkowsky and Saposnek (1978) have argued that 'the vestigial personality traits resulting from childhood learning disabilities which persist into adulthood can have a deleterious effect on the emotional development of the adult dyslexic and his family' (p. 52). Certainly many adult dyslexics presenting for assessment, counselling and training, including those who are ostensibly successful, express feelings of frustration and manifest a lack of self-confidence. It is for this reason that it is imperative that dyslexia be identified early in life. Many of the dyslexic people referred to in this book have experienced problems with confidence and self-esteem because their difficulties were not identified until well into adulthood. The earlier the problems are identified the less likely it is that confidence and self-esteem will be affected and that other secondary symptoms will develop.

Chapter 2
Identification of the adult dyslexic

Grounds for concern

A number of factors reasonably lead one to suspect that a person is dyslexic. Many definitions of dyslexia focus on the discrepancy between a person's literacy skills and their apparent intelligence. Although such definitions fail to focus on the true nature of the condition, they do describe what is frequently a salient feature of dyslexia. *Discrepancy definitions* have developed and their use persists precisely because many dyslexics display an inconsistency between their apparent general ability and their literacy skills. At the most extreme it is inconsistent, for example, that someone who shows good verbal ability and has spent the usual amount of time in school cannot read and write. It is also inconsistent that a professional engineer who has had a good education still has trouble with spelling. Evidence of such an inconsistency suggests that someone may be dyslexic.

Miles (1982) has suggested that incongruity is '...the key' to the identification of the dyslexic. However, this might lead to the incorrect conclusion that discrepancies must be obvious. Many adult dyslexics have compensated for their inefficiencies to a large extent and it is important to be aware that the incongruity can be very subtle: a lack of obvious incongruity does not imply that someone is not dyslexic. Listed below are some common characteristics which would suggest that further investigation is warranted.

1. A discrepancy between academic achievement and performance in practical problem-solving and/or verbal skills.
2. Excessive misspelling in written work, including errors such as confusion of letter order.
3. Difficulty with sequencing tasks that are usually automatic, such as reciting the months of the year and arithmetic tables in order.
4. Problems with organising work.
5. An aversion to writing notes or excessive note-taking.

6. Reluctance to write anything at all.
7. Evidence of difficulty with working memory tasks such as taking telephone numbers or messages.
8. Forgetting series of instructions or carrying them out in the wrong order.
9. Persisting illiteracy in spite of remedial help or attendance at adult literacy classes.
10. A tendency to talk rather than listen as a strategy for restricting the input of information.

Dyslexics do not have a monopoly on any of the above and, taken individually, any one of the behaviours described would give little cause for concern. However, when several occur together with no obvious explanation, such as a neurological injury or disorder, there is justification for assuming that the individual may be dyslexic. For example, if (1), (2) and (7) are evident then it is strongly possible that the individual is dyslexic. It is, however, important to distinguish between a suspicion that someone is dyslexic and convincing evidence that they are.

There are a number of quite plausible reasons why someone who is not dyslexic might exhibit typical dyslexic characteristics: many people of low intelligence, for example, exhibit behaviours, such as difficulties with literacy and working memory, which have typically been associated with dyslexia. There are also many intelligent people who, because of inadequate education, have poor literacy skills. Anne, for example, sought an assessment on the suggestion of a friend who thought that her poor spelling and writing might be due to dyslexia. In the initial interview and discussion Anne explained that she was having problems with aspects of her job as a receptionist. She had been working in this capacity for just under a month and had already been warned about her 'sloppy work' on several occasions. She occasionally had to take telephone messages and was having difficulty with this task; she complained that '...I sometimes put the phone down and then just can't remember what the message was. I try and write it while the person's talking to me but then I can't make out what I've written'.

Anne had a typical dyslexic behaviour pattern. She was clearly bright but was very poor at spelling and writing. In addition she appeared to have a working memory problem and, like so many adult dyslexics, she was anxious to hide her difficulties and felt embarrassed when people discovered her weaknesses. Formal assessment, however, indicated that she was not dyslexic. In-depth discussions revealed that Anne had received very poor schooling. Her parents had provided no encouragement for her to work and apparently felt that education was a waste of time for females. In view of her childhood experiences her poor literacy skills were quite understandable. In the assessment Anne performed poorly on tests of reading and writing but on all the other tests, including those tapping working memory, she scored above average. Careful questioning and observation provided an explanation for the apparent working memory deficit. Anne was stressed and anxious about a number of personal and financial problems; she was also depressed because she felt that she was of low intelligence. Her mental state was interfering with her concentration and attention. Her forgetfulness was just one result of this condition. This case illustrates the importance of formal assessment. Anne needed counselling for her personal problems and tuition in literacy; an incorrect diagnosis of dyslexia would not have assisted her in any way and it might well have added to her difficulties.

'Grounds for concern' should not automatically lead to the conclusion that a person is dyslexic. If suspicion is aroused, an investigative process should collect and carefully examine the evidence, and conclusions should be based on this alone. To be effective the investigation should be objective and systematic. To be of use to clients investigation should be structured so that they gain an insight into their own behaviour and functioning. This demands that professionals have the knowledge and skills to enable them to provide information, support, advice and guidance. Thus, formal identification has a number of distinct requirements. It is a four-step process:

- information gathering;
- psychological testing and diagnosis;
- developing an understanding of dyslexia;
- taking action.

The first step involves gathering information in a structured way. If this information indicates that the client is likely to be dyslexic then the next step is formal psychological testing and diagnosis. This requires very specific skills and should be carried out by an appropriately qualified psychologist. Only when the results of testing are available can the individual be identified as dyslexic. It is logical for the first two steps to be completed by a psychologist because the information from step one is used in step two; however, in cases where this is impractical it is reasonable for information to be passed on to the psychologist (assuming that the client agrees).

If individuals only wish to know if they are dyslexic or not then the process ends after step two; step one must be completed, because it provides important information, which is used diagnostically in the second step. In such cases, however, the information gathering can be less detailed than when a client is seeking help and advice as well as diagnosis. Step 2, the formal testing, should never be carried out in isolation. The information gathered in step 1 is critical to diagnosis.

Following step 2 those clients who are not dyslexic should be referred elsewhere for appropriate assistance with their difficulties.

Those clients identified as dyslexic should be offered support and guidance.

Step three involves raising awareness and understanding of what dyslexia is. Most dyslexics will benefit from knowing how their dyslexia has operated in their early life, how they have coped with it to date, how it continues to influence their life and how they can acquire new behaviours that will enable them to overcome the difficulties they face. The last step involves agreeing on what action is necessary and how to implement it.

The remainder of this chapter will be devoted to a description of step 1: the other three steps are discussed in following chapters.

Screening

Basic information that must be obtained includes details of:

- education;
- qualifications;
- work experience;
- present occupation; and
- family history, including details of the incidence of dyslexia within the family.

This information is best collected using a structured interview such as the one outlined on pages 23 and 24. This is only intended as a guide and interviewers are encouraged to ask clients to expand on their answers. For example, if clients reply 'yes' to the question 'do you write slowly?' it is important to ascertain what their concept of 'slowly' is and to whom they are comparing themselves.

It is common practice to substitute a questionnaire for the interview, but there have to be reservations about asking someone who has experienced problems with literacy to fill one in: it is akin to establishing a swimming school for beginners in the middle of a lake! Many dyslexics find any requirement to write something down extremely stressful; the horror one woman expressed when describing how she had been presented with a questionnaire in a waiting room confirms that dyslexics should never be asked to complete a questionnaire 'on the spot'. If one is used it may be helpful to clients if it is sent out before an appointment so that they can complete it in their own time and if necessary seek assistance from family or friends.

The basic information gathered from the structured interview must be interpreted in the following context: personal; needs and goals; understanding dyslexia; educational achievements; experience of other learning situations; medical information; coping strategies; and behavioural information. This is achieved by in-depth questioning and the investigation must be a dynamic and interactive process.

Adult Dyslexia Screening Interview

Full Name: ....

Address: ....

Date of Birth: ....   Age: ....

Part A (Biographical Details)

Are you working at present? ....

If you are working what is your job? ....

What other jobs have you held? ....

....

....

What educational qualifications do you have? ....

....

What were your best subjects at school? ....

....

What were your worst subjects at school? ....

....

Did you have any extra help at school? ....

Were you disappointed in your results at school?...............................

Did you work hard at school? ....

Are you studying at present? ....

What are you studying? ....

Do you have any particular difficulties with your studies? ....

....

Is your general health good? ....

Have you suffered any serious illnesses? ....

....

....

Do you have any problems with your hearing? ....

Do you have any problems with your vision? ....

Has anyone in your family had difficulty with any of the following:

reading   yes ....   no ....

writing   yes ....   no ....

spelling   yes ....   no ....

arithmetic   yes ....   no ....

memory   yes ....   no ....

Part B (Strengths and Weaknesses)

1. Do you have difficulty with any of the following?:

i. a. using a dictionary ....

   b. using a telephone directory ....

ii. following directions or using street maps ....

iii. time keeping, e.g. are you frequently late for appointments?

iv. taking telephone messages ....

v. writing letters or messages ....

2. Do you make mistakes when you speak, e.g. using the wrong words or mispronouncing words? ....

3. In conversations do you tend to lose track of what you wanted to say?..

4. Are you distracted easily?..

5. Do you have to have a special place where you need to go when you want to work?..

6. Do you tend to avoid talking? ....

7. Do you tend to talk a lot?..

8. Do you have difficulty remembering what you wanted to say? ....

9. Do you tend to make mistakes when writing? ....

10. Do you have difficulty with spelling? ....

11. Do you write slowly?..

12. Can you take notes when listening to someone speaking? ....

Personal

What difficulties have caused the client to seek help? It is necessary to gain some awareness of why, at this moment in their life, there is a need to investigate a problem. What is the reason for and/or who is the source of referral? Is it a self-motivated enquiry arising from a client's own feelings that they might be dyslexic? Have they been persuaded by others, for example, friends, relatives or employers, to seek advice?

The aim should be to find out whether the client is internally motivated to engage in assessment, is externally influenced by others or if there is some combination of both. The degree of commitment the client has will influence the outcome of any intervention.

Needs and goals

In what way(s) would the client like to change? The client's emotional and psychological state will have a powerful influence over their expression of what they need and want. They may have difficulty identifying goals, i.e. what they want to change or what would personally satisfy them, and therefore may speak in general and abstract terms. Frequently clients make general statements such as saying they want a less stressful job. This information is by itself unhelpful because it does not identify the problem in behavioural terms. While the information that is most useful relates to what the client could do and would be happy doing, they are often unable to specify this. In such cases it is valuable to identify what, specifically, they find stressful in their present situation: it may transpire, for example, that they are required to work with numbers, to write reports quickly and under pressure, to use filing systems, to do tasks in certain sequences or to carry out instructions given verbally – all of which place heavy demands on working memory. Specific information such as this can lead to the identification of work that would be more appropriate or it can lead to suggestions on how to develop coping strategies so that such tasks are less stressful.

Understanding dyslexia

What does dyslexia mean to the client? What do they think it means to those who have applied the term to them? Who first described them as dyslexic and why? Perhaps it resulted from a formal assessment in their childhood, or maybe it was the result of an informal (and possibly uninformed) judgement by a teacher. This line of enquiry leads naturally into obtaining detailed information about why assessments were carried out or informal judgements made. The existence of any assessment records and their availability should be established. It is useful to find out if any recommendations were made as a result of assessment and whether they were followed up.

Educational achievements and experience

The client's achievements, failures and preferences for particular subjects should be explored in detail. Someone who reports a strong liking for football may have developed this because playing football was a strategy they used to avoid difficult subjects, rather than from any intrinsic love of the game. Similarly, an explanation of failure as the consequence of 'messing around' in lessons or getting in with 'the truancy crowd' would merit further enquiry. Illness, difficult family circumstances or truancy may offer an explanation for lack of academic success. Ques-tions regarding their success relative to that of their peers can be of value in determining if poor teaching might have been a significant factor.

The most useful information concerns what tasks presented difficulties and what help, if any, the client received. What is their opinion about why they succeeded or failed? It is also important to investigate the reasons for success: perhaps it was due to extra help from a teacher to whom they related well or perhaps they had extra tuition or attended remedial classes. Learning a foreign language can be particularly difficult for dyslexics but this does not imply that someone who has a university degree in foreign languages is not dyslexic. They may have worked much harder and been considerably better organised than their peers; personal tutoring may have been employed to supplement the educational provision made by the university. By accident or design, teaching methods may have focused on multisensory learning. The client may have been fortunate enough to have sympathetic teachers and have received special provision during learning and examinations. Alternatively, someone who has consistently found it difficult to learn foreign languages, despite having made the effort to do well, is not necessarily dyslexic. They may simply have little talent for foreign languages, but have pursued an inappropriate course of study as a consequence of poor advice and guidance.

Someone employed by a major organisation may have achieved a senior position requiring very good literacy, numeracy, memory and organisational skills. Careful investigation, however, might reveal that they have developed strategies for dealing with the demands the job makes of them.

Asking about a person's preferences for teachers can often bring insight into patterns of success and failure. Furthermore, a discussion of what they experienced in terms of good and bad instruction can help to identify the difficulties they had at that time and will often cast light on the teaching methods that are most likely to succeed in their particular case.

Experience of other learning situations

Any training courses attended or special learning situations that the client has been exposed to since leaving school should be explored.

This enables one to determine whether patterns of weaknesses in processing information have persisted or if effective strategies for coping with learning have been developed. This is also useful for assessing self-image, i.e. how the client has compared their own ability to that of their peers. How do they perceive themselves in learning contexts? It could be that they have low expectations of themselves, have become resigned to failure; they may be overcompensating by being very persistent and working much harder than others.

Medical information

A history of neurological disorder and/or head injury is of significance as one could be dealing with acquired dyslexia. Sensory impairments may also have a bearing; impairment in hearing or vision can, for example, undermine the development of perceptual processes that underlie literacy skills. If there is any doubt concerning the integrity of hearing and vision an investigation by an appropriately qualified person should be recommended.

Coping strategies

Although some behaviours can be described as being typical of a dyslexic, it is possible for someone to develop strategies that obscure obvious signs. Some adult dyslexics will appear to be very good at remembering: paradoxically, they have a good memory because their memory is poor, i.e. owing to the problems that poor working memory presents in terms of everyday tasks, some adult dyslexics seek out very effective ways of improving memory and, because of their motivation and application, they develop an above average ability to recall material. They do, however, continue to have difficulties with phonological memory.

Behavioural observation

It is always as important to see how people do what they do as it is to investigate what they fail to do. This applies equally to interviewing, checklists or screening tests. A checklist in wide use requires people to respond simply 'Yes' or 'No' to questions such as

- Is your spelling poor?
- Is your writing difficult to read?
- Do you find it difficult to carry sums in your head without using aids such as fingers or paper?
- Do you forget telephone numbers or car registrations easily?

An analysis of the responses to 100 such questionnaires showed that a number of the items were not discriminating in that the numbers of people indicating 'Yes' and 'No' were more or less equal. Such questions are very subjective and there are no normative data against which responses can be considered. It is not enough simply to ask an individual if they are well organised or if they have difficulty with remembering telephone numbers. They may have developed strategies for overcoming such difficulties and not be aware of the fact that they are 'different' in the way they deal with such things. It is more important to ask *how* they deal with such tasks.

Screening tests

The focus on childhood dyslexia has meant that there is a paucity of appropriate screening procedures for use with the suspected adult dyslexic. This has resulted in the misuse and misinterpretation of tests that have been designed for and standardised on younger people. One of the best known screening tests in use in the UK is the Bangor Dyslexia Test developed by Miles (1983a). It consists of the following subtests:

- left/right confusions;
- repetition of polysyllabic words;
- subtraction;
- tables;
- saying months forward;
- saying months reversed;
- repeating numbers forwards;
- repeating numbers backwards;
- confusion of 'b' and 'd'; and
- reporting of familial incidence.

The Bangor Dyslexia Test is used with adults in a number of contexts but it was designed for young people of 7–18 years of age. In developing this test, it was found that only 'tables' and 'reversing digits' were sensitive in identifying dyslexics among the older teenagers in the sample. This means that most of the items on the test are not discriminating when used with adults. Until appropriate research and development of screening tests has been undertaken, their use requires very careful consideration. This is not to say that they are unhelpful, as systematic observation of the ways in which adults deal with the tasks set can yield valuable information.

When using such instruments, it is imperative not to administer them in isolation. The principle of 'specificity' (i.e. the notion that dyslexic people have an underlying neurological inefficiency) is central to the screening and assessment process. Consequently the accurate diagnosis of dyslexia requires the measurement of general ability and working memory. Any procedure that fails to incorporate appropriate cognitive tests is likely to produce both false positives (i.e. the incorrect identification of a person who has low intelligence as dyslexic) and false negatives (the failure to identify a dyslexic person as such because they have developed strategies to compensate for their dyslexia). The reliance on the assessment of literacy skills alone as the sole or main diagnostic procedure is inappropriate and uninformed: Klein (1993), for example, while offering a way of assessing an adult's literacy skills, fails to describe objective methods for the measurement of relevant cognitive abilities, without which an assessment procedure cannot be diagnostic.

People with general learning difficulties will often manifest signs similar to those who are dyslexic. It is therefore important to take measures of verbal and non-verbal ability as well as memory skills. Many tests of such abilities are available to teachers and other professionals who are not psychologists. For example, Raven's Progressive Matrices, a measure of non-verbal ability, is widely used, as are the Mill Hill and Crichton Vocabulary Scales which are measures of verbal ability. It is especially important to measure verbal ability as it is the more reliable predictor of academic performance. Whatever tests of ability are used, it is imperative that these can be administered without the client having to read or write answers.

Chapter 3
Formal diagnosis

Formal diagnosis of dyslexia involves psychological testing, careful observation and clinical judgement. It should be carried out by a psychologist because it requires the interpretation of 'closed tests' (i.e. those that are available only to qualified psychologists) as well as the exercise of judgements that require psychological understanding and knowledge. The individual carrying out the diagnostic procedure should interpret tests and make a clinical judgement in the context of the information obtained in the first stage of the assessment process outlined in Chapter 2. The importance of operating within this context will become clear later in this chapter.

Diagnosing dyslexia requires identification of a disparity between general intellectual functioning and functioning in certain specific areas. In Chapter 1 it was argued that dyslexia is essentially an inefficiency in working memory and that this makes it difficult for a dyslexic person to acquire certain fundamental skills. As a consequence of this individuals will, in spite of adequate intellectual functioning, appear to be less able in certain areas than their peers. This apparent lack of ability is most likely to manifest itself during childhood as a deficit in literacy skills but it is not necessarily restricted to this area. Furthermore, by adulthood the literacy problems have usually been overcome and performance in reading, writing and spelling can be within average limits. It is not unusual to find an adult dyslexic who has good literacy skills but has been unable to master other tasks which rely heavily on working memory, for example, mental arithmetic or activities that require steps to be executed in strict sequence. However, some dyslexics have developed strategies for dealing with most (or all) of their primary difficulties, although many continue to experience secondary psychological difficulties such as low self-esteem and poor self-confidence.

Compensatory strategies allow dyslexics to operate as efficiently as non-dyslexics but their acquisition does not mean that the dyslexia has gone away. As noted earlier, such strategies conceal incongruities that would usually point to the dyslexic condition – it is this concealment that needs to be uncovered in the course of diagnosis. The process of investigation using tests is intended to identify areas of fundamental weakness. If the person being examined is dyslexic they will perform poorly on certain tests, particularly those which tap working memory. Such weaknesses will, assuming the individual is of average or above average intelligence, stand in marked contrast to their functioning in other areas. The tests used in diagnosis must cover a wide range of abilities or the disparity between general functioning and functioning in specific areas cannot be measured and there is a risk of misdiagnosis. In addition to identifying a discrepancy, the procedure should allow the examiner to specify what weakness is causing it. When this can be isolated to an inefficiency in working memory, and there is no history of head injury or neurological disorder to account for this, then the diagnosis should be developmental dyslexia.

The testing procedure is described below. The order in which the individual components are undertaken will vary according to the client's history, disposition, personality and current situation. It is important to have regard for the particular difficulties the client has experienced. One man, for example, had been made redundant from the police force because he was unable to read written notes out loud in court – his poor reading was the source of great embarrassment and anxiety. Thus, in his assessment the reading tests were administered late in the procedure with sensitivity and supportive reassurance. Similarly, a young woman was experiencing anxiety in her place of work because she was unable to remember telephone messages. She had received a number of warnings from her immediate line manager, who apparently felt that she was not interested in the job and was irresponsible. This client was very concerned about her poor working memory skills and was visibly distressed when talking about the subject. Thus, in her assessment the tests that tap memory skills were administered following some counselling and relaxation work. Test anxiety is an important source of error when making measurements using psychological tests and it must be reduced as far possible if the test is to be valid and reliable. This necessitates the assessor making decisions about what is and what is not appropriate in terms of the order in which subtests are administered.

Testing intelligence

Thomson (1990) states that the appropriate assessment of intelligence is one of the most crucial factors in the diagnosis of dyslexia. He describes the four major functions of intelligence testing as being:

1. To obtain a measure of the intellectual level of the individual in

order to rule out slow learning or low intelligence as a cause of written language failure.

2. To examine the interrelationship between the individual's intellectual level and written language attainments in order to describe any discrepancies between these.

3. To obtain a diagnostic profile from the intelligence test used.

4. To describe the cognitive functioning of the individual in order to identify areas of deficit and help plan remediation.

Although Thomson was concerned with the testing of intelligence in children, the functions he describes are applicable to intelligence testing in adults (thus the word 'individual' has been substituted for 'child' in the list above).

There is considerable debate (and much disagreement) concerning the measurement of intelligence. In the context of dyslexia, however, the issues are relatively clear. The concern is to determine if, compared with a suitable reference group, an individual shows a discrepancy between performance in tasks that place heavy demands on working memory and performance on tasks that do not. In relation to the latter the measurements must be uncontaminated by the effects of working memory, so the tests used in diagnosis must not require reading questions or writing answers because these activities utilise working memory. Further, they must be administered individually. The test most widely used in the diagnosis of adult dyslexia is the Wechsler Adult Intelligence Scale (WAIS), originally devised in 1955 but revised and re-published as the Wechsler Adult Intelligence Scale – Revised (WAIS-R) in 1981 (Wechsler, 1981). The format of each subtest in the WAIS and the WAIS-R is essentially the same and therefore it seems unlikely that the performance patterns and psychometric properties of the two tests will differ significantly.

The WAIS-R is a normed test, that is to say there is information contained in the manual relating to how specified groups perform on the subtests. It can be used with individuals between 16 and 74 years. The WAIS-R examines different kinds of intellectual functions and allows the examiner to rule out, or diagnose, intellectual disability. When acquainted with the subtests the examiner can, with careful observation, become sensitive to behavioural nuances. This is particularly important in the assessment of dyslexia, where individuals may be completing certain tasks using compensatory strategies that can be detected only by careful observation of their responses. In the subtests described below valuable information can be derived from continuing to administer test items beyond the levels suggested in the directions, although these would not be included in the client's score.

The WAIS-R consists of 11 subtests, six forming a verbal scale and five forming a performance scale. It yields separate scores for verbal, performance and full-scale IQs, the last being calculated on the basis of all 11 subtests.

Verbal tests

Information

This measures the ability to access long-term memory by focusing on general knowledge. The standard instructions direct the examiner to end the test after five consecutive failures. It is imperative to adhere to this in the calculation of a score, but in gaining a picture of someone's knowledge and experience it can be useful to continue. A poorly educated person who is clearly bright may be able to demonstrate good knowledge in specific areas: they may, for example, have acquired through their work special expertise in science while remaining less knowledgeable about literature, history, geography and religion. In such cases selected questions can be given; for example, all the items can be related to the individual's work.

Digit span

This subtest is designed to measure auditory sequential memory but it may also measure item memory. Regardless of whether it taps item or sequential memory, it is a test of working memory and is particularly important in the diagnosis of dyslexia. It is made up of two tests: digits forward and digits backward. Each of these requires the examiner to read aloud random number sequences at the rate of one number per second. The first sequence has three numbers, the second four numbers and so on, until the last sequence, which has nine numbers. On 'digits forward' the examinee is required to listen to a sequence and then repeat the numbers in the same order as they were presented. On 'digits reversed' the examinee is required to listen to a sequence and then repeat the numbers in reverse order. In the WAIS-R the scores from the two tests are combined, but in terms of assessing dyslexics this may be misleading because important information can be lost. Dyslexics typically have more difficulty recalling lists of digits than people who are not dyslexic but they frequently overcome this by employing a strategy called 'chunking'. This is a method of improving recall based on a reorganisation of the material to be recalled. For example, if required to recall the six digits 4, 1, 6, 3, 9, 2 a chunking strategy would be to think of the information as three two-digit numbers (i.e. forty-one, sixty-three and ninety-two). An examiner can detect this strategy by observing carefully how the numbers are repeated; however, it is not always possible to discern that such a strategy has been used. 'Digits reversed' makes use of such strategies quite obvious; the examinee will either perform poorly or will perform well but obviously present the digits in pairs.

The WAIS-R scoring system could easily obscure the operation of a compensatory strategy such as this and so it is wise to examine performance on the two tests separately.

Vocabulary

This subtest, which requires the examinee to define words, is a good measure of both verbal and general mental ability. According to Lezak (1990), performance on this test reflects socioeconomic and cultural origins because vocabulary development is apparently more influenced by these than it is by schooling. In terms of adult dyslexia, vocabulary development can be affected by inefficient working memory and so the examiner must be careful when interpreting low scores. If the person being tested performs poorly, but has had good schooling and a rich home and cultural environment, then inefficient working memory could offer a logical explanation for the low score. Further, accessing the lexicon, or 'word finding' can be a problem for dyslexic people and their answers will often be rather vague.

Arithmetic

Although this test involves mental arithmetic it is not so much a measure of arithmetic ability as a measure of working memory skills. Because in assessing dyslexia we are concerned to distinguish between these two components, it is wise to check which is responsible for failures. One method of achieving this is to allow the test taker the opportunity of working out the answer using pen and paper after each incorrect response. It is important to examine the incorrect answers for evidence of understanding. If an answer is almost correct the individual has more ability than if the answer is completely wrong. This information would be lost if the WAIS-R scoring system was applied mechanically. The examiner should also be alert to the use of strategies that may inflate test scores: some adults, for example, will get quite a good score on this test because they have used their fingers to count.

Comprehension

This subtest is designed to measure common sense and practical reasoning but, as some of the questions are rather lengthy, individuals with inefficient working memory may be at a disadvantage. The examiner should be aware of this and make sure that all elements in a question have been registered. The marking requires some judgement as there are no single correct responses. Although the standard instructions require the examiner to stop after four consecutive failures, it can be useful to exercise discretion, particularly when dealing with individuals who are very anxious about their performance.

Similarities

This test measures verbal concept formation and verbal reasoning. It requires the individual to consider the relationships between objects and concepts by explaining what they have in common. This is a very good test of general intellectual ability because it is almost independent of any memory component and is not unduly influenced by social and educational background. Examiners should be prepared to give assistance if they suspect that the examinee is making mistakes because of performance anxiety; typically this may manifest itself as answers that identify differences rather than similarities.

Performance tests

Picture completion

This is a measure of general ability and visual recognition. The tasks require information from long-term memory and so, to some extent, the test also measures this component. The examinee must identify what is missing from a black and white picture presented on a card. The easiest item is a picture of a door with a handle missing while the most difficult item requires the examinee to notice that a stack of logs has no snow on it while all other objects in the picture do. This is one of the subtests which is not, in general terms, adversely influenced by inefficient working memory.

Picture arrangement

This subtest measures a number of skills, including sequential thinking ability. It consists of several sets of cartoon pictures that make up stories. The cards are placed before the individual in an incorrect order and the task is to arrange them so that they make logical sense. Lezak (1992) states that performance on this subtest '...reflects social sophistication ... [and] ... socially appropriate thinking...'. Thus it can give some insights into the social reality of the client, particularly if they are asked to explain the story. An average or above average score establishes that sequential thinking is intact. This is particularly significant if the client had reported difficulties with sequential tasks and performed poorly on the digit span test. It would imply that working memory was the cause of their difficulty rather than a general intellectual failing with sequential tasks.

Block design

This test measures visuospatial organisation. The test taker is required to construct, using small red and white cubes, replicas of designs printed on cards. This type of task involves the ability to perceive and analyse forms and patterns and as such is a good test of general intelligence. It is particularly useful for measuring general ability in intellectually able individuals who have not benefited from education or training.

This test can provide a wealth of information about the examinee, including information about problem-solving methods, work habits and thinking styles. Comments that the examinee may make can give insights into their self-perception. A tendency to give up quickly can reflect a feeling of helplessness, and a reluctance to change the way that the blocks have been arranged may indicate a lack of flexibility. The examiner should make notes of the types of error made and how the individual approaches the problem.

Object assembly

This is a reasonably pure measure of visuospatial organisation or spatial ability. It requires the individual to assemble some jigsaw puzzles of familiar objects (such as a manikin, a profile, a hand and an elephant). Poor performance would suggest a particular difficulty in forming visual concepts, difficulty in translating visual concepts into rapid hand responses or both. Average or good performance would eliminate these possibilities.

Digit symbol

This subtest is a symbol substitution task; it requires the individual to associate a number with an abstract symbol. It is one of the four WAIS-R subtests on which dyslexics tend to perform poorly and so warrants particular attention. It is a strictly timed test that requires speed and accuracy. It is generally considered to be a measure of psychomotor performance, which is not affected by intellectual prowess or learning. Performance is lowered as a result of poor vision, poor visuomotor coordination, poor or slow motor responses and so it is necessary to ensure that the test taker does not have deficits in any of these areas. This test relies to some extent on an ability to encode symbols verbally, which is the most likely reason for the dyslexic's poor performance (i.e. verbal encoding utilises the phonological store and is disrupted by inefficient working memory).

Calculation of a person's IQ scores provides a criterion against which their performance can be compared. A person who attains high IQ scores but whose academic attainments have been very modest has obviously underachieved. However, the matter of how the subtests are scored needs to be carefully taken into account because the WAIS-R scoring system and the administration instructions are not entirely appropriate to the context of diagnosing dyslexia. Too mechanical an approach to testing can lead to invalid conclusions. If, for example, the examinees are intellectually able but suffer from low self-esteem, lack of confidence and long experience of failure, they may well be predisposed to 'going through the motions' without being motivated to perform at a level commensurate with their actual ability. The possible consequence of this is misdiagnosis.

A comparison between estimated general intelligence and academic achievement is useful, but more specific comparisons can also be made. For example, people who have achieved good academic results and who have good literacy skills will usually achieve a high verbal intelligence score. Good verbal ability suggests that, ordinarily, someone should have well-developed reading, writing and spelling skills: if, however, an individual achieves a verbal score well below average, it can be expected that they would have experienced difficulty with the acquisition of written language skills. It is logical to argue that someone achieving a very low score on a subtest such as vocabulary would experience difficulty with reading at an advanced level because such reading requires an extensive lexicon. Similarly, a good vocabulary score would lead one to expect that the individual could read at an advanced level: if this is not the case then there is an inconsistency.

The third function of an intelligence test, described by Thomson, relates to the subtest scores. As well as providing a separate IQ for verbal, performance and full scales, each subtest yields a standard score ranging from 1 to 19, where 9–11 is the average range. Obvious discrepancies among the scores can be examined to establish if there are specific areas of weakness of the kind associated with dyslexia.

The most widely used test in the diagnosis of childhood dyslexia is the Wechsler Intelligence Scale for Children (WISC; Wechsler, 1976, 1992). A considerable amount of research has been devoted to identifying 'typical' dyslexic profiles of WISC subtest scores: Bannatyne (1974), for example, has proposed four groups of subtest combinations on which dyslexics and non-dyslexics are presumed to differ. These are:

- Spatial (Picture completion, Block design and Object assembly);
- Verbal conceptualisation (Comprehension, Similarities, Vocabulary);
- Sequential (Digit span, Arithmetic, Coding or Digit symbol); and
- Acquired knowledge (Information, Arithmetic, Vocabulary).

Dyslexics have been found to be equal to, or better than, non-dyslexics in spatial and conceptual ability but they do less well in sequencing ability and acquired knowledge.

A large number of studies have identified what is known as the ACID profile of WISC scores (i.e. Arithmetic, Coding (Digit symbol), Information and Digit span), which has proved very useful in diagnosing dyslexia as they are the subtests on which dyslexics typically do less well than non-dyslexics (Thomson, 1990). Each of these subtests places a demand on working memory and the pattern of weak scores reflects inefficient working memory skills. The ACID profile is, however, only significant when scores on the four subtests in question are lower than scores on the other seven subtests. Low scores on all, or most, of the subtests may be indicative of low intelligence, not dyslexia.

The identification of adult dyslexics using the WAIS has not been as well researched as the identification of dyslexic children using the WISC. However, several studies have provided support for both Bannatyne's clusters and the ACID profile (Cordoni and O'Donnell, 1981; Salvia and Gajar, 1988; Katz et al., 1993). A typical ACID profile would be as shown below: calculation of Bannatyne's clusters for this profile would show that this individual has better spatial and conceptual ability than sequencing ability and acquired knowledge.

WAIS-R IQ and subtest profiles for a dyslexic individual

Full Scale IQ = 107

Verbal IQ	*106*	*Performance IQ*	*109*
Information	7	Picture completion	12
Digit span	6	Picture arrangement	11
Vocabulary	12	Block design	13
Arithmetic	7	Object assembly	14
Comprehension	12	Digit symbol	7
Similarities	11		

Some adult dyslexics will readily exhibit patterns of scores that fall into the ACID profile and it is an obvious indicator. Clinicians, should not, however, examine only the subtest scores of the WAIS-R with a view to determining if this profile exists. They should, during the administration procedure, look for evidence of potential weaknesses on subtests, which may have been obscured by the use of compensatory strategies.

Refining the process

For a number of reasons it may be necessary to shorten the process of testing intelligence. First, when assessing a dyslexic person, one is inevitably dealing with someone with a history of failure who finds being tested extremely stressful. In such situations it is legitimate to minimise the amount of testing undertaken. Further, the educational achievements of some individuals will suggest that eliminating low ability as an explanation for specific difficulties is unnecessary.

There are short forms of the WAIS and WAIS-R that produce estimates and can give a fairly representative picture of someone's overall level of functioning. For example, Satz and Mogel (1962) developed an abbreviated set of scales covering all subtests. It uses a largely split-half procedure in which only odd items are administered, with the exception of Information, Vocabulary and Picture completion, for which every third item is given. Brooker and Cyr (1986) have produced data for calculation of full-scale IQ equivalents on the basis of scores on Vocabulary, Block design, Arithmetic and Similarities. They have also produced tables for full-scale IQ equivalents based on scores achieved on Vocabulary and Block design. Such short forms can, however, provide only an estimate of the overall level of intellectual functioning.

Memory testing

Administration of the WAIS will have provided some insight into memory functioning. It can, however, be helpful to explore this further for two reasons. Successful adult dyslexics will have developed compensatory strategies and may be able to mask their memory inefficiencies. Further diagnostic testing can therefore provide a clearer picture. Given the model of dyslexia described in Chapter 1, testing sequential memory is particularly important and focusing on tests such as Digit span is essential. It has been suggested that the best test of auditory sequential memory is digits reversed (Lezak, 1983). The difference between the performance on the two aspects of the Digit span subtest is consequently very important. It is, therefore, useful to administer the equivalent subtest from the Wechsler Memory Scale – Revised (Wechsler, 1987) as this yields separate centile rankings for digits forward and digits reversed. Often, although the scaled score for the Digit span subtest on the WAIS is average, the Digit span subtest from the Wechsler Memory Scale shows that the centile ranking for digits forward is average but digits reversed is well below average.

Many tests of sequential memory have been developed; for a description see Lezak (1983). The problem with a number of these tests is that they do not clearly separate visual, auditory and kinaesthetic dimensions. For example, the visual sequential memory subtest of the Wechsler Memory Scale requires the individual to watch the examiner tap out a pattern on a card of coloured squares. It is not easy to administer and involves both visual and motor memory. The problems in testing visual sequential memory have been described in Chapter 1.

A useful source of information about working memory is the Visual Aural Digit Span Test (Koppitz, 1977). This was devised for children up to the age of 13 years. However, the maximum number of digits a subject is required to remember is seven and as average digit span is 7 ± 1, it seems appropriate to use it with adults also. The examinee is asked to repeat series of numbers in the same way as in the Digit span tests of the Wechsler Scales. Unfortunately, it does not have a digits reversed component, but clients are asked to write down a series of spoken numbers and some adults find this much more difficult. Such a discrepancy would explain why someone is able to spell a word out loud but has difficulty in writing it down. It would also account for difficulties with tasks such as taking dictation. The visual dimension of the test also requires repetition and writing down of visually presented numbers. Again, as people often subvocalise, it is difficult to establish whether they are relying on visual memory, but their difficulty in writing down numbers presented visually can often account for problems with tasks such as copying.

Another reason for administering separate memory tests is that the results can have implications for training and teaching. For example, if an individual had good visual pictorial memory, it might be suggested that an effective way for compensating for an inefficient working memory is to use visual imagery. The reader is again referred to Lezak (1983) for a description of suitable tests. There are, however, risks involved in administering too many tests. When working with adults the best insights into how they remember things are often gained from asking them how they deal with particular memory tasks.

Attainments in literacy and numeracy

Once a level of expectation has been established on the basis of a measure of general intellectual ability, tests of proficiency in written language skills should be administered.

Reading

Assessment of reading skills should include tests of:

- single word reading;
- prose reading;
- reading comprehension; and
- reading fluency.

This is not as easy as it should be because there is a dearth of good tests designed for adults.

Single word reading tests

There are many single word reading tests that may be helpful in providing a measure of decoding skills and act as a guide to an individual's reading level. The best known tests are those developed by Schonell (1955), Burt (Scottish Council for Research in Education, 1976) and Vernon (1983). Only the last of these provides a score beyond the beginning of secondary school level. The New Adult Reading Test (NART), although occasionally listed as a single word reading test, was, in fact designed as a test of premorbid intelligence (Nelson and Willison, 1991). The Wide Range Achievement Test – Revised (WRAT-R; Jastak and Wilkinson, 1984) has two forms for reading, level 2 being for 12 year olds and upwards. However, like many single word reading tests its presentation gives it low face validity – the subject is presented with 90 words on a card, which poor readers can find quite threatening. Experience of attempting to use the WRAT-R with adult dyslexics is that they are frequently depressed by their failure to be able to get beyond the first few lines. Spreen and Strauss (1991) have questioned its use outside the USA because it lacks correspondence with academic curricula in other English-speaking countries. Spreen and Strauss argue that owing to a lack of availability of technical data regarding the properties of the test '...as well as shortcomings in the standardisation procedures the test should not be used as a diagnostic measure of academic difficulties' (Spreen and Strauss, 1991, p. 109).

Prose reading tests

Although they do have a place in the assessment of reading skills, single word reading tests are of limited value. In assessing adults' reading skills, we are really attempting to determine how well they can function in everyday life and in academic settings. Most people have to deal with prose rather than individual words. Prose reading tests usually consist of a set of passages graded in order of difficulty. Examples of these are the Neale Analysis of Reading Ability (Neale, 1989) and the MacMillan Reading Test (Vincent and De La Mare, 1990). The passages are read aloud, the time taken to read them is noted and then questions are asked about the content. Thus measures of accuracy, fluency and comprehension are provided. Again, however, such tests were developed for use with children and the maximum score tends to be around the beginning of secondary school level. Further, such tests are not good measures of reading comprehension as reading aloud places greater demands on working memory than does reading silently. The process of dealing with correct pronunciation and expression interferes with comprehension. Measures of silent reading comprehension are much more important as this is fundamental to being able to pursue formal education and most occupations.

In examining an adult's reading skills the prime objective should be to establish whether they have reached one of the four literacy levels:

- *functional* level, which is roughly equivalent to that which is achieved by younger primary school children;
- *vocational* level, equivalent to the upper stages of primary school (people who have reached such a level should have little difficulty in

reading and understanding most of the basic needs of jobs that require a moderate amount of reading);

- *technical* level is equivalent to the lower stages of secondary school – people at this level should be able to deal with post-secondary training such as for a trade or technical occupation;
- the *professional* level is equivalent to the standard achieved by college students. An individual who has reached this level is capable of independent reading and has the basis for development of the reading skills that should enable them to cope with a university education and training for a professional occupation.

If we were to choose a particular aspect of reading to measure that would predict success in an occupation it would be silent reading comprehension.

In the examination of people who, on the basis of their educational background, are likely to be at a functional or vocational level, the Basic Skills Tests (Smith and Whetton, 1988) are useful. These were designed for use in occupational rather than educational settings. The reading section focuses on silent reading comprehension (the examinee is required to answer questions about articles and advertisements in a mock local newspaper, which has good face validity because of its obvious relevance to everyday life).

For those functioning at technical and professional levels the Spadafore Diagnostic Reading Test (Spadafore, 1983) provides a very comprehensive picture. It includes tests of single word reading which are better presented than in most individual reading tests; there are ten words on a page for each grade level, which is far less threatening for the adult who has problems with literacy than a large number of words presented all at once. The single word reading test is given as a measure of decoding skills and there is a prose reading test of the same ability. The Spadafore test also has tests of oral reading comprehension, silent reading comprehension and listening comprehension. It has grade norms but is criterion-referenced, indicating whether an individual has reached independence, instructional or frustrational levels for each section. Further, it provides information about the level of reading skill required for specific occupations, so it can be useful in career counselling.

Writing and spelling

A sample of the client's writing should also be examined. The tester may suggest a simple topic or the client encouraged to choose one. Many dyslexics find this task difficult and it is important to suggest something that they do not have to think too much about, such as their journey to the assessment centre or a description of their hobbies. The Basic Skills Tests include specific tasks such as writing a postcard and writing a letter.

Dyslexics tend to be slow at writing. There is a dearth of information regarding the average writing speed for particular groups of adults, although it appears to be about 20 words per minute for an undergraduate student. To a large extent comparisons must be based on clinical judgement. A measure of writing speeds can be established by calculating the number of words produced per minute. It can be difficult to separate out writing and thinking speeds but a judgement can be made about the individual's verbal fluency on the basis of their performance on the intelligence test items and the amount of written work they produce.

The quality of the written work in terms of legibility, structure, syntax and punctuation should be evaluated. Again, the interest is in the contrast between this and verbal ability. Dyslexics will make characteristic errors such as omitting words and missing out prepositions and pronouns they intended to include, and they will have difficulty with spelling (Gregg, 1983). Spelling errors in a piece of written work can be analysed for characteristic errors such as letter order confusion. It can be helpful to examine spelling skills more closely by administering a single-word spelling test. There are many of these, including those developed by Schonell (1955) and Vernon (1983) and the spelling section of the WRAT-R (Tartak and Wilkinson, 1984). Although being aware of a spelling age or grade level can be helpful to a teacher, these are relatively meaningless to the client and may in fact be depressing. What is often more important is to go through the words on the spelling test and point out how close the dyslexic was to getting a word correct. The dyslexic who has been able to compensate through a good education will often make only minor errors, but this would still result in a very low score on a spelling test. Further, writing and spelling places a very heavy load on working memory. Some individuals will have a score on a standardised spelling test not significantly outside average limits, but their skills may deteriorate markedly when they are writing prose, particularly under pressure. Often these errors are construed as carelessness, so it is important to look at their nature: for example, confusion of letter order, omission of letters and phonic spelling or words spelled as they sound are characteristic of dyslexia.

Arithmetic

It can sometimes be useful to test arithmetic skills, particularly when difficulties with these have been raised by a client or an employer. However, arithmetic tests are usually simply measures of attainment and a low overall score may only reflect gaps in knowledge caused by poor teaching. Nevertheless, they can be of diagnostic value when responses are analysed carefully – an examination of the kinds of error made may determine whether they reflect inefficient working memory or poor learning. As well as difficulty in reading questions, a dyslexic can have trouble in dealing with symbols. It is common to find that '+' has been identified as 'x'. When a measure of elementary attainment in arithmetic is required the Numeracy section from the Basic Skills Tests is recommended.

Test scores and their analysis, together with information about family, educational and occupational history provides a basis for diagnosis.

Feedback to clients

Acceptance and understanding have been identified as essential factors in determining whether dyslexics are able to take control and overcome their difficulties. Feedback is therefore the most important part of an assessment. The goal is to enable individuals to understand their condition and how it affects them in order that they can take appropriate action. This is a part of the assessment that requires special attention, as dyslexics have problems with the organisation and processing of information. Through a proper explanation the client will be able to start developing their awareness and understanding. If, following an assessment, a client leaves without a greater understanding of the nature of their difficulties and what they can do to overcome them, then the assessment has been a waste of time. Psychologists conducting assessments should spend time explaining the nature of dyslexia to the client: too often one meets teenagers and adults who have known for years that they are dyslexic but who, when asked what it means, can only describe symptoms such as poor spelling . It is particularly important for adult dyslexics to know that their fundamental weakness is in working memory and that their problems with reading, writing and spelling are only symptoms of this. Feedback should take two forms: verbal and written.

Verbal feedback

Immediately after testing the client should be given a careful explanation of the test results and their implications. A simple operational model, preferably one which can be illustrated graphically, can be a useful aid to understanding. The client's strengths and weaknesses should be described and strategies for dealing with the latter outlined. Many adult dyslexics will have already developed their own strategies, in which case the way these can be applied constructively to deal with other areas of difficulty should be explained. Practical information about sources of further help, including names of agencies and appropriate literature, audio- and videotapes, should be provided. It can be particularly helpful to the client if the clinician records the feedback session on tape so that they can listen to it again at their leisure.

Written feedback

Verbal feedback should be followed by a written report. Essentially this should reiterate what the client was told at the end of the assessment session. In writing the report attention should be given to the educational level and literacy skills of the client. The inclusion of an abstract and interim summaries can aid comprehension, as can other factors, such as large print, which improve readability. Production of the complete report on tape as well as in a written form could be valuable.

Too many assessment reports written about adults are based on the format used by educational psychologists when describing assessments of children, but they are being written for a very different audience. A dyslexic adult should be able to derive benefit from the report themselves and should feel comfortable about showing it to people such as their personnel manager, who will not necessarily be trained in test interpretation. It has become regular practice to begin assessment reports with a page of test results. Because of the likelihood of misinter-pretation, this should not be done: it can be helpful for specialist teachers working with the client to have the test results, but these should be on a separate sheet so that the client can make them available at their own discretion. A sample report is provided in Appendix I.

Who should assess?

Securing relevant assessment can be more difficult than it should be. The difficulty arises because adult dyslexics, unlike their younger counterparts, require the psychologist to have a range of skills that cross over the established boundaries between areas of specialisation within psychology. To be specific, the assessment of dyslexia in adults requires as a minimum the following skills:

- clinical assessment;
- testing literacy;
- testing memory;
- counselling;
- understanding of work-related matters.

Although some psychologists have acquired these skills, the divisions within the profession of psychology are such that there is no one group of psychologists whose training would normally cover them.

Occupational psychologists have little training in clinical assessment and, in general, the development and testing of literacy skills is not one of their concerns.

Educational psychologists are not trained to work with adults or to deal with the problems people might experience at work. They are trained in the assessment of literacy skills but the psychological tests they use for this purpose are designed for use with children and are of little validity when administered to adults.

Clinical psychologists, although trained to work with adults and in clinical assessment, do not generally deal with work-related matters. Thus, while it is preferable for one psychologist to complete the process, it may be necessary for a dyslexic to have a series of assessments completed by different psychologists and educationalists. This would be a lengthy and largely impractical procedure in most cases but there may be no option if the assessment is to be thorough and relevant.

Chapter 4
Counselling the dyslexic adult

The word *counselling* is used in a variety of contexts. Miles (1988) draws a distinction between 'generalist' and 'specialist' counselling expertise. The former he describes as being common to all forms of counselling, i.e. the ability to be a good listener, show empathy and be non-judgmental. Counsellors with specialist expertise are those who have a '...technical knowledge over and above their ability to listen and discuss...' (Miles, 1988, p.103). In this chapter the word counselling is used in its generalist sense.

There are numerous different theoretical approaches to counselling, all of which have something to offer in helping adult dyslexics overcome the various emotional, personal, practical and work-related difficulties that they are likely to experience. Certainly the notion of 'unconditional positive regard' (i.e. complete and unqualified acceptance for a client's feelings and actions), which is central to Roger's client-centred therapy (Rogers, 1951) should underlie any generalist counselling. Given, however, that a dyslexic's understanding of the nature of their difficulties is central to overcoming those difficulties the 'cognitive restructuring' approaches are particularly apt: rational–emotive therapy (RET), developed by Ellis (1962), for example, assumes that maladaptive feelings are caused by irrational beliefs. Ellis argues that through mistaken assumptions people place excessive demands upon themselves. The adult dyslexic who assumes, incorrectly, that most people are very skilled in spelling and who consequently thinks that their own spelling skills are much worse than they really are is a typical example. Counselling involves challenging such assumptions. Likewise, Beck et al. (1979) attribute numerous psychological problems to the negative patterns in which individuals think about themselves. Their approach to counselling involves questioning clients so that they can discover for themselves the distortions in their thinking and can then make changes that are more consistent with reality.

It is necessary to recognise that dyslexics have constitutional difficulties that make certain tasks more difficult for them than they are for people who are not dyslexic. Counsellors need to be aware of how these difficulties have operated to produce further complications in the person's life and behaviour; the complex interaction of the psychological difficulties and the constitutional weaknesses must be fully acknowledged if the individual is to make progress.

In this chapter a distinction is drawn between two types of difficulties experienced by dyslexics: primary and secondary. The way in which dyslexics come to terms with their difficulties is then analysed along two dimensions, namely:

1. The level of awareness individuals have regarding their weaknesses.
2. The level of consciousness individuals have in relation to their compensatory behaviour.

A four-stage intervention model is presented and how it can be used to identify goals and objectives in a counselling context is explained.

Classifying symptoms

Primary symptoms

As a direct consequence of an inefficiency in working memory a dyslexic person will have more difficulty acquiring certain skills than a non-dyslexic of similar intelligence. Most notably, dyslexics take longer to develop literacy skills, and expend more time and energy in the process, than non-dyslexics. Less prominent features of dyslexia are difficulties with remembering facts, figures, sequences of instructions, messages, names and almost anything that places a heavy demand on working memory. Many dyslexics lack organisational skills; they are, because of a poor concept of time, frequently late for meetings and appointments. They can also have trouble following and keeping track of what is said in a conversation, lecture or interview. All of these difficulties arise as a direct result of their constitutional defect in working memory and are, therefore, *primary* symptoms.

Secondary symptoms

In contrast to the primary difficulties, these are additional complicating factors. Owing to the environmental demands, such as the need to learn in prescribed ways, the importance of competence in written expression, the centrality of the written word as a means of understanding the arts, sciences, politics and current affairs, dyslexic people can, understandably, feel overwhelmed by their inability to keep up with their peers. The often unsympathetic attitude and behaviour of other people undermines their confidence and contributes to the development in many dyslexics of profound and deeply ingrained low self-esteem.

Negativity is more potent when significant people in the dyslexic's life, perhaps members of their family or their teachers, have dismissed them as having low intelligence. An effect of low self-esteem and lack of confidence is to reduce or eradicate the motivation to do anything, which is then interpreted by others as well as by the individual as further evidence of low intelligence. Poor motivation, low self-esteem and a lack of confidence can lead to isolation, which in turn causes them to miss out on activities that would normally help them to acquire social skills – this isolates them further. Not surprisingly, dyslexics sometimes develop stress disorders and depression. These psychological difficulties are termed *secondary* symptoms.

The following case illustrates how the primary and secondary difficulties interact.

Susan, a 24-year-old woman who had worked in her father's corner shop since leaving school at 16, came for assessment following encouragement from a lecturer at the college where she was learning pottery. At school she recalled being initially interested in most of her lessons but, because she couldn't write well and because she made mistakes when asking questions (primary symptoms), she was labelled as unintelligent and was the subject of much ridicule. She soon learnt not to ask questions in class, not to do her homework and not to make an effort to learn. Subsequently her parents received school reports which labelled Susan as lazy and uncooperative. Her parents and family apparently became embarrassed by her lack of intelligence and encouraged her to take a back seat; she was the 'black sheep' of the family. Her two brothers and her sister all excelled academically and she was taunted by them because of her supposed stupidity. She was depressed and ashamed of herself. In response to the question 'how do you see yourself?' she replied 'I'm stupid, clumsy and ugly' – clearly something she believed. She had developed such a strong negative self-image that it extended to her physical appearance. Essentially, after years of negative feedback and constant suggestions that she should 'give up', she did; at the time of assessment she was nervous, self-effacing, lacking in confidence and had a remarkably low self-esteem (secondary symptoms). In Susan's case the secondary symptoms needed immediate attention because she was not prepared to do anything about her primary symptoms. Susan made rapid progress once she was given support and encouragement to reappraise her skills and potential. After several sessions she was able to focus on developing strategies to compensate for her weaknesses. She eventually acquired sufficient confidence, feelings of self-worth and appropriate learning skills to enrol on a course of training in business studies, where she achieved commendable results.

Awareness and compensation

Awareness is the first step to conscious control. At one extreme there are some dyslexic people who have a very clear and accurate knowledge of their strengths and weaknesses, while at the other there are those who for whom ignorance is bliss: they are not preoccupied with their weaknesses because they simply don't see them. It may seem strange to suggest that, with regard to the latter group, they should be changed in any way. The reality is, however, that such people are vulnerable. A change in their environment can throw them into disarray and the longer their ignorance has persisted, the greater the trauma will be. In practice it is usually following some change (such as losing a job or even gaining promotion; it could be that their children are starting to show an interest in books and are asking about words that the adult cannot read) that such individuals come to be diagnosed as dyslexic. Because awareness is so important, there is an onus on psychologists conducting assessments to provide a client with a proper explanation of their findings.

Compensation is control; it is most effective when it is fully conscious because when this is achieved strategies can be examined and finely tuned.

It is useful to combine these two dimensions to identify four levels.

1. People at level 1 are not aware of their weaknesses and have developed no strategies to overcome them.
2. Those at level 2 are aware of their weaknesses but have not developed strategies to overcome them.
3. People at level 3 are aware of their weaknesses and have developed compensatory strategies, but have developed them unconsciously.
4. Finally, people at level 4 are aware of their weaknesses and they have consciously developed strategies to overcome them.

Level 1

Adult dyslexics at this level are people who, to all intents and purposes, have learned to live with their particular difficulties and weaknesses. They are unaware that they are less able than those around them; they simply accept that there are certain tasks they cannot do and live with that reality. Individuals in this group have made no attempt to compensate for poor skill development.

Andrew, a 34-year-old telesales operator, was typical. He made various mistakes in his work but was fortunate (or perhaps unfortunate) enough to have colleagues who accepted his errors and corrected them without bringing them to his attention. This situation changed when his line manager retired and was replaced by someone who had experience of working with dyslexics. The new supervisor recognised typical dyslexic patterns in Andrew's behaviour and arranged for him to be assessed. The assessment established that Andrew was dyslexic, which came as a complete surprise to him. Andrew had managed to live in ignorance of his condition because he had, from his early schooldays, experienced environments in which few intellectual demands were made of him. Throughout his schooling his teachers apparently paid little attention to his academic performance. Strangely, perhaps, he experienced the same response in his place of work. This disinterest allowed him to carry on without developing a conscious awareness of his weaknesses.

Level 2

People at this level realise that they have specific weaknesses but have not developed methods of compensating for their difficulties. They may not be aware that they are dyslexic; when asked to explain their predicament they may attribute the cause to a poor education, low motivation or other external factors. Their most obvious difficulties are likely to be with reading, writing and spelling. People in this group may have quietly accepted their limitations or may have, in frustration, anger and distress, learned to live with them.

> Paul, an unemployed 29-year-old man, was typical. He was unable to read or write and had accepted his condition as the product of low intelligence. A girlfriend persuaded him to have an assessment, during which he detailed a remarkable list of activities that he was unable to master. Although he was of average intelligence he had made no attempt to develop strategies for coping with some fairly basic requirements and was quite open about his weaknesses.

Level 3

Dyslexics at this stage of awareness are similar to those at level 2 insofar as they acknowledge their weaknesses. They differ in terms of their response: this group is made up of people who, albeit unconsciously, develop strategies to improve their performance and overcome their difficulties.

> Mike, a 37-year-old cabinet maker, suspected that he was dyslexic and after reading about the condition concluded that he was. Nearly two years after he first decided this he came for assessment. He was very well informed about his condition and wanted help to improve his memory and his reading, writing and spelling. Mike was unassuming, rather nervous and quite self-effacing. He viewed himself as a failure and, despite the fact that he had received praise for his work, he laboured under the belief that he was performing poorly. He was anxious to acquire skills which in fact he had already acquired. Like many adult dyslexics, Mike judged his ability against extremely high standards, assuming that they were the norm.

Level 4

People at this level are exercising some control over their lives and tend to be the most successful of the four groups. The difference between people in this group and those at level 3 is that, in developing strategies, they are fully aware that they are involved in a process of making themselves more effective in terms of their study, their work or their lives generally. This awareness allows them to experiment with new strategies and variations of those they have already mastered.

> Anthony, a 31-year-old computer programmer, was diagnosed as dyslexic when he was 20 and immediately applied himself to developing memory strategies. He mastered a number of techniques and by the time he was 22 he could perform feats of memory that most people could not match. His ability to recall large quantities of material resulted from his use of visual memory. Anthony had experienced considerable difficulties during his schooldays; his teachers had apparently not identified his dyslexia and had more or less given up on him. Nevertheless he managed to gain two GCE 'A' levels (English literature and history) by working much harder than his peers, by focusing on organisation and by using memory aids. He was, however, unaware of the significance of these strategies; he was at that time at level three. Anthony decided to take a degree in computer science when he was 24. He was able to examine the strategies he had used during his GCE 'A' level studies and plan more effective strategies for his degree level work. He graduated when he was 28 and within months of graduating secured employment as a computer programmer.

Counselling at four levels

The starting point for any helper working with a dyslexic is to determine at which level the client is functioning. This information determines the intervention strategy. Without this there is the danger that genuine differences in need will go unnoticed and standard interventions will be applied as if adult dyslexics constitute a homogeneous group.

Level 1

Adults who are unaware of their dyslexia and who have not developed compensatory strategies to overcome their inefficiencies are frequently the product of a school and home environment that has focused on their weaknesses rather than their strengths. These people may have natural abilities which remain hidden or undeveloped because they have never been stretched intellectually or academically. There are cases of bright and very able dyslexics who were, during their school years, put in classes with children of low intelligence. Such experiences can mislead individuals, as well as the teachers and parents, regarding the true nature and extent of their intelligence. An analogy can be drawn with a high jump competition: if the rail is fixed at 1 m those who can jump 2 m will not be identified. Similarly, dyslexics who can potentially achieve a great deal, but who were only ever expected to achieve a little, may never risk pushing up the rail to test themselves.

By definition, people at level 1 are not going to seek help to improve their situation. There are, however, a number of ways in which such people are identified. A change in personal or working life increases the likelihood of dyslexia coming to light. A new relationship, parenthood, a new boss, a job change or redundancy can all be the source of someone realising that an individual is dyslexic. Career counsellors, particularly those who use general aptitude tests, are well placed to spot untapped talents. Counsellors may be alerted by a seeming discrepancy between a client's verbal and conceptual skills and their level of practical functioning.

Whatever precipitates the identification of dyslexia in someone at level 1, the response from the person identified will usually be a mixture of shock, denial, fear and anxiety.

Level 2

The reaction of someone at level 1 is in stark contrast to the probable reaction of a person at level 2: in this case the typical response is a mixture of relief, anger and happiness. People at level 2 have frequently experienced great frustration because of their inability to deal with basic tasks such as reading and writing, at acceptable levels. Many may have been written off by teachers, peers and family as lacking intelligence. After prolonged exposure to persistent messages that they are intellectually inferior they come to accept that explanation for their weaknesses. The eventual identification of their dyslexia may result from the same set of circumstances as for people at level 1, but someone at this stage is more likely to be identified because they have sought help to improve their weaknesses. An adult whose reading and writing skills are weak may eventually go to adult literacy classes; a decision which, if the teacher is sufficiently well trained to recognise the signs, may lead to the identification of dyslexia as the cause of their difficulties.

On finding that there is an alternative explanation, one that is less damning and offers them some hope, they are frequently overcome with a strong mixture of emotions. Their reaction to a positive diagnosis is not the surprise of someone who did not know that they could jump any higher but the relief of someone who has, usually for a long time, wanted to 'raise the bar'.

These two distinct groups of adults respond differently to the information that they are dyslexic. There are, however, some similarities in their responses. People from both groups are, on diagnosis, likely to be confused and disoriented and to disbelieve the information they are given. The questions clients ask and the comments they make illustrate these sentiments:

- 'How could I be dyslexic (for 5, 10, 20 years) and not know it?' (confusion).
- ' What does it mean and where do I go from here?' (disorientation).
- 'I can't be dyslexic, I went to a good school, they would have told me' (disbelief).

The counselling skills required to help these two types of people include those of the generalist counsellor such as active listening and careful observation to enable them to deal with their transition. Professional who finds themselves in the position of helping dyslexics should, therefore, acquire such skills.

Level 3

Adult dyslexics at level 3 who have developed, albeit unconsciously, some compensatory strategies to overcome weaknesses may still be coping with the complexity of emotions that were described earlier. Although they know the origin of their difficulties and have gone some way to overcoming them, they still lack the key to complete mastery over the condition: they have not achieved 'control'. This lack of adequate control can come to light in various ways: it may happen that a person's 'competence' in one task can lead others to expect that they will be able to complete other tasks for which they have not developed appropriate strategies. This situation is quite common. People at level 3 are often anxious about situations developing in which they will be unable to cope. This fear is made worse by the fact that others assume that they will be able to cope. Often they stay in the same job for a very long time, fearing change.

The input from a counsellor should be to help the dyslexic to understand and confront, assertively, the way other people perceive them. This point is well illustrated by the following case study.

Malcolm was a 43-year-old video producer who, following an industrial accident, could no longer run his own production business. He was offered a lecturing post in a college and, although happy in principle, he was terrified at the prospect of reading essays and answering students' questions. He had a very supportive wife who was not fully aware of her husband's difficulties with working memory. She knew he had a tendency to forget what he was doing but she explained this away as absent-mindedness caused by preoccupation with work. Malcolm had for many years allowed his wife to believe that he was simply absent-minded. His negative experiences as a child dyslexic determined that he was not going to be identified as a dyslexic when he had the choice of a less emotive description for his behaviour. Although this had been a convenient way of dealing with his weaknesses for many years, it was now adding to his problems. The intervention that helped him was a discussion of the nature of his relationship with his wife and the responsibility he had to inform her fully of circumstances that affected her and their family. Malcolm took part in exercises involving visualisation and role-playing, after which he was able to explain to his wife his dyslexia, his fear of failure and (importantly) his reasons for hiding it from her and the family. This breakthrough focused Malcolm's attention on how he had developed strategies, how effective they were, where they failed and how he could improve on them: the first steps towards level 4 were taken.

Level 4

Typically, it is the secondary symptoms of people who are at level 4 which are the overriding problem. The case of Anthony (described earlier) is a good example of someone who has very efficiently dealt with all of his primary problems but who is left with secondary symptoms such as low self-esteem and a lack of confidence, which he has not overcome. The requirement of a counsellor in this situation is heavily weighted in favour of 'generalist' expertise. There is, however, often the need to examine the way a dyslexic is compensating and to ensure that it is efficient. This requires specialist knowledge and can often be a sensitive topic. Many adults at level 4 have invested much time in developing their methods; they naturally feel proud of their achievements and respond with indignation to any suggestions that they could improve on them.

One dyslexic who had achieved conscious compensation developed the habit of preparing for shopping trips in his local supermarket by writing out cheques in advance of when they would be needed, while relaxed, in his own time, at home. However, he was suddenly faced with an unexpected request by the till operator to write out a cheque by hand because the automatic printer was not in action. Knowing that the till operator and the customer behind him would be watching him write out the cheque he panicked, abandoned the trolley and his family – he and his family had no food for the weekend.

Feelings of embarrassment, self-deprecation and helplessness are often the problems presented to a helper by people at level 4. They often report living in fear that at any time they could be 'found out'.

When working with dyslexics at this level the most helpful thing that can be done is to assist them to gain insight into their cognitive functioning so that they can assess for themselves whether what they do consciously is effective. Exploration of the strategies they use and finding ways of transferring strategies to other situations/tasks may be an appropriate starting point for an intervention with a dyslexic who has already developed many ways of compensating. Intervention of this kind is, in effect, a training role and will be discussed in more detail in the Chapter 5.

If the particular requirements and probable demands on counsellors from people at the four levels are borne in mind, the general nature and extent of the difficulties that arise when adult dyslexics are counselled and the type of assistance from which they will benefit can be examined. The stages in the four-level model represent a sequence of personal development that dyslexics can be helped to work through.

The purpose of any helping intervention can be to assist an adult dyslexic to progress through these stages to the point at which they successfully compensate and are able to fulfil their potential. This is an admirable goal but there is need for caution. Dyslexic people vary widely in terms of their own understanding of their condition and their ability to function. Helping a dyslexic adult move from, for instance, a stage at which they are conscious of their difficulties to one at which they feel competent and confident can be satisfying for both the client and the person working with them. However, if intervention is to be truly effective, it is crucial that someone in a counselling role pause to ask themselves 'What is the purpose of my intervention?' and 'Is it appropriate for this particular individual?'.

The aim must be to enable a dyslexic to function effectively in one or other context. This may be their current one or one they are working towards. Care should be taken to try to effect change only if people appear to have the psychological resources to deal with it, or if they are aware of and prepared for the possible consequences. This is a delicate issue because with experience a counsellor knows that there will be some effects which a client will not be able to anticipate. For example, in many marriages or close personal relationships a non-dyslexic will often be covering up for their dyslexic partner. As the dyslexic's self-awareness and confidence develops, the balance of dependency within the relationship will drastically alter: the implications of this are obvious.

Unfortunately, some dyslexics have been moved by their 'helper' from lack of awareness about their dyslexia (through formal diagnosis or just a casual remark) to an acute self-consciousness of their abilities, which they now construe as a 'problem' made worse by having been given written evidence of this in the form of a professional assessment. A diagnosis of dyslexia without further support, or given out of the context of the client's awareness and understanding so that they do not realise that they can move to a stage of greater competence, is as serious as giving someone a medical diagnosis without offering treatment. Certainly, some of the secondary difficulties that dyslexics suffer stem from having been given inappropriate 'help' in the past. There are those for whom heightened awareness of their difficulties and lack of knowledge or insight as to how they can overcome them has caused unnecessary distress, serious psychological problems and even mental breakdown. It is therefore important that a counsellor/helper acknowledges the risks of inappropriate intervention.

Although the development path for dyslexics can create feelings of vulnerability, shake their self-identity, cause repercussions in their personal life, their relationships with others and their work, it can also excite self-development and enlightenment and facilitate practical success. Anecdotal accounts of dyslexics who have been able to take control of their development, together with results of independent research, support the notion that it is possible for someone who is dyslexic to move from an existence of frustration and low achievement to competence, confidence and success.

There are many professional groups who, in the course of their work, will be required to provide adult dyslexics with help and guidance. Inevitably such contacts will demand some basic counselling skills. Many people working with dyslexic individuals, be they medical practitioners, personnel managers, social workers or teachers, will require counselling skills. In certain cases it may be appropriate to refer the client to a psychologist or trained counsellor, but in many cases the reality is that no referral can be made and therefore it is wise to have some knowledge of what is required.

Requirements of counsellors

More important than the theoretical stance or knowledge underpinning skills is an understanding of both the primary and secondary difficulties experienced by dyslexics. In presenting the four-level model, the aim is to provide a foundation for anyone helping a dyslexic. Used as a structure by the helper, this model will allow intervention appropriate for the client, while at the same time allowing them to retain their working style and to operate within the constraints on time and resources.

Level 1

The types of skill required to help dyslexics at level 1 are both general, in that qualities such as empathy are important, and specialist, in that a knowledge is required of what dyslexia is and, should the client need assessment or training, where assistance can be sought if the helper is not qualified to continue the intervention.

Level 2

Dyslexics at level 1 seeking help are typically grappling to make sense of things external to them, such as other people's reactions or comments.

Those at level 2 are typically more inward-looking and feel that there is something about them that is amiss. The focus of an intervention for someone helping dyslexics at level 2 will therefore be different. A helper dealing with such a case will typically be enabling the dyslexic to deal with their own emotional responses to their situation. Often the dyslexics feel that they have been misjudged by others and they are very angry. They are generally confused because they are aware of their difficulties but have not yet understood the nature of their dyslexia; they are not compensating and are distressed by their symptoms. Clients at this level will include those who have recently been diagnosed 'dyslexic'.

Level 3

Dyslexics at level 3 require assistance in other ways. A helper could usefully draw on counselling skills and a variety of therapeutic approaches as well as the knowledge and ability to explain what dyslexia is. Often the change of circumstances have thrown the client into sudden confrontation with their dyslexia. They may have coped with their situation to date but are suddenly unable to do so. Furthermore, a person's 'competence' at a task for which they have effective compensation strategies may have led to them being required to do other tasks which, to the outsider, seem clearly within their competence but which in fact are not. The dyslexic at this level is often overawed by the fear of being unable to cope in a future situation. This can be exacerbated when the expectations of other people, including family and friends, are too high. A helper dealing with this type of case would need to assist the dyslexic to learn how to deal with other people's perceptions of them.

Level 4

Generally, people at level 4 are competent and usually successful. However, on occasion they will seek counselling, often because they are experiencing some kind of transition in life and need reassurance. Counselling should focus on this and must provide objective feedback about the issues they raise.

Chapter 5
Dealing with dyslexia: strategies and solutions

Basic principles

Dyslexia is an inefficiency in working memory and dyslexic people need to learn in ways that compensate for this. By using methods that suit their learning style they can overcome many of their difficulties. There are three basic principles which, if adopted, can enable a dyslexic to become more efficient: learning should be

- manageable;
- multisensory; and
- make use of memory aids.

These are referred to here as the three Ms.

Making it manageable

To accommodate their limited memory skills dyslexics need to make any material being learned or any task more manageable. For example, series of numbers can be made more manageable by reducing them to smaller units: the sequence 5, 9, 8, 3, 6, 2 would become 59, 83, 62. A dyslexic is able to deal better with these units than the original; this is why most of us reduce seven-digit telephone numbers to three numbers followed by four numbers.

Making it multisensory

The effectiveness of multisensory teaching/learning has been referred to in Chapter 1. Essentially, it compensates for the dyslexic's inefficient working memory. The pathways to the memory are the senses; the more one uses at a time the more direct and powerful the input. Simple examples of this are learning a foreign language in its country of origin or watching a television programme rather than listening to the radio.

Making use of memory aids

To facilitate recall it is important that the dyslexic learns how to use memory aids such as mnemonics for irregular words and factual material. Visual imagery can be particularly powerful.

The above principles can be applied to everything dyslexics need to learn or do to help them overcome their inefficiencies. They can be applied in training and teaching: dyslexics have, for example, been helped to improve organisation by examining how they might make tasks more manageable and multisensory and by considering what memory aids they can use. Avoiding clutter on a desk makes dealing with the task to hand more manageable; reading material aloud or recording it on audiotape and playing it back can make it multisensory; using visible year planners, calendars and notice boards can both make organisation multisensory and provide memory aids.

Training

In work with adult dyslexics brainstorming can provide a useful way of generating solutions to particular problems. Brainstorming involves thinking about as many solutions as possible, first without making a judgement about them and then evaluating the feasibility of each. It can be particularly useful if the possible solutions are considered within the framework of the principles outlined above.

Being able to take control of situations is very important to a dyslexic but stress undermines the ability to function effectively. It can, therefore, be very beneficial if training courses include the teaching of simple relaxation techniques. Each training session should begin and end with a relaxation exercise.

Relaxation techniques are well documented and include the following:

- Progressive relaxation – focusing on the major muscle groups of the body; group by group the person tenses and then relaxes (e.g. 'Focus on your right foot, tense it, hold the tension, now relax it).
- Visualisation – producing feelings of calm and well-being by training people to use the right half of their brain to produce pictures in their minds of themselves in safe, warm and comforting environments (e.g. 'You can now see yourself lying on a warm beach and you can feel the heat of the sun on your body').
- Deep breathing, which stimulates relaxation and reduces stress and anxiety.

The above techniques are well-established, widely used stress-reduction methods. There are many explanations of how they achieve their results. The simplest is that they reduce the activity of the nervous system and therefore the body's resources are preserved, preventing it from becoming run down with the consequences of ill health. Relaxation techniques reduce activity in that part of the nervous system which prepares the organism for flight or fight. The techniques relax muscles and, because muscular relaxation is incompatible with anxiety, the latter it is reduced in its intensity.

The following examples from a training course illustrate how these methods can be integrated. At the first meeting of a group, participants were asked to list their concerns. The following, which are typical of the issues which arise, were listed:

- having the confidence to progress;
- feelings of inferiority;
- communication (both verbal and written) problems;
- time keeping;
- remembering to do things;
- lack of organisation;
- dealing with large volumes of reading;
- concentration;
- noticing spelling errors.

Participants were asked to focus on one of these issues and a brainstorming session followed. The solutions generated were then classified according to the 3 Ms.

Spelling problems

Eric ran his own office cleaning company. As an exercise in quality control he used to visit sites after the staff had finished their work and inspect what had been done. Where there were problems he needed to leave notes. However, because he had a good deal of difficulty with spelling he found that he needed to telephone his wife to ask her how to spell even simple words. He did not have a major problem with reading, so the suggestion was that he prepare a form that listed all the jobs needing completion on a particular site. He then needed only to place a check mark against any tasks that had not been completed satisfactorily and leave it for his staff. This made his job more manageable in that he no longer needed to write; made it multisensory because he had a visual list to work from; and provided him with a valuable memory aid in that it meant he had a reminder of the areas he should be checking himself.

Problems with left and right

Remembering left and right quickly is a difficulty sometimes raised by adult dyslexics. How this was resolved for another participant is demonstrated in the following case study.

Jenny had a major problem with distinguishing between right and left. As part of her job she needed to visit various factories and was usually the driver, with her colleague giving directions. We brainstormed a number of possible solutions, which included wearing a ring on her left hand, attaching a piece of tape to one side of the steering wheel, having the letters L and R marked on the dashboard of the car. The final solution was to have a red air freshener hanging at the right-hand side of the windscreen. This made the task more manageable in that it was in her line of sight and she did not need to look elsewhere or do something like feel for a ring; it made it multi-sensory in that she had something she could see and it acted as a memory aid.

Improving concentration

An inability to concentrate, probably a direct result of inefficient working memory, is a commonly reported difficulty. Concentration can be made more manageable by working for short periods because this places fewer demands on working memory. Further, theories of memory tell us that we remember best the things we learnt first and the things we learnt most recently: working for short periods is therefore much more effective. The best guide as to the optimal length of a study period is to ask someone how long they are able to concentrate. People will express surprise when approval is given for what they consider to be a fairly short period of time. However, an explanation of the benefits of working for short periods will enable them to become more comfortable with the idea. Concentration can be made more manageable by working in a place where distractions are at a minimum. Studying is made more effective by using multisensory strategies such as watching videotaped material.

Organisational problems

Dealing with organisation is a common problem. Adult dyslexics need to work very hard at organising themselves. They may have even more difficulty when they have to organise others as well. The application of the three Ms can provide a solution; by focusing on one specific task, usually the simplest, they can make organisation more manageable. When efficiency in dealing with a number of small tasks is improved the ultimate goal of becoming better organised will be achieved.

Improving memory

As a dyslexic person's fundamental area of weakness is in memory, training in the use of appropriate memory aids is essential. Some people will need to be taught very basic memory strategies, others will have their own. One way of establishing how people remember is to ask them about things they can recall and how they do this. The technique that they are employing can be identified and applied to other tasks. As well as having inefficient working memory skills, dyslexics often lack confidence in their ability to remember, which exacerbates their difficulties. It is, therefore, very important to focus on simple memory strategies. Many standard techniques are quite complex and dyslexics sometimes find these difficult to learn and apply. For example, a popular strategy for remembering people's names is to associate a physical characteristic with the name. Sometimes dyslexics fear that they may make the wrong association, causing even more embarrassment than forgetting the name. A simpler way of remembering a person's name is to say it frequently: when, for example, somebody introduces themselves as Michelle, one would respond by saying 'Pleased to meet you, Michelle', following this with a question such as 'So, Michelle, whereabouts are you from?'.

Distortion of perspective

Adult dyslexics often have a distorted perspective of what is the norm and may have higher expectations of their skills than they should. It is therefore helpful to provide a realistic comparison of their level of competence in specific areas with that of other people. One man, for example, expressed concern that he was unable to write down names and addresses. He was encouraged to find out for himself whether other people have this problem and he concluded that it is not uncommon and that asking people to write down their name and address is acceptable.

Teaching

The teaching programmes that are effective with dyslexics are described in detail elsewhere; see Thomson (1990). The basic principles outlined above apply to the teaching of literacy skills. The common component of the specialist programmes for dyslexics is that they are structured and phonetically based, making the language more manageable. A knowledge and understanding of the rules and logic underlying language make it easier to manage. Multisensory methods are an integral part of the teaching programmes, making learning more powerful. Memory aids, such as mnemonics and visual imagery, are incorporated as a way of improving recall. The programmes in use have been designed for dyslexic children and require modification in their content and presentation when working with adults: the basic approach derived from the work of Gillingham and Stillman (1969) has, however, been shown to be effective with adult dyslexics (Guyer and Sabatino, 1989; Kitz and Nash, 1992).

It is particularly important that tutors acknowledge that they are working with adults. Working on a one-to-one basis is essential, at least initially, because many people will need to overcome their self-consciousness before they can feel comfortable with groups. There are, however, benefits in adults working together (for example, their shared experience can contribute to understanding and motivation). A great deal of sensitivity is required when deciding who should work with whom. An adult should never be paired with a child because they find it humiliating; the anger one young man expressed about an occasion when he arrived at a teaching centre to find that he was having a lesson with a 7 year old is entirely understandable. People should work with others who are at more or less the same level in terms of the development of their literacy skills. Teachers need to be able to respond to each individual's needs and require a great deal of flexibility.

Klein (1991) describes three essential criteria for establishing a successful learning programme:

1. It must be completely relevant to the student's individual needs and goals.
2. It should give students immediate (or almost immediate) experience of success.
3. It should enable students to participate in, and eventually take charge of, their own learning.

Adults are prompted to seek help with their literacy difficulties for a number of reasons: there are people who have problems with basic literacy and who have been prompted to seek help because their young children expect them to read books to them; others have been prompted by a fear of being 'found out'; others have developed skills that have enabled them to cope for most of their lives but promotion or the demands of undertaking further education have revealed inadequacies.

Life is a process of transitions; from school to college or work and then from one organisation to another. Each of these moves places demands on reading comprehension, written expression and organisational skills. Gerber et al. (1990) advanced this as one explanation for the fact that, in their survey of adults with learning disabilities, a quarter or more reported an ever-increasing difficulty with aspects of literacy skills.

Adults who have summoned up courage to seek help frequently have high expectations and it is therefore important to set realistic goals. For example, there are those who will never achieve average literacy skills; this should be made clear to them and strategies for overcoming this discussed. A tutor should establish why an individual needs tuition; this information can help with goal setting and indicate appropriate course content. People's daily living and work demands determine what literacy skills they need: some adults will be satisfied if they can achieve a basic functional level, others need to develop vocational or technical levels and there are those who, because of their work, need to be able to work at a professional level. Regardless of what skills are needed, it is imperative that appropriate materials are used. These include books with a high interest but low readability level and practical materials such as newspapers and magazines.

Part of goal setting is putting problems in context. Time and time again we hear adult dyslexics say 'my spelling is terrible!' but on examination their spelling skills are near to average. Further, their unsuccessful attempts at spelling are often very close to being correct. These facts should be pointed out, as such knowledge can improve confidence and self-esteem; it also suggests that quite rapid progress is possible.

Essential for every dyslexic person is the development of efficient learning skills. This may involve learning how to deal with basic tasks more effectively, or may entail developing advanced skills for those in demanding jobs or formal education. Efficient learning skills are fundamental to the achievement of managerial or professional effectiveness. Learning and study skills must be developed, refined and maintained throughout life. The many systematic approaches to learning are particularly important for a dyslexic because they make tasks more manageable. They should be an integral part of specialist tuition from the beginning. The earlier one acquires good skills and strategies, the less one has to unlearn later in life; a point that has implications for curriculum planning.

Some appropriate strategies relevant to particular areas are described below. These are not a universal panacea and it is important that they are 'customised' to suit individual needs. Dyslexic people should be encouraged to develop their own learning style, as often they will have found by trial and error what suits them best.

General learning skills

One of the best known and oldest systematic approaches to study skills is known as SQ3R (Cheek and Cheek, 1983). This method follows five procedural steps: *survey; question; read; recite; review*. It involves first *surveying* introductory statements, headings and summaries in an attempt to grasp the main idea of material. The survey step also includes specific attention to diagrammatic aids. The learner then formulates *questions* about the material in an effort to identify the purpose of reading it. This includes who, what, where, how and why questions. The third step involves *reading* the material and attending specifically to the questions generated. Upon completion of the reading, the reader should then attempt to answer the questions without direct reference to the material. Finally, they *review* the material and any notes compiled during the reading to verify their answers. Writing down the questions derived can ensure that the process is even more effective as it makes it multisensory. It has also been suggested that dyslexic students write their answers to the questions as soon as they are found, rather than wait until the entire selection has been read, as this makes it more manageable (Hoover, 1989). Some dyslexic people find SQ3R difficult to use: Devine (1981) has suggested that in such cases alternatives such as OARWET (*o*verview, *a*chieve, *r*ead, *w*rite, *e*valuate, and *t*est) and OK5R (*o*verview, *k*ey idea, *r*ead, *r*ecord, *r*ecite, *r*eview and *r*eflect) might be more suitable.

Another approach, known as PANORAMA (Edwards, 1973), involves three stages. In the first, the purpose for reading the material is determined and the most appropriate reading rate is decided upon; questions about the material based upon the headings therein are formulated. In the second or intermediate stage, the material is surveyed to determine the organisational format of the selection. The student reads the materials and takes notes relevant to the formulated questions. The final stage involves memorising the material with the aid of outlines and summaries. It includes an evaluation component to determine what should be retained.

Comprehension

Reading comprehension is one of the most important skills. Comprehension generally (Faas and D'Alonzo, 1990), and reading comprehension in particular (Spadafore, 1983), has been described as the best predictor of successful transition from school to employment and thus warrants particular attention in learning or study skills programmes.

Appropriate reading comprehension strategies include the more general approaches described above as well as specific ones such as RARE (Gearheart et al., 1986). This strategy emphasises reading for specific purposes and involves four stages: *r*eview the questions at the end of the reading selection; instruct students to *a*nswer all questions already known; *r*ead the selection; and finally, *e*xpress the answers and obtain those to the questions students were unable to answer initially.

PQ4R (*p*review, *q*uestion, *r*ead, *r*eflect, *r*ecite, *r*eview; Cheek and Cheek, 1983) is a variation on the SQ3R method and is designed to assist students to become more discriminating and systematic readers. It is similar to SQ3R but the *reflect* element has been added. This emphasises that the student should reread various parts of the selection which were initially unclear.

Listening skills and note-taking

Being able to follow training courses and presentations means that dyslexic people need to become good listeners. Systematic approaches to this include TQLR (tuning in, questioning, listening, reviewing). This suggests that listeners must be ready for verbal communication, that they should attempt to identify the position the speaker will take and then listen for the actual stance taken. As the material is presented, the listener should generate questions about the topic and, at the end of the training session, should mentally review the material to ensure that the important points are remembered.

Note-taking can be a particularly difficult task for a dyslexic as it places a heavy load on working memory. The mind mapping techniques developed by Buzan (1974) can be helpful in this area. Taking notes in mind map form allows one to listen discerningly to the content of a training session or presentation – as opposed to taking reams of notes without learning anything.

Checking and proofreading

It is often difficult for dyslexics to check their own work. Proofreading one's own work is difficult because one anticipates what should be, rather than what actually is, written. Reading something from right to left can be helpful in that it takes away meaning and focuses attention on the individual words. Systematic approaches such as COPS (checking capitalization of letters; examining the overall appearance; punctuation; checking spelling; Schumaker et al., 1981) exist.

Examinations

The systematic method SCORER refers to schedule time, search for clue words, omit difficult questions, read carefully, estimate time for answers and review the work. When using this strategy students begin by planning time for taking the test. They should review the entire test initially to identify easy and difficult items, varying point values per item and numbers of items. Students should also search to identify clue words used in different items such as 'usually', 'never' or 'sometimes'. In true–false tests, the words 'usually' and 'sometimes' often indicate a true statement, while the words 'never' or 'always' frequently pertain to false items (Hoover, 1989). As students complete the test, the more difficult items are left until last. These should be marked for easy identification. Careful reading of the test questions and directions is also necessary. Also, for those items that require calculations, an estimate of the answer should precede actual calculation in an effort to eliminate obviously wrong answers and reduce careless errors. Once the test has been completed, each answer should be reviewed carefully. Highlighting key words when reading questions can make reading comprehension both manageable and multisensory.

The most difficult task dyslexics have to deal with is putting their ideas and thoughts on paper. Examples of difficulties with written expression have included undergraduates trying to write essays; a young woman working for a recruitment agency who took considerably longer to write short reports than her colleagues; an ex-army officer, working in public relations, who could sell people ideas over the telephone but had great difficulty writing reports of the conversation.

Even for dyslexics who have, to a large extent, compensated for their difficulties and are normal readers, written expression is a very difficult task. The most effective way of making written expression more manageable is through planning. In particular, the mind mapping techniques referred to above (Buzan, 1974) are very effective ways of making writing a report more manageable. The first task is to get down the important ideas, concepts and words without giving thought to their organisation. Following this the results are organised by grouping and numbering them. The writer then structures the material by establishing links and using this as a plan. However, some people prefer a more conventional linear type approach to planning and it is thus important to consider individual differences.

Complementary skills

As well as improving their literacy and learning skills, dyslexic people need to develop what can be called 'complementary skills'. This involves exploiting the wide range of technological aids currently available. In their study of successful adult dyslexics Gerber, Ginsberg and Reiff (1992) found this to be an important factor in determining the success of dyslexics. Many dyslexics continue to have residual difficulties in areas such as spelling. Learning to type and use a word processor can provide them with a long-term solution: as well as enabling them to produce better presented work and check their spelling, it can improve the organisation of their written work. The editorial capacity of a word processor is probably its main advantage. Even a slow typist has only to produce one draft of a document, which can then be edited. Word processing demands less of working memory because it makes written expression more manageable, i.e. the writer can focus on content because neatness and legibility are no longer a concern and spelling and reorganisation can be improved once a first draft has been completed.

Dyslexic people can also take advantage of electronic organisers and spelling checkers. Electronic organisers can be particularly helpful, if one is interested in using such technology, because many of them have a spell-check capacity as well as an electronic calculator. They can also be helpful with organisation, timekeeping and storing information. Some people will, however, be more comfortable with an old-fashioned diary or a Filofax. It is very important to encourage dyslexic people to choose the aids that suit them best.

Many dyslexics will always have a gap between their verbal ability and their ability to put their ideas on paper. The most effective way of bridging this gap can be through learning to give dictation and relying on the services of an audio typist. When computers we can talk to become more generally available, dyslexics will have the perfect solution.

A cassette recorder can be a very valuable aid in giving dictation and as a note-taking device. Dyslexic people should take a cassette recorder into learning situations such as training courses and presentations. Ideally, the machine should have a counter on it so that they can note down the number at which specific points are made. Listening to the whole tape again can be very effective but being selective means that they do not have to 'attend' the session twice. If they have taken notes in sketch form, a first piece of revision can then be to add detail by reference to the tape as well as to text books.

Aids such as telephone answering machines can also be an asset. For some dyslexics taking a telephone message can be a nightmare. However, recording it on an answering machine can make life easier.

A good secretary or personal assistant can often be the most effective aid to organisation. Nevertheless, some people are reluctant to delegate in this way and often it is important to help them feel more comfortable with the idea. One man who had recently become self-employed was finding it difficult to deal with the organisational demands of his business. He was losing business because he did not follow up calls and was experiencing cash flow problems because he neglected to send out accounts. When asked why he did not have a secretary or a personal assistant, he said that he believed he should be able to do it all for himself. When it was pointed out that most professional people rely on secretarial support and he might be better devoting his time to what he was good at he seemed happier. Several months later he had employed someone, business was on the up and he was generally feeling much more relaxed.

Special arrangements in further education and training

One of the most difficult situations a dyslexic person has to deal with is a formal examination. Often, even those who have overcome the worst aspects of their difficulties still have problems with reading comprehension and are slow at writing. Timed tests can be very difficult to cope with, because stress exacerbates memory difficulties. Increasingly in education and training special arrangements are being made for dyslexic students. Gilroy (1991) has made the following suggestions:

1. Use a tape recorder or a reader – to read the rubric and questions aloud.
2. Allow extra time, usually at least 30 min in a three-hour examination.

Ideally, extra time should be at the beginning rather than at the end of the examination so that the student can finish when everyone else does.
3. Use a combination of oral and written testing.
4. Allow a student to write out an examination paper then read it into a tape recorder.
5. Allow use of a word processor.
6. Produce duplicate copies of examination papers, which enables the students to see both sides of the paper at once.

Extra time

Making such special arrangements has been, and continues to be, a matter of controversy. Academics have expressed the concern that dyslexic students are being advantaged over their non-dyslexic peers, particularly by being given extra time to complete examinations. This is fuelled by the fact that there has been little systematic research on its effects.

One of the few systematic studies (Runyan, 1991) looked at the effects of extra time on reading comprehension among university students with and without learning disabilities. Her findings were that, on a reading comprehension task, students without a learning disability were able to perform up to their capability under timed-test conditions and there was little room for improvement, but those with learning disabilities were less able to perform up to their capabilities in timed conditions. However, they showed considerable improvement when allowed extra time. In other words, allowing extra time did not advantage them but minimised the impact of their learning disability. In this study the amount of extra time needed by learning disabled students was found to vary considerably, ranging from 4 to 29 min. The author concluded that this supported the idea that students with learning disabilities have varying rates of processing printed information and therefore a fixed amount of extra time for all students with learning disabilities on a standardised test may not be appropriate. Runyan also suggests that students should be given a specific amount of time according to their skills. However, further research is required into the amount of time needed to complete specific tasks and suitable procedures for assessing this. Until this information is available, dyslexics should be given a fixed amount of extra time.

Use of word processors

The use of word processors in examinations is a particularly contentious issue. This may simply be because of practical difficulties in ensuring that word processors and invigilators are available but, as the capabilities of computers are still widely misunderstood, there is possibly a fear that the candidate could access information to their advantage in an examination. Both problems could be overcome by having students sit their examination in a computing centre using a machine that is not their own. For many dyslexics the word processor has become their main way of communicating in writing. Those who have developed their typing skills to such an extent they can type as quickly as (or more quickly than) they can write by hand should be allowed to use a word processor. It will be their enduring way of dealing with written work and the one in which they can display their knowledge and learning most effectively. The formal examination system has not kept up with the available technology but eventually we hope that all students will be able to take examinations using a word processor.

Frequent reassessment

The fact that dyslexia persists and that even ostensibly successful people continue to have difficulties in areas such as reading comprehension and writing fluency has implications for the practice of reassessment. Regulations insist on frequent assessments. This means that people are being put through what amounts to a diagnostic assessment at regular periods, which is unnecessary. The dyslexic student who needs special arrangements when taking an examination at one stage of their education and training will need it at another. They will be no less intelligent, nor will they have 'grown out' of their dyslexia. The demands on and expectations of their skills will continue to increase. Although a full diagnostic evaluation is not warranted, in some cases (particularly where the use of a word processor is being requested) it might be important to re-examine a student's literacy skills. This would establish that such provision is justified and that they have the requisite complementary skills. It is also to the benefit of students as some tend to be a little naive. They do not realise that, under timed conditions, their typing speed may be too slow. Likewise, there are cases of difficulty with reading and writing such that it would be appropriate to provide an amanuensis. However, this is not a facility one can make use of without practice, as giving dictation is an acquired skill.

Chapter 6
The dyslexic at work

As outlined in Chapter 1, dyslexia is essentially an inefficiency in working memory. This can manifest itself as a variety of difficulties in a work setting.

Literacy

It appears that, because of their inefficient working memory, dyslexics have persisting problems with reading, writing and spelling. The prognosis for many dyslexics is that, provided that they are taught in a way which suits their learning style, they learn to read, write and spell as well as many adults. However, this is not always the case and the importance of literacy skills in securing and maintaining a job cannot be underestimated. The embarrassment faced by the dyslexic whose difficulties with literacy persist are encapsulated in the following abstract from a piece written (on a word processor) by a 34-year-old dyslexic male, William.

> ...It is a damning indictment of the British educational system that in the 1960s I left school virtually illiterate without one teacher realising this. No one was to know this when I applied for a job with my present employer. I would have failed at the first hurdle if I had not brought a list of past employers as I certainly could not spell their names. The first question I was asked after the interviewer read through my job application form was 'What job are you applying for?' This was the only question that I had omitted on the form because the three different versions I had scribbled in the palm of my hand did not look like anything I had recognised. I was not going to let this embarrassing fact be known to the interviewer. Hiding my anxiety I replied 'Well, what sort of jobs are you trying to fill?' and after some discussion he agreed that I should apply for the guard's job.
>
> My anxiety was to reach an all time high when I was taken into a room where I sat an entrance examination. A booklet was placed in front of me. It was opened at the first page and I was asked to answer the first question in the presence of the examiner. Each question had a choice of three answers – (a), (b) or (c) – and I had to tick the appropriate box for each question. I was

unable to read the questions and so had to resort to looking at the answers to guess the questions. I was unable to finish the questions because of my hidden handicap but nevertheless I passed the exam. It was six weeks later that I found myself in a classroom environment and subsequently had to employ a number of subterfuges in order to avoid detection.

William has held the job for which he applied since the episode he describes above. He has also received specialist tuition and, being bright, has made good progress. The anger and frustration felt by him are clearly evident in what he wrote. These emotions are common in adult dyslexics who, because of other people's ignorance and misunderstanding regarding the nature of dyslexia, are made to feel so embarrassed by their weaknesses that they feel forced '...to employ a number of subterfuges to avoid detection'. Adult dyslexics are frequently reluctant to admit to their illiteracy because of its association with stupidity. This can sometimes have dire consequences, as the following cases illustrate.

Jack was a police officer who had worked in the force for over 20 years. He was known by his colleagues as someone who was very conscientious; he took copious notes whenever he attended the scene of a crime or an accident and he kept a very detailed diary. This daily record contained his hour-to-hour activities, both on and off duty, for every day of the week and he had six such diaries for previous years. His friends interpreted his excessive note taking as nothing more than a habit acquired in the course of his work. Following an incident which involved him confronting an armed robber, and because of the resulting stress, he was transferred from 'walking the beat' to court duty. This new position required him to read aloud statements and other written material. Jack could manage to read only very slowly and he made many errors of pronunciation. He was frequently criticised by judges and other court officials for his slow and clumsy presentation. He was clearly unable to do this job and was given early retirement. Jack had managed to hide his difficulties with reading and writing from his colleagues, his friends and his family and as a result never received any help to overcome these difficulties – which eventually cost him his job. Furthermore, Jack had probably failed to progress in his career because of these difficulties; the strategy he employed was to avoid situations in which his poor reading and writing were a disadvantage.

For some people problems with literacy can result in them being on the other side of the law:

George left school illiterate and took a succession of jobs as a labourer, dish washer, factory hand and so on. At 35 he was a self-taught chef and was very successful. He was eventually offered and accepted a partnership in the business. However, after several months he was arrested and charged with fraud, his partner having been involved in 'shady' contracting and accounting. George's defence was that he could not have been a party to such activities as he was unable to read and write. Assessment established that he was in fact dyslexic and was still almost illiterate. He had spent his adult life covering up and relying on his wife to deal with his paperwork. As a result of evidence submitted to the court about his dyslexia, the charges against him were dismissed.

Some dyslexic people decide, as a result of experiencing difficulties with literacy at school or college, to adopt a strategy of avoidance, i.e. they give up trying to acquire the ability to read, write and spell and develop ingenious (and occasionally bizarre) ways of achieving their goals without exposing their illiteracy. This strategy frequently extends to choice of job or occupation. However, no matter how unimportant literacy skills appear to seem, it is nearly always the case that job performance and/or progression in an occupation requires some grasp of basic literacy. The case study below illustrates this.

David, a 25-year-old video production assistant, left school at 16 with no qualifications and a collection of school reports that consistently identified him as bright but lazy and uncooperative. Although some teachers made remarks about his handwriting being illegible, apparently none of them realised that he deliberately made it unreadable so that his very weak spelling and use of punctuation would not be detected. In fact, during his dyslexia assessment David demonstrated that he could write, if not neatly, certainly legibly. In the nine years between leaving school and seeking help for his dyslexia David had never attempted to improve his level of literacy; he simply found ways of manipulating other people to complete, on his behalf, tasks involving reading and writing. Thus, when making deposits in banks he would, squinting at the deposit slip, explain to the bank clerk that he had lost his spectacles and ask her to complete it for him. The 'lost spectacles' strategy was one David used frequently but it entailed him using many different banks because he was too scared to use it on the same person twice. In terms of work David was acknowledged as very creative and talented – so much so that his employers were encouraging him to do a day-release course at a local college. On two successive occasions David declined to take the opportunity, giving some plausible excuse each time. He realised, however, that this was holding him back and that progress with this company would not be possible unless he could take such courses. This realisation was his first step in a process that involved a dyslexia assessment, a course of training in literacy skills, study skills and memory improvement. David eventually enrolled on the video course and was successful. Interestingly, he discovered that he was by no means alone with his dyslexia; he reported that two other students in his class of 19 were also dyslexic. This is a rather high proportion but, if indeed there were 3 dyslexics in a class of 19, it could reflect the fact that many dyslexic people see working in video, films or television as an attractive choice because of the perceived low demands for literacy skills.

Literacy is so fundamental to modern society that it is highly unlikely that any job or profession could be found that did not require reading and writing to some degree. Although avoidance is an understandable response it is not always an appropriate solution and, in general, dyslexics who adopt this strategy experience a good deal of anxiety and guilt, as well as feelings of inadequacy.

Symbols and coding

We live in a world in which we are surrounded by symbols: traffic signs, filing systems, libraries, telephone directories, advertisements in newspapers and magazines, computing and informal conversations which frequently demand the decoding of symbols. Even finding the right toilet can be a problem when the pictorial representations used are not readily identifiable as male and female or when 'Sailors' and 'Mermaids' have been substituted for 'Men' and 'Women'. Decoding symbols is a demanding task for dyslexic people; even relatively common symbols such as the letters of the alphabet can cause difficulty. As Critchley (1978) points out, dyslexic people cannot rapidly consult a dictionary or a telephone directory and as a filing clerk they can be a failure. He mentions that one of his clients telephoned Directory Enquiries rather than spend ages searching through a telephone book, a very common occurrence.

Thus, given that many people with good memories report difficulty in dealing with symbols and abbreviations, it is hardly surprising that dyslexics can be lost in a world where this is an important skill. Remembering how certain coded functions available in the word-processing package used to type this manuscript are accessed is not easy, even for people who are not dyslexic! Some dyslexics working with computers almost write their own manual by entering the codes for operations in a separate indexed book. The following case study highlights some typical experiences of a dyslexic.

> Jane, a 23 year old, sought an assessment after she saw a television programme on adult dyslexia. She was an articulate young woman of obviously high intelligence who had good literacy skills. She was working as an interior designer and was already well established in this field. She was conscious of not having a degree whereas most of her colleagues did and so she was pursuing a degree course on a part-time basis. She was advised by one of her tutors, who noticed she had some difficulty with memory-related tasks, that she might be dyslexic. Assessment established that she was dyslexic.
>
> During the assessment interview Jane related a number of anecdotes which illustrate the problems of decoding acronyms. She related an event where a colleague had sent her an invitation to a small gathering, which she subsequently attended. She later discovered that the colleague was annoyed at a number of invited guests, including her, because they had failed to reply to the invitation. Jane could remember that there were some letters written on the invitation but could not recall what they were; when written down for her during the assessment interview she could make no attempt to decipher 'RSVP'. In a similar fashion she could not explain the meaning of 'ono' in an advertisement stating ' £450 ono'.

Regarding her college work, she had essays which had been marked by the lecturer with abbreviations that were a mystery to her. She did not realise that 'ss' indicated that here sentence structure needed attention, or that 'punt' indicated that her punctuation was at fault. Other difficulties she was experiencing included using a dictionary to look up the correct spelling of words, using a thesaurus to find alternative words and finding books in the library.

Jane was relieved to find firstly that she was not alone in her lack of ability to decipher abbreviations, codes and symbols and secondly that she could be trained to overcome this weakness to some extent. She eventually felt confident enough in her work to explain her dyslexia to close colleagues who accommodated her by explaining acronyms and abbreviations whenever they were used.

Organisation

Many dyslexic people have a general and fundamental weakness in organising information. Typically they have difficulty with organisation and so it is not unusual to find that dyslexics are late for meetings or that they forget such arrangements altogether.

Caroline was someone who had never been diagnosed as a dyslexic. She had well developed reading and spelling skills but found it difficult to put ideas on paper. It was, however, the difficulties she experienced in organising her working day which prompted her to seek advice.

Organising materials, such as papers or documents, in a logical order is another difficulty. In the case of a dyslexic whose work involves managing other people there can be considerable difficulties. It is, however, not necessarily the case that all dyslexics exhibit the lack of organisation described above. In a surprisingly large number of instances the basic weakness in organisational skills acts as a catalyst, leading some people to compensate by becoming exceptionally well organised. Thus, a person who was initially known for their lack of organisation may become so meticulous that every event is recorded in a diary. Their determination to plan and organise their activities results in them becoming very reliable. Paradoxically, it is the fact that they are so well organised that indicates they have a fundamental weakness in organisational skills.

The dyslexic person's weakness in terms of organisational skills is a direct result of their inefficient working memory. Organisation involves sequencing information and behaviours as well as keeping track of sets of instructions. For example, a receptionist needs to be able to hold in memory a sequence of instructions or facts long enough to organise them on paper, or she will not be able to accurately record telephone messages; a secretary asked to file papers needs to be able to locate the correct file if he is to keep the files organised; a dispatch rider needs to be capable of holding information about directions and routes and be capable of translating such information from maps into behaviours if she is to get to the destination. The case of Max illustrates how a lack of organisational skills can lead to significant difficulties in a work context.

Max, a 33-year-old solicitor, was made redundant when the housing market collapsed. He started his own practice and employed a part-time secretary for two days a week. Initially, because there was little business, this arrangement worked well but when business started to improve Max found that the two days of secretarial support was not enough. Being rather reluctant to employ a secretary full-time until he was financially better off he tried doing some of the office work himself. The result was that when the secretary came in she would spend most of her time looking for information that had been wrongly filed, changing appointments that had been incorrectly made and dealing with annoyed clients who had arrived to find they could not have their appointment. Max soon accepted that his involvement in the office work was counter-productive: it did, however, lead him to investigate his weakness and discover that he was dyslexic.

Organisation also involves sequential memory as it requires sequencing in several dimensions. This has implications for operating a keyboard or other machine having a different layout of controls, organising one's work and workload and for scheduling and organising others. Organising one's work and workload is a commonly reported difficulty. If people have trouble organising themselves, being promoted to a managerial position can be stressful as they then have to organise others as well. Alas, difficulties with work tasks deriving from poor sequential memory can often be misinterpreted: dyslexic people have reported accusations of laziness by their employers because they have forgotten to complete tasks. Sometimes they perform well because their poor memory is accommodated for in some way by the work environment:

Peter, aged 25, had held 27 jobs since leaving school. During the initial training period in a new job he did well. The close supervision and reminders enabled him to perform his duties well and employers were tolerant of his mistakes because he was new to the job. He found it much more difficult to cope when the supervision was reduced and so would leave. It was always easier for him to get another job while still employed and he was given good references. He presented for assessment as someone who was concerned about his poor memory, dyslexia never having been considered.

Peter's case not only illustrates the difficulties that a dyslexic person can experience but also gives clues about solutions. Supervision and reminders were acting as Peter's memory aids. He simply needed to develop his understanding of how these were helping and learn how to apply them on his own initiative.

The adult dyslexic's difficulties are not unidimensional; it is not simply a question of being disorganised, forgetful or having poor literacy skills. All of these factors can occur in a variety of combinations.

For example

> Yvonne is a clerical worker and over 20. She has five 'O' levels, including
> English language, although she was successful with this only at the fourth
> attempt. Her original choice of occupation was that of hotel receptionist but
> she was not very successful: in fact she was sacked from several different
> hotels before deciding on a career change. As a hotel receptionist she was
> very inefficient. She gave people the wrong keys to rooms, recorded mes-
> sages incorrectly and her accounting was chaotic. She changed her job, tak-
> ing up data processing, but found this difficult as well. The data she was
> entering into the computer bore little resemblance to that which she had
> been given. Although Yvonne can read and write as well as many adults, her
> spelling is a little weak, but her job difficulties did not stem from this: her
> dyslexia is responsible for poor performance with memory tasks and organi-
> sation.

What all the people mentioned above have in common is the fact
that they have been able to 'get by' to some extent. The difference in
their literacy skills is the result of factors such as better schooling. Further, they have developed strategies that have enabled them to overcome many of their difficulties, but as demands have increased they
began to struggle. They are people who have compensated unconsciously. This is common among adult dyslexics and for this reason the
problem is sometimes not identified until well into adulthood. It seems
that many cope quite well but reach a point in their lives at which their
dyslexia results in some kind of crisis. In a sense, the 'Peter Principle'
operates, i.e. we all eventually find our level of incompetence. For
example:

> Anthea is in her thirties. She has a lower second-class degree from a universi-
> ty, but had been expected to get an upper second. She has done very well
> with her career and now holds a senior management position. She has
> always suspected that she might be mildly dyslexic but has never been sure.
> It was weak spelling and lack of organisation in her examinations which was
> advanced for her failure to get a better degree. She was now finding that the
> demands of her current position were making her more acutely aware of her
> weakness in memory. She could not remember names of important people,
> the notes she took at meetings were scant and she could not therefore
> remember decisions which had been made. She was also having trouble
> organising her workload. Although she had no obvious written language dif-
> ficulty, psychological testing revealed that she had the inefficiency in work-
> ing memory and consequent sequencing problem which characterises
> dyslexia.

Being dyslexic does not mean that a person cannot progress, but it
usually indicates a need for them to develop new strategies for the tasks
that they are finding difficult. For example, Anthea was given advice on
memory and organisational strategies which might help her cope better
with the increased demands upon her. It does, of course, take time and

a reluctance to change jobs is common among dyslexics. This seems to stem from anxiety precipitated by having to develop new strategies and a fear of being 'found out'. It is often for this reason that people change jobs so frequently. Working as a temporary rather than a permanent employee is another way of avoiding being found out. Some people report that they appear to have to work much harder at tasks others take for granted and, as a result, find work more tiring.

The employer's role

A survey by Minskoff and Sautter (1987) of employers' attitudes towards people with learning disabilities revealed that employers have more reservations about employing the 'cognitively disabled' than they have about employing people with physical disabilities. This was attributed to a lack of understanding of, and experience with, conditions such as dyslexia. He concluded that intensive educational and public relations programmes for employers were necessary.

The least one can ask of an employer is an awareness of the possibility of there being a significant minority of dyslexics among their workforce. There will be those whose problems are obvious and relate to basic literacy skills, but as the cases described in this chapter illustrate, there will be those whose difficulties manifest themselves only subtly. Considerations of equity in employment contexts demand that employers go further than simply making themselves aware of the condition. An examination of literacy skills should be included in the selection process. Where selection tests are used it is important to ensure that the skills required to complete the tests successfully are similar to, not greater than, the skills required to do the job. In particular the use of timed tests needs careful consideration as these can unfairly discriminate against dyslexic people. Discrepancies between performance in particular areas should be explored further. The obvious conclusion is not always the correct one – difficulties with literacy do not necessarily mean lack of intelligence or education.

When an employer suspects that an employee might be dyslexic, he or she should recommend that confirmation be sought through formal assessment by a psychologist. This would lead to a diagnosis of the problem and would provide information about how the employee can be helped to overcome their difficulties and carry out their job more efficiently. Developing skills and strategies can take time and employers should be patient, allowing the dyslexic the opportunity to work out strategies for dealing with new tasks.

Dyslexics should not be discriminated against by employers or potential employers, though it may need to be acknowledged that their problems present an unwarranted risk in some occupations, particularly where safety depends on a memorised sequence. However, it should be remembered that it will have been more difficult for the dyslexic to have achieved the same qualifications as a non-dyslexic. Some dyslexics become very organised to deal with their lack of organisation; others appear to have excellent memories as they have worked on developing strategies. One of our clients is, in her twenties, one of the highest paid recently graduated surveyors in a well established firm. She checks all her calculations twice (but that would seem no bad thing). She certainly possesses a quality of determination which should commend her to any employer.

As well as in training, the basic principles (i.e. the three Ms described in Chapter 5) can be applied to work settings in the following way:

1. Training courses, presentations and instructional methods should incorporate multisensory techniques. The use of diagrams should supplement written or verbal explanations. Where possible, an explanation should be accompanied by a demonstration of 'how it's done'. Employees should be allowed and encouraged to practice behaviours as part of their learning and skill development.

2. When written material such as policies, procedures, rules and regulations is presented to employees, it should be presented in logical sequence with good indexation. Particularly important points should be highlighted in some way and, if summaries can be included, they should be. Special attention should be given to the readability level of such material; the use of jargon, technical terms and uncommon words should be avoided.

3. When a job or task involves following a sequence of steps, these should be set out clearly on a wall chart, manual or instruction sheet. Such information should include clear diagrams or pictures wherever possible.

Chapter 7
Career guidance

Approaches to counselling

A variety of competing, theoretical and practical approaches to career counselling have been developed. These include the simplistic trait factor approaches (Parsons, 1909), the social learning theory approaches (Krumboltz, 1976) and the developmental theories of Ginsberg (1972) and Super (1969).

Yost and Corbishley (1987) argue that, although there are contradictions between the various theories of career and career choice, there are nevertheless central themes which have implications for career counselling generally. These include the assumptions that:

- people make career decisions within the context of their lifetime of experiences;
- people have strong expectations of work and, therefore, the exploration of intra-personal satisfaction they expect or derive from work is important;
- there is a need for skills specific to job selection, acquisition and retention to be assessed or taught;
- there are personal, social and environmental factors which need to be explored as these can be a barrier to deciding on or pursuing a particular career.

On this basis, and in the absence of a comprehensive career theory, Yost and Corbishley take a pragmatic view and argue for a decision-making model which acknowledges the influence of the central themes of the various theories. A decision-making model, they argue, has the advantages of focusing on the established core of career choice – i.e. the centrality of decision making. Furthermore, it allows a good deal of flexibility, it is practically oriented and people perceive it as both relevant and worthwhile. The decision-making model of Yost and Corbishley involves eight steps:

1. *Initial assessment*, the aim of which is to gather personal and employment information about the client and to arrive, in collaboration with the client, at a feasible career counselling goal that the client is motivated to pursue.
2. *Self-understanding*. The client explores the values, interests, experience and abilities that relate to their present goal. In addition, assessment is made of psychological issues that may affect career counselling.
3. *Making sense of self-understanding data*. The information gathered in stage 2 is synthesised into a coherent set of statements which indicate the client's desired outcomes for a career choice. These will be used as a reference point in future stages. Personal and environmental barriers to success in pursuing the desired career are summarised.
4. *Generating alternatives*. Using the information acquired so far, counsellor and client develop a list of possible career alternatives without making any judgement about the value of the options.
5. *Obtaining occupational information*. Learning as much about each option as is necessary to make an informed choice. The list of options is narrowed.
6. *Making the choice*. The client makes a choice among options – any psychological problems that arise should be dealt with at this stage.
7. *Making plans to reach the career choice goal*. Contingency plans are worked out to handle any setbacks that might arise.
8. *Implementing plans*. The client takes whatever action is necessary to achieve the selected career goal. This could include further training or education, learning how to present oneself, both on paper and in person, to prospective employers and conducting a job search.

Career decisions and dyslexia

The issues that are involved in the career counselling of dyslexic people include some that are specifically related to dyslexia, and others which, while applicable to career counselling generally, are more pronounced for dyslexic people. Low self-esteem and lack of confidence are frequently encountered in career guidance work but these are much more common among, and significant for, dyslexics. Inefficient working memory is not usually encountered as a weakness needing attention in the course of a career counselling programme but will typically be a significant issue in counselling dyslexic people.

It is important to bear in mind that dyslexics may have decided to avoid certain areas of work, or focused on certain occupations, as a result of their dyslexia. As we saw in Chapter 6, such decisions are frequently based on assumptions that are not well founded in fact: assumptions, for example, that certain occupations, such as video production work, do not require literacy skills when they do or that certain occupations, such as the legal profession, are inappropriate for dyslexic people because they demand good levels of literacy. People with dyslexia are not automatically barred from jobs that require good levels of literacy; some dyslexics have overcome their literacy weaknesses and perform efficiently in such occupations whilst others can do so after specialised training. Thus, in carrying out career counselling of dyslexic people it is advisable to explore their reasons for expressing preferences for certain types of jobs. Such an exploration, combined with knowledge of their interests, skills, abilities and experience, can result in a successful match between a job and the person's knowledge, skills and abilities which might otherwise have been missed. Career counselling should focus on how a dyslexic can acquire strategies for coping with the demands of most jobs. It should not reinforce the false perception that there are large numbers of occupations that dyslexics should avoid. Furthermore, the possibility of return to some form of education or training should be explored: however, because it is likely that people's previous experience of learning might have been very negative, some work on improving confidence and self-esteem could be needed.

A television advertisement drawing attention to the plight of the disabled portrayed a physically handicapped man complaining that people too often see the wheelchair at the expense of the person. There is a similar risk with dyslexia, which is often thought of just as a difficulty or a weakness. It has been argued that we should talk about 'difference' rather than 'disability'. Further, it has been suggested that dyslexic people have many strengths, although this can sometimes be taken to extremes.

In an effort to convince the public that dyslexics are not stupid, publicity has been given to 'famous' dyslexics such as Churchill, Rodin, Edison and Einstein. Posthumous diagnosis is purely speculative and, although it might have '...helped draw attention to the problem and provide a vivid image to aiding in fund-raising... it is the type of shoddy enterprise the field can readily avoid by relying more on living examples to provide inspirational models and attention catching images' (Adelman and Adelman, 1987). Moreover, it has created a mythology that could be to the dyslexic person's disadvantage. For example, drawing attention to famous people who have been very creative has encouraged the belief that all dyslexics are good at creative tasks. This has been reinforced by the assumption (and it seems no more than this) that dyslexics are over-represented in professions such as architecture and engineering.

The research into Bannatyne's cluster profiles, referred to in Chapter 3, indicates that dyslexics are better at spatial than sequencing tasks but it does not indicate that they are necessarily better than anyone else –

nor is this indicated in any other research. Nevertheless, some writers believe it to be the case. In a widely read introduction to the subject of dyslexia (Hornsby, 1984) the author maintains that dyslexics have a natural talent in spatial ability. She writes that '...many of my clients have become successful scientists and engineers, both professions that require good spatial ability' (p. 30). She goes on to discuss the implications of this for certain occupations, particularly in working with computers. Hornsby does not, however, investigate whether her clients chose such professions and occupations because they were less good at others. This explanation is quite plausible but it has not yet been addressed in any systematic way.

In a study of high-school students Hearne et al. (1988) found that learning-disabled students were no worse or better than their non-disabled peers in terms of an aptitude for working with computers. Another study of senior school students (McLoughlin, 1990) suggests that generalisations about the superior or inferior ability of the dyslexic are inappropriate. Dyslexic students in the sample did have more difficulty with language activities such as spelling and verbal reasoning, the latter possibly because of ongoing difficulties with reading, but they were no better or worse than non-dyslexics in terms of abilities such as numerical ability, abstract reasoning, clerical speed and accuracy. Thus, there is little evidence to support the assertion that dyslexics have particularly good spatial ability, or that they are particularly suited to working with computers. Spatial ability is probably as normally distributed in the dyslexic population as it is in any other section of the population.

If dyslexics are not necessarily better or worse at many tasks than their non-dyslexic peers, providing them with vocational advice and career guidance is essentially the same as for any other group. Persisting problems with literacy do, of course, make a difference. Prima facie, high general intelligence indicates that the individual is suited to university-level study but very limited reading and writing skills would make this impossible. Even residual difficulties, such as slow reading and writing, would make some occupations onerous. Problems with literacy can also create other difficulties, William (referred to in Chapter 6) being a good example. In their study of the needs of learning-disabled adults, Hoffman et al. (1987) found that filling in application forms, knowing where to find a job and how to get training were major problems. One client sought help because preparing applications presented her with a problem despite the fact that she had a degree in fine art and a postgraduate diploma.

Essentially, dyslexics should pursue occupations and careers for which they are appropriately equipped in terms of their abilities, aptitudes and interests. The case material described in Chapter 6, however, suggests that it is not quite that simple. There is no doubt that dyslexic people can find some aspects of work more difficult than others; generally speaking they are likely to have difficulty with tasks involving working memory. However, because they can develop strategies for dealing with memory tasks and improving their organisational skills, there is no reason why they should be excluded from particular occupations. Developing a list of unsuitable occupations similar to that which has been prepared for people who are colour blind would not be helpful. The same argument applies in the context of further and higher education. Many people find study programmes that rely more on course work than examinations easier to follow and this option is likely to be attractive to a dyslexic person. However, there is no reason why a dyslexic should be prevented from studying any subject they choose, assuming that they can meet the usual entry requirements. It is desirable that they make their choice from an informed position (i.e. they should be aware of the demands of the course or job) and that they have developed effective learning strategies for meeting those demands. If this criterion is met they have as much chance of success as anyone else.

As stated above, vocational guidance counsellors working with dyslexics may find themselves needing to encourage their clients to pursue courses of training for occupations which they had ruled out because of their difficulties. Plata and Bone (1989) studied the way in which learning-disabled adolescents perceived the importance of particular occupations. They found that their subjects considered skilled, semiskilled and unskilled occupations to be more important than managerial and professional occupations, despite the fact that some were of well above average intelligence. It might therefore be that the school experiences of some lead them to underestimate their capabilities.

Helping dyslexics to identify their abilities and to understand their inefficiencies is an important aspect of vocational guidance work, particularly when dealing with someone who has reached a transition point in their working life. The evidence suggests that objective self-assessment in dyslexic people is not well developed. In a study of 33 learning-disabled adults Buchanan and Wolf (1986) found evidence of the lack of ability to assess their own strengths and weaknesses. Some did identify personal strengths but their perceptions were often inaccurate. They had little understanding of the nature of their difficulties and how these were affecting their lives. Miles and Gilroy (1986) believe that an increase in self-knowledge is likely to be beneficial and that if there is a problem, however mild, it is not very sensible to 'shove it under the carpet' by denying its existence. The case of Anthea described in Chapter 6 is a good example of this: it was only when the nature of her difficulty was identified that she was able to take steps to overcome it.

It is important to make dyslexics aware of the difficulties that might arise as a consequence of their condition and to provide advice on how they could overcome them. Further, it is important to make them aware of the possibility of their dyslexia adding to normal occupational stress and fatigue. For example, the teenager who wanted to become an air traffic controller need not have been dissuaded from pursuing this occupation, despite the fact that she had trouble with sequential tasks and with labelling (including right and left) correctly. She could have used strategies to overcome such difficulties; however, it was pointed out that she would be putting more pressure on herself in an already stressful occupation.

Career guidance and the dyslexic: a model

Yost and Corbishley's decision-making model can be adapted for use with dyslexic people in the following way.

1. *Initial assessment*. The aim of this is to gather personal and employment information about the client, including the usual information about aptitudes and abilities. Careful thought should be given to the question of aptitude and ability testing. For example, Holland's (1985) Self-Directed Search is useful because it provides a self-rating with regard to interests, competencies and abilities. This facilitates the process of improving self-understanding. It has the added advantage of offering two assessment forms, one of which has a low readability level. Although there are a number of other tests on the market, timed tests generally, and those that require people to write responses (particularly under timed conditions), should be used with caution. Such tests often provide more information about the client's dyslexia than they do about their abilities. In being diagnosed as a dyslexic the individual will have undergone an assessment process that will usually have involved some form of intelligence testing and such information, when available, can be helpful.

   Personality testing is a contentious issue because the relevance of personality characteristics to job performance is not well established. In addition, because there are no right and wrong answers to questions on personality inventories, they are easy to fake. However, in the context of career guidance they can be of some use because the client is unlikely to fake responses and the outcome can lead to greater self-understanding. Some qualities such as the determination a client has shown in attempting to overcome their learning difficulty can be assessed informally. It is also important to consider the extent to which their difficulties have affected their confidence and self-esteem.

2. *Self-understanding*. The extent to which a dyslexic understands their condition and how it affects them is particularly important. Such insight can be achieved by assisting them in an exploration of the values, interests, experience and abilities that relate to their goal. Denial of their weaknesses, or failure to recognise the possible problems these might create, could interfere with counselling.

3. *Making sense of self-understanding data*. The information gathered is summarised into statements or goals which can be used as a reference point. For the dyslexic, listing the possible difficulties a job could present and identifying the skills they will need to acquire to overcome them is very important.

4. *Generating alternatives*. Using the information acquired thus far, counsellor and client develop a list of possible career alternatives without making any judgement about the value of the options. The options should be based realistically on the information provided from the previous stages.

5. *Obtaining occupational information*. This involves learning as much about each option as is possible and narrowing the list. Like anyone else, a dyslexic must address the question 'How good is the match between my knowledge, skills and abilities and those demanded by the job?'. Other issues include qualifications and training. Some routes are better than others because they involve working towards short-term, rather than long-term, goals. A short course of training that leads to the next stage of a programme is more manageable than undertaking a lengthy one. Success on such a course would build confidence and allow development of skills needed for the future.

6. *Making a choice*. The client makes a choice among options based on all the above information.

7. *Making plans*. The purpose at this stage is to make plans to reach the career choice goal. Where the choice might be affected by the outcome of examination results, contingency plans should be worked out. Alternative routes to the same career goals should be considered.

8. *Implementing plans*. The client takes whatever action is necessary to achieve the selected career goal. This could include any of the following:
   - Pursuing further education or training – essential for those who need further education or training is the development of learning skills, including strategies that aid memory and organisation.
   - Starting a job search – this is a time-consuming process that involves examining advertisements in local and national newspapers, relevant magazines, newsletters and information sheets. Regular visits to job centres and career information centres as well as libraries are an important part of the process. Telephone calls and exploratory enquiries to key people within potential employing organisations are also advised.
   - Learning to deal with interviews – being able to present oneself in person in a confident manner. It requires good verbal communication and interpersonal skills. A fundamental issue is how to explain dyslexia to an employer. First, a dyslexic person must

decide whether they will inform the prospective employer. This issue must be considered with the client so that they are clear as to how they would deal with it if it arose. Secondly, they should be able to describe what dyslexia is, how it affects them and how they compensate for it, to ensure that there is no misunderstanding. A phrase such as 'I am dyslexic, which means that my writing is untidy and my spelling is weak but I can type and use a word processor, so will deal with any written work in that way', is clear and honest and shows that they have admitted to and developed a solution to the problem.

- Preparing application letters and curriculum vitae – being able to present oneself on paper is important. The emphasis should be on getting information about the client across effectively. Help might be required with filling in forms and preparing a curriculum vitae so that the weaknesses in the written language skills are not immediately obvious. Typed applications are better than handwritten ones but if an employer insists, this might be an important indicator of whether the client is likely to achieve 'goodness of fit'. The client could insist on typing the application and add a note saying that they are dyslexic. Another way to look at this is that insisting on handwritten applications means that the employers are either fussy about neatness (so if this does not come naturally to the client they will not fit in) or that they require handwriting to analyse writing as part of the selection procedure. Handwriting analysis is such an unreliable way of predicting occupational success that its use says something rather negative about the organisation.

- Developing complementary skills – as mentioned in Chapter 5 skills such as word processing and the use of other technology provide long-term solutions to many inefficiencies.

- Confidence building – if people are to present themselves well in interviews, group exercises and other similar activities, they will need to feel confident. Rehearsal using role-playing techniques can be useful in this regard, as can providing positive feedback concerning strengths.

Case studies

Case study A: Patrick

Initial assessment

Patrick is 22 years of age. In his final year at school he passed four GCSE subjects, including English language (at the second attempt). He started sixth-form courses but found these too difficult. At the time of interview he was working as a factory hand. His supervisor noted that he experienced difficulties with spelling and organising his work. Knowing something about dyslexia, the supervisor suggested an assessment.

Patrick was examined by a psychologist. Assessment showed that he was of above-average intelligence. He read accurately but slowly and had difficulty with reading comprehension. His spelling skills were quite poor and, as a consequence, he had trouble putting his ideas on paper. Diagnostic testing showed that he was dyslexic in that his working memory skills were below average.

Patrick was encouraged by the outcome of the assessment. Realisation that he is quite able led him to seek career counselling as he was bored with and frustrated by his present job.

In an interview Patrick presented as a shy but self-conscious young man. He was quite articulate. He believes that he was misunderstood at school and that his constant failure affected his motivation. He was now expressing a determination to do better.

Self-understanding

The psychologist who examined Patrick had explained the nature of dyslexia and Patrick now understood more about it. Patrick reported that he had done quite well at art and design subjects when at school and wondered if there might be a career for him in that area. Completion of the Self-Directed Search showed him to be an AI type, where A stands for artistic and I for investigative (as in scientific). This is consistent with his expressed interests and it suggested that pursuing training leading to a qualification in design work might be appropriate.

Making sense of self-understanding data

Examination of Patrick's psychological assessment report, discussion of his educational and work history as well as his behaviour in the interview suggested the profile shown.

Strengths	Weaknesses
Good spatial ability	Low self-esteem
Good problem-solving skills	Reading comprehension
Interest in and aptitude for design work	Poor spelling
Good general intelligence	Difficulties with written expression
Improved motivation	Poor organisational skills

Generating alternatives

Reference to the Jobs Finder devised for use with the Self-Directed Search listed the following occupations of interest to Patrick:

- furniture design;
- computer-aided design;
- product and package design.

Obtaining occupational information

Careers in the above areas could be pursued by completion of GCE 'A' levels, followed by a foundation course and then a degree course. Alternatively, a first certificate, diploma and advanced diploma could be gained by pursuing BTEC courses.

Making a choice

Patrick decided that he would like to pursue a course in design so that he could get a more interesting job. He chose the BTEC pathway, starting with a part-time certificate course, so that he could work towards short-term goals, and so that he could be assessed on the basis of his performance in coursework rather than take formal examinations.

Making plans

Patrick sought information about courses in the area where he lived. He discovered that there was a suitable course at his local college and that he would be able to gain a place as a mature student.

Implementing plans

The course chosen would not begin for 6 months. This gave Patrick some time to prepare. He was advised to seek tutoring directed towards improving his basic writing and spelling. It was suggested that he took help in developing study skills, including note-taking strategies, and that he learn how to use technological aids such as a word processor.

Case study B: John

John is 25 years old. He was identified as being dyslexic during his primary school years. He was moderately successful when he completed GCSE and 'O' level examinations, and when he left school he went into sales and marketing. He was very good at his job and did very well – to the extent that he was offered a senior job with a major firm. He was nervous about taking the job but it was a good opportunity and his application was successful.

Within a very short space of time after starting he began to find things difficult. Producing memos and reports was a problem and he was having trouble organising his workload. Further, he needed to live away from home and did not have his usual support network around him. He had not told his employers that he was dyslexic, assuming that it would not be a significant problem.

In a career counselling session John expressed a good deal of frustration and was obviously very anxious about his current situation. He described his difficulties and we discussed his dyslexia and how it affected him. He clearly did not understand the nature of his problem; some time needed to be devoted to developing his understanding of the condition and how it was affecting him.

John had also enjoyed the type of work he was engaged in, but the increased demands on his organisational, writing and spelling skills were causing him problems. It was quite clear that he wanted to continue in the same field but that he did not know what action to take.

Various options were discussed and it was decided that he should try to develop strategies to enable him to pursue his new job more effectively but that ultimately he should leave as he recognised that even if he was successful, increasing demands would mean that he was also under pressure. He developed some strategies that enabled him to work more effectively, including taking a laptop computer to work so that he could produce reports and written work. However, his eventual solution was to become self-employed, which meant that he was able to create his own organisational structure and employ people to deal with the tasks he found difficult. The small business he has established has been very successful and he is a relaxed and happy man.

Case study C: Pippa

Pippa, a 25-year-old arts graduate, sought career guidance after working for three years in various jobs. The testing session and interview established that she was very interested in working in video or related areas, that she was sufficiently qualified and that she had relevant experience and skills which would be valuable in such work. It was agreed that an appropriate career goal would be to focus attention on developing an existing private business venture which Pippa was already involved in with two other people and at the same time search for related employment until the business was established

In exploring her interests, experience and abilities with a view to determining the types of work she could seek and enjoy doing, it became obvious that a lack of self-confidence, developed as a result of her childhood experiences of being dyslexic, was a major barrier to her success. Her fear of failure and rejection and the frustration of trying to overcome a pronounced memory problem were conspiring to undermine her career progress. A programme of memory training, self-presentation and confidence building was agreed and implemented. This included training to identify the sources of negative feelings and attitudes, the effect of these factors in terms of gaining employment, self-assessment of skills (compared with the skill demands of specific jobs), training in how to be effective in interviews and techniques of improving recall of factual information.

Pippa was assisted in the identification of a list of occupational areas and specific jobs which warranted further investigation. Once this list was compiled she undertook an information gathering exercise to narrow down the list to make it manageable; Pippa eventually had three alternatives, of which teaching media studies in the tertiary education sector was her first choice. Pippa contacted all tertiary education colleges in her area, arranged to see the appropriate staff and eventually acquired part-time posts that provided her with a sufficient income and free time to pursue her private business venture.

Appendix I
Sample report

Alistair, aged 26 years

Introduction

Alistair was examined with a view to determining if a specific condition such as dyslexia might account for his persisting difficulties with aspects of literacy. He has also experienced difficulty in organising his work and with memory tasks.

Alistair left school at 16 years of age with five low-grade CSE passes. He failed English at the first attempt and has since been unsuccessful in both GCE 'O' level and GCSE English language examinations. Since successfully gaining a BTEC certificate in engineering he has worked as an engineer. He has done well in his work and is now seeking promotion but experiences difficulty with spelling and written expression, which is a disadvantage when report writing. Further, he fears that the greater demands that promotion will place on his organisational and memory skills will make it difficult for him to gain and maintain a supervisory position.

In an interview Alistair reported that he had worked hard in school and when taking his BTEC course but he believes that his results are not an accurate reflection of the effort he made. He reported a lack of confidence and feelings of frustration. His general health has been sound and both his vision and hearing are within normal limits.

Alistair's responses were such as to indicate that he has difficulties with geographical orientation, mental arithmetic, remembering telephone numbers and concentration, as well as with spelling.

Test behaviour

Alistair presented as an articulate young man. He was, however, somewhat anxious and self-conscious in the assessment situation. Nevertheless he made a consistent effort throughout the session, gaining confidence as he met with success. Following feedback from the interview and testing he seemed to be relieved that an explanation for his difficulties was possible.

Intelligence

Assessment of Alistair's intelligence by the administration of the WAIS-R showed him to be within the above-average range. There was no significant difference between his verbal IQ (112) and his performance IQ (116) but there was a wide variation among his subtest scores. He showed strengths in verbal reasoning (similarities), vocabulary, comprehension, perceptual reasoning (block design), non-verbal reasoning (picture arrangement) and spatial ability (object assembly). He attained below-average scores on information (recalling factual material) and digit symbol (copying symbols at speed) tests, which suggests some inefficiency in his working memory. Further, although he attained an average score on arithmetic (mental), it was noted that Alistair was overly reliant on concrete aids such as his fingers to help him deal with even simple calculations. On the digit span subtest Alistair had much more difficulty in reversing the order of numbers than he did in repeating them in the order in which they were given. It was obvious that he was using a 'chunking' strategy of grouping numbers into pairs but could not operate this strategy when reversing them.

Memory skills

As Alistair's performance on the WAIS-R suggested an inefficiency in working memory, this was investigated further. The digit span subtest from the Wechsler Memory Scale was administered. Consistent with his performance on the WAIS-R he scored at the 60th centile when repeating numbers in the order in which they were given. This is average. However, when reversing numbers he scored at the 20th centile – he did less well than 80% of his age group. This confirms that his working memory is inefficient.

Written language skills

Reading

Alistair's reading skills were assessed by the administration of the Spadafore Diagnostic Reading Test. He read at the 'independent' level up to Grade 10, having difficulty with pronunciation when reading more advanced words and prose. Nevertheless, this suggests that in terms of word reading he has sufficient skill to enable him to deal with advanced study and much professional work. However, although he read fluently he had difficulty in answering questions about material he read aloud or silently. He therefore still has trouble with reading comprehension.

Writing and spelling

An examination of a piece of Alistair's written work showed that he writes legibly, but somewhat untidily, in cursive script. He expresses ideas clearly but the structure of his written work and his use of punctuation are unsophisticated. Further, he writes slowly (16 words per minute). He also makes spelling errors and on a standardised single word spelling test (Vernon, 1983) his score was below the average adult level. His performance was erratic and he made errors at a basic level whilst being correct with more sophisticated words. His errors reflected inefficient working memory in that he omitted letters and confused letter order but many of his attempts were very close to being correct.

Summary and conclusions

Alistair presented as an articulate young man whose intelligence (both verbal and non-verbal) is above average. However, he has a significant problem with working memory, which has undermined his acquisition of literacy skills and prevented him from fulfilling his academic potential. He also reports difficulties with orientation and organisation. There is a history of written language difficulties within his family. It is therefore appropriate to describe Alistair as being dyslexic.

Recommendations

Skill development

1. Alistair's remaining difficulty with reading is in the area of comprehension. To overcome this he needs to learn efficient comprehension strategies such as the discussed with him, SQ3R.
2. Alistair would benefit from structured help with his spelling. Tuition in spelling should involve multisensory teaching. The upper levels of a programme such as *The Hickey Multisensory Language Course* (Augur and Briggs, 1991) would be suitable.
3. It would also be helpful if he could acquire some of the techniques and strategies known as study skills. In particular the use of spider plans or mind maps to help with planning written work would be of benefit. These could also be used to make note taking more efficient.
4. Although it is important that Alistair tries to improve his spelling skills, it is as important that he develops complementary skills such as touch typing. This would enable him to use a word processor

effectively and he would then be able to produce better presented and organised written work as well as to check and correct his spelling electronically. An alternative way of dealing with written work would be for him to develop his dictation skills and use the services of an audio typist.

5. It is particularly important that Alistair devotes some time to developing memory strategies. He needs to become a maker of lists and should be reliant on a Filofax or detailed diary. He might find one of the electronic personal organisers a helpful aid, particularly as these can often include a spell-check function. Essentially he needs to be able to see what he has to do rather than rely on his memory. Memory strategies that involve visual imagery might be helpful. Likewise, he would be able to deal with such problems as orientation more effectively by focusing on visual cues and landmarks rather than on street names or compass directions. He has already developed a number of strategies unconsciously and needs to learn how to apply them to the other tasks he has to deal with.

6. Above all, Alistair should exploit his strengths and acknowledge his achievements. His difficulties and failures have obviously undermined his self-confidence and lowered his self-esteem. The fact that he has been successful despite his problems should enable him to believe that, with greater self-understanding, he can meet increasing demands.

Special arrangements in examinations

Alistair has obviously worked very hard to overcome his problems and is therefore deserving of every consideration. His dyslexia need not be an insurmountable barrier in his employment setting and he should be given appropriate support.

He has expressed an interest in improving his qualifications. If he does decide to do this it would be appropriate to make special provision for him during a course of study. In particular, he should be allowed extra time to complete formal examinations as his slow writing and problems with reading comprehension will be a disadvantage (10 minutes per hour of each examination would be sufficient). In the assessment of his performance an allowance should be made for his untidy handwriting and weak spelling. This is the minimum provision which should be made for him. If he can develop his typing skills, he should be allowed to use a word processor during examinations. He will always be able to demonstrate his knowledge verbally better than he can in writing and, should his performance be borderline, a *viva voce* examination is recommended.

Appendix II
Useful addresses

The following are national organisations for the promotion of provision for dyslexic people of all ages. They are a good source of general information about dyslexia as well as advice on sources of support.

Australia

Australian Federation of SPELD Associations
129 Greenwich Road
Greenwich
NSW
Australia 2065
Tel.: (02) 906 2977

EC

European Dyslexia Association
c/o British Dyslexia Association
96 London Road
Reading
Berks RG1 5UA
UK

New Zealand

SPELD New Zealand
PO Box 13391
Christchurch
New Zealand

United Kingdom

British Dyslexia Association
95 London Road
Reading
Berks RG1 5AU
UK
Tel.: (0734) 668 271

United States of America

The Orton Dyslexia Society
724 York Road
Baltimore
MD 21204-2540
USA

The following are specialist services for adult dyslexics in the UK.

Adult Dyslexia and Skills Development Centre
5 Tavistock Place
London WC1H 9SN
Tel.: (071) 388 8744/387 9681

A centre for adult dyslexics providing professional assessment, counselling, training and teaching.

Adult Dyslexia Organisation
336 Brixton Road
London SW9 7AA
Tel.: (071) 924 9559

A support organisation run by adult dyslexics which can provide information, advice and arrange access to professional services.

People At Work
78 Albert Road
London N22 4AU
Tel.: (071) 624 8187

A firm of chartered psychologists offering specialist counselling and occupational advice.

References

Adelman, K.A. and Adelman, H.S. (1987). Rodin, Patton, Edison, Wilson, Einstein: Were they really learning disabled? *Journal of Learning Disabilities* 20, 270–279.

Augur, J. and Briggs, S. (1991). *Hickey Multisensory Language Course*, 2nd edn. London: Whurr.

Baddeley, A.D. (1986). *Working Memory*. London: OUP.

Baddeley, A.D. and Hitch, G.J. (1974). Working memory. In: G.Bower (Ed.) *Recent Advances in Learning and Motivation*, Vol. viii, pp. 47–90. New York: Academic Press.

Baddeley, A. and Wilson, B. (1988). Comprehension and working memory: A single case neuropsychological study. *Journal of Memory and Language* 27, 479–498.

Bannatyne, A. (1974). Diagnosis: A note on recategorization of the WISC scaled scores. *Journal of Learning Disabilities* 7, 272–274.

Beck, A.T., Rush, A.J., Shaw, B.F. and Emery, G. (1979). *Cognitive Therapy of Depression*. New York: Guilford Press.

Brooker, B.H. and Cyr, J.J.(1986). Tables for clinicians to use to convert WAIS-R short forms. *Journal of Clinical Psychology* 42, 983.

Buchanan, M. and Wolf, J.S. (1986). A comprehensive study of learning disabled adults. *Journal of Learning Disabilities* 19, 34–38.

Buzan, T. (1974). *Use Your Head*. London: BBC Publications.

Chasty, H. (1985). What is dyslexia? A developmental language perspective. In: M.J. Snowling (Ed.) *Children's Written Language Difficulties*, pp.11–27. Windsor: NFER-Nelson

Cheek, E.H. and Cheek, M.C. (1983). *Reading Instruction Through Content Teaching*. Columbus, OH: Merrill.

Coltheart, M. (1978). Lexical access in simple reading tasks. In: G. Underwood (Ed.) *Strategies of Information Processing*, pp. 151–216. London: Academic Press.

Cordoni, B.K. and O'Donnell, J.P. (1981). Wechsler Adult Intelligence Score Patterns for Learning Disabled Young Adults. *Journal of Learning Disabilities* 14, 404–407.

Cowen, S.E. (1988). Coping strategies of university students with learning disabilities. *Journal of Learning Disabilities* 21, 161–164.

Creasey, G.L. and Jarvis, P.A. (1987). Sensitivity to nonverbal communication among male learning disabled adolescents. *Perceptual and Motor Skills* 64, 873–874.

Critchley, M. (1964). *Developmental Dyslexia*. London: Heinemann.

Critchley, M. and Critchley, E.A. (1978). *Dyslexia Defined*. London: Heinemann.

Devine, T.G. (1981). *Teaching Study Skills: A Guide for Teachers*. Boston: Allyn and Bacon.

Edwards, P. (1973). Panorama: A Study Technique. *Journal of Reading* 17, 132–135

Ellis, A. (1962). *Reason and Emotion in Psychotherapy*. New York: Lyle Stuart.

Farnham-Diggory, S. (1978). *Learning Disabilities*. London: Fontana.

Faas, L.A. and D'Alonzo, B.J. (1990). WAIS-R Scores as predictors of employment success and failure among adults with learning disabilities. *Journal of Learning Disabilities* 23, 311–316.

Frauenheim, J.G. (1978). Academic achievement characteristics of adult males who were diagnosed as dyslexic in childhood. *Journal of Learning Disabilities* 11, 21–28.

Gathercole, S. and Baddeley, A.D.(1990). Phonological memory deficits in language disordered children: Is there a causal connection? *Journal of Memory and Language* 29, 336–360.

Gearheart, B.R., De Ruiter, J.A. and Sileo, T.W. (1986). *Teaching Mildly and Moderately Handicapped Students*. Englewood Cliffs, NJ: Prentice Hall.

Gerber, P.J., Ginsberg, R. and Reiff, H.B. (1992). Identifying alterable patterns in employment success for highly successful adults with learning disabilities. *Journal of Learning Disabilities* 25, 475–487.

Gerber, P.J., Schneiders, C.A., Paradise, L.V., Reiff, H.B., Ginsberg, R.J. and Popp, P.A. (1990). Persisting problems of adults with learning disabilities: Self-reported comparisons from their school-age and adult years. *Journal of Learning Disabilities* 23, 570–573.

Gillingham, A. and Stillman, B.W. (1969). *Remedial Training for Children with Specific Disability in Reading, Spelling and Penmanship*, 5th edn. Cambridge, MA: Educational Publishing Co.

Gilroy, D. (1991). *Dyslexia and Higher Education*. Bangor: University College of North Wales.

Ginsberg, E. (1972). Towards a theory of occupational choice. *Vocational Guidance Quarterly* 20, 169–176.

Goswami, U. (1991). Recent work on reading and spelling development. In: M. Snowling and M.E. Thomson (Eds) *Dyslexia: Integrating Theory and Practice*, pp. 108–121. London: Whurr.

Gregg, N. (1983). College learning disabled writer: Error patterns and instructional alternatives. *Journal of Learning Disabilities* 16, 334–338.

Guyer, B.P. and Sabatino, D.(1989). The effectiveness of a multisensory alphabetic phonetic approach with college students who are learning disabled. *Journal of Learning Disabilities* 22, 430–434.

Hall, J.W., Wilson, K.P, Humphreys, M.S., Tinzmann, M.B. and Bowyer, P.M. (1983). Phonemic similarity effects in good v's poor readers. *Memory and Cognition* 11, 520–527.

Hearne, J.D., Poplin, M.S., Schoneman, C. and O'Shaughnessy, E. (1988). Computer aptitude: An investigation of differences among junior high students with learning disabilities and their non-disabled peers. *Journal of Learning Disabilities* 21, 489–492.

Hoffmann, F.J. Sheldon, K.L., Minskoff, E.H., Sautter, S.W., Steidle, E.F., Baker, M.B. and Echois, L.D. (1987). Needs of learning disabled adults. *Journal of Learning Disabilities* 20, 43–48.

Holland, J.L. (1985). *The Self-Directed Search*. Odessa, FL: Psychological Assessment Resources.

Hoover, J.J. (1989). Study skills and the education of students with learning disabilities. *Journal of Learning Disabilities* 22, 452–454.

Hornsby, B. (1984). *Overcoming Dyslexia*. London: Optima.

Hulme, C. (1981). The effects of manual tracing on memory in normal and retarded readers; some implications for muli-sensory teaching. *Psychological Research* **43**, 179–191.

James, W. (1890). *The Principles of Psychology*. New York: Henry Holt.

Jastak, S. and Wilkinson, G. (1984). *Wide Range Achievement Test – Revised*. Los Angeles, CA: Western Psychological Services.

Jorm, A.F. (1983). Specific reading retardation and working memory: A review. *British Journal of Psychology* **74, 311–342.**

Katz, L., Goldstein, G., Rudshin, S. and Bailey, D. (1993). A neuropsychological approach to the Bannatyne recategorization of the Weschler Intelligence Scales in adults with learning disabilities. *Journal of Learning Disabilities* **26**, 65–72.

Kitz, W.R and Nash, R.T. (1992). Testing the effectiveness of the Project Success Programme for adult dyslexics. *Annals of Dyslexia* **42**, 3–24.

Klein, C. (1991). Setting up a learning programme for adult dyslexics. In: M. Snowling and M.E. Thomson (Eds) *Dyslexia: Integrating Theory and Practice*, pp. 293–301. London: Whurr.

Klein, C. (1993). *Diagnosing Dyslexia*. London: Avanti.

Koppitz, E.M. (1977). *The Visual Aural Digit Span Test*. New York: Psychological Corporation.

Kreiner, D.S. and Gough, P.B. (1990). Two ideas about spelling: Rules and word-specific memory. *Journal of Memory and Language* **29**, 103–118.

Kronick, D. (1983). *Social Development of Learning Disabled Persons*. Toronto: Jossey-Bass.

Krumboltz, J.D. (1976). A social learning theory of career selection. *The Counselling Psychologist* **6**, 71–81.

Lefly, D.L. and Pennington, B.F. (1991). Spelling errors and reading fluency in compensated adult dyslexics. *Annals of Dyslexia* **41**, 143–162.

Lenkowsky, L.K. and Saposnek, D.T. (1978). Family consequences of parental dyslexia. *Journal of Learning Disabilities* **11**, 47–53.

Lezak, M.D. (1983). *Neuropsychological Assessment*. New York: OUP.

McLoughlin, D. (1990). Masters' dissertation, University of East London.

Miles, T.R. (1978). *Understanding Dyslexia*. London: Hodder and Stoughton.

Miles, T.R. (1982). *The Bangor Dyslexia Test*. Wisbech: LDA.

Miles, T.R. (1983a). *Dyslexia: The Pattern of Difficulties*. St. Albans: Granada Publishing Co.

Miles, T.R. (1983b). On the persistence of dyslexic difficulties into adulthood. In: J.B. Bath, S.J. Chinn and D.E. Knox (Eds.) *Dyslexia: Research and Its Applications to the Adolescent*, pp. 88–100. Bath: Better Books.

Miles, T.R. (1988). Counselling in dyslexia. *Counselling Psychology Quarterly* **1**, 97–107.

Miles, T.R. (1990). Towards an overall theory of dyslexia. In: G. Hales (Ed.) *Meeting Points in Dyslexia. Proceedings of the first International Conference of the British Dyslexia Association*, pp. 50–53. Hull: British Dyslexia Association.

Miles, T.R. and Ellis, N.C. (1981). A lexical encoding deficiency II. In: G.Th. Pavlidis and T.R. Miles (Eds) *Dyslexia: Research and Its Applications to Education*, pp. 177–215. Chichester: John Wiley & Sons.

Miles, T.R. and Gilroy, D. (1986). *Dyslexia at College*. London: Methuen.

Miles, T.R. and Haslum, M.N. (1986). Evidence for dyslexia in a nationally representative sample of 10 year olds. *Dyslexia Contact* **5**, 5.

Minskoff, E.H. and Sautter, S.W. (1987). Employer attitudes toward hiring the learning disabled. *Journal of Learning Disabilities* **20**, 53–57.

Neale, M.D. (1989). *Neale Analysis of Reading Ability (Revised)*. Windsor: NFER-Nelson.

Nelson, H. and Willinson, J. (1991). *National Adult Reading Test (NART)*, 2nd edition. Windsor: NFER-Nelson.

Papagno, C., Valentine, T. and Baddeley, A.D. (1991). Phonological short-term memory and foreign-language vocabulary learning. *Journal of Memory and Language* 30, 331–347.

Parsons, F. (1909). *Choosing a Vocation*. Boston: Houghton Mifflin.

Patton, J.R. and Polloway, E.A. (1992). Learning disabilities: The challenges of adulthood. *Journal of Learning Disabilities* 25, 410–415.

Plata, M. and Bone, J. (1989). Perceived importance of occupations by adolescents with and without learning disabilities. *Journal of Learning Disabilities* 22, 64–71.

Rogers, C. (1951). *Client-centered Therapy*. Boston: Houghton Mifflin.

Runyon, M.K. (1991). The effect of extra time on reading comprehension scores for university students with and without learning disabilities. *Journal of Learning Disabilities* 2, 104–107.

Ryan, A.G. and Price, L. (1992). Adults with LD in the 1990's. *Intervention in School and Clinic* 281, 6–20.

Salvia, J. and Gajar, A. (1988). A comparison of WAIS-R profiles of nondisabled college freshmen and college students with learning disabilities. *Journal of Learning Disabilities* 21, 632–635.

Satz, P. and Mogel, S. (1962). An abbreviation of the WAIS for Clinical Use. *Journal of Clinical Psychology* 18, 77–79

Schonell, F.J. (1955). *Schonell Graded Word Spelling Test*. Edinburgh: Oliver and Boyd.

Schumaker, J.B. Deshler, D.D., Nolan, S., Clark, F.L., Alley, G.R. and Warner, M.M. (1981). *Error Monitoring: A Learning Strategy for Improving Academic Performance of Learning Disabled Adolescents*. Lawrence, KS: University of Kansas Institute for Research into Learning Disabilities.

Scottish Council for Research in Education (1976). *The Burt Word Reading Test*. Sevenoaks: Hodder and Stoughton.

Siegel, L.S. (1992). An evaluation of the discrepancy definition of dyslexia. *Journal of Learning Disabilities* 25, 618–629.

Singleton, C.H., Ed. (1991). Computer applications in the diagnosis and assessment of cognitive deficits in dyslexia. In: *Computers and Literacy Skills* pp. 149–159. Hull: British Dyslexia Association.

Smith, P. and Whetton, C. (1988). *Basic Skills Tests*. Windsor: NFER-Nelson.

Spadafore, G.J. (1983). *Spadafore Diagnostic Reading Test*. Novato, CA: Academic Therapy Publications.

Spreen, O. and Strauss, E. (1991). *A Compendium of Neuropsychological Tests*. New York: OUP.

Stanovich, K.E. (1991). Discrepancy definitions of reading disability: Has intelligence led us astray? *Reading Research Quarterly* 26, 1–29.

Super, D.E. (1969). Vocational development theory: Persons, positions and processes. *Counselling Psychologist* 1, 2–9.

Thomson, M.E. (1984). *Developmental Dyslexia*. London: Edward Arnold.

Thomson, M.E. (1990). *Developmental Dyslexia*, 3 rd edn. London: Whurr.

Thomson, M.E. and Watkins, E.J. (1990). *Dyslexia: A Teaching Handbook*. London: Whurr.

Torgesen, J.K. and Houk, D.G. (1980). Processing deficiencies of learning-disabled children who perform poorly on the digit span test. *Journal of Educational Psychology* **72**, 141–160

Vellutino, F.R. (1987). Dyslexia. *Scientific American* **256**, 20–27.

Vernon, P.E. (1983). *Graded Word Spelling Test*. Sevenoaks: Hodder and Stoughton.

Vincent, D. and De La Mare, M. (1990). *New MacMillan Reading Analysis*. Windsor: NFER-Nelson.

Vonnegut, K. (1991). *Hocus Pocus*. London: Vintage.

Wechsler, D. (1976). *The Wechsler Intelligence Scale for Children*. Windsor: NFER-Nelson.

Wechsler, D. (1981). *The Wechsler Adult Intelligence Scale (Revised)*. New York: Psychological Corporation.

Wechsler, D. (1992). *Wechsler Intelligence Scale for Children,* 3rd edn. Sidcup: The Psychological Corporation.

Wheeler, T.J. and Watkins, E. (1978). Dyslexia: The problem of definition. *Dyslexia Review* **1**, 13–15.

Williams, E.G. (1965). *Vocational Counselling*. New York: McGraw-Hill.

Wing, A.M. and Baddeley, A.D. (1980). Spelling errors in handwriting: a corpus and distributional analysis. In: U. Frith (Ed.) *Cognitive Processes in Spelling*, pp. 251–285. London: Academic Press.

Yost, E.B. and Corbishley, M.A. (1987). *Career Counselling*. London: Jossey-Bass.

Index